Carom Shot

By

J·J·Partridge

Carom (Kăr′əm) n. In pool, a shot in which the object ball strikes another ball and rebounds into a pocket.

A CHUKAR BOOK

"She came from Providence,
born in Rhode Island
Where the old world shadows
hang heavy in the air."

A Chukar Book

Published by Chukar Books, a division of Gryphon Corporation

First Printing, November, 2005

10 9 8 7 6 5 4 3 2 1

Copyright © John Partridge, 2005

All rights reserved

® REGISTERED TRADEMARK — MARCA REGISTRADA

Library of Congress Control Number 2005908063

ISBN — 0977307808

Printed in the United States of America by Meridian Printing
Book design by Don Paulhus Design

BOOKS ARE AVAILABLE AT QUANTITY DISCOUNTS WHEN USED TO
PROMOTE PRODUCTS OR SERVICES. FOR MORE INFORMATION PLEASE
WRITE TO CHUKAR BOOKS, A DIVISION OF GRYPHON CORPORATION AT
JJP@GRYPHONCORPORATION.COM

PROLOGUE

She drew breaths easily. Her small, even teeth were barely visible behind puffy lips. Her expression was placid, belying the bruises on her cheeks. In her dream, she was in the cavernous Refectory and students carrying trays passed her table; some faces loomed at her while others shrank from her glare. As her killer straddled her body, the shiftings in the tired mattress provoked no reaction. She exhaled as a pillow was lowered to cover her face; when a cough didn't clear the obstruction, her mouth opened, the pillow pushed against her teeth, her throat caught in a muffled gurgle.

A bad dream.

She awoke, more confused than alarmed, drew up her knees, and began to coil to her left side; her killer responded with a move up on to her chest that compressed her ribs and pinned her shoulders to the mattress. Resolute hands pushed the pillow into her eyes and flattened her nose. She managed to free her right hand and found the pillow—instantly, she knew what it was—but without leverage, its flimsy cover slipped from her grasp, leaving her hand to flail in empty air.

I can't breathe!

In panic, she thrashed beneath the unyielding weight of her killer. Her collapsed lungs burned in a blast of bloody ruptures; garish sparks and dying points of light streamed behind throbbing eyes as a rushing sound, like wind emerging from a tunnel, rose in her ears.

It is not happening!

1

Her mouth stretched in a silent scream—*Oh God, No!*—and the pillow entered her gaping mouth. Its taste gave rise to a spasmodic butt of her head that allowed her hand to regain the pillow and rip it off a corner of her face so that a bruised eye opened into blackness. For seconds, she stared without seeing until a vice-like grip wrenched her wrist away and her nails raked across the pillow.

I am going to die!

Her writhing, intense and unavailing, continued until almost theatrically, her arm gave up its struggle and slumped to the mattress. Under the pillow, facial muscles trembled, cramped, retracted, and were still. All light, sound, and pain faded to vanishment as her brain shut down, leaving her stomach to convulse on its own; her heart sputtered out of rhythm.

After her last contortions, the pillow fell to the floor. The dim light from a table lamp across the room exposed a slack jaw, a trickle of blood, saliva, and vomit oozing to her chin and throat, and a single, not yet sparkless eye swelling within its socket.

A hand lifted the lacy fringe of the slip covering her breasts in a silence broken by irregular hisses of breath and distant street noises: a racing motorcycle, the squeal of brakes, a car horn. The mattress creaked as her killer straightened and began to slide off her body. Then, from the blackness behind the lamp, came the scrape of wood rubbing against a hard surface. A doorknob creaked as it was released. A finger touched her neck, feeling for a pulse.

A moan began—

Monday

CHAPTER ONE

There is something about the investigation of a murder. Especially the murder of a young woman. We bring all of our baggage, our guilty consciences, and our less than pure motives into play even as, ostensibly, we seek justice for the victim and society. A lesson of my first case.

At a minute or so before nine, I was alone in the Provost's conference room. I ignored the coffee setup on the credenza, tossed a Uni-Ball pen and legal pad on the oblong table, and sat in a leather-backed chair facing the door to the adjoining office. I expected it to open momentarily—there were voices within and the Provost demanded punctuality from the senior staff—but it didn't. After finger rolls of impatience on the table, I turned to the room's only window.

Following a weekend of intermittent drizzle and fog, I could almost smell the damp. Through the lingering mist, The Green had an early winter-in-Providence quality—bleached-out sky, frost-killed grass, and shoals of dead leaves from ancient elms and oaks—against a background of the motley facades of Federal, Greek Revival, Romanesque, and Beaux Arts buildings across its expanse. Its spaciousness and the classic architecture evoked sentiments of stability and continuity appropriate for the physical center of a great university; my view from the second floor of College Hall gave no hint that the institution was in crisis, that its core was churning.

The Chapel Bell broke the calm with the first of nine dissonant clangs and classroom buildings disgorged throngs of kids with backpacks and carryalls, wearing hooded Carter U. Cats sweat-shirts, quilted vests, ponchos, windbreakers, and droopy raincoats, on to puddled brick walks; skateboarders and cyclists soon weaved in and out among them like fish in eelgrass. From William Street, a white pickup pulled up; two maintenance men in yellow slick-ers got out and began tossing leaf bags into the back of the truck. It was, I thought, a snapshot of this time of day, this time of year, in any year, except for the huge banner strung across College Arch: "STOP THE STALKER."

"Mornin', counselor." Bill Tuttle, Carter University's Chief of Security, dropped a manila folder on the table and removed his raincoat and tan Kangol cap. It was Tuttle's before dawn phone call that had summoned me to this emergency meeting. His decid-edly Gaelic face was grim and pale, even his freckles seemed faded, making his kelly green tie over a white shirt too buoyant for our somber business. "Where's everybody," he said, more as a com-ment than a question, as he poured coffee into an oatmeal colored Carter mug.

The door to the Provost's office snapped open. Artemus Vose's bushy eyebrows barely rose above rimless eyeglasses in acknowl-edgment of our presence when he folded his lanky frame into the chair at the head of the table. He has been Provost for four of the six years I've been here, before that a senior executive of two *Fortune* 500 corporations, and that's the way he is: all business as soon as he arrives in College Hall at seven a.m. His slate gray eyes held pin-pricks of anger as he tugged at the cuffs of a blue oxford shirt; then, giving us a profile of craggy jaw, roman nose, and mane of white hair, he spun in his chair. I followed his glower and my jaw dropped. In the doorway to his office was the diminutive Leon Goldbloom, Esquire, a.k.a "Puppy Dog" Goldbloom, Providence's

City Solicitor; hulking behind him, stood an angry Dwayne McAllister, the Dean of Student Life.

Tuttle and I barely squelched comments as Puppy Dog slinked his way into the conference room like a cat seeking the protection of shadows. Since Puppy Dog is Mayor Angelo "Sonny" Russo's lackey, his *cucciolo*, his political and legal lap dog, our dismay as to his presence at a cabinet level meeting had to be apparent to the Provost. Would we be able to stop ourselves from blurting out Puppy Dog's behind-his-back nickname in surroundings where it was in common usage?

Puppy Dog's rat-catcher eyes surveyed the conference room before he dropped a greasy poplin raincoat on a chair back, gave Tuttle and me a nod, and chose the chair to the Provost's immediate right. The conference table hid Puppy Dog's shiny black trousers and some of his faded green blazer but not a formerly white shirt or a stained, midnight-blue tie that almost matched the shade of a sweep of hair pasted to his balding pate. A deficient chin gave his beak-like nose a Cyrano quality. He was already into his irritating habits of impatient lip slicking and rapid eye blinking as he pointedly ignored McAllister's scowl. That wasn't easy because the Dean, at six-four and weighing in around two-seventy, had sat heavily opposite him, splayed his elbows on the table, and balanced his shaved, black, bullet head on the tips of two fingers. "Shazam" McAllister's persona radiated menace as it probably did years ago when he steamrollered opposing linemen as Carter University's All-American defensive tackle.

"The Mayor called this morning," the Provost began, enunciating each word to get our attention. "Asked to have Leon meet with me and I invited him to sit in." The stress was on *I* and his expression cautioned us to be cool. The Provost, the University's chief administrative officer, has a lot of responsibilities—although Puppy Dog is usually my turf—so I had to take comfort that his decision was in keeping with his reputation as a sure-handed administrator as well as ocean sailor, someone who assimilates angles, speeds, and directions with preciseness and alacrity. "Okay," he said, "the President is coming back from Washington around noon, and Larry"—meaning Information Officer Larry Gregson—"has the flu so I told him to stay home." Since Gregson, despite, or maybe because of, years of public relations experience, had stubbornly refused my advice to bring in crisis management counsel, I was disappointed that he wouldn't be here to squirm through another short-noticed meeting. "Bill, bring us up to speed."

"This is what we know," he said, referring to a yellow pad he had taken from his folder. "Her name is Anne Sullivan. Twenty years old. Lived in Hastings Hall first year and Johnson last year. Reasonable academic record, took grades second year, no fails." He hesitated, cleared his throat, and continued. "Local girl. Graduate of St. Xavier's Academy here in Providence. Partial scholarship and loans each of the first two years. Didn't register for junior year." He flipped to the next page. "Father is a Providence policeman—"

Without warning, Puppy Dog leaned so far forward that his nose barely missed the table. He straightened, sucked in a portentous breath, and addressed us in his nasally alto. "The Mayor instructed Chief McCarthy to make this homicide a priority!"

Um? Huh? What else? We waited for more. But, there wasn't any; with his fingers laced together, he rested his hands on the table like a well-behaved first-grader. Blinking rapidly, he peered over my head and out the window.

I didn't try to restrain my rueful expression. There is a serial crazy on the loose! For over a month, despite public and private pleas for more police support to augment our security officers, the University had virtually been ignored by the Mayor and his Police Chief, Daniel Patrick McCarthy. Not that this malfeasance was a surprise; Sonny Russo had made a career out of painting the tax-exempt University as a free-loading, snooty, drug-ridden, haven of liberal hypocrisy. Even the few additional patrol cars grudgingly assigned to the campus area on weekends and the ineffective, lack-adaisical efforts of McCarthy's less than enthusiastic Detective Division were accompanied by City Hall's loud complaints as to the "enormous" additional burdens being placed on "the backs of Providence taxpayers."

Tuttle broke the silence. "They're going to autopsy this morning. So far, it looks like she was assaulted and murdered sometime Friday night or early Saturday morning." Tuttle raised his eyes to the Provost, perhaps considering what details to discuss in front of Puppy Dog, and getting no reaction, returned to his notes. "Lived in an apartment on Veasey Street. No roommate. Found by her landlady on top of her bed, nude from the chest down. Slip over her head. The apartment was a mess. Probably beat her up before she was raped. No evidence of a knife." His eyes went down the page. "Death by asphyxiation, not strangled as I was told last night. Pillow over the mouth, probably." He pulled a photograph from the folder. "Anne Sullivan, sophomore year ID photo," he said, and handed the photograph to me.

In the grainy blow-up, she came through as pretty, a blonde with long hair over each shoulder, square face, large, expression-less eyes, freckled nose, and generous lips around a wide mouth. I gave the photograph to the Provost. Puppy Dog looked over the Provost's shoulder before it was passed on to McAllister. "Well," Puppy Dog said, "she certainly doesn't *look* like any of the others."

Even the Provost shifted his eyes to McAllister who, thank God, seemed intent on the photograph and not on Puppy Dog's hapless comment. The "others" were six black Carter women assaulted at various off-campus locations on Saturday nights during October and November.

"Immediate reaction is that the perp was The Stalker," said Tuttle, lapsing into police-speak in a voice now edged with hostility. "Weekend night assault, Carter connection, two blocks off campus. Autopsy today, as I said. No witnesses. They also want to question a boyfriend." He ran his hand through his clipped gray hair as though considering a further comment, but held back. "That's it."

"Won't make much difference, white or black," McAllister interjected as he tossed the photograph on the table. "She was murdered and it was the weekend and she was raped, and so what if she dropped out and stayed around campus. That's how they'll see it. With the kids coming back from Thanksgiving break last night and today and the news getting 'round, the place could bust wide open or shut itself down—"

The Provost interrupted. "We are *not* shutting down!" he said, plainly irritated that the subject had been raised in front of Puppy Dog. "The President needs options, including something that will let the kids, the parents, everyone, know that we can be *in loco parentis* when we have to."

Reactions to *in loco parentis* varied considerably. Tuttle looked puzzled, McAllister's forehead furled, and Puppy Dog looked on from a distant planet. Eyes shifted to me and I was caught off guard. *In loco parentis*—long a pejorative phrase in College Hall—essentially means a paternalistic relationship between a university and its students, a concept that died in the sixties when higher education abandoned its traditional role in regulating student life. All curfews, dress codes, parietal rules, and such were eliminated and the kids were given charge of their private lives at eighteen.

McAllister, usually an advocate of leaving students alone whenever possible, pressed me. "How far can we legally go, Algy? What are we talking about? Getting the kids back on the campus? Monitors? Room checks...?"

The Provost responded for me. "That's not what I mean," he said, maybe annoyed at himself for harking back to campus rules he could remember. "I meant actions that demonstrate concern, and more importantly, show that we are doing something!"

"Ah-h-h," said Puppy Dog, whose eyes had brightened in an expression that could only be termed *pious*. "Let me repeat, Artemus, it's time for cooperative action. The Mayor is willing to join with President Danby in a major cooperative event of some kind. The University and the city! Together! You know what I'm saying? Police, administration, faculty, students..., all together! Raise their consciousness! Get the safety message across! Get everybody to calm down...." His voice trailed off.

Tuttle's face didn't bother to conceal contempt while McAllister's, if anything, was even more grim. The Provost, however, remained poker-faced. We all recognized that Sonny Russo and Puppy Dog were tweaking us; they knew, as we did, that getting our fractious campus community into any facility would be like dropping a lighted match into a box of fireworks. Got to hand it to Sonny, though; by making the proposal, Sonny had the cover of offered cooperation in case the media asked. It was the University's fault, not Sonny's, if we couldn't follow through.

We waited for the Provost to respond but he sat stolidly, and I wondered if this "cooperative event" had been discussed and dismissed earlier.

Tuttle shifted in his seat, reached into his folder, and said ominously, "We may have another problem," as he passed out sheets of eight and a half by eleven copy paper.

I took mine, surprised that it felt damp, and studied a photograph of a stern, black face within a crudely drawn circle cut through with vertical and horizontal lines, like a gunsight's cross hairs. The target's name—Reverend Jesse Kingdom, the date—this Friday, the time—noon, and the place—The Green—were printed below. The same flyer, without the cross hairs, had been affixed to utility poles, tree trunks, and bulletin boards all over campus and adjoining streets for at least two weeks.

"These were blowin' around early this morning outside the Refectory. With this wind, even with them soppin' wet, they were all over the place before Security was alerted and we picked them up. No idea how they got there or who produced them."

We fingered our copies. Jesse Kingdom is Providence's Al Sharpton or Jesse Jackson or Martin Luther King, depending on your outlook, and W.A.R., Kingdom's We're Against Racism organization, has long been a hair shirt for Sonny Russo and Chief McCarthy, even more so after the ugliness of last August's night of violence in mostly black South Providence. With bullhorn in hand, surrounded by belligerent supporters, Jesse Kingdom's rallies and speeches decried Sonny's and his police department's "record of shame": discrimination, brutality, racism, and the bullying of minorities. Kingdom had entered into our crisis early on, denouncing the Providence cops as incapable of "finding their own behinds with both hands when it came to a white man attacking black women." The announcement of a Kingdom rally on our campus at the invitation of the Black Student Caucus had infuriated Sonny and he let it be known, through a call from Puppy Dog to me, that he viewed it as nothing less than a "hostile act" by the President and the University.

"The Reverend sure has enemies," Puppy Dog said, addressing the Provost. "Violence breeds violence. As I said to you earlier, Artemus, the Mayor wants you to consider postponing Kingdom's appearance until everything calms down. You're inviting trouble. Why take the huge risk of letting him rile up your students? They're already worked up and when he shows up with his rabble-rousers, there'll be an explosion. You watch!" When the Provost didn't even flick an eyelid, Puppy Dog shrugged, picked up his raincoat, and stood. "Our men are stretched as it is, and if it gets unruly...." The sentence ended in a weary rasp.

Loose translation: You want our help, then cancel Jesse Kingdom.

The bullying had been so blatant that it even got to the Provost. "I don't think we have to go that far, Leon," he said slowly and almost dismissively. "In any event, we expect the police to take it seriously." He tapped his finger on his copy of the flyer and addressed Tuttle. "Make sure Reverend Kingdom is informed about this, whatever it's supposed to mean, in case *he* wants to postpone—"

McAllister thrust a flyer across the table at Puppy Dog and barked, "Are you going to *ignore* this?"

Puppy Dog responded as though addressing a not very bright child. "Oh, let's not overreact! God knows where it came from. Some crank, no doubt." A cunning expression crept into his face. "Of course, people like Jesse Kingdom love the publicity of a threat. Know what I mean? Creates sympathy."

I thought McAllister was going to lose it. He pushed back his chair as though to reach over the table and grab his nemesis by the throat, prompting Puppy Dog to snatch a flyer off the table and take a backwards step toward the hall. "I'll bring this... *threat*..."— his eyebrows rose in a question—"...personally to Chief McCarthy" and with that, he smirked at the Provost, nodded to me, ignored McAllister and Tuttle, and left us.

Nobody spoke. Sometimes, in the aftermath of a situation like this, you wonder if you should give voice to your inner thoughts or you should best ignore that which you have to ignore. The Provost decided the issue.

"What a *jerk*!" he said, wearily. A smile played at the corner of his lips—that was about as much as you could ever get from him— and disappeared as he said, "Look, this isn't easy. Like it or not, we've got to keep communications open with City Hall." He took off his glasses, found a handkerchief, breathed on the lenses, and methodically began to polish them. "I don't see a lot of options. We've had Security on overtime, patrols everywhere, buddy-up programs, escorts, what else is there? We can't get into their apartments. We can't protect everybody all the time, and certainly not someone who dropped out of here!" He paused for a moment and, maybe, there was a trace of a sigh. "But, we move on. The President has ruled out closing down. Meanwhile, we've got to get ahead of the reaction—"

"We shouldn't assume it was The Stalker," I offered.

The Provost put his glasses back on and joined the others in their puzzled expressions.

"They're looking for a boyfriend, too...." I glanced at Tuttle, who nodded. "It was Friday night, not Saturday night. And, as important as anything else, she's not black! This is different...." Tuttle began another affirmative nod but stopped, hesitant about going too far with me. "We've got to have a response. Sure. But let's not make the message self-fulfilling."

Even as my words were spoken, I recognized they sounded hollow and disingenuous. The killer had to be The Stalker. It had only been a matter of time for his rampage to reach the level of a death. Why did I get this far on a limb?

My assertion, however, struck a chord with the Provost. He left his chair, a familiar move at prescient moments in his meetings, and walked behind me to face the window, his hands linked behind his back. After at least a long pause, he turned and said, "I agree. We shouldn't get ahead of ourselves, even if turns out to be The Stalker. What we put out to the campus and in the President's statement for the media and the *Crier* should be consistent with what we know, not what we might assume. And we need a show of security today and tonight, Bill, especially in and near the women's dorms and at the Refectory. Dwayne, you have to get to the off-campus kids..., e-mail, calls, visits, whatever you have to do."

McAllister's face remained stoney.

The Provost then raised a palm to his mouth, surely considering what else might be done. "Maybe, the President goes to the Refectory and into dorms tonight and..."—his face revealed an idea being formed— "...unannounced, without a retinue, speaks to small groups, especially to black women. He'll know what to say and how to keep moving...." He was on a roll. "And Alger..."—he never used my nickname— "...with Larry out, crank out a draft statement so the President's got something to review." He paused and directed himself to Tuttle. "See what you can find out about this flyer and get the information to the police. If the Kingdom rally goes off, it has to be as secure as we can make it." With that, he nodded to each of us, as though affirming our respective duties, and returned to his office.

My companions stirred. McAllister, visibly upset, stood as Tuttle gathered the victim's photograph, the flyers, and his pad into his folder. In contrast to McAllister, Tuttle had relaxed. "The Detective Division and the patrols gotta jump into this now. We'll get cops for sure this weekend, whether Sonny likes it or not. Has to. The girl is Terry Sullivan's daughter. Been a cop longer than me. *Big* McCarthy supporter. *Very big* in the Fraternal Order of Police, the FOP. Different ball game now." He shook his head, put on his cap and his raincoat, and exited.

I packed away my pen and picked up my unmarked pad, feeling a little pleased with myself until McAlister grumbled, "Won't fool anybody. The kids will think it's a ploy if we ignore The Stalker. A murder? Can't hide that. We're heading for shutdown, Algy."

I didn't want to agree with his characterization of our plan as a "ploy" although I recognized that it was defensive and smacked of a stratagem. After two weekends, including the long Thanksgiving weekend, without a reported assault, I had hoped that Tuttle's much derided security operations had finally been effective. Maybe The Stalker, although not caught, had been scared away from the campus. Now it seemed that The Stalker had taken the weekends off to build up to this tragedy.

McAllister reached into his suit coat pocket, removed a folded sheet of paper, and handed it to me. It was captioned "Black Student Caucus" and "Speakers" over a list of names. One was brightly highlighted in yellow: Martine Danby, the daughter of Carter University's new President. "She's completely wrapped up in this rally. I thought you ought to know."

"Thanks for the heads-up," I said, my face certainly betraying my concern. When Sonny Russo found out, the "hostile act" would become open war.

CHAPTER TWO

I trudged up a flight of stairs.

My paralegal, Marcie Barrett, was in her office; Maria Lopes, our shared secretary and imperturbable veteran of two previous University Counsels, was in command at her imposing desk in the middle of our suite. Each looked up at me in expectation; their greetings were barely audible so I surmised that news of the murder had reached the third floor. I stood between Marcie's office and Maria's desk and confirmed the murder of Anne Sullivan, a former student—I stressed *former*—on Friday night, *not* Saturday night, that the cops hadn't actually said it was The Stalker, and that the victim wasn't black. Marcie's face registered a lot more than professional concern as I finished; Maria, her Azorean features darkly troubled, returned to her computer and started keyboarding.

As I hung my suit jacket on the hook behind my office door, my Blackberry—compact in its cell phone, e-mail, and some other features I'd never learn to use and mandated by the Provost for all senior staff—vibrated at my belt. I checked the caller ID. Puppy Dog! Damn! Circumstances grant him unwelcomed access to my otherwise private number. Without any salutation, he recapped his argument of thirty minutes ago, this time without any subtleness: if Providence politics has a texture, it is sandpaper. "It's budget time, ya know, and Sonny's got the University down for four million."

What was I suppose to do, have a case of the vapors? Arguing would be futile. In each municipal budget since his first election,

Sonny had put in a revenue estimate for the property tax-exempt University, knowing full well he wouldn't get a dime unless he would engage in good faith negotiations, trading in-lieu-of-tax money for better municipal services for the University. When he didn't, because good faith was alien to Sonny and he liked having the University as a convenient whipping boy, he had his annual excuse for another tax increase on Providence's long-suffering ratepayers.

"Too bad you can't see Sonny's position on Kingdom."

I didn't respond. My gaze fell on two silver gelatin prints of Providence's WaterPlace Park and RiverWalk behind my desk. Sonny got a lot of credit, most of which he didn't deserve, for the city's recent economic and cultural resurgence. I thought of the dichotomy: the revitalized, attractive city and the mendacity of its mayor.

"You just don't know what Kingdom's rabble is gonna do. Look what's happened to your buddy Tramonti...."

At that, I took in a deep breath. One way I've learned to deal with Puppy Dog is to take the posture that I had no idea what he was talking about and let him ramble on until he was over his latest gripe; however, I couldn't do that after his potshot at my closest friend, Police Commissioner Tony Tramonti. Another tactic is prolonged silence since it irritates him and he would eventually fill the void. I mentally started to count the seconds. Through the room's only window, the granite dome of Shay Library masked all but the upper floors of the office buildings downtown; in the distance, an American flag waved from the top of an orange and red crane at some unseen building site. At fifteen, he said, "Ya know, a little help on this would go a long way to patch things up."

"Leon, it's not going to happen. With what we've been experiencing, Jesse Kingdom is the least of our problems. We can't get into it—"

"You've got to be practical," he whined. "Practical...."

I got to ten studying a recent addition to the office, an earth-tone monotype of the Tuscan Crete, its chalky cliffs and orangey light captured by a Providence artist, when he resumed bellyaching.

I interrupted. "Look, if anything changes with Kingdom, I'll let you know. But don't count on it," and got off the call. I would speak to the Provost even though nothing was going to change: neither the Provost nor the President could be intimidated or would make a deal with crooks. Puppy Dog's crack about Tramonti, to let *me* know that he was aware of my relationship to Sonny's nascent political rival, also sharpened my aversion to any deal. Six degrees of separation? Not in Providence, the home of the "knowing wink," where ignoble politics and "doin' business" are joined at the hip.

"Ugh," I said aloud.

○ ◯ ○

University Counsel, according to the position description, is "...the principal legal counsel to the Board of Trustees, the President, and the Officers of the University...." Since I had been my alma mater's litigation counsel at Champlin & Burrill, Providence's largest law firm, and had worked with my predecessors, the advantages of the "in-house" university position were known to me when I accepted the offer: no time sheets, a single client, the stimulation of an Ivy League campus, regular hours instead of a schedule set by arbitrary demands from clients and court calendars, and the end of the peaks and valleys of a litigator's life—intense trial days, followed by weeks of reading memos, depositions, and client hand-holding. The disadvantages? I could accept that I'd be more of a legal manager than before but I did not foresee the effects of three occupants of the President's office within six years—the one who hired me retiring after a heart attack, the one in the middle a disappointing academic politician, and the third, Charles Danby, Jr., only six months from his inauguration—and I was naive as to the enervating, dopey, schedule-filling effects of what Marcie and I call the "Carter dialectic."

To describe this phenomenon succinctly, you first have to appreciate that an Ivy League campus is a distracting, noisy place, populated with concentrations of the politically correct and culture war militants, all of whom have micron-thin skins and memories like elephants. Thus, even mundane University decisions require multiple discussions with various interest groups who argue interminably with throbbing moral certainty among themselves, causing issues to end up in our office in a convoluted, legalist form. Ironically, the web of administrative rules and regulations that created these obstacles to action has one positive effect: Presidents and Provosts involve me in administrative and policy matters that are only remotely legal, such as dealing with contentious city officials. A sympathetic colleague at another Ivy League school located in a town not unlike Providence once described her own job this way: it's like being Attorney General in a mini-state inhabited exclusively by the smart, the opinionated, and the stubborn, surrounded by antagonists who would like nothing better than to rub our collective faces in the *merde*!

The office had begun to percolate: a phone rang and was answered by Maria, the fax machine began to chirp away, I heard the mail messenger arrive, and above us on the fourth floor, an electric drill whirred, stopped, whirred, and stopped. I settled in behind the old yellow oak desk that had once been my grandfather's and entered my password on my iMac. On my desk lay this morning's *Crier*, the tabloid student daily, along with manila folders, redwell files, the mandatory name plate identifying me as "A.M. Temple" in case I harassed someone, and a photograph of a smiling Nadie Winokur under a red umbrella on the patio of Osteria Pazanzo in Chianti. I touched Nadie's photograph and felt a tad better. She'd be back in town today after spending Thanksgiving with her mother in Miami.

I missed her; a few days without her and my senses dull.

Marcie came in, brusquely I thought, carrying a brown folder and a legal pad. Always put together for work, she wore a blue tweed suit and white blouse accented by a strand of amber beads. The only thing out of the ordinary was the solemnness of her normally lively face. She removed a document from the folder, placed it on the desk blotter, and took the chair in front of the desk. She sat rigidly.

"Thanks," I said.

"Fine," she said in non-response. Anger stirred in her washed-out, greenish eyes.

Evidently, she wanted to know more about the Provost's meeting and our course of action so I expanded on Puppy Dog's outrageous attempt at intimidation and my "ploy" for handling the expected campus reaction to the Stalker's latest outrage. She listened; her fingers went to her beads as the intensity in her eyes suggested the active mind that had earned a degree in English at Carter and, years later, a paralegal degree at Roger Williams University. Since she abhorred anything that was even a tiny bit devious, I expected a complaint and was surprised when she said with rigid certainty, "Of course, it wasn't The Stalker. Anyone can see that. Why would he rape and murder a *white* girl after weeks of attacking only blacks?" Her fingers brushed her curly, prematurely white hair. "It's not him."

She said it so confidently that I sat back, needing a few seconds to formulate my response. That gave her the opportunity to click her ballpoint pen, open her folder, and begin our Monday morning rundown of litigation, campus appeals, and miscellaneous projects in the office. Crisply, she described a series of evidentiary motions in a highly publicized sexual bias and harassment case that was our litigation priority, followed by a summary of a meanly fought tenure denial coming our way from the English Department. I made notes, more like doodles, on my copy of her memo, more intent of formulating my challenge to her than listening carefully. She finished with routine real estate and contract issues, a list of speech code and student rights appeals, and importantly, the status—almost done—of her draft of the federally required Campus Crime Report.

Finished, and before I could get back to The Stalker, she abruptly stood to leave, saying, "In case you missed it, the Reinman memorial service is scheduled for tomorrow morning. First Congregational, at eleven. Heard we can expect all the conservative poobahs from the cable networks to be there. Details in the *Crier*." A wry smile was playing on her face when she sniffed, "*You* really should be there."

I nodded—which she took at point taken—because I had read his obituary in the *Sunday Journal* and because I didn't want to get into the political discussion that clearly was her purpose. Marcie, whose politics is the stuff of NPR and Bill Moyers, loathed Carl Reinman, Carter's most well-known and most controversial faculty member. More than once over the years, she had referred to Reinman by the nickname hung on him by his enemies on campus: the "apostate".

She left the office, albeit, disappointed I had not risen to the bait, leaving me to wonder if even in death, Reinman would be forgiven by the Marcies on our campus. As an undergraduate, she along with her classmates had idolized Reinman, then the iconic leader of faculty radicals who made Carter University the *hot* campus of its day, a place of no grades, open curriculum, Third World Studies programs, and a deconstructionalist view of the world. Years later, when Reinman morphed into an ideologue of the political right, Marcie, along with her contemporaries on Carter's faculty and elsewhere, felt betrayed. Pens were dipped in vitriol as academia complained that he had sold out to the Republicans, that his highly publicized conversion was all too pat and opportunistic, and the disparagement of his motives and ideology remained unabated to this day. Personally, my few conversations with him had been friendly enough, even if it didn't take much, I recalled, to get his back up whenever the liberal bent of our faculty or the current campus cause was the topic.

The Chapel Bell began to toll eleven, reminding me of schedules and work. I turned to the computer and scrolled through files. I intended to read what the Information Office had previously released as coming from the President on The Stalker but stopped at my saved files and clicked on "Incidents and Victims." A list of names and dates filled the screen. "Sarah Tyson—October 10; Yvonne Kafume—October 17; Maria DeGoes—October 24; Francine Johnson—October 31; Juanita Jones—November 6; Latoya Chapin—November 13." Then, two Saturdays without attacks. I started to type in "Anne Sullivan" when Marcie's certainty slowed my fingers.

That neat chronology was at the heart of the University's dilemma. In point of fact, until the rape of Francine Johnson, the fourth Stalker victim, none of the assaults had been reported to any University office through the ignorance, indifference, or embarrassment of the victims, and the complete disregard for common security concerns by the Providence police. Each of the first three victims had been saved by the chance intervention of others: Ms. Tyson, thrown into an alley next to a student hangout at Hope and

Gower Streets, by bar-goers entering the alley to relieve themselves; Ms. Kafume, cornered in the vestibule of a rooming house at the RISD end of Benefit Street, by the arrival of another lodger; and Ms. DeGoes, a graduate student from Recife, Brazil, attacked while jogging after midnight on Arnold Street, by a late-night walker and his rottweiler. Ms. Tyson and Ms. Kafume filed complaints with the cops although neither contacted the Security Office—as all students are instructed and continuously reminded—and the police hadn't bothered to inform us either.

Francine Johnson's rape changed everything. He broke into her apartment on Young Orchard Street, waited for her to return, held a black handled knife at her throat, threatened to slash her face, gagged her, pulled off her jeans, and raped her, all the while muttering loathsome, racist filth. Although seriously injured, she dragged herself to the nearby Infirmary and the assault was reported immediately to both the police and Security Office.

Francine was the first to be threatened with a knife.

I recalled vividly how College Hall blew it then and there. We couldn't get ahead of the news. While Francine Johnson's rape drew an inside story in the *Journal* and didn't make television news, the *Crier* naturally blasted away; since she was a member of the Student Council, her rape had a tremendous campus impact which gave impetus to the other victims to surface with crushing rapidity. On Tuesday, Yvonne Kafume gave the *Crier* an interview on her assault, replete with a graphic recitation of her attacker's choice of language. Sarah Tyson went public on Wednesday, and when Maria DeGoes went to a counselor at the Women's Center, she was in the *Crier* on Thursday. Providence television news and the *Journal* as well as Boston and New York newspapers were now into the story and a headline writer at the *Boston Herald* came up with the name "The Carter Stalker"—which made the Admissions Office cringe—when it became clear that the victims' descriptions of their assailants matched: medium height and bulky, dark leather jacket, black gloves, black wool cap, mesh nylon mask, guttural voice, fetid breath, and body odor. An artist depiction, useless without a face, was generated for the campus and by the weekend, the cops, College Hall, the Security Office, and the *Crier* put it together: "Fingers" had returned, with a vengeance.

"Fingers!" I spit out and sat back. Last spring, Fingers had been a creep who jumped out of late night shadows to get his jollies with a grope at female flesh before running off at the first resistance. A burly guy in a black jacket, black gloves, and black wool cap, with breath like a toad that every victim remembered. Back then, he exhibited no obvious racial bias in his choice of victims and — maybe this was the reason the Security Office matched the cops in lassitude—he didn't use a weapon. Shamefully, with so many other things on the agenda in College Hall, including the inauguration of a new president, and with the Security Office in caretaker mode after its chief resigned in frustration at the University's ambivalence on security issues, College Hall tacitly accepted the kids' take of Fingers as a wimp so feckless in his attempts that he deserved his dismissive nickname. Sure, flyers were posted and campus patrols beefed up but when his attacks ceased after Commencement, and the summer session passed without incident, he was off our screen.

Until now.

I went to the next victim, Juanita Jones. The first week in November was memorable. Nothing went right. College Hall's responses to the crisis smacked of a whiney "it's not our fault!" while the Security Office, its ignorance of the three prior assaults admitted, was castigated by the usual anti-everything campus activists along with the justifiably concerned. It didn't help when Tuttle, who had been hired in August, told the *Crier* that coordination with the Providence police was "inadequate," which, of course, infuriated Chief McCarthy, a man known to glory in his disdain of the University. Within the inner sanctum of his third floor office in the Public Safety Building, McCarthy, Tuttle learned, had given us a Providence salute: "Fuck'em! They want a cop on every corner, fer chrissakes, and here they are marchin' with Jesse Kingdom and his mob. Fuhgeddaboutit!" There went any chance of a focused investigation or a dragnet and questioning of past offenders.

The lack of police support kept us vulnerable on the following Saturday night, when despite a full force of security officers deployed on and near the campus, Juanita Jones, captain of the women's track team, was assaulted outside an apartment building in Fox Point. She managed to fight him off, report the incident that night, and leave for her home in Chicago the following morning. Her absence led to wild rumors and it took days to get the story out with some semblance of truth.

Not that truth mattered much; with this attack, the activists and campus fringies had momentum. An over-the-top rally on The Green the following Tuesday brought out hundreds of students shrilly demanding protection and threatening a campus shutdown. Not unsurprisingly, a significant portion of the faculty, especially younger ones who thought they had missed out on the thrill of campus militancy enjoyed by a prior generation—a *nostalgie de la boue*, a nostalgia for the mud, according to one of the deans—agreed or acquiesced or accommodated and their classes became little more than consciousness-raising sessions. The routine of the University began to grind to a halt.

I was now at the last screen. Latoya Chapin, a senior from Baltimore, vice-chair of the Black Student Caucus, the daughter of a congressman, a charming young woman with crinkly, intelligent eyes, and hitting me close to home, my student intern last year, second semester. On the following Saturday night, despite safety admonitions of every kind, our entire security force and even a few cops in the neighborhood, she answered a knock at the door of her second floor apartment on Olive Street and The Stalker was inside, his knife at her throat. Before, during, and after her brutal rape, he spewed humiliating, racist trash. After he left, she called 911 and collapsed. With the lurid facts reported in Monday's *Journal*, embellished on local television, and exaggerated in the *Crier*, the campus roiled with strident condemnations of the University and the police—which didn't go unnoticed in the Public Safety Building or City Hall. The shutdown movement gathered steam as the media invaded the campus: when they didn't interview victims, they got to victim's friends, or friends of friends, or anybody else with a gripe with the University or Providence cops and time for a sound bite. The *New York Times* ran a front page story headlined "Campus in Crisis" and Oprah found Juanita Jones and paired her with other college rape victims for a weepy, chilling hour. Parents bombarded College Hall with complaints, alumni around the country sounded alarms, the local NAACP chapter president wondered loudly about the University's "inaction," Reverend Jesse Kingdom blasted our Security Office as well as the cops, and the Admissions Office noted a sharp drop in applications and campus visits. Carter University was living its worst nightmare: national and bad, very bad, publicity with the potential for shutdown.

"Ugh!"

As I closed the file to begin drafting Danby's statement, I recalled his empathetic demeanor only a few days earlier as Latoya's father, the congressman, paced the President's office. His palms pounded each other in rage. His daughter had been raped! The University was culpable! He was hiring a Johnnie Cochrane! "*This* should not be happening to *black* women under a *black* man's care!"

Danby's expression indicated to Dwayne McAllister and myself that we shouldn't respond, so we didn't. Only nine months earlier, Charles Danby had been the surprise choice of the Board of Trustees who had plucked him from obscurity at a small, midwestern liberal arts college and installed him as Carter's fourteenth president and the first black president of an Ivy League institution. He was beginning to resolve the leadership vacuum left by his predecessor but watching him take the father's wrath, the depth of weariness in his dark eyes was palpable, as though his presidency was about to be overwhelmed by events. Already there were nasty rumblings, repeated meanly even among some faculty and administrators, that maybe Danby wasn't up to the challenge. Even more despicable was the rumor that The Stalker's attacks were the direct result of the massive, positive publicity attending Danby's selection and inauguration as President. How else, the gossips whispered, to explain that in a city with eight other colleges and universities, with thousands of women students, a substantial number of whom are black, all The Stalker's victims are Carter women. *Black* Carter women.

CHAPTER THREE

After finishing my draft of Danby's statement and reviewing Marcie's edits, I e-mailed the finished product to the Provost, the President's secretary, and the Information Office. The draft and editing had taken longer than I expected—it was close to one o'clock—and I was pleased that the statement was not especially trite, despite the difficulty of trying to say something that hadn't been already repeated *ad nauseam*. I was hungry enough to brave a frigid wind that was warning Providence of the imminence of winter for a take-out lunch. When I felt my Blackberry's vibrations, I was on Thayer Street, heading back from Johnny Rockets with a paper bag containing plastic tubs of chili con carne and salsa, and an Orangina. Its screen displayed a number that I knew well and which could not be dealt with on the run.

Back in College Hall, Maria flagged me down as I passed her desk; she cradled her phone with her neck and held up a pink "while you were out" note. She mouthed to me, "Your mother called."

"I know," I said, and touched the cell phone at my belt. I snatched the note, aware of the knowing look from Maria. Victoria Elizabeth Mason Temple did not use voice mail. Nor e-mail, as she found it intrusive as soon as the first bit of porno spam hit her computer screen. I took off my Burberry and suit jacket and sat at my desk to decipher Maria's scribbles: "Reverend Thomas called Sylvia. Police…" and something illegible "…student. Member of church…Needs help. Call before 3:45."

I was glad that I had a clue as to her concern before returning the call. Sylvia Odum has been my mother's cook, maid, confidante, and companion for decades. Reverend Thomas is Sylvia's pastor, the elderly minister of a black Baptist Church on Halsey Street, and a not unfamiliar figure to me when there was a pastoral request for the church's needy, fuel bills, repairs to the roof or pipe organ, or other expenses that my family had traditionally and anonymously underwritten. I touched the microphone and speaker buttons on the telephone console and one labeled "home". Sylvia answered.

"Hi, is she there?"

"She's upstairs. Let me tell her you are on the phone." I was put on hold as Sylvia used the intercom. That meant that Sylvia was in her kitchen, comfortable in its dated décor of pastel pink and green tiles, vintage appliances, and triple sinks, maybe with freshly baked bread cooling on the table. *Mmmm.* I removed the lid from the chili container, poured in the salsa, put a paper napkin under my chin, and had dipped in a plastic spoon when I heard my mother's beguiling, Low Country accented voice.

"I wish Reverend Thomas had called you di-rectly. I spoke to the *po*-or man. Always something, isn't it? Seems the son of a church member knew this girl..., the student..., who was murdered over the weekend..., the Carter student? And the police are looking to question the boy. Now, with all of these racial problems in the city, he needs some advice and wants to talk to you...."

"Reverend Thomas or the boy?"

"Reverend Thomas." Pause. "I think."

"This is a murder investigation, Mom, and I—"

The serene self-confidence of a grand dame in her late seventies was in her voice as it rose ever so slightly. "Of course, I *to*-ld Reverend Thomas that you would as soon as you could. In fact, I *to*-ld him I'd see if you could be here around four o'clock."

My mother's aplomb had been nurtured by her Beaufort heritage and a friendship, beginning at Sarah Lawrence, with socialite Jacqueline Bouvier, grown through marriage to my father—a war hero, Jack Kennedy pal, Democratic fundraiser, and heir to the Temple fortune—and matured as she took on his leadership role in civic, charity, and political fundraising when he died after a horrific battle with cancer when brother Nick and I were ten and eight respectively. Nick and I grew up under her strict but loving guidance, watching others comply with her gently given orders; to this day, she remains our family's conscience and arbitrator of standards. "You should speak to him in the study. He'll be comfortable there."

I shook my head, resignedly. I knew the drill. Reverend Thomas' church and its congregation remained a family responsibility. Okay, it sounds patronizing, but there it is. Within my family, racial inequality is America's greatest tragedy, its greatest injustice, and you do what you can. Victoria Elizabeth Mason Temple would expect my full attention, despite complications and time constraints, and so would Sylvia, even though the church my mother remembered fondly for its religiosity, its traditions, and service to the black community was now a dwindling congregation of white-haired women and a few old men, a church that had lost out to more socially active, evangelical or mainstream denominational churches throughout the East Side. Not that it would have made any difference to Victoria Elizabeth Mason Temple. Family responsibilities were timeless.

My failure to respond quickly brought a subtle rebuke. "Reverend Thomas is..., we are all..., getting on. Only more reason to assist when we can. I'm going to be at your Aunt Vera's at four for tea. See what is troubling that *po*-or man, dear, and help him out if you can."

And that was it. I agreed to meet him and we said goodbye. I had once again been called for duty. I finished my rations like a good soldier and arranged my work schedule to meet her challenge.

○ ○ ○

At five minutes before four, after checking the *Journal*'s website—nothing on the murder—I was walking past the brick-faced dorms of the Old Quad and down Carter Street to the smooth cobblestones of Boone Lane, my hands deep inside my raincoat's pockets. Within moments, I reached the driveway gap in the mossy brownstone walls of Mary Street where the wide, ornately embellished iron gates to Temple House were open. As I turned into the rising, graveled drive, a shaft of sunlight escaped pewter-gray clouds, illuminating the mansion's ruddy bricks and flashing off its white balustrades and three floors of double-width, multi-paned windows. The scene was so striking that I paused.

Temple House had been on my mind since Thanksgiving. Nick, up from New York City with his family for the holidays, suggested, as we played billiards after dinner, that we ought to be thinking about what was going to happen to the house after our mother passes. Neither of us would reside there. Would the University accept a donation? Or the Historical Society? Probably both would if we pledged enough capital to insure the maintenance, in perpetuity, of the house with its outbuildings and its two acres of landscaped grounds, ancient copper beeches, elms, oaks, and mock cherry trees, and formal gardens.

Since our conversation, my mind had been uneasy as to the inevitable change. For six generations, the mansion had been not *Temple House* to our family but our home. Even now, there stirred within me a pang of family pride. Sitting on the highest ground of Providence's historic East Side, with views to Narragansett Bay and a downtown where the oldest structures are still known as Temple Bank and Temple Exchange, Temple House, a paragon of early American design and craftsmanship, rightly deserves the compliment bestowed by John Quincy Adams: the "most elegant formal house in New England."

An impatient car horn on Benefit Street ended my rumination. I resumed my walk up the drive, past beds of impatiens and nasturtiums, to a turn-around in front of a four stall garage and a narrower continuation that ran under a porte-cochere at the rear of the house. My mother's ten year old Volvo station wagon was missing from the drive which meant she had already left for English tea, bite-sized sandwiches or sponge cake, and gossip at the home of my maiden aunt a few blocks away on John Street. I unlocked the door, wiped my shoes on the cocoa mat, and went through the rear hall, pantry, and kitchen to the spacious center hall. Its massive crystal chandelier was, as usual, unlit and what sparse light there was passed through the famously decorated stained glass window—Rhode Island's state seal of a golden anchor wrapped by a banner proclaiming "Hope"—over the double front doors. Sylvia was sitting on a bench under a seascape of storm driven surf by William Troast Richards, her green cardigan sweater covering her more than ample figure. Next to her, almost hidden by her bulk, was Reverend Thomas.

I greeted them and they stood. Sylvia, at five-three or so, is no taller but has twice the girth of her pastor. Her full, multiple-chinned face, beneath pulled-back, steel colored hair, registered strength and kindness and her eyes gave me a *take care of this* look as she took my raincoat and retreated to the kitchen. Reverend Thomas offered me both his hands and I felt bones as fragile as a bird's as he grasped mine. He followed me across the hall to the study, a stooped figure in a tight black suit, black cloth bib and clerical collar, his posture hiding a deeply lined face the color of

37

worn Navy shoes, protuberant eyes, wispy white eyebrows, and flat nose with flaring nostrils.

The study reeks seriousness. With its enormous granite fireplace and blackened hearth, closed beige draperies, walnut floor-to-ceiling bookcases, and numerous portraits illuminated by overhead lighting that went on as the door opened, the room's formality limits its use to important matters, such as when Nick, our family's public man, the Brown Brothers partner, and face in the *Forbes 400* listing, discusses our complicated family finances. I turned on both a table lamp and a floor lamp as I led the old man across a plum-colored Shiraz carpet to a leather chair in front of my father's marble, Italianate desk. As he lowered himself slowly, arthritically, into the chair, I pulled out the desk chair, and finding the room remained too dark for intimate conversation, tugged at the beaded chain on the desk's green-shaded banker's lamp.

Reverend Thomas's acorn colored eyes measured the room, feeling its familiarity and security, while we made small talk about the weather and his church. I had to concentrate to avoid the dry-throated, too well-bred, Bertie Woosterish voice that can sneak up on me when I'm uncomfortable in situations like this. In contrast, he spoke in the style of the pulpit, disarmingly simple and a little repetitive. It took all of several minutes for him to get to his purpose.

"It's about the murder, the one on Veasey Street." His eyes, which had been fixed on me, searched the desktop. "This boy, his name is Williams. Lavelle Williams. His mama is in the church. His pa, a house painter, died years back. She worked houses until she got sick some time ago. A strong, god-fearin', church goin' woman. The boy used to come to church with his mama until he got into high school and started to get into things, ya know, and dropped out. Left here a year or so ago, then came back this summer."

The old man hunched closer to the desk and his words surged out of him. "He started going 'round with this girl, this white girl, the one that was found killed, y'see? He stayed with her, I guess, some of the time." He pulled a large white handkerchief out of his back pocket, wiped his forehead, and left it open on his lap. "Anyways, he went to his mama's this morning. Said the po-lice was lookin' for him, that they wanted to know about the girl 'cause she'd been killed. Now, I said Missus Williams is *strong*! She didn't want him shot or somethin' runnin' away from the po-lice, what with all the troubles we've been havin'. She brought him to me." His long bony fingers played within the circle of light under the lamp. "Nowadays, I suppose most of our people would go runnin' to a lawyer or to the councilman or to somebody like Jesse Kingdom..."—his voice betrayed disapproval—"...but Missus Williams came to her pastor. I need to help her if I can." He looked straight into my eyes. "She got it out of him. This girl. He didn't do it but he was with her last Friday night before she got killed!"

Tuttle's report at the Provost's meeting flashed in my memory. Was the boyfriend being *black* the cause of Tuttle's seeming hesitation? Why? Puppy Dog? McAllister?

"They met and went to her apartment. He...slept...with her, he says, then they had an argument. A bad fight. He said she had a bad temper, called him names..."—he paused, unclear as to whether to repeat the names—"...bad stuff, and he left her. He swore to his mama that is all that happened. He didn't kill her! She's a strong believer. She made him put his hand on his father's Bible and swear it was true, and he repeated it to me."

My reaction was expressed too curtly and portentously. "It sounds to me that he needs a lawyer—"

"His mama wants him to tell the truth to the po-lice but he's scared 'bout what'll happen. Seems some po-lice warned him about bein' with this girl before, ya' know. No tellin' what is goin' to happen, so many stories 'bout that these days. If he runs for it, that's like sayin' he did it. And, he'll get caught and...." He ran his hands over his balding scalp and blinked his baleful eyes. "I don't think the po-lice are goin' to waste a lot of time on a black boy who's been livin' with the daughter of a white po-lice-man—"

"She was a student of ours—"

"Now," he said, expectation in his eyes, "I thought if *you* could make arrangements for him to talk to Commissioner Tramonti, he's a good man, I hear, and Miss Odum says he's your friend. Maybe Lavelle gets a chance to tell his story without some lawyer gettin' in the way, makin' it appear he's guilty by not lettin' the truth talk! This way, they gotta treat him right! If he comes in through you and your friend, he'd be protected!" Bitterness crept into his voice. "Maybe they'll keep lookin' for who did it, not just close it up 'cause they caught a black boy who's been sleepin' with a white girl who gets herself killed!"

He slumped back into his chair, the energy that had propelled him here exhausted.

I couldn't let the lawyer advice go. Reverend Thomas was naive to expect anything but hostility despite any arrangement as to how Williams was delivered to the Public Safety Building. "If he's wanted for questioning, he should go in with a lawyer. The lawyer will advise him as to whether he tells anybody, anything. There are technical evidence rules at play here. The lawyer will protect his rights." Almost as an afterthought, I added, "I can't be that lawyer."

He pushed his chair away from the desk and stood up, trembling with emotion. "I know what I should do, Alger," he insisted, his eyes burning. "I haven't been preachin' the gospel all these years not to know to get the truth!" His voice filled the room, perhaps reaching out into the hall. "Aren't we protectin' his rights by makin' sure he gets there safely, makin' sure that he isn't hurt? Those the rights I got to worry about! We gotta protect that boy and that woman's faith in her church, and *do the right thing*!"

In the silence that followed, I realized that it was *my* predicament that made me hesitant. Chief McCarthy would throw up at any involvement by Alger Temple, the hated University's lawyer, on behalf of a suspect in the murder of a cop's daughter, complicating the University's already fragile relationship with the police. Puppy Dog would be on it in a minute! But, then, the old man had every reason to expect Temple family help. We had always been there. Even the room gave off a sense of familial duty. Maybe, I concluded, I could arrange *something* with Tramonti, without getting identified as the go-between. Why would he have to let anyone know?

"I'll try to reach Commissioner Tramonti," I said warily. "But," I said sternly, "Williams has to have a lawyer!"

His face relaxed immediately. "Praise the Lord," he said slowly and sat down, his eyes evidencing triumph in the use of the powerful in the name of the church. *He* had moved the moment, not some cheap politician, no lying lawyer, no Johnny-come-lately reverend strutting with a bullhorn! "Maybe you could call him right now, Alger," he urged, "before the boy stops listenin' to his mama."

Tramonti took my call and didn't interrupt or ask questions when I explained Reverend Thomas's request. When he responded, he was unusually direct. The preliminary examination of Ms. Sullivan's body found dope in her system, with more in her apartment. Williams, her boyfriend, ran a "page boy" operation, selling drugs on the East Side and its campuses with cell phones and pagers, for Nestor Flores, the biggest, meanest drug lord in the West End, the heart of the city's drug turf. Most of the city's street dealers, he said, are Latino or a member of one of the Asian gangs but on the East Side, a lot of the dealers were black and Lavelle Williams was in Flores's "crew."

Ugh! Reverend Thomas depicted Lavelle Williams as a scared kid and it turns out he's a dealer!

The murderer could be The Stalker, Tramonti went on, and just as likely not. If Williams came in, he'd be tested, fingerprinted and samples taken, there'd be lots of questions, and he'd better have an alibi. All of this was delivered in an uncharacteristically laconic monotone and it seemed that Tramonti would refuse to meet at all; then, in a roundabout way, he seemed to talk himself into it. "Okay," he said firmly. "Eight o'clock. In my office. I'll have detectives here who will be straight. Let's see what Williams has to say. And you and your reverend friend had better accompany him."

"What?"

"If I go out on this limb for you, your presence is my guarantee that this was a serious request and worth the risk."

"Wait a minute, I just—"

"Algy, don't push it. I'm doing this only to get him in here before something else happens. The girl is the daughter of a cop, remember? Lots of my heroes are out looking for Williams as we speak. I'll put a hold on picking up Williams on your personal assurance that he'll be here tonight. If you can't live with that, forget this call, no meeting, and he'll get picked up eventually." I remained silent. "You get into the parking lot behind the Public Safety Building a few minutes before eight. I'll be there, and we'll go upstairs. You don't have to stay."

With resignation, I agreed. His "good-bye" could have been a groan.

I put down the telephone and repeated the plan to Reverend Thomas. He would deliver Williams to my home at seven forty-five and we would drive downtown. My everyday car, a Mini Cooper, wouldn't fit us all and my new Ranger Rover HSE might seem over the top for this short trip but I let the thought go by and gave him two names of criminal defense attorneys who our students sometimes used and who accepted modest retainers.

We shook hands and left the study. Sylvia was back on the bench in the hall; her face wore a concerned expression until Reverend Thomas's smile perked her up. "It's going to be all right," I heard her whisper in his ear as we entered the kitchen, with the same tone she used, when as a child, I scraped my knee or confessed some venial sin. She took him by the arm and directed him through the pantry to the rear hall where I heard her say, with more conviction, "It's going to be all right!"

She held his nondescript black overcoat as he slipped it on and when he turned to face us, his eyes were hopeful. "The Lord will be with us. I know it." He laughed, winked at Sylvia, we said good-bye, and he walked out into the courtyard. I returned to the kitchen and its always full cookie jar on the baking counter.

I took out a handful of Sylvia's homemade oatmeal and raisins, and was about to caution her as to too much optimism when she surprised me with a wide-armed, pressing hug.

That's why I get into things.

CHAPTER FOUR

I had a choice. It was six blocks either to my house or to Jimmy's in Fox Point where I could get a drink, play a little pool, have a quiet dinner, and take a cab home in plenty of time for the arrival of Reverend Thomas and Lavelle Williams. I chose Jimmy's.

On the walk over, I checked my voice messages and e-mails on the Blackberry and responded to a message from the Provost with a call. Sometime after four, he said, the police had released a surprisingly bland and inconclusive statement which didn't stress The Stalker's possible involvement, although Chief McCarthy had made a crack to a *Journal* reporter—who called the Information Office for comment—that The Stalker may now be going after "white girls" too. *What?* McAllister reported grisly rumors were rolling through the campus; Danby's press release—which had been altered to fit with the police account—was out to the media and e-mailed to students. Danby had been interviewed by the *Crier* and would visit the Refectory and two of the women-only dorms on the Meeting Street campus. The Provost hazarded a guess that the victim's race, the murder not on a Saturday night, and her no longer being a student might dull the immediate impact although the relative calm wouldn't likely survive tonight's television news, Refectory gossip, and the *Journal* and *Crier* tomorrow. I told him about Puppy Dog's follow-up call on Jesse Kingdom; he grunted in disinterest and mused aloud as to how long Danby could avoid a shutdown.

"Ugh."

45

○ ○ ○

Jimmy's in Fox Point, at the corner of Wickenden and Otis Streets, is named for James Aloysius Hannigan, the *Jimmy* of Jimmy's Billiard Room, a pool room-cum-bookie parlor which right into the seventies had successfully ignored city ordinances prohibiting "the transport of alcoholic beverages from a licensed premises" and service of the same where games of "...pool, billiards or snooker are played not otherwise licensed..." through the judicious use of a dumbwaiter on call from Jimmy's Tap downstairs, also operated by the wily Mr. Hannigan. Like most of the buildings on the block during that era, it was a two-story and gambrel roofed, rundown, with uneven clapboards and peeling paint; a Narragansett Beer sign hung askew over the door to the Tap while the Billiard Room was entered by climbing a tremulous outside staircase at the rear.

To a teenager of my time, the Billiard Room was thrillingly disreputable, murky with stale smoke and redolent of last week's beer, a hangout for gamblers, off-duty cops and firemen, pool junkies, and neighborhood characters with bellies hanging over belts and White Owls or Phillies in the corners of their mouths. These worthies tolerated the presence of me and Tony Tramonti only because James Aloysius Hannigan's son, then and forever after known as "Young Jimmy," was a buddy of Tony's from the Boy's Club downtown and, eventually, mine as well.

Tramonti, Young Jimmy and I "racked 'em" whenever there was a free table, shooting games like eight ball, nine ball, and straight pool in all of their variations, along with local favorites like Stop-Dog, Fox Trot, and Minus, games unknown in the billiard room of Temple House. Early on, I knew I had some talent for the game; my almost embarrassingly long arms and fingers were advantages, particularly in finesse and middle table shots where other players strained and stretched or resorted to what we derided as the "crutch," the perfectly legal bridge stick. Since my father was a crack billiards player, as was my grandfather, maybe genetics played a role. In any event, pool gave a shy, gangly kid confidence and experiences in a slice of society that otherwise would have likely been denied to me.

That was over thirty years ago, and now Fox Point's East End, while still a Portuguese and Cape Verdean neighborhood, has also attracted the gay community and is in the process of gentrification, the first floor saloon is now a restaurant renowned for authentic Portuguese food, and the pool parlor has gone respectable as a private club. For fifty dollars a month, you can become a "friend of Jimmy", an "FOJ," provided Young Jimmy liked you and you can shoot pool. That got you a key to the door up the back steps and into the members-only, refurbished billiard room where the serious players among FOJs sharpen their skills during the week, the *bangers* play on weekends, and Young Jimmy sponsors the occasional big money game, with all the drama and cash of *The Color of Money*.

The place exudes male-only, despite several women members, with its bare brick walls, subdued lighting, classic billiard posters of turn-of-the-century masters, and one advertising the "match of the century" between Willie Hoppe and Willie Mosconi, New Orleans, 1954. Until recently, there was a cigar case next to the twenty foot long, mahogany, BYO, self-serve bar, and smoking is still officially sanctioned in the private club although discouraged by Young Jimmy's frowns after his wife's bout with breast cancer. Comfortable leather couches on a raised platform face either a projection screen television or the four tables—nine foot Brunswicks and Gabriels, each illuminated under three shaded lamps and covered with green Simonis cloth—placed so play on one didn't invade another's space. Racks of Vikings, Predators, Intimidators, Schoens, and custom cue sticks line the outer wall.

Five-thirty was too early for any FOJs, and when I entered, I had the place to myself. I made a Gordon's gin and tonic with makings from my labeled stock behind the bar, pulled a Viking cue from the wall rack, and loaded a nine ball layout. The feel of the cloth under my fingers and the smack of the break gave me a needed lift; I had no particular game in mind and took shots, including virtually impossible combinations and double banks, for fun. After fifteen minutes or so, a few other FOJs arrived and then Young Jimmy came up, pulled a cup of Poland Spring water from a dispenser behind the bar, and checked the room. He came over to me and watched my play without comment.

I'm thought of here as a pretty good shooter, eligible for master status in the club's standings, tournaments, and the occasional stakes game, but not in the same league as Young Jimmy. He learned pool from people who beat you and took your money so he critiqued FOJs only when he gave a formal lesson or exhibition. He had been a club player, too early for ESPN and the big cash pay-offs now offered in Las Vegas, a "Fast Eddie" who was into the rat race of "tournaments" in every small city on the East Coast. In his prime, he had been a shark among the fish, the best in a city of pool players and probably in New England, a natural shooter who never quite understood why others don't see the angles and the ball paths, or have the stick control, or remember shots that they'd seen or made or missed, like he does. But then, damn few players are like Young Jimmy.

Young Jimmy asked after Nadie, a frequent dinner companion in the restaurant, and mentioned a weekend exhibition match he had set up for a couple of pros, then made his rounds to the other tables, and went downstairs. I had my Blackberry out to reserve a cab for seven when it buzzed.

I read the number and pressed the green phone symbol. It was Tramonti—and he was pissed!

"Lavelle Williams was picked up about thirty minutes ago. He's in interrogation. Somebody here decided to break up our party. He was at his mother's place on Camp Street, with your minister friend. Caused enough of a commotion that back-ups were called in. Anyway, he had junk on him, enough to get him for possession, maybe intent to sell. By now, he's been charged, fingerprinted, blood tested, and photographed." Tramonti coughed, then continued. "I'm home, but I'm going downtown. Do you want to come? I owe you that much."

I accepted immediately and told him where I was; he said he'd pick me up in ten minutes and hung up. Only then did I think of Reverend Thomas and his likely reactions: disbelief, followed by betrayal. I punched in 411 and got the number for the parish house.

"He's not here, Mr. Temple." The voice that answered was cool, elderly, and female. "He's with Missus Williams. They—" She stopped abruptly.

I felt embarrassed as only a do-gooder can when the do-good goes badly. "I'm going down to the police station with Commissioner Tramonti." There was no response. "Mrs. Thomas, do you know if your husband contacted a lawyer?"

"I don't know for sure, but I don't think so, 'cause he was relying on you...." An accusation hung in her voice.

The whole thing was such a goddamn mess. "Would you tell your husband that I'll call as soon as I have any news, and that I'm sorry..., really, very sorry—"

"I'll give him the message, Mr. Temple. Goodbye."

In my frustration, I kept the line open until the phone emitted a high-pitched squeal, then gulped down my drink, grabbed my Burberry, and went outside to the parking lot. The air felt cold, sour, and sooty. I thought of Lavelle Williams in custody, picturing him as scared, angry, and betrayed, until I recalled the drug dealers and gang members I had prosecuted so many years before—fiercely insubordinate, smirky, bravado oozing out of every pore, operating on the assumption that all was temporary— and my empathy wavered.

Tramonti's black GMC Envoy soon pulled in; I slid into the passenger seat, primed with questions, only to be ambushed by the slobbering tongue of Oboe, Tramonti's chocolate English Lab. "Sit!" came a gruff command and Oboe retreated to the rear seat with a disappointed whimper. As we peeled off, I snapped my seat belt into its lock. Tramonti was staring straight ahead, his large head rigid, his lips moving in and out, signaling conversation would not be welcomed.

We crossed the Providence River on the Steeple Street Bridge in front of Citizens Plaza and slowed only when faced with a bank of red brake-lights on Exchange Terrace between the skating rink and the refurbished railroad station complex. Tramonti's ill humor piqued at the traffic heading towards the Civic Center and Mall; he hit a switch on a flasher light on the dash, its globe burst into white and blue brilliance, and with Oboe howling and his master threatening punishment, we snaked through the bottleneck, ignored a traffic signal and irate car horns, roared past the Westin Hotel and Convention Center into LaSalle Square, and entered the parking lot behind the darkened hulk of the Public Safety Building. Tramonti parked in a space designated "COM'NER" next to three concrete steps that led to a battered metal door bare- ly illuminated by a red bulb in a wire cage. I followed Tramonti, with Oboe on a leash, up the steps where he paused to look through an eye-level, wire-reinforced window in the door, used a key, and charged inside.

Immediately, we were enveloped by the overheated air of a Providence municipal building, a dry, stale odor of disinfectant mixed with grime. The Public Safety Building is a graceless concrete pile—its façade gives the appearance that the architect just gave up—meant for, and filled by, unhappy people. Led by the dog who clearly knew his way, we ran up two gloomy flights of worn, metal-tread stairs, guided by paint-flecked banisters. At the third floor landing, Tramonti flung open a metal door to a starkly lit corridor with pea green walls and black and yellowish squares of linoleum. Oboe's claws echoed off the flooring until we stopped at a door marked "308 Commissioner, Enter Through 310" with an arrow pointing down the hall. Tramonti unlocked 308 and flipped a switch for fluorescent lights that reluctantly blinked on.

The office was crowded with non-descript furniture under a stained, dimpled tile ceiling and badly needed an air purifier. A dusty, fly-specked venetian blind hid a single window above a battered air conditioner. Oboe was taken off his leash and, after intently sniffing in each corner, found a place in front of a metal desk, his huge brown head resting on his paws. His master plunked down heavily in a squeaky, oak-backed swivel chair behind the desk, then stood to rip off his raincoat and suit jacket and throw them angrily to the floor behind his chair. His white shirt and Gucci tie maintained the veneer of the business lawyer he had once been—until the tie was yanked off, his shirt collar was unbuttoned, and his sleeves were rolled up over hairy forearms. A pack of Salems and a lighter were tossed on the file cluttered desk. He pushed in a button on a telephone console.

"O'Neil," somebody by that name answered.

"Tell the Chief the meeting is in here," Tramonti responded in a bellow; he released the button, put a cigarette to his lips, and motioned me—still standing—toward a chair. "This might take a while."

I closed the office door, dropped my Burberry over one of the three vinyl chairs facing the desk, and sat. Tramonit's cigarette remained unlit, maybe out of deference to me, maybe because in a moment of virtue, the city had banned smoking in public buildings. He used a remote for a CD player in a bookcase behind me and The Eagles' *Hell Freezes Over* began with "Get Over It". With the cigarette hanging from his lips, his icy eyes, curly black hair, swarthy complexion, and stony face begging for confrontation, he could have been one of the fellas from *Goodfellas*.

I didn't pursue conversation even as I wondered why he had asked me to come with him. It was then that I noticed there was no touch of *famiglia* here, not what I would expect from a Tramonti whose lineage demanded acknowledgement. The yellowish walls were unadorned except for a certificate of Tramonti's appointment as Police Commissioner. Was it a signal to all, especially to Chief McCarthy, that it was a place of transition?

Sonny Russo had appointed Tony Tramonti as Police Commissioner as a pay back for the generous campaign support Fausto Tramonti, Tony's brother, had given Sonny in past elections, with the expectation that the position would continue as a part-time ceremonial post and that Tony was just another uniform-enraptured dilettante who craved a city car and driver and the trappings of medal award ceremonies and press conferences. Which meant that the department—despite being racked by low morale, petty corruption, promotion-for-pay politics, cheating on entrance and promotion exams, well-publicized incompetence, and alleged racism—would remain Sonny's fiefdom.

It didn't go according to Sonny's play book. Within weeks of his confirmation by the City Council, despite being a civilian and a Harvard graduate to boot, Tramonti went full time and was exercising rights given exclusively to the Police Commissioner by the City Charter without so much as a "how're ya" to Sonny, who was insulted and embarrassed by this treachery. Tony's easy going personality and community roots meshed well with rank and file cops with whom he went on night patrols and drank with at their hang outs, never demeaning their modest educations or working class backgrounds as reformers often unconsciously do. When he bucked Sonny on promotions, secured a pay increase from the City Council for patrolmen, authored a settlement of a long-running discrimination suit on admissions to the Police Academy, and began community outreach in minority neighborhoods, his leadership began to pick up allies.

Sonny tried to fire Tony but lacked sufficient votes among the fractious Council members, some of whom also "owed" Fausto. Then, he resorted to sabotage. The FOP, the police union controlled by Chief McCarthy's mostly Irish and Italian contemporaries, "grieved" every personnel change to arbitrators but couldn't make the appeals stick—which gave Tramonti more clout—leaving the Chief to swallow his resentment and stay short of open defiance in day-to-day operations. Sonny seethed as Tramonti's accomplishments garnered admiring *Journal* editorials, more so when Providence politicos gossiped that this "comer", a tough-minded scion of the city's most well-known Italo-American family, was preparing to challenge Sonny for City Hall.

Tramonti abruptly silenced The Eagles. "I hear Jesse Kingdom will be up there on Friday."

I told him about the flyer, which he indicated he knew all about, and Puppy Dog's message from Sonny.

"This time, Puppy Dog just might be right," he grumbled.

I started to defend the University's decision but stopped. Wouldn't have made a difference. Since last August, Jesse Kingdom had become Tramonti's nemesis.

It began with a routine bust of an after-hours sip joint in South Providence. A black off-duty cop who tried to bring calm into the rowdy crowd was killed in a crossfire between patrol officers Ryan and Cabone and someone with a .38. False rumors, drunkenness, and a legacy of racism set off the arson, looting, and assaults the next night and into the next day, bringing on a police clampdown resulting in a plethora of allegations of police brutality. No doubt, the churls on the force used their privilege of street power against the "yoots" of South Providence; you could surmise that from the number detained rather than arrested, and the number of brutality complaints. Sonny and the Chief immediately rallied to the "rights" of "their" cops and attacked the "bleeding hearts" who didn't get their hands dirty "dealing with criminals." A state law, the *Policemen's Bill of Rights*, the legalization of the "blue wall of silence," required Tramonti to convene closed internal hearings into the allegations before he could refer them to the Attorney General for prosecution. When the hearing panels, by law appointed by the FOP and the Chief, found no cause for prosecution, Jesse Kingdom and his W.A.R. organization blasted away at Tramonti, not understanding—or seemingly interested in—the limits of the Commissioner's authority or the realities of directing a police department reeling with shock and fatigue.

In the aftermath, Tramonti, caught in the middle of controversy and without a political base of support, saw his election prospects plummet. Jesse Kingdom, more than even the caustic *Journal* editorials, was responsible. Many reformers who had indicated support for Tramonti did not want to back someone who earned Kingdom's condemnation while others shied away from opposition when Sonny was riding high. Sonny, scenting blood, rejoiced in the crippled candidacy of his rival but wanted the kill. The trials of Ryan, Cabone, and two other white officers under federal civil rights laws were set to begin next week at the federal court on Kennedy Plaza. Jesse Kingdom's announced courthouse rallys, Tramonti's inner circle believed, would be a suitable opportunity for Sonny to again whip up support and marginalize Tramonti.

The outer office door opened and slammed shut. Oboe sprang to his haunches, ignoring Tramonti's commands to sit. With a perfunctory knock at the office door, Chief McCarthy, resplendent in a blue blazer, gray slacks, and white turtleneck sweater, his chin forward and his chest puffed out, strode in. "I know what you're going to say," he said breezily, "and—"

He saw me and stopped in mid-stride. Oboe's muzzle rose as a low growl rolled in his throat.

"I think you know Alger Temple, Chief."

McCarthy recovered enough poise to acknowledge my presence with a hand offered only out of habit. I attempted to stand but he crowded me into remaining seated; he was so close I could smell his Aqua-Velva. "Good to see ya, Alga," he said as he crunched my hand, his voice not concealing irritation and making my name sound absurd.

Tramonti took the cigarette from his mouth and used it to stab the air. "They went against my direct order," he said in a deliberately staccato voice.

Twenty-five years of police force experience, and as many in the political wars of Providence, earn a survivor like McCarthy a doctorate in guile. His demeanor expressed the confidence of a self-possessed man used to command and he gave off more than a little insolence as he picked an imaginary mote of lint off his expensive-looking blazer. "Nothin' to get boiled about. He's part of Flores's gang and had some junk on him. Somebody didn't get the word and he got rousted—"

Tramonti, his face even darker than before, popped out of his chair and stormed around the desk; Oboe's ears went back and his teeth bared; Tramonti yanked back the dog's chain collar. "I gave specific orders. Williams was coming in, voluntarily, with his minister... *voluntarily*, I said, and these guys go in a black neighborhood, no warrant, and they bust into his mother's house! His *mother's* house? With his *minister* screaming that he's supposed to be meeting with me?" He caught his breath. "They knew what they were doing so I don't want any bullshit about a good bust!"

Tramonti's ferocity left McCarthy open-mouthed; the muscles on his neck stood out like cords and his already florid complexion flushed. He sucked in a deep breath, stuck out his chin, and braced his shoulders, a move only slightly less exaggerated than one from Rodney Dangerfield. "Look, it may make ya feel good to bring someone up on charges but that's not going to make anyone around here too popular. There are plenty around here who don't like the idea of a 'how-de-do' with this scumbag, especially when he's involved with Terry Sullivan's girl." When Tramonti didn't flinch, McCarthy shifted gears. "Anyway, he'll be here for awhile." He sat in the chair next to me and, with a coolness I had to admire, slipped into a patronizing "we know best" mode. "Y-o-o-u people up at Carter, y-o-o-u think all we got ta deal with is this Stalker. Let me tell ya, we—"

Tramonti was barely audible when he interrupted. "Get this. Anybody involved is in deep shit. The deepest." He was sitting on the edge of the desk, not more than a step from McCarthy. "Don't they get it...," his voice falling into a real wiseguy tone I hardly recognized, "...that this might blow the case? They had better grow eyeballs in the back of their heads!"

McCarthy's face had gone from surly to a twitchy recognition of a predicament: there *was* a problem if you screwed up a "family" case. "We got him so I don't see the beef," he said and shrugged.

His mean eyes made me wonder about how Williams was faring, either under questioning in an interrogation room facing some of McCarthy's finest or in a holding cell two floors below immersed in smells of dirty mattresses, sweat, and drunkenness from the tank down the hall. Right now, because of Tramonti, he'd be protected from any rough stuff, but for how long?

"Has he got a lawyer?" Tramonti demanded.

"I don't know. I just got here."

Tramonti responded by pushing the telephone console towards McCarthy. "Find out."

McCarthy grabbed the receiver, punched in three buttons on the console, and spoke to someone named Kelly. McCarthy's eyebrows raised appreciably. "He did?" he said with evident disbelief and listened for another moment before he hung up. "Jerry Franks," he said, sounding somewhat deflated. "He just showed up. LaVoie set the hearing for nine-thirty on possession and intent to sell charges."

The office was hushed as we absorbed the news. The criminal defense bar in Rhode Island is like everywhere else: a lot of ham-and-eggers live on DWIs, assaults, and other petty crime, and a few top guys in Canali suits, Zarella shoes, and Armani ties grab the big cases and fees. Jerry Franks, however, didn't need Milanese tailoring or other indicia of the criminal bar's success. He was above the top-of-the-top, the dean of the criminal lawyers in the state, for decades the successful, flamboyant, crafty defender of the mafia dons, indicted politicians, major drug dealers, embezzlers, and anyone else who could afford his services. All the biggest dirt bags of Rhode Island hired him because he was smart, crafty, a workaholic, and incredibly successful before Rhode Island judges and juries. How could a street kid like Lavelle Williams retain a Jerry Franks?

"Shit," Tramonti said with disgust, "the kid's protected! He's on Flores's tab!"

McCarthy, beginning to look as though he needed a handful of Rolaids, slowly got to his feet. "Let me find out who we got handling the hearing." Ignoring me completely, he left the room.

When the outer office door slammed shut, Tramonti stood and closed the inner door. To my amazement, there was a glint of victory in his eyes. "You've got to take advantage of any situation around here," he said, slapping me on the back. "The Chief has a problem. Some of his very own picked up Williams and will have to take the fall. Nobody likes that. How about some coffee?"

Without waiting for an answer, he opened the side door and went out into the corridor; Oboe, tail swishing madly, got up and almost beat him over the threshold. I sat back, trying to get a fix on what had been another skirmish in the grinding day-to-day war between the reformer Commissioner and the truculent Chief, a fight so intense that the combatants would pummel one another without care as to who was present. Anthony Michael Tramonti may be savoring a win right now but Daniel Patrick McCarthy would be planning his counterattack. There was no checkmate in this power game.

Tramonti returned, carrying two styrofoam cups; he waited for Oboe and then kicked the door closed. The tepid, greasy brew could have been sucked directly from the nearby Woonasquatucket River but that didn't seem to bother Tramonti. "LaVoie, the bail commissioner, is Franks's man. He'll do about anything Franks asks, unless we've got enough to embarrass him into letting us hang on to Williams for a few more hours. If not, LaVoie will let him out on personal recognizance on the junk charges." He sat on the edge of the desk and leaned toward me. "Williams plays into the politics here. The Detective Division guys McCarthy owns have put out the word that The Stalker is a suspect until shown differently. McCarthy doesn't like the picture of an Irish blond shacked up with a black dealer. It shames Terry Sullivan. One of his guys. Not the brightest, or the nicest. A survivor. Used to be secretary of the FOP. If she's a random victim of The Stalker, we don't have to get into her drugs or her love life. Fortunately, McCarthy doesn't own everybody and we'll get to the bottom of this eventually. So, what was he going to tell us?"

"As far as I know, no confession. What he would tell you...?" I covered my obvious hesitation with a sip of coffee. "It's all sort of hearsay, anyway."

"Hearsay?" Tramonti clapped his right hand to his forehead, a sound loud enough to prick up Oboe's ears. "Did you say 'hearsay?' Give me a break! You were a prosecutor, right? A long time ago but nothing's changed. You know we can hold him on hearsay! Even hearsay two steps removed! Or as a material witness!"

Tramonti's black eyes searched my face, expecting a lot more than I felt that I could give. "All I know is that his mother and Reverend Thomas talked him into coming in. Doesn't seem likely it was either a confession or an accusation." What I had somehow rationalized was that whatever Williams told Reverend Thomas, a clergyman, was privileged under Rhode Island law, and what Reverend Thomas told me would be privileged if he claimed I acted as his lawyer.

Or, something like that.

"Look, Algy, I was, *for you*, going to give him a chance to tell his story, and now it turns out he's a walking drug store, he's got Jerry Franks as his lawyer, and he'll be out of here in an hour. I'll look very stupid, Algy, very stupid. Nothing better for Sonny and the Chief."

I got the message. Tramonti and I go back to seventh form at Moses Brown Academy and were roommates at Harvard Law; I was his best man and godfather to his eldest daughter. That would be McCarthy's spin: the Commissioner was backing his old East Side buddy instead of one of the "blues."

Tramonti shook his head in frustration and went around the desk where he rolled his shirtsleeves even further up his muscular arms. "I should have known better than mix you up in this. A mistake. Because this will be nasty and very public before it's over and you are now up to your neck in this as far as the Chief is concerned. So is the University. Sonny and McCarthy can't separate things."

Better to leave it there, I thought. "I need a ride home."

His hand slapped the desk top. "I've got just the thing. A cruiser with siren, maybe lights flashing? Let everyone on The Hill know Mr. Temple was out fighting crime!" This came out as very sarcastic but ended with a trace of smile. "Better yet, I should just call Nadie to come and pick you up. She'd know how to get through to you."

Ugh.

CHAPTER FIVE

By the time the cruiser dropped me off, without blue and white strobe flashes or siren, it was after nine. Except for asking my address, the surly-faced cop at the wheel didn't say a word except "yuh" when I thanked him for the ride home. Already, I had the mark of a pariah.

I live in an 1830 Greek Revival nestled into the steep rise of The Hill on Congdon Street, a five minute walk up to the campus and a five minute walk to the downtown. The shambles I had purchased for its magnificent view of the city required two years of restoration, including a slate roof replacement, deleading of clapboards, granite buttresses to support the embankment down to Pratt Street, a new kitchen with a den facing the city's skyline, and a functional loft-like space out of most of the second floor. As I put my raincoat in the hall closet and hung my suit jacket over the banister, today's efforts by Mrs. Pina, my twice-a-week cleaning lady, were evident in the gleam of the hall table and the pervasive scent of Garden Fresh Glade. In the kitchen, a room of open chrome shelving, limestone flooring, and granite countertops, all traces of my bachelor weekend—dirty dishes in the sinks, pots on the Viking range, empty Sam Adams bottles, and the odor of pepperoni pizza—had been whisked away in her whirlwind of dust cloths and generous use of Windex. A large hand-painted ceramic bowl from Portugal, adorned with flowers, birds, leaping hares, and hounds and filled with gorgeous looking apples, was on the counter.

I opened the Sub-Zero for a beer, went into the adjoining den, and looked out into the night. In its blackness, the office and apartment towers of downtown were defined by layers of lights separated by Providence's boulevards, streets, and sweeping curves of its rivers; the domes of the State House were bathed in uplighting that magnified their size and presence. Yet again, the view confirmed that despite the cost, the haggles with the Preservation Commission for permission to create the den and the loft, and the irksome lack of city services on The Hill, it was worth the investment.

After a large swig of beer, I unclipped my Blackberry from my belt and called the parsonage. Reverend Thomas didn't interrupt as I told him that the arresting cops had acted against Tramonti's orders and that Lavelle Williams had a lawyer and would be released within the hour. After a long pause, in a voice that began in disappointment and became one of humiliation, he described the cops hammering at the door, the mother's wails, Lavelle Williams's attempt to escape out of a window and cries of betrayal, and his own pleas to the cops that Williams was on his way to the Commissioner's office. I assured him that his intervention might have saved Williams from harm, in words that came out as an apology. His response was a short and unequivocal statement of failure in his personal, redemptive mission. "Nothin' to do now," he said and ended the call with a "thank you" spoken so weakly that my embarrassment was acute. The thought of repeating the story to my mother and Sylvia was so unpleasant, I decided to put that off until tomorrow.

"Ugh!"

I needed a friend! Where was Nadie? Earlier, I had left messages for her at her apartment and at the Psychology Department, hoping that a few days away would reduce some of her recent prickliness toward the University—and me—for the "impotent" security efforts and their "underlying causes." Nadie the Psychologist is big on "underlying causes."

I reached her at the Women's Center. She said matter-of-factly, "I'm hungry. Why don't you pick me up and we'll get some Chinese." I promptly agreed. "I've only been back since four and all I've heard about is this murder. We've got two overcrowded groups going on here right now. Apparently, Danby went to some of the dorms tonight. The rumors...!"

"Ten minutes," I said.

Nadie was waiting in the vestibule of the Women's Center, a converted two-story residence across from the women's dorms on Peckham Street. We kissed and I felt her willowy body under her light raincoat. It was an inappropriately long kiss that was perhaps unexpected by both of us. She took a step back, looked at me as though startled, then faced a hall mirror where she swept her black hair over her shoulders. She smiled and my eyes lingered over the face in the mirror: prominent cheekbones and narrow chin, pale skin with a scattering of freckles over her nose, black eyebrows and eyelashes, a thin-lipped mouth with a natural pink that gave them measure, and green eyes that can be opaque as sea glass one second and exotic as emeralds the next. Catching my expression, she broke into a waif-like smile that can break my heart.

Ah, Nadie.

With a black bag slung over her shoulder, we went out into the chilly, foggy night where our breaths immediately clouded and were blown away by a sharp wind. As we approached Thayer Street, I was into an account of the last few hours, ending my excitedly-told tale with what I knew of Jerome Franks. "You should have seen McCarthy and Tramonti when they heard Franks was involved!"

Nadie didn't immediately respond. I'm in love with a woman who espouses the Shakespearean view that it would be a public good to get rid of all the lawyers. For her, most are over-paid, morally inert, agents of the propertied class; the only lawyers worth their salt worked for social agencies, the ACLU, or as public defenders. Criminal lawyers who defended Mafiosi or crooked politicians or corrupt corporate executives were worse than their clients, hence, her apparent quandary: an abhorrently notorious mouthpiece was defending a young black man from the mercies of the Providence police! After a moment of consideration, she said, in that whithering yet nonchalant Lauren Bacall-ish voice she has when edgy, "Whatever."

I knew better than to push.

Thayer Street, the campus's main drag, is alive, trashy, nondescript, and very non-Ivy, having had the benefit of haphazard growth which permitted the funky, the offbeat, and the counter-cultural to prosper, survive, or disappear without notice. The University, always ambivalent towards neighborhood complaints of any sort, usually maintains a deaf ear to the frequent merchant promoted, ambitious redesign projects, realizing that backing any plan would offend any number of campus groups. Anyway, our students like Thayer Street the way it is.

Tonight, the glistening sidewalks reflected the resplendent garishness of its jumble of bookstores, head shops, clothing stores, music stores, pizza and sub joints, clubs, Dunkin' Donuts and Starbucks, tea bars, restaurants, video stores, tattoo and body piercing parlors, hairdressers, and convenience stores. Multi-colored flyers, along with a zillion stapled bits of their predecessors, festooned utility poles and message kiosks; stands for alternative newspapers and entertainment and real estate guides competed with Keep Providence Beautiful trash bins for space at street corners. The beaded finishes of parked cars—too many of them sleek

BMWs and Audis and bulky SUVs to belie all of Sonny's prejudices towards our students—and rows of motorcycles at the curb reflected the storefronts' neon. Knots of students of both sexes flowed toward us from the Sisson Street dorms; a single white and blue police cruiser, its wipers swishing slowly back and forth, had a lone occupant who looked routinized to the streetscape. His token presence constituted tonight's city-provided protection from The Stalker.

We avoided an aggressive panhandler with a "veteran" sign looped around his neck as I remarked that not even the threat of The Stalker seemed to affect Thayer Street.

Nadie tugged me forward at a faster pace. "You think if something affects you in a certain way, it's like that for everybody. I don't know if it's sentimentality or the way you were brought up." She paused. "Either way," she said lightly, "it might be saner."

I didn't reply. When she begins a psychological excursion, I know better.

A group of teenage girls, perhaps thirteen or fourteen years of age, exploded from a pizzeria and walked noisily toward us, laughing, wide-eyed, two on their cell phones, all smoking cigarettes awkwardly. One in particular had enough makeup to qualify for a Rocky Horror Picture Show contest. I wondered aloud "Why aren't they home doing *something*? Where the hell are their parents! The Stalker could be one of those guys right over there," and gestured with my free arm towards some dark figures standing under the canopy of the Thayer Mini-Mart, "or anywhere."

Nadie drew me a bit closer. We were a block away from the China Dragon, our destination. Her head was bent slightly forward, her voice was so low that I had difficulty hearing her.

"When I was at Harvard," she began, "there was a rape, right off the Square, a block or so from our Radcliffe dorm. The victim was a grad student. A single, isolated rape. Not like this epidemic but it was really played up in the *Crimson* and in the *Globe* and on television." We waited at the corner of Olive Street while a rusty VW van held together by Grateful Dead bumper stickers and duct tape noisily turned into the street. "It's all we talked about," she continued. "Precautions, how terrible it would be to be assaulted, what would we do to defend ourselves. We got mace. We got instructions. We had meetings. Solidarity! Sisterhood!" We crossed the street in a miasma of the van's exhaust fumes. "It was...surreal, the sessions in which we discussed it, tried to deal with it. Then they caught him and it turned out to be a mentally challenged guy thrown out on the street when the state closed its mental institutions. He must have been a sex-starved time bomb and the state was responsible for—"

A passing motorcycle's rumble interrupted. She looked up at me sharply and was about to continue when she pointed towards the marquee at the Avon Cinema, the art film house down the block. It was a Monday night Kevin Spacey double feature, *Usual Suspects* and *L. A. Confidential*. "We could use a hard-boiled cop around here right now. Instead, we get the Providence version of Inspector Clouseau!"

The China Dragon, sandwiched between a comic book emporium and a crystal-happy holistic artifact store, was steamy with soy sauce, hot peanut oil, and spices. Huge handwritten signs on the walls lied "No MSG." Somehow, despite its meager décor of time-warped prints, yellowed fans, red lantern lights with dusty red tassels, worn linoleum, and scarred booths, it had survived competition from newer and glitzier Thai, Vietnamese, and other Asian restaurants by serving enormous helpings of inexpensive, really good food. The always disinterested manager flashed a gold incisor as we entered and led the way to a booth adorned with a bottle of dark sauce, a sprig of plastic flower in a tiny plastic vase, a container of napkins, and stained plastic-coated menus leaning against an imitation knotty pine wall. He continued through a bamboo curtain into the kitchen where pots clanged and crashes erupted as he got someone's attention in loud Cantonese over the strains of something twangy from the Hong Kong hit parade. We hung our coats on a pole next to the booth, slid in, flattened the menus on the Formica-topped table, and ordered a "number sixteen" for two from a diminutive waitress who neither greeted us nor thanked us for our order. She disappeared into the kitchen and returned to deliver a chipped ceramic teapot and two companion cups. Nadie poured and we clinked cups, sort of a salute to being together.

Nadie propped her head on her open palms and smiled. She was wearing a dark green blouse with a silver moon-shaped pin. Her skin glowed although her eyes were tired, with tiny crow's-feet in their corners. As a lead into telling her how much I missed her, I described my Thanksgiving and asked about hers. She recounted a weekend of mother-daughter bickering—not married, no grandchildren, you never call—and went on about the only child problem of a mother more than a thousand miles away, getting older, crankier, and lonely. Listening to her, I realized it was unlikely that she had lightened her perspective on the University's response to The Stalker: Nadie was of the fiercely held belief that College Hall had flubbed-the-dub on its handling of the crisis which, among other effects, resulted in extra hours for her as a volunteer psychologist at the Women's Center.

When she finished, I mentioned Reinman's death over the weekend and Marcie's unforgiving comments. Nadie's face screwed into a frown and she began to fidget with a paper napkin, wrapping it around and around her fingers. I assumed her reaction was because of his conservative politics and said so.

"Which doesn't put me in a distinct minority since he was—" She was interrupted as our meal, chicken with almonds, scallions, pea pods, and mushrooms, with a mound of white rice, arrived in a clatter of thick serving dishes pushed around the table by the waitress. As I started to serve the food, she said, "He made a pass at me when I first came here, and—"

The serving fork and spoon were caught in mid-air. "You've never mentioned it." She let me fill her plate, took two quick bites of the spicy chicken, and put down her fork. I filled my plate. "Beat me to it," I said and smiled, even though the eyes which met mine, didn't.

"No, you don't get it," she said soberly, patting her mouth with a napkin. "He was aggressive. He was playful but *very* aggressive. It was as though he could sense some vulnerability. To tell you the truth, after our first encounter, I was...wary of him."

It is hard for me to imagine that Nadie would be *that* put off by Reinman, or anyone else, for that matter. She is basically fearless, assumes yoga positions you don't see on Fit TV, and earned a belt of some color in karate. However, the expression on her face convinced me that she was serious. I stopped eating and said, "Should I ask...?"

Her fork prodded her food. "It was right after I took the job here. I met him at the College Bookstore. He knew who I was; that flattered me. Then he got me into..., what was the name of that coffee house next to the Avon? Peaberry's? In a few minutes, he was coming on to me. I couldn't believe it; it was all so smooth, so practiced. When I said 'no,' he laughed as though it had all been a joke, that I had misunderstood his obvious interest. It was eerie, the way he did it. A couple of months later, at a party, he did it again, almost as though the first time was a dry run, to get the idea into me that he would do it again, and that it would be worthwhile to have it happen." She shrugged her shoulders. "It didn't, and he never suggested it again, even though we would bump into each other from time to time. Anyways, his politics are…, were…, odious!"

With that, she began to devour the meal. I remained silent because I couldn't see them together in any circumstances, not Nadie the Radical and Reinman of the Right! Anyway, I wasn't sure how to react.

Eventually, she put down her fork. "You and Reinman," she said with eyes at once more serious and sentimental than I would have expected, "you are completely different." She twisted away a strand of hair from her forehead. "He was handsome, confident…, *charming* comes to mind, and such a celebrity." Her voice dropped to a more intimate level. "And he was a practitioner of the art of seduction, I'll tell you that, and he *had* to use it. You could feel it in him…."

I stopped eating, waiting for the rest of this complicated distinction that I wasn't sure was going to be flattering.

"You…,"—she searched for the right word—"…you're just… *you*. You have a kind of integrity and character and depth that Reinman never had, couldn't aspire to, probably didn't even know existed." She dropped her earnestness, probably because I was blushing or close to it, and then she smiled *that* smile. "And, I bet a much better, more constant lover."

"Thanks." Pause. "I think."

Abruptly, she pushed her plate away. "I think we ought to blow this place."

"Your place or mine?" I said too flippantly.

"No," she said with exasperation. "I mean a break…, away…, together. R and R. We need it."

I covered her hand with mine, lacing my fingers with hers. "How about a weekend in New York? I'll get tickets for a show. We'll stay at the Carlyle…?"

Her eyes brightened. "When?" she asked expectantly. "Next weekend?"

Pop. Burst of balloon. The Stalker, forgotten for the moment, came back to our minds simultaneously.

"As soon as it's over, sweet thing," I said, pressing my hand on to hers. "As soon as it's over."

Tuesday

CHAPTER SIX

It was before six when I awoke to flittering images of the teenage girls on Thayer Street. Their obliviousness bothered me and I turned to Nadie. Who wasn't there. After the China Dragon, we had walked to her apartment, my arm around her waist, the movement of her hip against mine a real turn-on, and promises had been made for tonight. We'd get together early, I'd cook dinner, there would be romance....

I doubled up the pillow under my head and stared at the barely visible ceiling of the loft. The teenage girls. For those kids, I thought, a menace like The Stalker doesn't penetrate their roaring hormones, even if the danger is immediate and gruesome. Fear belongs to their parents. The parents of Carter's students had to be loaded with anxiety, making panicky calls, pulling their kids home. The Stalker had shattered the University's carefully crafted image of a protected environment worth paying for. Was it worse for the black parents? Sure, but after Anne Sullivan, any complacency among white parents would be gone: their Jennifers, Karens, and Lisas would now seem as vulnerable as Francines, Yvonnes and Latoyas. What's next? Exodus? Shutdown?

"Ugh!"

I pressed the button on the gizmo that electronically raises the shades on the four oversized windows facing west towards downtown and the loft filled with pale light. Across the room, the light played on the gold background of a four screen panel of water lilies and serenely signaled the day would be clear and bright. I rolled over, felt something hard, and found that I had gone to sleep with Inspector Morse; the Colin Dexter mystery I finished last night shook out from the blankets and I found it a place among the shelves of thrillers and whodunits that lined the walls on either side of the entertainment center. I exchanged pajamas for sweats from an oversized armoire that holds a season's clothing, put on sneakers, and trotted down two flights of stairs to the exercise area in the basement.

The remote hanging on the handle bar of the Nordic Track reminded me that I usually watch "Daybreak News" on Channel 11 on the eye-level television across the room while exercising and I clicked it on—and immediately off. Not today. I was already on Stalker overload. The bad news could wait for the office. Instead, I raised the tension bar on the machine and pounded the Nordic Track; by the end of the workout, my pace was almost punitive and I felt better for it. After toweling off, I opened the door to the other side of the basement, touched the rheostat, and illuminated a refurbished, nine foot Brunswick-Balke-Callender pool table.

The shaded fixtures over the antique table directed light that shimmered on the balls scattered on its immaculate green cloth; diamonds of inlaid mother-of-pearl glowed from within the mahogany rails. I selected a cue from among several in a vertical rack, lined up the ivories, and began a sixty ball drill of shots off the second diamond into the middle pocket on my side, one of my oldest practice routines, one I should handle with ease. But this morning, I couldn't shoot worth a damn! Who knows why? My strokes and stance seemed the same, yet today, one missed shot, including a couple of shanks, for every two in the pocket. Young Jimmy, his fingers holding the cue like a violin virtuoso, his concentration as hard as a rock, would have probably been perfection.

When I finished, my stomach was grumbling and I went upstairs for two English muffins spread with dabs of Rose's lime marmalade while an espresso brewed noisily in the shiny Ruffino machine on the kitchen counter. I took the coffee to the upstairs bathroom, a funky relic of the pre-renovated house, preserved with its original wainscoting, a scrolled mirror over a stand-up sink, black and white diamond floor tiles, an enameled tub standing on four lion's paws, and what Nadie has always referred to as the "throne", a water closet with a black oval seat not designed for her trim bottom. I finished the espresso as I waited for hot water to gurgle its way upstairs, showered using a loofah and bath gel recommended by Nadie, and completed the rest of my ablutions.

Returning to the loft, I met images of a naked, middle-aged man in the full-length triple mirror that serves as a room divider when needed and as a source of eroticism when desirable. Nadie says fifty is a good age for a man—why, I never asked—but I can't fully accept her compliment since the mirrors revealed some of life's battering, even when exercise, reasonable habits, and a vigorous lover have me thinking thirty. Not that all is hopeless; there remains a certain symmetry to my six feet three inches and one hundred and ninety-five pounds. No washboard abs but no middle age sagging either. Broad shoulders, longish arms, and, as was once said of East Side gentlemen, "otherwise of a piece."

My hands were at my hips and I realized that I had struck a pose, with a sucked-in stomach and straightened back. That pulled me forward to inspect the not exactly handsome faces in the mirrors. There is little to be done with an oversized jaw to which other facial parts struggle to conform, a nose that is longish, straight, and too narrow, a mouth that seems always in a slight curl that could come off as smirky if not controlled, and ears large enough to match those of Prince Charles tucked into thick, gray-flecked hair. Nadie says I possess one distinguished—or was it "distinguishing"—feature on which I now concentrated: blue-gray eyes inherited from my father that confer a self-possessed look.

The thought of Nadie brought a grin. She'd love to see me checking myself out. Enough! I put my thumbs in my ears, wiggled my fingers, and stuck out my tongue!

I dressed quickly in a lawyer's uniform of a glen plaid suit, yellow tattersall shirt, and paisley tie, packed my briefcase, and moments later was out of the front door, retrieving the plastic wrapped *Journal* from the walk. Despite an almost cobalt sky and a bright sun, frost decorated the windshields of parked cars and sparkled on crusty fallen leaves and puddle edges; the blustery wind coming down Angell Street was biting enough to water my eyes and I was glad I had decided, for the first time this fall, to forego the Burberry for an overcoat. By eight, I was at my desk with both the *Journal* and the *Crier* at the ready. The red message light on my phone console was flashing.

I decided to leave the *Journal* for lunch at my desk, and the phone message until after the *Crier*. Its banner headline read "Former Student Murdered" with "Stalker Victim?" below. Anne Sullivan's ID photo was above two columns taken from the police report, McCarthy's sally about The Stalker, and an interview with a former roommate who described Anne as "free spirited," "fun loving," and "neat." A half-dozen women representing feminist groups and the Student Council were quoted, all of whom had criticisms of the cops and the University's response to The Stalker. On the left side above the fold, enclosed by a black border, was an editorial headlined "McCarthy Must Go!" an acidly written piece that compared the Chief's intelligence quotient to that of a single-celled animal and his department's efficiency to the Keystone Kops. Danby's statement and dormitory visits were squeezed into a sidebar next to a schedule of crisis related campus events, including a meeting of student leaders with Danby, another conscious-ness-raising gathering in Chancery Hall this afternoon, sign-ups for Jesse Kingdom's demonstration at the federal courthouse the day after tomorrow, and a special Faculty Senate meeting today to discuss the University's "chronic failure" to deal effectively with The Stalker. The predicted head of steam was clearly building.

I put the *Crier* down and went into voice mail. Puppy Dog! Had to be from last night or very early this morning. His whiny voice managed to come across as stony cold. "Just some friendly advice. It's one thing to jerk us around with Jesse Kingdom. It's another to screw up a homicide investigation when it's a cop's daughter. Nobody, particularly Sonny or the Chief, like having their noses rubbed in it. Makes dialogue impossible. Don't call me unless you want to discuss."

Ugh!

Marcie appeared at my office door; despite her white blouse and dark skirt, she looked somewhat less put-together than usual and her frown didn't change as I confided to her the happenings of the previous evening. In the middle of the telling, I focused on a disconnect—is the kid that runs to his mother and her minister when there's trouble with the cops the same kid who is a drug deal-ing, out and out punk? I mentioned the concern in passing.

She had listened without comment, or maybe better expressed, she was mute and appeared unconvinced as she took a step into the office, put her hands on the back of a chair, and said earnest-ly, "If this kid is her killer...?" as Maria squeezed past her with an open box from Dunkin' Donuts and saved me from a fumbling answer. I picked out a cranberry muffin; Marcie declined.

"Whole bunch of kids just millin' around on The Green," Maria said gruffly. "This murder. First I can remember of a stu-dent. Maybe we'll get some action from the johnnies now. Maybe not, since that McCarthy is such a jackass." With that, she closed the box and left the office. Another county heard from, and in spite of ourselves, Marcie and I both had to smile.

○ ○ ○

An hour or so later, Maria was back in my office. She was huffy. "There is an Attorney Pine to see you. Not on *my* calendar. Says it won't take a minute."

Eustace Pine? What could he want? Damn! A senior partner at my old law firm, "Ew" as he was universally addressed, could not be denied to anyone connected to the University, especially me. Born on an Iowa farm, he had found his way to Carter, and after law school, returned to marry into a prominent local family, and spent the next forty years at Champlin & Burrill perfecting his "white shoe" trappings in harmony with his East Side and Sakonnet neighbors and clients, becoming the legal architect of the city's largest estates and trusts, and chancellor of the Episcopal Diocese. More important to me and College Hall, he is also my mother's lawyer and a senior member of the University's Board of Trustees.

"Conference room," I said.

"And I got another attorney, Jerome Franks, on my line. Says it is important to talk to you."

Jerome Franks? Williams' attorney? Maria eyed me coolly, knowing well who this "another attorney" was. "I'll take it," I said, smiled, and waited while Maria maneuvered her heavy figure in a reluctant shuffle from the doorway.

I don't know what I expected. I'd never met Jerome Franks or even spoken to him on the phone, that's the yawning gap between a strictly civil practice like mine and the criminal bar. I had seen him in the courthouse, usually with clients and two or three acolytes in tow, knew he was flamboyant in his haberdashery, courtroom style, and oratory, and had heard his unmistakable voice that had mesmerized Rhode Island judges and juries for decades. I picked up the phone, stated my name, and the syrup started to flow.

"Jerome Franks," he responded. "I'm Lavelle Williams' attorney." He paused to give me time to be impressed. "My client informed me that you and his minister tried to intervene last night. I wanted to convey his thanks, even if things went wrong." His voice slid in to a tone of shared confidentiality. "He's out on bail, but they'll have him back in for questioning sooner or later. He was the victim of an old cop trick. They keep a little bag in the patrol car for situations like this. Slap it on the accused. Used to be marijuana, now, its crack cocaine." A pause for a heaving concern. "I doubt they'll pursue it. But, you can't tell. The atmosphere in the department is so *venomous*. They wanted him in custody long enough to force something incriminating out of him. You prevented that."

Prickles went up my neck. While the voice was deep, resonate, and demanding of attention, it also conveyed a forced sincerity, as though he was used to a role and had little regard for honest emotion.

"I wonder if you could drop by my office... today, if possible? We're down on South Main."

His answer was a silence engendered by my surprise. No Providence lawyer *ever* asks another lawyer to change his immediate schedule, to "drop by", because availability is an indication of lack of business or weakness in your case. Perhaps he sensed he had overreached because his tone immediately changed to one of petitioner. "I know it's short notice but believe me, it's for a very good reason. Which I would prefer to discuss in person. Could you spare some time at lunch... or right after?"

I was free during the noon hour, so the choice was between

reading the *Journal* at my desk with some takeout or meeting a legal legend on his own turf. Put that way, my decision seemed easy. Way too easy since, obviously, Franks had planned some further involvement for me. Was I prepared to say "no"?

● ○ ●

I have to admit this moment was pivotal to what happened. If I had refused, which would have been my better choice then, I would never have experienced the next few days of angst, of being inside a mental Rubik's cube, wrestling to link together facts, personalities, and devious motives.

● ○ ●

"All right, twelve-thirty."

"Fine, twelve-thirty it is." He gave me his office address and hung up.

It crossed my mind that Franks was a good lawyer: when he got the answer that he wanted, he was finished.

Two minutes later, enough time to second guess myself on why I had been rash enough to agree to meet Franks, I greeted Eustace Pine in our tiny library-conference room. Despite his age, he exuded energy as he rose from his seat; his skin was tanned and firm, his handshake vigorous, and there was a spark in the blue eyes nestled beneath white brows. Only the pucker in his cheeks, a certain roundness to his shoulders, and sparse, white hair evidenced his seventy-plus years. In a vested gray wool suit, white shirt and maroon bow tie, he looked every bit an East Side probate lawyer.

"Well, Algy, it appears that we'll be working together."

I didn't reply, not grasping his meaning.

"You know," he urged, "the Reinman estate."

He didn't wait for my response.

"Referral from a classmate of mine up in Brattleboro. Interesting matter, valuation of copyrights and royalties on the Roosevelt book and his other writings. I haven't met the widow yet. Took his death very badly, her mother tells me, although I gather it was not unexpected." He cleared his throat loudly and I waited for him to explain what seemed gibberish. "Unfortunately, his estate plan consists of a simple will which leaves everything to his wife. No tax planning at all! Mrs. Reinman will be well provided for. Still," he said in his condescending way when addressing the work product of other lawyers, "with a little planning, we could have saved—"

I had waited out of politeness long enough. "Ew, how can *I* be involved?"

He was flustered at my question. "Why, I thought you knew. You are the nominated executor."

"Executor? *Me?*"

Pine sputtered his response. "Yes, you! I have the document right here," and reached into a battered briefcase beside him. He rustled through papers, then said, "No, I don't. Must be in the office. But, I remember when it was executed. About two years ago. May, I think...."

Nonsense! Reinman should never have nominated me without my assent. He was only a campus acquaintance; I didn't have anything like a friendship or professional bond with him that might give him the right to call upon me for such duties. "Well, Ew, I refuse. I knew him, of course, but executor...?"

Pine was deaf to my complaint. "The document was drawn by the Stimson office over on Benefit Street," he harrumphed. "You could call there, I suppose. The mother-in-law, a Ms. Cabel, sent the will over yesterday. As I say, not much planning..." and he began long seconds of throat-clearing, and went on to point out the draftsman's failure to use living trusts to avoid probate and tax-saving techniques. Every conversation with Pine, even when he was going on about fly-fishing, or was into his second or third Beefeater Gibson at the Benevolent Club, or retelling one of his magpie collection of East Side family stories, contained a reference to good estate planning.

"Ew..., sorry. I've got too much on my plate right now. There must be an alternate named."

"No, and that's strange. It's just you, I'm afraid."

I tried to collect my thoughts. "Well, you can get an administrator appointed...."

"I suppose so," he said reluctantly. "Of course, that will *really* delay things for the family. Advertisements, bonds, etc..., and the probate judge might end up appointing one of the Mayor's favorites as administrator. You *know* how expensive and time consuming that can be! And the delay, Algy, the *delay*! I'm told that Mrs. Reinman wants to have everything wrapped up quickly so that she can move up to Vermont...."

I felt trapped and told him so.

"Well, really not much I can do, Algy. Not with these time pressures." He shrugged, paused, and started to cajole. "It won't be *that* bad. We'll do everything at the office, take care of all of the probate issues." More throat-clearing. "We'll have a professional appraisal of valuables, segregate personal effects, you know the routine. The houses, one on Benefit Street and a summer place they have in Little Compton, they're in joint names so the real estate won't be any problem. The federal estate tax return could be complicated by copyright and royalty issues, but we'll take care of that," he added hopefully.

He was convincing enough to make me feel like I was overreacting. How bad could it really be? At most, maybe a couple of hours at Champlin & Burrill. I was there often enough because of the University-related litigation and real estate matters that C & B handled. Pine and his staff would take care of the details efficiently and it could be a costly mess for the family in the not unlikely event that Judge Cremascoli, Providence's probate judge and a former Ward Ten councilman, appointed one of Sonny's cronies as administrator with the prospect of a whopping big fee and costly delays. Added to such good reasons, Eustace Pine might wonder aloud to mutual acquaintances why Alger Temple refused a colleague's call for a final service.

"Okay," I said after deep breaths, grimaces, and moments of indecision, "but your office really has to do everything! All I want to do is sign the papers."

"That's grand, Algy," he said enthusiastically, his expression reflecting self-assurance and self-importance. "Would it be convenient to drop by the office tomorrow morning to execute the probate documents? I've given Mrs. Cabel the probate petition for execution by her daughter so we can waive newspaper advertising of the probate and, well, you should meet her...."

I knew I was scheduled to be at Champlin & Burrill at eleven for a meeting with Steve Winter, its principal litigation attorney, on the sexual bias and harassment litigation so I agreed to meet with Pine an hour earlier. I escorted him to the elevator down the hall and when I returned to my desk, I used the calendar function of my computer to note both new appointments and saw an e-mail from the President's secretary that he had rescheduled our every-Tuesday-at-eleven meeting until three because of Reinman's memorial service.

The service! I had forgotten. Should I, as the putative executor, attend?

I didn't relish the thought. Except for checking out Marcie's "conservative poobahs," Reinman's service at First Congregational would likely be an hour's oleo of piety, following the hoary track of a reading from St. Paul, Emerson on the virtues of the teacher, a snippet of Old Testament, hymns loudly sung or mouthed depending on the familiarity of the music by those in attendance, and a brief eulogy by the church's long-in-the-tooth minister who would use the word "challenge" a half dozen times. Reinman would be portrayed as a *solicitous* husband, a *brilliant* scholar, a *committed* member of our community and if the minister was "on," the assemblage might momentarily forget the need for lunch. Before and afterward, the chatter of the University's attendees would likely have little to do with the deceased. Academia tries to avoid the unpleasantness and inconvenience of death. Would that be true in Reinman's case? How many of his colleagues would be there? The few who accepted him? Those who were ready to forgive and forget? The curious? Would I be prepared to defend him as his executor if things got a little abrasive?

I decided I wouldn't be missed.

I leaned back in the chair with my hands clasped behind my head. Wait until Marcie hears about this! It was then I recalled my last, and very brief, contact with Reinman at the beginning of the semester.

I had barely noticed the stooped figure standing at the curb in front of a medical building on Waterman Street. When he called to me, my face surely registered shock as I took in his protuberant black eyes and sallow skin that made each whisker a dark pockmark. I asked him how he was getting along and he shrugged listlessly, and clung to my arm as though to continue the conversation, only to be interrupted by a metallic green BMW driving up to the curb. He struggled opening the passenger door and I supported his elbow as he angled himself inside. A women's voice thanked me for my assistance; I bent down and looked inside the car.

Deborah Reinman reintroduced herself. We had met years before at a faculty party where she had seemed to blend into the draperies as her center-of-attention husband held forth. She had been heavy set, in unfashionable clothes, with limp, long brown hair, out-of-place and uncomfortable in the company of the glib and slim. So, I was surprised by the trim appearance of the attractive woman behind the wheel, even when her smile awkwardly gathered her features into the center of her face. She was neither the pale nor exhausted-looking wife I might have expected; instead, she seemed robust, with clear eyes, a focused expression, and spoke easily, not at all the near invisible wife I recalled.

Some people thrive, I remembered thinking, on caring for others. Deborah Reinman must be one of them.

I glanced outside: it was no longer sunny, and a closer look revealed a high gathering of gray clouds, a sure precursor of rain. Geezus! Providence's late Novembers and early Decembers are filled with days like this: low pressure systems shoot up the coast, knock out the clear-weather highs, and are followed by dizzying sequences of sun and wet weather. I decided I would work until noon—it was likely to be fairly peaceful with most of College Hall at Reinman's service—and walk down The Hill to South Main Street and the five blocks or so to Jerome Franks's office.

Where connivance and trouble awaited me.

CHAPTER SEVEN

The mournful toll of the Paul Revere bell from high in the elaborate steeple of First Congregational Church beckoned those interested in Reinman's service and accompanied me out of College Hall and down The Hill. The peals stopped as I approached the church and almost in response, the clammy mist clinging to downtown changed to a drizzle.

The service must have been well-attended, based on the number of cars parked bumper-to-bumper on Benefit, Thayer, and Waterman Streets. On the flagstones at the church's front entrance, a gaggle of state troopers in Smokey the Bear hats, brown rain gear, and polished riding boots brandished umbrellas underneath its ornate portico, no doubt serving as escorts for the VIPs to and from the line of limos parked conspicuously on North Main Street. The drizzle soon became a wind-driven downpour noisily spattering the brick sidewalks, causing me to huddle under a raised overcoat collar and to pick up my pace. A car horn sounded ahead of me and a black Cadillac DeVille left a line of traffic and maneuvered between orange traffic cones to the curb. Under flipping wipers, its windshield brandished a blue, square ME sticker. A darkly tinted passenger side window slid down and Gershwin's *Rhapsody in Blue* boomed out on to the street. A plaid cap and Tariq Faud's cherubic face, in that order, appeared. "Faculty Club?"

"Got an appointment on South Main."

"I'm due back at the hospital. So I'll drop you off?" Faud's declarative sentences inevitably end in question marks.

"Thanks but don't bother," I begged off even as a squall of rain blew in my face.

The car door opened. Isn't life easy when you can ignore anything you choose?

I reached for its handle, unsure if I was getting in or going to push it shut. Faud had learned to drive on the Shari Qasr al-Ali and kept to Cairo's tradition of hand-to-horn, bumpers are there for a purpose, driving, which neatly melded with his fellow Rhode Islanders' abhorrence of turn signals, disrespect for stop signs, and catch-me-if-you-can mockery of speed limits. My hesitation ceased when rain began to seep down my coat collar.

As I opened the door wider to get inside, Faud raised the window and cleared the passenger seat of chartreuse colored parking tickets which he tossed on to a pile of books, papers, and more billets-doux from the Municipal Court covering the rear seat. A medicinal odor, antiseptic and vaguely vinegary, greeted me as a chime signal, over Gershwin's horns and violins and the roar of the Cadillac's engine, cautioned me to lock my seat belt. Faud lowered the radio's volume, maybe a decibel, and the car abruptly swung into the traffic.

I wiped my head and face with a handkerchief and turned to Faud. Under his cap, his dark eyes set above chubby cheeks were focused intently at a spot directly over the steering wheel; the behemoth was directed by his leather gloved hands which were an inch or two above his lap. His torso, buried within a green macintosh that had seen a few winters, was set deeply in his seat. While he might dress like Apu from the Kwik-E-Mart, Tariq Faud, Professor of Pathology at University Medical School and Chief of the Department of Pathology at City Hospital, grows orchids in elaborate greenhouses next to his mini-mansion on the Blackstone River, has children studying at Carter, Harvard, and Stanford, and owns lots of big, solid things like Cadillacs. He's come very far from his days as a penniless medical student and Legal Aid referral who enlisted my help to convince the Immigration Service to lay off his mother who had become ill, according to his diagnosis, during a visit from Egypt. The beginning of her twenty year *visit* and our friendship.

"I'm so exhausted from Sunday night? So late!" He looked to me for some sign of cognition or sympathy. I had none; I was too busy watching for accidents waiting to happen.

"The girl...? The homicide in the newspaper?" he insisted, his voice filled with impatience, either at me or the rain-slowed traffic, or both. "Really, Algy," he continued, undaunted although peeved at my slow reaction, "they call me at home..., after midnight on Sunday night? Too late, much too late? 'Call somebody else,' I said. 'I don't do crime scenes,' I said." Faud's hands left the steering wheel for a frustrated wave as he braked, reluctantly and with an epithet, for a traffic signal. "Excuse me, Algy, but I remind you that College Hall is always urging more *cooperation* between the faculty and the government. Do you know what that means? Asinine telephone calls in the middle of the night? More work for me and less for some nincompoop state employee?"

"You're Chief of Pathology," I said defensively.

"What, Algy, you joke?" The light changed and we continued up North Main Street toward Pawtucket, in the opposite direction from Franks office. "They called me because the Chief ME and the associate are both out of state for Thanksgiving! The first assistant, *he* went to the Cape for the long weekend and couldn't be called back for some hocus-pocus reason? And the second is out on maternity leave as of last week? So, besides the fact that this girl was dead more than thirty-six hours before she was found, nobody could get to her for another couple more! The police finally got hold of the Chief ME who runs down his list and tells them to call me, you know, because I'm on this panel? Stupid! I'm supposed to cover in *real* emergencies? So because I got a title, I have to go down to this crummy tenement and I start *cooperating* at two in the morning?"

He muttered something like *ara fi ardak* which I took to be a pithy Arabic curse; I was focused on how close the Cadillac was to climbing up the rear of a slow moving Kia. "Am I a forensic person? No! But they got to have somebody with a title to get the body out of there! I take the temperature, scrape the blood, and give her a prep. No rape kit. I had to use Q-Tips from her medicine cabinet! Then, I get to check her into the morgue? I get to go home after five? Pardon me, Algy," he said, "but I get tired cooperating."

"Well, what happened?" I tried to sound polite but disinterested, even as I disposed to mine any information he possessed.

"Damned if I know! Asphyxiation, I said. Pretty obviously, the pillow on the floor. Blood stains on it and she had cotton threads under her nails, pressure points on her face, lint and threads in her mouth, up her nose? Not strangled though, like they said on the news. Suffocated! The rigor was gone..., you know, 'twelve hours on and twelve hours off?' Bruises on her face and lips where she was hit before her suffocation. More on her chest and shoulders, like maybe somebody sat on her and pinned her shoulders?"

He blasted the horn to express frustration with the Kia, spun the steering wheel, and the huge sedan lunged up The Hill on Knowles Street where cars parked illegally on both sides of the narrow incline induced me to hold my breath to squeeze through unscathed.

"But rape? Was she raped? Like these others?" The car slowed but didn't stop at Prospect Street where we made a right turn and began a circle back towards downtown. "The assistant ME, who finally gets in from his tryst on the Cape, said 'probable rape'. How come? I'd like to know? When I left, it wasn't rape. No scrapes, no cuts, no skin under the nails, no lacerations in the vagina..." He pressed the car horn impatiently at two pedestrians who scurried across the slickness of the street in front of the Woods-Gerry Museum, unaware of their peril. "Sex? The swabs showed that. Semen all over, sure. From when? From whom? And any connection?"

I've heard Faud on other occasions when he got wound up in the nauseating details of his specialty. Basically, I'm squeamish and came damn close to fainting at my one and only autopsy. "I guess everyone assumed it was The Stalker."

"Oh," he said disparagingly, "of course. Of course, The Stalker. That's all the cops could talk about? But since the rigor was gone, best guess would be sometime late Friday night, maybe early Saturday? Not Saturday night into Sunday, I pointed out, and she's white, but... no, it *has* to be The Stalker?" His right index finger went next to his nose as he turned his face to me, leaving the car's piloting to its weight and momentum; my hands went palm-down on the dashboard. "Sure there was sex. Pizza and sex. Pepperoni and onion pizza and... sex. Sex from the obvious and pizza from the Ronzio's box on the floor!" He took a sly, fleeting glance at me and nudge, nudged me, Eric Idle-like, with his elbow. "Maybe it was The Stalker? Who knows? Suffocation can take a couple of minutes and she looked like a healthy enough specimen. She wasn't tied up or anything like that? Maybe he held her down, killed her, and that's when he did his business?"

With that particularly repulsive thought, he gave the car's brakes a good test at the bottom of The Hill at South Main Street, near the Cable Car Cinema. I gave him Franks's address and almost immediately, he pulled over and double-parked. His voice was terse when he said, "Her slip was over her head, with nothing else on, no panties, no bra. The cops said there were latents all over the place, mostly smeared, but lots. There will be hairs, short and curly with roots, so a microphoto analysis will give up something as to the sex? Maybe they'll match The Stalker. From the semen, they get a blood type, and there's enough of everything for lots of DNA tests. But, Algy, you still have to work backwards from that. You got to have matches for DNA and fingerprints. By the time they get it analyzed, even assuming the cretins at the state lab get it right, if it was The Stalker, he'll still have plenty of weekends to ply his trade."

"True," I replied and thought that if Lavelle Williams had sex with the victim before the murder—as Reverend Thomas had intimated—he'd be a match!

I said, "thank you" as I shook Faud's offered hand and left the car's protection. Faud leaned over the passenger seat to catch the closing door and looked up at me. "You know, Algy, it's so emotional again? No sense of anything but right now and how screwed up it is? All these groups and marches and with these assaults and what's going on downtown...? Is it crazy time again? If it is, forget more *cooperation* from me or anyone else."

◉ ◯ ◉

Jerome Franks's office was in a line of nearly identical, buff-colored, two-story clapboard buildings from the early 1800's which, when I was growing up, housed plumbing suppliers, paper jobbers, and secondhand stores and now served as prime office space for lawyers, accountants, and insurance agents. The sagging asbestos roofing of yesterday had been replaced by neat rows of slate and shingles, grimy shop windows were now mullioned and clear, and chimneys were no longer vulnerable to any stiff breeze off the Bay. To the right of each doorway was a brass plate etched with italicized script that discreetly indicated the present occupant. It was all so pristinely *historic* that it made me nostalgic for the neighborhood's remembered tawdriness.

When the door to the Jerome A. Franks Law Offices opened to dark purple walls, a mauve rug, and chairs covered in a wretched orange, it was jarring. Adding to the claustrophobic effect were two large oil paintings on the facing walls of the reception area, great smears of orange, yellow, and red. Equally unsettling was the big hair brunette in a bulging green sweater layered with gold chains, who gave me the once-over from behind a glass-topped desk. A name plaque, next to a nail brush, identified her as Angela DeMartini.

"Yahess?" she said with classic Cranston nasalness.

"I have an appointment with Mr. Franks. My name is Temple." To myself, I sounded like a self-important ass but there was no reaction in the big brown eyes under smudgy mascara and false eyelashes. In fact, no reaction at all as though her mind was off shopping at Garden City. Then, she blinked and brushed aside shoulder-length ringlets to glance at an open engagement book. "Yer early. Mr. Frah-anks will be wid ya shortly." She made an elaborate gesture with a multi-braceleted hand toward a grouping of chairs under one of the smears.

A faint recollection of Michelle Pfeiffer as Angela DeMarco in *Married to the Mob* stirred in my memory—this Angela could have been her first cousin—as I hung my overcoat on a rack by the door. Ms. DeMartini was now on the telephone and it was all "yadda, yadda, yadda" and jingling bracelets. How did she get the job? Was she some Mafia don's niece?

I sat where directed and took a tattered *Sports Illustrated* from a pile of magazines all about six months old. As I flipped through its soiled pages, I considered: when had I last been in the office of a criminal defense lawyer? Ever? Not while at Champlin & Burrill where my partner, Jim Bryan, a former deputy attorney general, handled cases when a corporate client or a government official had a brush with the criminal law or was accused of corporate skullduggery. Years ago, when I was a fledgling prosecutor? No, not for the level of crime I dealt with; the lawyers came to me to cop misdemeanor pleas in the windowless cubicles of a justice factory also known as the Manhattan Criminal Courts Building. Very few pleasantries and a lot of wheedling characterized those brief encounters, where the justice dispensed had little to do with the noble sentiment carved into the building's façade: "Equal and Exact Justice To All Men Of Whatever State and Persuasion."

I put down the magazine and sat back. My career as an assistant Manhattan County DA had been brief. After law school, I followed my father's path with an ROTC commission in the Marines, where my two years of court martial experience after two years of fleet and intelligence duty, decided me on a career as a prosecutor. I would use any talent I had to put away bad guys under the naïve impression that it was the same as protecting the good guys. I would be a star!

Through family connections, I wrangled the DA job, only to receive the in-your-face treatment I should have expected, but didn't. Supervised by a series of inept, civil service protected mediocrities who loved to play with my given name, I endured a year of night court arraignments of pickpockets, pimps, druggies, and prostitutes, where the absence of "mister green" meant a night in the slammer. That was followed by a tour at housing court, and then, something where I thought I could excel: felony arraignments. Murder, rape, violent assault, and big drug busts. Within six months, my illusion of the moral imperative of a prosecutor in *real* criminal law evaporated. I experienced remorseless defendants joining their buddies at Rikers Island, bored prosecutors and judges, hardened cops, and both slickster and regular Joe defense attorneys for whom it was all a day's pay. I saw the corruption of spirit in an atmosphere of continuous chaos and a day-to-day moral pollution that eventually broke too many in the system.

That belated realization coincided with the end of my brief, argument-filled marriage to an associate in a Wall Street law firm, so I was primed when I got the offer from Champlin & Burrill to come home and join its young and aggressive litigation team.

I rubbed my eyes. It seems like a million years ago....

My name was spoken loudly. A blimp of a man, his rounded bulk barely contained within a tent-sized white shirt accented by a red tie and pleated gray flannel trousers clutched to his body by a black shiny belt, braked in front of me. Heavy-lidded, old eyes, under unkempt brows, inspected me as he grasped my hand and almost pulled me out of my seat. The impression of force was so overpowering that I hardly heard his introduction or his order to follow him. As we passed Ms. DeMartini, did she pucker her enhanced lips and give me her almost-smile?

I heard him say something about the growing size of his firm as we passed secretarial carrels and a line of offices for Jerry Franks wannabes and stopped before a set of imposing, elaborately carved, double doors with *Jerome A. Franks* in gold lettering on the right-hand side. He opened both doors with a flourish and urged me inside.

Everything clashed. A wall hanging, an orange disk sinking into a green colored stew, adorned one wall and great daubs of green, mauve, and ochre filled a canvas on the wall opposite. A deep blue rug, chairs, a sofa, and a massive mahogany desk filled the room. Directed ceiling lights illuminated photographs grouped behind the desk, a rogues gallery of Rhode Island legislators, governors, senators, and congressmen, with Mayor Sonny Russo right smack in the center. There apparently was no need for the traditional display of diplomas.

Franks maneuvered himself into a brown leather chair and motioned me to an uncomfortable-looking, straight-backed chair in front of his desk. I sat and realized that Franks's chair was set several inches off the floor, giving him the ability to look down at me—which he now did—for physical and psychological advantage. It was impossible to sit comfortably in my assigned chair.

There followed a moment of mutual appraisal. Who knows what *he* thought as I began to measure his silver, coiffured hair, pouchy eyes, bulbous nose, puckered chins, and the glitter of gold on his fingers, his wrists, and at his cuffs. A musky cologne reached me. I realized I was on my way to a discernable aversion to Mr. Franks.

"Well, Alger...," his voice was breathy and deep, "...I don't recall that we've actually met..."—we hadn't—"...but we get a number of referrals from your old firm these days, some things your Mr. Bryan doesn't handle, DWIs, drugs, petty stuff like that. Still, it's a living."

I struggled to retain a vacant expression which seemed to vex him as he made a show of putting on a pair of half-lens glasses.

"Lavelle Williams," he intoned, peering over the glasses to find my eyes, "we produce too many Lavelle Williamses these days, don't you agree?"

My face remained deadpan and I didn't reply.

Franks' expression showed his disappointment as he opened a folder, displaying a pinky ring with a diamond the size of the top of a golf tee, and picked up a sheet of paper. "The possession charge was a frame-up. A plant. As I explained on our call, happens all the time," he said dismissively. "The judge could see that and set bail on personal recognizance. They should drop the intent to sell charge even before the prelim." He let the paper fall to the desk. "They don't mind arresting but they *hate* to testify."

It was time to say something. I probably winced before I said, "Interesting, but what has all this to do with me?"

The lawyer cocked his head back and leveled a cold, steady stare at me. "The murder, of course. He's a suspect because he's black and had an unfortunate liaison with the victim. The police don't care that Williams has an alibi for the night she was murdered—if they can make up their minds *when* she was killed—especially if the alibi witnesses are minorities with prior scrapes with the law." He sought my acknowledgement which he didn't get. "And this Ms. Sullivan, to hear my client tell it, was an erratic, *very* erratic, young woman!" With that declaration, he removed his glasses, looked through the lenses, and wiped them with a tissue from a box on the desk. "Difficult to understand what she would have seen in my client. He's young, uneducated, streetwise..., not exactly someone with whom you would expect a Carter undergraduate to be spending her time."

Franks was too busy wiping to see my reaction which was becoming near physical.

"Her father's an old-timer on the force. I'd hate to think what could happen to Williams if he's in the wrong hands for just a few hours. People still get hurt resisting restraint, even commit suicide while in the lockup. Blacks and Latinos seem particularly prone. You haven't had to deal with your local police, Alger. Sometimes they're reasonable, sometimes absolute—you'll pardon me—absolute pricks. Mostly, pricks."

At that, he pushed his glasses back on his nose and searched my face for a reaction. It was now obvious that Franks had not bothered to vet me before our meeting; if he had, he would have known of my stint as a prosecutor from the Martindale-Hubbell law directory. Maybe, then, he would not have assumed that I would agree with his made-up-for-me assessment of the moronic, cruel, and homicidal Providence police. I hadn't made the same mistake: Franks was from Philadelphia, attended Temple undergrad and its law school, somehow got to Rhode Island where he had always practiced criminal law, and had listed two columns of his successes in the directory.

As seconds went by, he picked up a thick, red-lacquer and gold, Mont Blanc fountain pen which he twirled impatiently; his voice, the *famous* voice, became engaged when he continued. "Your support was critical to his safety last night, what with the emotions running down there. We were one step away from manifest injustice!"

Ugh! was almost verbalized as he dropped the pen on to the desk for emphasis.

"Let me be plain," he said, trying to pierce my forced obtuseness, "Williams will be picked up again and it could be hours before I know. That's extremely dangerous for him. And, I think, unnecessary. I've become aware of facts that could change the focus of the homicide investigation, assuming, for discussion purposes, it wasn't your Stalker. For instance —"

My Stalker? He had taken a page from Sonny Russo.

I raised my hand. "Before you say anything," I said, with my voice beginning to inflect the 'ahhh's' I hate, "I didn't act as Williams's lawyer. We have no attorney-client relationship and no privilege is involved in anything you tell me."

Franks scowled, conveying to me, "Look, stupid. I've practiced criminal law for thirty years. Don't I know what I'm doing?" Still, his proposition stirred in my brain. While part of me was primed to leave, there was also something akin to curiosity, or whatever it was that had brought me to his office in the first place. I saw the shrewdness around eyes that never wavered and despite the urge to get behind them, maybe even to get them to blink, I nodded.

"Good! Fine!" he said, practically beaming at my epiphany, glad that I was on the team. "Ms. Sullivan had a savings account totaling nearly twenty thousand dollars. Think about it! A college drop-out with twenty thousand dollars in the bank. Or more! The initial deposit, ten thousand, was made in early June, even before Williams returned from New York! Then, multiple deposits, every month, he says, that she picked up at the post office, right up into October. She bragged about it. He didn't believe her so, once, she showed her bankbook to him. According to Williams, she didn't work, spent a pile of money on clothes, trips to New York City, concerts, and whatever turned her on. The rest went into the bank. He says the payments stopped in November but the night she was killed, she told him the money would start again. The police either don't know about the money and the bankbook or are ignoring both. Williams thinks that she might have given the bankbook to her sister...," he checked the file "... Patricia for safekeeping. Apparently, the cops don't have it."

I had to admit that her money and how she got it was intriguing and was about to so comment but he didn't give me the opportunity. He moistened his lips with a rather pointed tongue and said, "There are obvious questions running through your mind...."

He was going to supply the questions—who gave her the dough, where did she get twenty grand plus, and why—and had all the answers.

"The payments had to come from someone who had good reason to make them." His eyes narrowed with cunning. "Ms. Sullivan had an abortion last summer. Thousands of dollars in payments to a young woman who had an abortion?" His face brightened as though his case had been made.

My response came almost mechanically, spoken with what I hoped was a suitably deprecating shrug. "A blackmail scheme, I take it. She was blackmailing someone. With the inference that blackmail is a motive for murder. If the police look for the source of funds, or even where the money is now, that would take the heat off your client." He rewarded my logic with a smile and rested his jowls on the points of two touching fingers. I continued. "But whomever impregnated her, presumably, got what he wanted. The abortion. So it has to be more than that."

His response showed his annoyance. "Could be anything. What she might say. There could have been letters, a diary, recordings, maybe a video or two, who knows what she had on him."

Despite a deep reluctance to give Franks any credence, I was buying into it. The source of the money had to be investigated. Was Franks telling me the truth about what the police knew? How would they know if the bankbook wasn't at her apartment? How diligently would they question the family, one of their own, or search records? Or did the police know and had chosen to ignore it because of racism or Williams being so convenient? Or Chief McCarthy's predilection for The Stalker?

And why was he confiding in me? I asked him.

"You've never practiced criminal law, Alger." Did I grimace? "It's a practice with unspoken rules and more gamesmanship than you are used to. I'm always up against the same people..., police, prosecutors, judges..., and you've got to be consistent." My back stiffened as he continued to educate me. "I do not provide any information to the police or the Attorney General without some concession, which, under these circumstances, and without the physical evidence of the bankbook, I am unlikely to get. Without a charge, I can't get the information I need by subpoena." He paused, anticipating a question. "An anonymous tip? No reason to believe it would be investigated in the present state of affairs. No, this information, if it is to be respected and acted upon, must come from a disinterested source, an unimpeachable source, from someone whom the Commissioner might feel obligated to honor with a meticulous search of bank records. That," he said with a dramatic flourish of his hands, "could be you."

Satisfied that he had succeeded with his gambit, his chins, which had emerged during his discourse, withdrew into his jowls. He was preening!

Whoa! I'm not going there! Even as I realized he had almost hooked me.

I stared at him and he reciprocated. I saw not a fabled defense lawyer but a bad Rumpole impersonator. His obvious attempt at manipulation really pissed me off! To use my relationship with Tramonti! How did he know? I looked up at the photograph of Sonny. Through Puppy Dog? McCarthy? And to do it, not because of empathy for his client, but because of Williams's relationship to drug boss Flores. For all I knew, the money had been stashed for Williams and this was all an elaborate ruse!

That did it! I abruptly stood and moved behind my chair to look down on Franks. "Je-rome," I said, stretching out the two syllables of his name as he had mine, "you overestimate my interest in your client." My voice gained insouciance and upper class intonation. "You've misjudged the situation completely. If you have something to discuss with Commissioner Tramonti, I suggest you do so. Quite frankly,"—I wanted to say *frankly*—"I see no reason to be further involved with your client."

There was a slight bobble to his head as his pulpy cheeks reddened, his eyes hardened, and his mouth contracted into meanness. "If Williams is picked up and something regrettable happens to him...." His voice trailed off in dramatic disappointment and he began to study the file in front of him.

I was supposed to feel the sting of dismissal, but I didn't.

I said goodbye and left his office and walked quickly down the hallway into the reception area where a group of Latino men with shiny dark hair and black leather jackets, two in their twenties and two a generation older, all with tough, suspicious faces, became silent. I put on my overcoat, feeling their stares at my back, glanced briefly at Ms. DeMartini, who flashed her eyelashes, and left.

It was no longer raining as I walked toward a downtown blanketed by low, leaden clouds. Words like *asshole* and *dipshit* were on my lips. I needed a quick change of scenery and went south a block to Water Street to the newly constructed brick walk along the Providence River. A blustery wind blew a plastic Pepsi cup ahead of me until it slipped under the decorative iron railing into the oily, umber-colored water; I stopped, leaned forward on the railing, and watched it bob in a swirl of eddies and head toward the Point Street Bridge and the Bay. I took a deep breath of the chilled, sea-tanged air, only to remember Franks' musky, overpowering cologne.

Damn him!

I forced myself to stare at the trails of leaves floating on the river. The tide was going out, exposing slimy mud banks and the barnacled pilings at the ferry dock where two inflatable dinghies rubbed noisily against ballasts. Out in the channel, a lone seagull hovered, then glided to the wind-rippled surface, ruffled its feathers, and took on a self-possessed look. As I cooled off, my cockiness dissipated. I questioned my motives in meeting with Franks. I wasn't just out of law school where saving the innocent was an imagined adventure. Lavelle Williams was likely lawless and self-destructive, up to his eyeballs in drugs and maybe a murder, even though, for some reason, he sought safety with his mother. I'd seen too many like him. And Franks? I know the shenanigans of criminal lawyers; why wouldn't I have expected some angular ploy like this?

But, if Anne Sullivan had an abortion and *did* receive all that cash, then....

I had to stop. Franks's scheme had succeeded to some extent. "Scumbag," I said aloud and startled an elderly man passing me on the walk. Embarrassed by my outburst, I left the railing, abashed and even more angry than before.

CHAPTER EIGHT

Nasty retorts to Franks were still percolating when I reached Verrazzano Park in front of the Supreme Court building and walked past the rust covered sculptures—forms that reminded me of huge alphabet letters and metallic doodles—near the fountain. Even in this weather, a few hearty souls were on benches by the herb and sea grass plantings at the river's embankment and grungily dressed teenagers slapped their skateboards on the granite steps circling the Peace Monument. A solitary woman, bundled up against the cold and woolen hat down around her ears, was feeding a pair of swans with what may have been the remains of her lunch. Flags snapped noisily in the wind above the granite pylons of the Korean War Veterans Memorial. Parkside, a favorite casual restaurant renowned for its grill and rotisserie menu, was across the street, but the immediacy of my postponed meeting with the President compelled me up University Street to the campus.

At a few minutes before two, I closed the door to my office and ate a Dark Milky Way purchased in the second floor canteen. I remained agitated and fell to the mindless distraction of straightening up my office, a process best described as shifting files from one bookcase, chair, or table to another bookcase, chair, or table, until my desk phone rang.

Danby said, "I'm going to be tied up all afternoon. I still need to get together with you. How about tomorrow, my house, at eight-thirty? Any problem?"

My calendar is flexible for him and it wouldn't be the first time we met at President's House when his schedule was tight. "I can be there."

"...Got the *Globe* in a few minutes and the *Times* around four. *Newsweek* this morning. Just raising the flag. Lots of race-related questions. You can imagine how it's going to be written up." He paused. "McAllister says more women are packing their bags and there's talk about a sit-in somewhere but he doesn't think it will go off. The Faculty Senate is meeting now. I've given them my views and I'm hopeful they'll be supportive when it comes to a vote." His voice hardened. "I've told them I'm determined not to close down." Before I could respond, he said, "I appreciate the courtesy" and hung up. The strain in his voice was palpable.

I put the phone down. "Damn!" When would the man have the opportunity to implement his announced agenda—one that was already raising the hackles of the opposition—of a common under-graduate exposure to Western and Third World traditions, with community service as the skeleton for the flesh of academic curriculum, and smaller, quality-driven graduate schools. Not expressed as such, he also had told senior staff of his intention to heal the general malaise, mulishness, and downright incivility that had been aggressively rampant during his predecessor's short but chaotic term. If the Trustees hadn't quickly recognized their mistake and bought out her contract, I would have resigned. Danby, I knew instinctively, had the leadership qualities to get Carter back on track, that is, if the cancer of disrespect hadn't metastasized. Plus, after months of feeling each other out, he seemed to trust my judgment, evidenced by asking for it with increasing regularity, which pleased me.

My musing was cut short by Maria who rapped at the door and delivered a clutch of message slips. One was from my mother.

This was as good a time as any to explain last night's fiasco. Sylvia must have been out because my mother answered the phone. It was quickly evident that Sylvia had already given her a vivid picture of Lavelle Williams's arrest and Reverend Thomas's humiliation. My assurances that Williams had a lawyer, that I had met with the lawyer, and Williams was out of any physical danger seemed to satisfy my mother that family obligations had been acquitted. I didn't get into Williams's dubious character or my impression of Franks. "You did your best," she said sympathetically. "That's all we were asked to do," and I finished the call somewhat morally lightened but wondering what the old man had told Sylvia and what she would be thinking of me.

I fussed about that for awhile and then got to work. A priority project was an analysis of the University's potential financial liability to The Stalker's victims, to be presented at the Trustees' December meeting. I found the file on the iMac and read again my draft memo which explained, in layman's terms, all the theories of potential liability for the University, such as common law negligence, breach of contract, and *in loco parentis*. The memo was sprinkled with sufficient references to case law, law review notes, articles in *University Counsel* magazine, and the *Chronicles of Higher Education* to satisfy even the lawyers among the Trustees, although my conclusion was unsettling. The status of the law in Rhode Island, where the cases would likely be brought, was, not surprisingly, unclear since case law is often a laggard when it deals with societal issues. Was the University liable for student pranks or brushes with booze and drugs or injuries, depression, and suicides or plain, old-fashioned stupidities? And, what if it all happens off-campus?

The last few pages contained an analysis of the University's insurance coverage and two problems I foresaw: first, the University had liability insurance coverage in the millions but the deductibles on the policies were huge, making the University virtually self-insured for the expected large claims; second, the off-campus locations of the assaults created the probability that the insurers would "reserve their rights" under the policies—that is, the insurers might say "maybe we'll defend you and maybe we'll pay, and maybe we won't, but keep us posted." Nobody, not the President, the Trustees, the Risk Management Office, nor the broker who had earned huge commissions on the insurance premiums, would want to hear that.

Revising the draft and updating legal research on Lexis/Nexus, a computerized case retrieval system accessed through a terminal in our library-conference room, took an hour or so. As I logged off and walked by Marcie's office, I remembered her concern as to security for Jesse Kingdom's rally on Friday. I had better call Tuttle before she reminded me.

I liked Tuttle. He was resolute, a leader, a person of integrity sorely tested by Sonny Russo. His career with the Providence police had been unblemished, with departmental citations for personal courage, and he had earned a college degree in law enforcement from Salve Regina University in Newport. Blocked from further promotion by his refusal to play ball with Sonny, he had seemed the perfect choice for our Chief of the Security Office, bringing a sterling reputation, knowledge of the local police, and people skills to the job. With some prompting from Tramonti, I managed to push him through the elaborate selection process the University had established for this sensitive position. Yes, he rode in *vehicles* and his *people responded* to calls, and some of the campus fringe groups were not to his liking; still, he had patience, common sense, and unlike a lot of ex-cops, was not too full of himself. So far, he seemed able to handle the University's two minds on security issues—*protect me but don't bother or offend me.*

Tuttle picked up immediately. I asked about the flyer and he said that they still didn't know the source, that Kingdom had dismissed it as a crank threat, and that the extra cops for the rally was under consideration in McCarthy's office, "...but I'm not holding my breath."

He didn't have to elaborate. I could imagine how the pouchy, caustic, world-weary veterans that constituted McCarthy's intimates would react: *in a pig's ass!*

He continued. "I've made a few additions to the Event Plan..."—that was a euphemism for a standard campus security plan for potentially unruly crowd events on The Green, everything from reserve units of security officers to the litter pickup—"...and I'll e-mail it to you and the Provost. We'll have fifty of our people ready." Then, he surprised me. With a quiver in his voice, he asked, "Got a few minutes? Mind coming over here?"

I glanced out of the window; the taller downtown buildings were wrapped in haze but it wasn't raining and getting out of the office was better than letting Franks gnaw at my innards.

The University's Security Office is in a nondescript, yellow brick building in the East Campus on Maxfield Street. Tuttle was waiting for me outside its glass vestibule, next to an aluminum stanchion which supported one of the campus's ubiquitous call boxes under a purple security light. He wore a brown raincoat with a loosely tied belt; a thin, unlit cigar was clenched in his mouth. There was a rigid set to his face. "Thanks for comin' over," he said, removing the cigar. "How about a walk?"

I nodded as he lit the cigar and started off towards Brook Street in a loping kind of stride, as though his legs needed uncramping. I followed in a wake of cigar smoke because the sidewalks were too narrow for both of us to walk side by side, or "side by each" in Rhode Island-ese. Twice we stepped into leaf filled gutters to avoid blackish puddles formed by roots breaching the sidewalk's asphalt surface; at our approach, skittish squirrels circled the trunks of maples, plane trees, and Bradford pears, fleeing to higher branches black against the gun metal sky.

Tuttle's arms swung back and forth, making little whispery noises as his sleeves rubbed the sides of his raincoat. We were a block away from his office, and by now, I had expected him to get to whatever needed airing outside of the office. Since he took the job, I've never seen him without a jacket and tie, or totally at ease in a staff meeting, and I've wondered what he really thinks of his new chain of command and the people he protects. At Waterman Street, as we waited for the traffic light to change, he squinted over his shoulder, took the cigar out of his mouth, and I sensed he was ready for our talk.

"I've heard from both McCarthy and the Commissioner. Guess you had a busy night," he said without any inflection indicating approval or disapproval.

So, I concluded, we were going to talk about me—not him.

When the "walk" signal flashed, we crossed the street and it took me about a block to get out a coherent summary of what happened. Somehow, I sounded almost apologetic and I expected his practical advice about not getting mixed up in police politics. Instead, with head down and cigar curled in his fingers, he said, "I got a problem. That is, Security's got a problem. My people are tired. Losing respect. They're not used to anything like this..., assaults, rapes, and now a murder. With Kingdom up here, and these marches and rallies, and maybe sit-ins.... I'm still a rookie around here. I don't have the feel for the job, if you get my meaning. And they know it." He stopped and looked me squarely in the eyes. "I got to know. Do you guys take me seriously? Or am I just a new pain in the butt."

I had my answer as to where his mind was. I responded that he would know if the Provost was on his case, that his efforts were appreciated, and that I honestly thought he retained the full backing of the administration. His expression showed a reluctance to accept my comments.

"I know her father," Tuttle said gravely as we crossed Angell Street and continued north. "Know or met most of the family, I guess..., the wife, his brother. He's a priest down in Warwick. For years, we were in the same parish, St. Michael's, before I moved the family to Mount Pleasant. Our kids went to the parish school. I probably met her somewhere along the way, at Mass or CYO or something." He said defensively. "I didn't mention that yesterday. Seemed not to fit there somehow."

That explained his hesitation at the Provost's meeting. The murder was too close to home.

"Must be rough on her family," he said. "You know, when I came up here, part of it was getting away from crap like this. But right away, there's a homicide and I know the family!" He took a last puff on the cigar, flipped it on the sidewalk ahead of us, and stopped to grind it out deliberately with the sole of a shoe. "The wake is tomorrow night. Delayed because of the autopsy. Closed casket, I hear. Half the force will be there, the rest at the funeral Thursday. I'll go to the wake."

We had reached the corner of Veasey Street. Tuttle pointed at the street sign and shrugged again. "Right down there. Seventy-two." I started to make the turn but Tuttle crossed the street and I followed. "I don't know if you can really appreciate this, and no offense intended," he added quickly, "but you're not trying to make twenty or twenty-five years for the pension, disability, too, if you can finagle it. For Terry Sullivan, his whole life is being a cop. I think his father was a cop. What's he got besides his family? A house in the city because of these stupid residency requirements, the pension?" He stopped and looked up at me. "That, and your kids. When you've got kids, and you're workin' a cop's schedule, you do it for them. You don't start out like that but that's what happens. You just suck it up. You take all the bullshit and suck it up. You work the eleven-to-seven shift, angle for the weekend event details and double time, maybe get a part-time job, too. Most everything you do is for them, so they'll do better... or at least no worse. I know, I've got two grown daughters, just like Sullivan—"

A beeping noise emanated from Tuttle's raincoat; he reached into an inside pocket of his coat and pulled out a cell phone. "Tuttle," he said, listened, grunted an acknowledgment, and put the phone back into his coat pocket. "Better be getting back," he said. "Always something. Some clown blocked the parking lot behind the Physics Building with a truck and nothing can get in or out." We turned and began to retrace our steps.

The wind was now at our backs, pushing thick, gray, wet clouds that kept pace with our quickening steps. When we reached Veasey Street, he paused, took out another cigar, cupped his hands, lit it, and eyed me squarely. "I know just how Terry feels. You do everything you can for your kids. Your wife works a job besides the home. You send them to parochial school because the public schools are lousy. When you get time to think of them, in your mind's eye, they're like they were when they made First Communion, all dressed up in white lace like little brides, with flowers, and the beads. Then, one day, they're gettin' a job or off to college or runnin' off to the malls or to the beach, and they're dating and never at home. You wonder what happened. 'When did they grow up?' you ask yourself. 'How did they get to be grown-up women?' 'Where the hell was I?'" Then, his tone changed. "Anne Sullivan?" he said, using his cigar as a pointer. "Everything her parents worked for ends up naked in a crappy apartment, killed by someone who thought her life was nothing." He paused and spat into the gutter, clearly out of disgust.

Three hours ago, Franks called her erratic and accused her of blackmail; Tuttle, it seemed, also had an opinion.

"I've been wondering about her, why she dropped out after last year. Maybe she needed help. Maybe the University could have made a difference...."

Tuttle halted, using his hand to stop me. When he spoke, I heard an unexpected scorn. "What could the school do? She made her own choice, led her own life. Gave up a scholarship! To do what? Hang around with a punk we know is a dealer. Not exactly the family's pride and joy any longer." Unpleasant emotions clouded his face. "Her family's mourning her loss and her shame. She was a cop's daughter."

He turned away from me and I had to walk faster to keep up with him. I recalled a line from somewhere that seemed appropriate: "the dead are always defenseless."

"In my experience," he continued, "more often than not, victims are not very nice human beings. Most get murdered because they hang around vicious people. If it was my investigation, I'd say it was just the usual thing. Drugs, for instance. But no *way*," he said with conviction, "no *way*, is it The Stalker."

"Because she's white...?"

"More than that," he answered. "I seen this before more than once. This guy, he starts off pawing 'em, but that gets him nothing, no satisfaction. He's *Fingers. A joke!* He wants an FFFF. Ever hear of that? A "fist full of female flesh." For some reason, he starts hitting on black women students. There's some connection to Carter and them, something we can't guess. He's paying back, taking his revenge. Maybe, 'cause he knows what the campus reaction will be if he gets it right. He adds the rough stuff. But still he gets run off. Three times! And he can't even make the papers! No publicity! Worse than last spring! Then, he gets a knife and rapes Francine Johnson. On the Student Council. That finally does it. All hell breaks loose. Publicity up the wazoo! The three previous victims show up. More publicity. It's clearly a Carter thing, with the blacks screaming to have him caught. He gets a new name. Forget 'Fingers'. He's on to something. He's getting his kicks outsmarting us. Then, he assaults the Jones girl and better yet, he hits on Latoya Chapin whose father's a big shot in Congress, a perfect target for more publicity. Cripes, they're talking about closing the place down! It's going better than he thought! He's pretty smug now, what with the reaction on campus, and the dimwits downtown like McCarthy don't get it. Don't want to get it. Nothin' random about this now. He's pickin' and choosin' his victims."

"You mean, so why kill a white girl, somebody not even at the school?"

He almost snorted with impatience. "Look, this time there was no knife, far as we know, and she was suffocated. Yeah, lots of bruises and raped, sure, but before, he had the knife. And fingerprints, enough for ten investigations, some good, some blurred, and maybe wiped. Can you imagine The Stalker wiping fingerprints? It's not The Stalker but it makes no difference to McCarthy. McCarthy wants it to be The Stalker. It would be The Stalker making McCarthy's point: 'White girls, don't fool around with black dudes.' Fits into McCarthy's view of life. And, he needs to protect Sullivan and his family. It's not such an embarrassment to the family if she was The Stalker's random victim—"

He stopped but kept his head down and his shoulders hunched forward, as though his thoughts had gotten too intimate; then, he gave me a flinty look. "It's personal now for Sonny and McCarthy. The Stalker is the *Carter* Stalker. In their twisted logic, he's Carter's creation, so Carter is the problem. It's all Carter's fault. Especially now. They didn't like you..., us..., before, and they're steamin' now because of last night. The President gives the go ahead to Kingdom for his rally and they've got you pegged as an interfering busybody who's buddy-buddy with Tramonti. So no matter what, they'll keep The Stalker in it to stick it to the

University. Funny, but to do that, McCarthy's got to give us more tactical support this weekend." I must have looked quizzical. "To get The Stalker. The Sullivan's kid's murderer. We'll get a load of cops on double time Saturday night."

We waited at the corner of Brook Street and Waterman for the traffic streaming towards Wayland Square. "As for The Stalker, my bet is he's been stoked up by the publicity on the murder. Somebody else is getting *his* coverage. The guy *is* a serial, even if he takes a Saturday night off now and again. He'll make up for this one. I think it'll get worse. He's going to be back to make his mark."

With that, he threw the cigar into a puddle; it sputtered out and we walked the next few minutes in silence.

CHAPTER NINE

t was after four-thirty, with darkness only a few minutes away and the on-and-off drizzle starting again. As I shook Tuttle's hand in front of the Security Office building, I lamented that I hadn't brought an umbrella. He responded, "No problem" and ushered me into the Security Office's waiting area where a dozen or more of his officers were pulling on greenish raincoats and flat brown hats over gray shirts, gray ties, and gray trousers with belts loaded with cell phones, walkie-talkies, key rings, and flashlights. There was little camaraderie in their conversation and only a few nods or other dry acknowledgements to Tuttle as we made our way through the room. "Shift change," Tuttle remarked and signaled the duty officer behind a Plexiglas enclosure to buzz us through a door marked "Personnel Only."

We walked down a corridor to its end where he produced a key on a ring that would have made any janitor jealous and unlocked a door. Fluorescent lights revealed a storeroom, its walls lined with shelves filled with wire baskets marked by black enamel numbers, its floor covered by canvas bins overflowing with what could only be lost or abandoned property. "We keep everything but the bikes and the really big stuff in here. Should have umbrellas up the yin-yang."

He poked around in one bin, then another, and another, and even a fourth, but he was wrong. I thanked him for the thought and turned to leave when Tuttle reached to a top shelf and pulled down a scruffy, wide-brimmed, brown fedora adorned with a black ribbon at its crown. "Try it on." he said. "Better than gettin' soaked." He gave it a buff with his coat sleeve, snapped its brim, and pinched the crown. Somehow, I was not surprised when it fit nicely. Tuttle smiled as he checked me out. "Makes you look like a regular shamus."

○ ○ ○

A phone call to Marcie confirmed there was nothing pending that couldn't wait until tomorrow as I followed a group of male students shuffling along in their hightops toward the main campus. I crossed Brook Street in front of a Security Office patrol car and became acutely conscious of my *shamus* appearance—overcoat with turned up collar and fedora fixed at a rakish angle—something Richard Widmark or Victor Mature or Robert Ryan might have worn in a fifties-ish *film noir*. All I needed was a blond on my arm and a revolver strapped to my chest. A Security Office van rolled by, followed by two campus buses, on their way to the Refectory. At the rear of the Computer Center, two security officers, a man and a woman, stood in conversation under an entryway light; they glanced in my direction before they split up, with the man heading up the mall to the main campus while the woman let me go by and then traced my steps through a parking lot and out into the brightness and hubbub of Thayer Street. Was I being shadowed? I stopped at a window of the Gap to see if she would pass me, which she did without even a squint in my direction. So much for fantasy.

I continued down the crowded sidewalk, head down in the swirling wind, intending to cross Thayer Street and take a left at Bowen Street toward home. I was on auto-pilot, considering Tuttle's comments about Anne Sullivan, as I maneuvered around a bike frame chained to a utility pole, stepped off the curb, and barely missed becoming a hood ornament on a red Cadillac Escalade.

I retreated to the sidewalk as the SUV sped away and realized I was at Veasey Street. The *scene of the crime* was down that gloomy block, in one of the nondescript triple-deckers I had walked by a hundred times with hardly a glance. I had to take a closer look.

Seventy-two Veasey Street met my expectations. It was three floors of peeling brown shingles, probably divided into four or five apartments, three in front and one or two in back; picket fences with broken and missing slats separated it from its equally dilapidated neighbors. No driveway. Utility wires extended from its second floor out to the street. A half-dozen trash cans, overloaded cardboard cartons, and several bulging green plastic bags lined the sidewalk in front of a crumbling retaining wall which held back a skimpy front yard. Four concrete steps, without railings, ran up to a few feet of asphalt leading to rickety-looking stairs and a front stoop. A dull glow shone through an oval glass set in the front door; more lights were visible from behind misshapen blinds on the first floor right and in the single, shadeless window on the third floor.

I had a shoe on the first concrete step as I tried to picture last Friday night—the rain, or maybe it had been fog, the single street-light maybe fifty feet away barely penetrating the gloom, The Stalker, or whomever, following his victim into the tenement or spotting her by a window, somehow gaining entry into her apartment—when the front door opened and a woman wrapped in a bulky coat, head covered by a babushka, and arms around two brown trash bags, appeared. One of the trash bags left her grasp and bounced to the asphalt with enough momentum to keep rolling to the steps where its twisty-tie must have come undone and tubes, jars, and boxes cascaded to my feet.

It happened so quickly that I barely avoided being ankle deep in trash. I could have, should have, skulked away right then, but I didn't and instead called out loudly, "Let me help you" as I went to my knees to pick up the debris.

There was no acknowledgment of my offer, only low mutterings as she waddled her way to pick up the errant bag and stand over me. She found its opening, shook it, and in a voice that combined the gruffness of Ma Kettle with the accent of Eastern Europe, commanded, "Put that stuff in here!"

I did as I was told as she began a stream of righteous indignation about cops not protecting women, swilling coffee, interfering with her life, and never around when you need them while I collected and deposited the "stuff"—Band-Aids, shampoo, aspirin, face creams, toothpaste and other items that had to be from a bathroom cabinet—into the bag she jiggled impatiently.

"That's her stuff, ya know," she grunted. "I can't keep the place empty so that you can come back here whenever you want. It's been two days! I've gotta make a living, too. Hard enough to rent that place now. And I got a party in back who tells me she's moving out!" I deposited the last piece of "stuff," a Kleenex box, into the bag which she closed up, spun around to make an end, and tied off. "Throw it in one of them cans by the curb. Tomorrow's pickup day."

Gingerly, I took the bag, picked up the other one that lay at her sneakers, and squeezed both into a battered can. As I pushed down its lid, she added, "How about cartin' down a load for me? I got a box or two left. It's better'n standing out here in the rain and cold. Oy!" Her hand went heavenward as she turned, not waiting for me to answer.

It was my chance to leave. Plainly, she thought I was a cop on some sort of surveillance of the murder scene! It took only a couple of seconds for the shamus in me to overcome caution, and at her cry of "C'mon! Can't wait all night!", I followed her inside the tenement and up a dark, musty-smelling staircase. On the second floor landing, where a greasy food odor took over and the only light was cast by a low-wattage bulb on a pull-chain fixture, I was ambushed by a recycling bin full of bottles, cans, and bags of newspapers. My clumsiness engendered more mutterings as we climbed another flight of bannister-less stairs. At the top of the stairs, with a scrape of floor and a creak of the doorknob, the door opened into her. She backed away from its arc, tottered for a moment, and took the last stair into the apartment. I followed, pausing to push away strands of yellow plastic tape, curled like flypaper, on the door-frame. There was enough light to read "CRIME SCENE DO NOT REMOVE PPD."

What struck me first was a chemical odor. Even though it had been years since I had encountered the smell, you don't forget the odor of formaldehyde and chloral hydrate or their association with a crime scene. Her apartment turned out to be what University Housing would have prissily described as a "studio", a converted attic with a kitchen area demarcated by a waist-high counter and a small bathroom crammed in the corner. Although it probably didn't come close to housing code standards, it was commodious, with a pine board ceiling following the pitch of the roof. The sparse furniture was straight out of the Salvation Army store: two uncomfortable-looking overstuffed chairs with sagging cushions, a floor lamp with a bulb-burned shade, a round table with two folded chairs leaning on it, an empty bookcase, a bureau emptied of drawers, a flimsy coffee table and lamp, and seemingly out of place, a wardrobe, at least six feet in height, with full-length doors and inlays of various woods in triangle designs. One door of the wardrobe was open, revealing a clutch of empty wire hangers and garment bags on a single pipe. One bag read "Saks," another said "Chicos." The only wall decorations were two faded concert posters for Eminem and The White Stripes attached with thumbtacks. Against one wall rested a steel bed frame with a stained yellowish mattress laying flat against it.

The doyenne, who had started making odd sucking noises as though she was admonishing a dog, caught her breath. From the center of the room, with both hands on her ample hips, she grumbled a "let's get a move on" and went into the kitchen area while I crossed over to the room's only window and looked down to where I had been standing moments ago: it was clear that anyone in the apartment who crossed within a few feet of the window would be visible from the street. I turned and found her glaring at me—an obvious slacker—and pointing at a wicker laundry hamper next to the bed frame. "See them magazines?" she directed, shifting her aim to a pile of magazines scattered about on the rugless floor. "Stuff 'em in that hamper. I'll get this other stuff and we can close up. The furniture goes tomorrow."

I obeyed as my one attempt at conversation failed. "It must have been a shock to discover her," I said. She didn't answer because, I thought, she was deaf or uninterested and I gathered up the magazines as directed. Their variety surprised me: TIME, Atlantic Monthly, Rolling Stone, New Yorker, Newsweek, and a bunch of Sunday Times Magazines. One or two were fairly current and some were months, even years old, with covers barely stapled on, maybe the leavings of more than one occupant. As I stacked them on the coffee table for better handling, I noticed the subscriber label on the top magazine: "Shea Library, Carter University, Carter Station, Providence, RI 02905." The same for most of the others. Strange, I thought but couldn't put it in any context. Students are always ripping off non-essentials from the library, but why so many? For what purpose? I thought of returning them to the library until I considered the explanation I'd have to give its staff and dumped them into the hamper.

The light in the kitchen area went off and she deposited a cardboard box, containing what sounded like glass containers at my shoes. "Her family cleared out the big stuff, the good stuff, all the clothes, books, all her electronic stuff..., that girl had all kinds of stuff..., and left *me* her ratty furniture and all this crap!"

With that, she squinted a farsighted stare into my face and I saw she was a crone: hatchet faced, long-nosed, with black sharp eyes and gray whiskers at the corners of her sagging mouth. She made her now familiar sucking sound and pointed to the floor.

"Spread-eagle. Right there. See them chalk marks? That's where the bed was. Nothing on except that slip over her head. Terrible. I've never seen nothin' so shameless." She shook her head vigorously, causing a strand of dingy white hair to fall out of her kerchief. "I came up here Sunday night. Like to check up on these people when they leave the lights on at all hours. The door wasn't locked. Place was a mess. One look at her and I called ya right away." She jerked her face close to mine. "And I didn't touch nothin', neither!"

I stared at the faint chalk markings as she went on about how she was a good landlord, had to stay up all night with cops, and answer the same stupid questions over and over, while in my mind's eye, I saw Anne Sullivan's body, her head hidden under the slip, her breasts loose, her body flaccid and waxen as her blood followed gravity to her backside, until a poke from the crone's elbow brought me back to reality. She said, "Why'ya take my fingerprints? Do ya think I did it?"

She blinked at me, not caring if I responded, snapped off the floor lamp, picked up her carton, and started down the stairs. I grabbed the hamper by its handles and followed, scraping my knuckles on the staircase's wainscoting as I honed in on the landing light. That beacon went off even before I had inched my way around the recycling bin. At the front door, she piled her carton on top of the hamper. "Just put 'em by the trash cans. Hope it don't get too cold out there," she said, and opened, and almost pushed me through, the door.

On the stoop, I listened for the snap of a lock, but there wasn't any—either there wasn't a lock or she hadn't bothered with it—and managed to maneuver to the sidewalk with my load without killing myself. I deposited the hamper and carton next to the trash cans as ordered, wiped my hands with a handkerchief, and faced the tenement. It had been as dark on Friday night and probably as wet. Likely, few to no passerbys, and who would notice anyone on the tenement's walk or steps? It was a perfect place for an intruder. Anne Sullivan could have been randomly picked by her attacker when she passed by her apartment's window or could have been followed inside and when she opened that awkward apartment door, she wouldn't have been able to close it against any kind of resistance.

Her killer had it made.

CHAPTER TEN

Since the kitchen lights were on, I called "hello!" as I closed the front door and put away the fedora and my coat in the hall closet, expecting a suitable response from Nadie. None came. I pushed open the kitchen's swinging door to find her sitting at the counter, an empty coffee mug beside her. She was wearing an Eileen Fisher-ish loose mauve sweater, black blouse, and grey wool skirt. The small screen television on the counter was turned to *Jeopardy*. She shut it off.

"So-ooo...?" she said—which meant 'where have *you* been?'—and glanced at her watch. "It's after seven."

"Sorry." I brushed a kiss on her forehead and got no reaction. "It's been a long day. How about a drink?"

"No, thanks," was the cool reply.

Okay, what was going on? I was late, but not that late. Or was I? Anyways, I wasn't going to let her mood spoil my expectations for the evening. I left the kitchen for the drinks cabinet in the dining room, thinking that instead of wine or martinis, sherry would be appropriate. In a moment, I was back with sparkling Lismore glasses and a decanter of pale dry Jerez. She gave me "the look" when she saw two glasses.

"I said 'no, thanks', didn't I?"

"C'mon," I said, purposefully ignoring her sourness as I filled a glass for myself and began to pour a second, "it'll warm you up."

Her back stiffened. "Five-thirty," she said tightly. Her chin came forward and she trained unnerving bottle-green eyes at me.

"Remember?" She took her glass, gave me her fine-boned profile, and tossed the sherry down in a single draught that accentuated the arch of her long neck and the black hair sweeping over her shoulders. That image made me conciliatory, even when she placed the glass firmly on the counter and practically impaled me with her glare. Stubbornness on my part would lose the prize—her bubbling Mediterraneanism lies just beneath her professional calm—so the better part of valor would be an abject apology.

"I lost track of time. Things were so damned confused today. I—"

"Did you lose your cell phone, too?"

"Hey, I said I was 'sorry.' Why are you so upset?"

She slid her empty glass across the counter towards me. I wasn't sure whether she wanted a refill or it was a gesture of rejection. "I'm not upset," she said, much too evenly. "I'm goddamn mad! I switched off tonight at the Center despite the crowd signing up for counseling so that we could have some time together..." and now, her voice rising, "...and you show up an hour and a half late!"

I ignored her exaggeration. "Na-die," I said and sat across the counter from her, reaching for her reluctant hands. "I know I said 'early' but..." and with a kind of nervous exhilaration, I recounted my ride with Faud and his clinical details of Ms. Sullivan's death, Franks's attempt to inveigle me into being his pipeline to Tramonti, Tuttle's strong belief that the murderer was not The Stalker, and my excursion on Veasey Street. Early on, I knew I was coming off disjointed and confusing; like last night, there were too many facts to marshal and no time to digest any. Halfway through my spiel, she reached for the decanter, poured half a glass, and sipped the sherry as I continued. As I went on, her listening mode changed from sulky disinterest to professional to annoyed. As I wound down with speculations about Anne Sullivan's relationship with Lavelle Williams, I braced myself.

"I can't believe that you actually went into that apartment!"

"I didn't plan it. And I was invited," I retorted, maybe with more defensiveness than needed.

She stood up, her hands pushing back her open sweater. I imagined the ominous glare she was aiming at me and heard exasperation in her voice. "What is wrong with you?"

I looked up with a face feigning surprise.

"The women on this campus are scared for their lives, they're leaving in droves, while the University Counsel is slinking around, hiding in the shadows like a voyeur, sneaking into a murdered woman's apartment under false pretenses." She stopped only for a deep breath. "While you were satisfying your morbid curiosity—"

"Whoa! Wait a second! It wasn't *morbid* curiosity! It just happened."

"Nothing like that just *happens*!" She turned her back to me in disgust. "And don't you dare say 'ugh'!"

Ugh! How did I screw this up? I had dinner and romance on my agenda, not an argument. With a sheepish expression, I went around the counter to face her. "Why are you so upset?" I said softly and reached for her hands which she released tentatively. "I didn't ask to be everyone's father-confessor today. Could we begin this all over again? Hello. I missed you. I love you."

Her eyes lowered and I felt her tension ease. What the hell did I know, anyway? Maybe it was morbid curiosity. Tentatively, she let me draw her body close and I put my arms around her. A shiver ran under my fingers as I held her.

She was silent for at least half a minute before she raised her head; a forgiving smile crossed her lips. I ran my fingers through her hair, took her head in my hands, and kissed her forehead lightly; she responded with a kiss that was warm, longing, and passionate and we were again lovers, not quarrelers. "I'm really sorry," I said and meant it. "I just didn't think about the time. Let me make some dinner. I've got some nice sole and...."

"Forget the *sole*," she said, recovering her verve. She took my arm and pushed me toward the kitchen door. "I need some *body*...!"

I love this woman!

○ ○ ○

She lay quietly next to me, her warmth, her perfume, and the covering of a sheet my only sensations. My right hand was enfolded over her left hand, at our sides. She turned her head and nuzzled my shoulder, nibbling at the base of my neck. Then, she rested a cheek on my shoulder. Her breath was sweet on my face.

I was content. We have been together for almost three years. No breaks, no excursions, no interruptions. After my divorce, there had been more than a few women and affairs without grand passion, all founded on lust, boredom, or natural needs, that ran their courses. Anyway, I didn't fall in love and gradually, there were longer, drier spells between affairs, followed by indulgence and hangover. At fifty, I was on the verge of becoming someone incurably polite and unflappable, the proverbial "extra man" at dinner parties, a stiff who had come to guard his freedom to do what he liked when he liked and avoided the inconveniences of a life impacted by someone close. In other words, I was socially constipated.

Until *il folgore*, the *thunderbolt*.

It had been a routine faculty cocktail party—one of those where to keep sane you say "okay" and "right" either because you didn't feel like contributing to tales of holidays abroad, private schools, cars, and campus gossip or because it is pointless to interject any fact, reasoned opinion, or nuance into the conversation without risking the "Carter dialectic." Two martinis were helping me through the guests' spurious laughter and discreet checks on the time, when Professor Nadie Winokur challenged an idle point being made about something political and not very important. I knew of her egalitarian views from snatches of prior conversations in similar venues but this time, I found myself really listening and watching as she went on, parrying objections with fervor. When I later engaged her in conversation, the way she responded made me feel better looking and wittier for the effort, even as she disagreed with most everything I said. Way back in my brain, there was a buzz of warning which I ignored: she's too earnest, a naif in a nasty world, passionate about people and poverty and the avoidance of cruelty to any person or animal — in fact, all hurts that can be averted by money or planning. Besides, too young for me.

It made no difference. Within weeks, we were lovers — tentative lovers, then risk-taking lovers. She frankly admitted that she wanted a mature lover, one who would bind her to himself without choking restraints, who could love her enough to let her ease into a relationship and test its strength. I was all too willing, even as I remained cautious and pragmatic about commitment, especially when confronted by her initial refusal to ignore our markedly different backgrounds and economic circumstances. Over time and not without strain, Nadie — from Prospect Park, Brooklyn, the only child of school teachers who were precinct leaders for New York's Liberal Party and grandchild of immigrants who brought their socialist ideals from the old country — and I have learned to cope. Her open love and relentless humanity help me accept her penchant for political, social, and psychological analysis for every occasion, and she stopped trying to convert me to her opinions after a mutual admiration developed between Nadie and my devotedly liberal mother.

Yet, I feel vulnerable as a schoolboy in a first love because most of the time we live together only on weekends or vacations; in this terribly modern relationship, there is always the danger of a drift to nowhere.

That would be devastating!

She unclasped our hands and propped herself up to lean into me. Her ripe breasts pressed against me but she didn't get her expected, and immediate, response. My mind had drifted elsewhere and she sensed it. "Now what?"

In fact, and terribly inappropriately, I was thinking about how you suffocate someone with a pillow, how do you get close enough, how do you keep it on the face when the victim struggles..., and it took a second or two to refocus.

"You're thinking about your goddamn murder, aren't you!"

How did she know?

She grabbed a pillow and whacked me squarely, and not particularly playfully, on my head.

"Hey, that hurt!" I fended off the next blow with my forearm. Was she kidding or not? Nadie's emotions flip so very, very quickly. "And, it isn't *my* goddamn murder!"

"You deserve it," she said in a mock pout. "Any normal man would give up a lot to be between your sheets right now." She sat up and brought her knees up to her chin, and wrapped her arms around them. I sat up, kissed the back of her neck and ears, and fondled her breasts. She turned to face me and her tongue touched mine. Slowly, she sank back on to the bed and lay still. Her eyes were half closed, her smell enveloped me.

"Still," I murmured, "Faud and Tuttle...."

Her eyes ignited and she bolted off the bed.

"I'm teasing," I said.

Too late; the magic was gone. At the triple mirror, she ran her hands through her hair so it fell over her shoulders and let her nakedness taunt me: her hands went to her breasts and down her slim muscular body, the result of a daily regimen of running and exercise at the Sport Complex and a strict, mostly natural foods, diet. She clasped her hands behind her neck. "If you're going to go on with this, even lovemaking can wear thin," she said curtly and left for the bathroom.

What a stupid tease! When will I learn?

She returned to the loft to dress quickly. I stayed in bed, bringing a cotton duvet up to my chin, keeping the peace by being silent until, as she took her sweater off the back of a chair by the bed and put it over her arm, I remembered Reinman. "Geez," I said, "I forgot to tell you. How's this for a coincidence? A lawyer from my old law firm visited me. Said that Reinman named me executor of his estate! I can't believe it!"

She took a step toward the bed, interest in her face. "Are you going to do it?" I explained the time predicament if I refused and she shook her head ruefully. "You do get in the middle of things..., or is it the muddle of things?"

"Damned if I know," and I smiled my most winning smile.

She came to stand over me. Her face had softened. "I think it's time you drove me home." When I didn't immediately respond, she leaned over and pulled off my covering. "Well," she said, "look at you. Pennants flying. Alas, too late. C'mon, laddie, get dressed, you've had your dalliance for today."

"I'm starving. Aren't you hungry?" I asked. "I—"

She hesitated before she allowed she was and I baked the sole with some Old Bay seasoning and little carrots, and we shared a nice bottle of Orvieto Secco. Not once did we discuss Anne Sullivan, The Stalker, or Reinman.

Not that Anne Sullivan was far from my mind.

Wednesday

CHAPTER ELEVEN

Nadie stayed the night; we were up early so that she could get back to her apartment for clothes and prepare for class. There was no time for exercise or my regimen of pool drills. I made espresso and grilled cappicola and provolone on sliced focaccia, drove her to her apartment, came back, showered, and dressed. A glance through the *Journal* showed that coverage of the Sullivan murder had been relegated to the *City* section and contained nothing new; demonstrations at the women's dorms and yesterday's Faculty Senate meeting merited short items in the wrap-up of The Stalker coverage—again, nothing new. I packed two copies each of Tuttle's Event Plan for Kingdom's rally and the insurance coverage memo, and left for my appointment with Danby.

○ ◯ ○

President's House is a rambling, ruddy-bricked affair facing Gower Street, with a Victorian porch add-on which begins at its front door and swings around the house on its easterly side to a sculpture garden in the side yard. At eight-thirty, Gower Street was lined with cars parked for the day despite the "two hour max" signs hung on every utility pole. I rang the bell and Martine Danby opened the door, greeting me with an almost inaudible "Hi" as I stepped inside. Her slender figure was hidden by an oversized purple and gold Carter warmup jacket that fell well below her hips; her hair was held back by a white scrunchy, sharpening the soft features of a pleasant, oval face. She gathered a pile of books from the hall table and said "They are in the study" as she swept by me.

I watched her through a window in the doorframe as she crossed Gower Street and started down Carter Street toward the campus. There was often a kind of remoteness about her, something disguised by her politeness and a seriousness that you wouldn't expect in a first semester junior. When her mother died unexpectedly of cancer only a few months after Danby's selection as President, Martine had decided, against her father's wishes, to move out of the dorms and live with him here, where she quickly assumed duties as unofficial hostess at many University functions. She was also, I suspected, her father's extra eyes and ears on campus.

It was only as I dropped my Burberry on a hall chair that the "they" hit me. "They?"

I entered a beige-papered, formal living room and crossed to the door of the study. The voices within stopped at my knock and I entered. The wall of glass windows overlooking the sculpture garden let in a brilliant light which cast the man on the leather couch facing me in a stark shadow. It took a second for me to discern the face of Jesse Kingdom. In my surprise, I looked quickly around the room to find Charles Danby who was standing off to my right, pouring coffee into a cup from a carafe on a sideboard next to his desk.

"Thanks for coming over," Danby said. "Coffee?"

I declined.

He was dressed in dark slacks, pinstriped shirt, and informal floral tie. His chestnut-colored eyes looked directly into mine, his full jaw set, his square face untroubled. He finished pouring and said, "I don't think you've met Jesse Kingdom. Jesse, Alger Temple, my legal counsel."

He was right, of course; I hadn't met Kingdom—but I sure as hell had been giving him a lot of thought these past few days! As Danby well knew.

Kingdom stood. Behind him, the sunlight gleamed on the metal shapes of the sculpture garden, giving him a background of shimmers of brilliance. He was handsome and about forty-five, my height, athletically built, dressed in an almost black suit, starched white shirt, and plain blue tie. Above a neck that was at least a size seventeen was a face of large features that radiated self-assurance, at once stern and calm. Like Danby, the grayish curly hair at his temples enhanced his face's authority; a close-cropped beard sprinkled with white added to a general seriousness. His eyes locked mine as he thrust his hand forward. As I shook it, I managed to say something like "glad to meet you" in a voice that caught my uncertainty.

Kingdom returned to his seat and I sat across from him in an armchair; Danby took his cup to an upholstered club chair that permitted him to face both of us. Maybe as a mediator, I thought. "Jesse doesn't even drink coffee," he said lightly. "No bad habits, probably."

Kingdom laughed in a self-deprecating manner. "I could give you my standard 'high on life' sermon in response to that, Charlie, but it wouldn't do much good here," he said, his voice richer and softer than I'd imagined.

Danby, rubbing his hands together as though he was anxious to get started, addressed me in his measured cadence. "I know you didn't expect Jesse to be here, but there are a few things that you should know, both as my friend and as University Counsel." Danby often speaks in paragraphs and I had the feeling that there were going to be a number of them. "Jesse and I are both Philadelphia boys. Grew up on the same block, went to the same school, same church, and have been friends for years. I don't mean that we talk on the telephone every week, although we always stayed in contact. I knew Jesse was preaching in Providence before I took the job here." He nodded toward Kingdom and his voice softened. "Then, when Holly... got sick, Jesse's friendship was very important to me."

I found myself compelled to glance at Kingdom; his eyes were half closed and his hands lay loosely in his lap.

Danby continued. "We haven't seen that much of each other here since Jesse's been so... busy. Talked on the telephone a number of times. Jesse suggested we meet because of the rally on Friday. He's concerned that he might be a source of embarrassment to me. I told him that I'm a big boy. That he didn't have to look out for 'Junior' anymore."

Kingdom reacted to Danby's gibe by sliding a meaty hand across his mouth. Maybe, he was embarrassed.

"It would've been unfair to have this meeting without you, Algy. Security for the rally is important and I wanted you to be aware of our friendship. Other than Martine and Artemus, I don't suppose anyone else here knows." Danby's face now opened up. "The Black Student Caucus had every right to invite Jesse to the campus, and I know he thought long and hard about accepting it, but he did, and that's fine. That's between Jesse and Martine, and her committee." He nodded toward Kingdom. "As far as I am concerned, Jesse is an invited guest to the campus for legitimate debate."

He sounded so ingenuous that I almost interrupted; when their relationship became known, Danby's critics would harp on his poor judgment in taking sides in a volatile, politically divisive, Providence *thing*, the ultimate "no-no" in the traditional Carter view of town and gown affairs. And, then there was Sonny! Danby knew this and was apparently comfortable with his position.

So, I had better be, too.

I waited for Kingdom to respond with a hint that he understood his friend's predicament. He remained silent and the quiet became awkward so I suggested to Danby that we review the Event Plan, with the thought that laying it out might help gauge

Kingdom's reaction and Danby's level of concern. I got the documents from my briefcase, kept one, and gave the other to Danby; Kingdom looked on as though it had nothing to do with him. Danby followed my summary of the plan carefully, occasionally indicating agreement, but asked no questions; Kingdom maintained an aloof silence which, for some reason, irritated me. "Tuttle still believes he might get some reluctant cooperation from the police." I heard a chuckle from Kingdom and continued. "Our security force will be at full strength, with personnel stationed around The Green...discreetly. We can expect a large crowd, the kids and anyone else that might arrive with Reverend Kingdom. The usual concerns about a building occupation are covered...."

Kingdom's eyes betrayed bemusement at such details. "It's just a contingency," I added, feeling defensive. "We don't expect anything of the sort. We always plan for the worst."

When I finished, Danby handed his copy to me, leaving me to wonder if his easy acceptance was due to Kingdom's presence. He said, "I know I could've told you all about Jesse and me in the office but I wanted you to meet Jesse. I want you to know that he and I disagree about a lot of things but we don't disagree about his right to speak here. He—"

Kingdom hunched forward toward me. "Charlie's about to make a speech and it probably will be long and complicated. Let me cut to the chase for you, Mr. Temple. You've got here a racist city, a racist police department, maybe a lot of racism here on your own campus, what with this Stalker terrorizing black women. The message is the same wherever I go—and if you haven't heard it before, let me summarize it: It's got to end. It's got to end *now!*"

His voice had developed a richness and I knew that I was in the presence of an orator.

"These rapes and goings-on. It's racism at its worst. I'm going to say that the same people who run the police and don't take action to find this Stalker are the same people who let a rotten police force run amuck. They have got to be targeted and driven out."

I almost complained, but didn't, that his accusations had weakened Tramonti, a reform candidate with the political will to address such issues.

"I'm going to say that this University and every educated person in this state has got a stake in convicting cops who beat up people and get away with it. They've got to recognize that a grinding racism is immobilizing this city." He took a deep breath. "Every day, it's my duty to move people. Like tomorrow, our largest rally yet. From the federal court to the Public Safety Building. We are carrying the message to *them*."

I had expected victimhood or some such stance after the way he had ripped into Tramonti but found nothing of that in his demand for justice. His indignation was genuine.

"I respect your right to bring your message, to be on our campus. As for Friday, though, I have a real concern." I turned to Danby. "With your permission," I added. He nodded, so I stared at Kingdom and gave it a go. "To protect our kids, the University needs cooperation from the police. So far, they haven't been responsive or effective. But, we need them. We also want our kids to cooperate with the cops and our security people, and, more importantly, pay attention to their own security. The Stalker is out there and Carter women are in danger." I edged forward in my chair for emphasis. "It wouldn't negate your message to urge common sense and stress individual responsibility. You could get that message through to some of them in a different way—maybe better than anyone else."

Kingdom's eyes didn't give any clues as to whether my argument was getting through.

"I didn't mean to lecture," he replied, his voice resuming a conversational softness. "I hope you realize that. I just wanted you to understand where I'm coming from and why I do what I do. Your boss here is my friend. Our mothers diapered our behinds together, that's how close we were when we were kids. Lots of things have changed and we've gone separate ways, yet underneath, we've got the same commitments. We've got loyalties. I'm not going to get in Charlie's way; Charlie isn't going to get less cooperation because I'm here."

He said all of this with such a warmth of feeling that I was touched.

He stood up, and so did Danby and I. "Got to go. Have as many meetings as I have anything else. Just like you, Charlie." He smiled a wide open smile. "Well, not actually a meeting this time. I have to tape an interview for one of those cable public affairs shows." He shook his head. "I wonder if anyone watches those things? They usually show them opposite the games or when the church-goers are in church or the revelers are sleeping."

Danby chuckled and slapped his friend lightly on the back. Kingdom and I shook hands and Danby accompanied him out of the room. I sat down, with confused thoughts about Jesse Kingdom, the disruptions that his message could cause, and friendship and loyalty. When Danby returned to the study, he was still smiling. "He's quite a guy. You should've seen him play streetball. There wasn't anybody better. He could still knock a few heads if he had to."

I slid the Event Plan back into my briefcase. Danby remained standing. "The Faculty Senate couldn't decide yesterday whether to support me or a class suspension motion. Postponed a decision until Monday. I'm losing support. If anything happens this weekend, it will be gone. As for the kids, it wasn't too bad at all. Only a hundred or so showed up last night and another group will meet me this afternoon. God knows what I'll say differently." He shook his head in doubt. "This thing has just got to end. We're losing ground."

I remembered that I had the insurance coverage memo to review with him but now it seemed like small potatoes. I did, however, deal with McAllister's caution. "I assume you know that Martine is on the rally's speaker list."

"Yes, she told me. She's very proud of her friendship with Jesse. I rather guess she's the one that got him to come up here. Otherwise, I bet he wouldn't have accepted out of some misguided deference to our friendship." His voice was steady and it was clear that he had thought through the ramifications of Kingdom on campus. "There will be some who will be disturbed by my association with Jesse," he said, his eyes exploring my face. "So be it. We all take risks with who we are." He said it easily and that made me feel more confident about his position. "I appreciate your concern."

I left the room and Danby followed me out to the hall. He held my raincoat as I slipped it on. For conversation, I mentioned that I had been named Reinman's executor. Danby said, "Met him just once, at a party last spring. Have to say that in two minutes of conversation, I was kind of put off by his view of his colleagues. Then, after his heart attack, we spoke on the telephone, a short 'how are you doing?' Got him a TA to help out. Even then..." — he paused to find a word — "... prickly?"

He had found the right one.

We shook hands and he held on to mine for a moment. "Martine is a wonderful kid, and I know McAllister keeps his eyes on her. And it's important that she has something of a regular college life, even if she insists upon living with her old man." His face became somber. "If you ever hear anything that I should know, friend to friend, I'd appreciate it."

"Sure," I said, and went out the front door, leaving him standing in the doorway. As I walked down the steps, I knew I had seen a glimpse of the man's loneliness as well as his sense of himself and his mission. Was The Stalker and Jesse Kingdom about to frustrate both?

CHAPTER TWELVE

Champlin & Burrill—Founded In 1818.

The words were etched in burnished silvery metal on a slab of cherrywood which faced the elevator bank on the twenty-third floor of the Bank of America Tower. Lorrie Stevenson, the firm's principal receptionist, a gray-haired, gentle-faced woman, was at her wide, teak desk when I asked for Eustace Pine. She instructed her assistant at the telephone console beside her to call Pine's secretary and the assistant complied amidst a constant repetition of "Champlin & Burrill...," pause, "...one moment please." As I hung my Burberry—now with its lining zipped in—in a closet behind her desk, Lorrie began her ritual discussion of the vagaries of Providence weather—the sky now had a suspiciously yellowish cast—and after agreement as to the likelihood of imminent change, I left her desk and sank into the comfort and familiarity of one of the reception area's upholstered chairs.

Nothing garish here, no smears of paint on the walls, just appropriate furniture and carpets, silk flowers in celadon glazed bowls, paintings like the one facing me—a FitzHugh Lane of a Newport yacht knifing through the swells in front of Beavertail—and a panoramic view of WaterPlace Park. Instead of aging *Sports Illustrated*s, the table in front of me held a fan of current issues of *Smithsonian, American Heritage, Forbes*, and *Antiques*. I admit to smugness: *this* was what a lawyer's reception area should be: comfortable, radiating civility, giving the client a feeling of security, not fright.

Eustace Pine, in a three-piece brown suit, striped shirt, and polka dot bow tie, took my hand in a two-handed grip as he thanked me for meeting on short notice, said that Mrs. Cabel had arrived, and led me down a hall to the glass door of the firm's main conference room. Since it was usually reserved for partners' meetings, bond issue closings, and other transactions involving a host of clients, lawyers, paralegals, and secretaries, I mentioned that I was surprised we would be meeting there. Pine stopped at the doorway, ran a bony hand over his scalp, and said, somewhat abashedly, "Seems as though the others are busy." Had I caught him trying to impress his new client?

He opened the door for me. Almost lost in the somber luxury of the conference room, in one of the twenty or so high-backed chairs spaced around an oval, green leather topped conference table, sat a plain-faced woman in a gray cardigan over a gray blouse, gray hair pulled back and knotted, hands clasped primly on the table next to a large cloth handbag. No jewelry lightened her appearance. From where I stood, the scene had the quality of a studio portrait sitting: a pale yellow wall with an elaborately framed landscape of a verdant pasture by Edward Bannister, and below the painting's center, the motionless study in gray. Pine made introductions while I crossed to her, offering my hand. She gave me a few fingers, rough to the touch, to rest in mine as I expressed condolences; her mouth relaxed slightly and I was struck by a flickering wariness in eyes that may have been blue but also seemed gray.

Pine recognized the awkwardness and quickly suggested I sit across the table from her, next to a stack of documents. I passed behind her, catching the scent of lilies of the valley. Pine sat next to Mrs. Cabel, took out a slim glasses case from his coat pocket, elaborately perched reading glasses on his nose, and began in a practiced manner to review Reinman's will. Deborah, he said, was the sole beneficiary since there was no "issue," a fact he repeated several times. He explained the documents I would be executing: a petition for probate, a waiver of notice of newspaper advertisement of the hearing, a form of bond, and two insurance forms. The hearing would be before the Honorable Judge Cremascoli of the Providence Probate Court at nine o'clock on Friday morning and there was no doubt the will would be admitted to probate and I would be appointed executor. As Pine rambled on about probate procedures, timetables, and estate tax returns, Mrs. Cabel, who had roused herself from passivity, stared at him intently; her face, showing the clefts and lines of age, with sags under her chin and indentations under the cheekbones, had the lack of color that one finds in elderly people who have suffered tragedy. I discerned a likeness to my recollection of Deborah Reinman in their shared narrow noses and thin-lipped mouths, but what appeared to be in proportion on the mother's face was oddly pinched when replicated on Deborah's.

"... Of course, once the formalities are through and, Algy, you're appointed executor, the firm will assist in every way possible. Algy would be entitled to a fee but has agreed to waive it." Had I? Or had Pine assumed that I would? "We'll prepare the Rhode Island and federal estate tax returns, the inventories...." He peered over his glasses at me. "I imagine, Algy, that you'll be appointed appraiser as well. We have the names of several experts to assist with the valuation of his copyrights and stream of royalties, and will contact them promptly. We've requested that there be a suitable widow's allowance from the probate estate for Mrs. Reinman, just in case, but there seems to be more than adequate funds in a checking account and a money market account with..."—he checked a document—"...Merrill Lynch."

Mrs. Cabel spoke for the first time. It was a dry voice with a slight Vermont twang, and I sensed a person who spoke when spoken to, who led a self-contained life. "Before his heart attack, he took care of all the major bills and Deborah had an allowance for household expenses," she said evenly. "He handled the investment sort of things by himself until he was stricken. Then, Deborah took over the accounts—"

Pine raised his hand slightly. "Of course, of course. Mrs. Reinman can use the accounts and will be permitted a widow's allowance as a matter of course. From what you've told me, I think six thousand a month would amply cover all expenses including the mortgage on the Little Compton property. The Benefit Street house is mortgage-free, so we really only have to worry about usual living expenses, the Little Compton mortgage, and of course, taxes."

"As I told you," Mrs. Cabel addressed Pine, "Deborah is determined to move back to Vermont." Her hands went to her lap, as did her stare. "Deborah is..."—she struggled for a word—"...overwrought. We took her back home last night. Her sister's come down from Burlington to be with her. The houses should be sold as soon as possible." Her eyes blinked twice as though for emphasis.

Pine reassured her. "Not to worry at all. With Algy's help, we'll move right along. I'm sure that whatever you..., whatever Mrs. Reinman decides can be accomplished promptly. House prices have been firm and...." He continued on, tilting his head fractionally towards Mrs. Cabel as he gave her his insights as to the realtors to be contacted while I wondered why the widow had such a reluctance to stay in Rhode Island where she'd lived for probably twenty years or more. Maybe it was this determined old lady who didn't want to leave Vermont. In any event, it seemed to have been decided.

Pine handed me a gold plated Cross ballpoint pen which I used to execute documents flagged by red gummed tags. I came to a personal property inventory form and stopped. "Who will be doing the inventory, Ew?"

"One of our paralegals, Connie Adams. Do you remember her? Very astute. She's going through personal property at the homes today with Mrs. Cabel."

I continued with the signing. "What about his University office? Can I be of help there, to get Connie in?" Reinman had an office in Ramsden Hall, the faculty office building for the History Department.

"That's next. A teaching assistant has been assigned and Mrs. Reinman, fortunately, had been there frequently during her late husband's illness, and had an office key." He rummaged through a redwell file and removed a key on a long string which he laid on the table. Mrs. Cabel's forehead wrinkled with seeming impatience at the imposition of a TA and Pine's paralegal going through her late son-in-law's possessions.

"It's really routine," I offered, feeling she should see me as somebody more than a mere endorser of Pine's legal documents. "Traditionally, class outlines and teaching notes are left with the Department, a resource for anyone teaching similar courses. The same with books that the family may not want or need. Everything gets inventoried, and Deborah can decide what she wants to keep or leave."

"If that's what's done," she said resignedly. "The idea of strangers going through his things...."

Pine replied to both my feeling of being supercilious and her reaction to the law's and the University's intrusive fussiness. "Connie is scheduled to be at his office Friday morning at ten. She's quite capable. Lots of experience. Of course, if you'd like to be present...."

She pursed her lips as if balancing competing pressures on her schedule. "No, that won't be necessary." She reached for her handbag.

The meeting seemed over but Pine couldn't leave well enough

alone. "Algy, you might want to stop in on Friday." He smiled, maybe even winked, thinking he had bridged the gap between myself and Mrs. Cabel by offering me some useful activity, and dangled the key from a string. "Won't take but a minute. Just to get things going?"

Mrs. Cabel gave me a quick but penetrating glance. In her estimation, I was, like Pine's paralegal, a practical necessity to be tolerated, and that irritated me. "I *would* like to move things along...."

Pine smiled in anticipation and slid the key across the table. It was then that I realized Pine hadn't explained to her that I hadn't known about Reinman's nomination of me as his executor.

Damn Pine! Damn Reinman!

I made my face into a half smile, nodded, and took the key. I said, "Friday at ten."

Mrs. Cabel stood. She was short, barely five-four, and slight, so different than her daughter. When she came around the table to me, I stood. "Mr. Pine has told me about you being the University's lawyer, so I guess you're familiar enough with this kind of thing. Carl must have felt you could do the job, that Deborah might be too upset—"

"I'll do my best to assist Mr. Pine," I replied, and shook the limp hand which she offered to me.

She peered up at me, maybe with some kind of acceptance in her eyes. "I guess we ought to thank you, so I will," she said evenly. "I hope it isn't too much of a chore. Mr. Pine says it won't be. Deborah's much too upset, especially about not being home when Carl died. Barely made it through the service yesterday. The one time she takes a break from caring for him, just an overnight down to their place in Little Compton, that's when he goes.... Now, she can't bear the thought of living here." She lowered her eyes, turned, and left the conference room without another word, followed by Pine.

Well, that explained the quick return to Vermont, even if it seemed an overreaction.

I put Reinman's office key in my jacket pocket. Pine returned and while I executed the remaining probate forms, he filled in some details on Mrs. Cabel's parting words. Deborah Reinman, he said, had been in Little Compton, a respite from her nursing of Reinman, when he suffered a fatal heart attack. Died in his sleep apparently. Mrs. Cabel had come down from Vermont to replace her as his nurse for the weekend. "Tragedy," Pine said quietly, "a young man," and put Reinman's will—which had a pale blue cover with his name typed and underlined—on top of the documents I had executed.

I touched the will; as far as the law was concerned, it represented the formal winding-up of Reinman's life.

Somehow, it was not enough.

CHAPTER THIRTEEN

During the next hour, Steve Winter, the co-chair of Champlin & Burrill's litigation group and usually an optimistic sort, briefed me on *Zerma v. Carter University*, the sexual bias and harassment case that was high on my anxiety barometer. His predictions were bleak; the federal court magistrate judge would likely allow the plaintiff, Associate Professor Isabel Zerma, to use pretrial discovery—over fifty noticed depositions of administrators and faculty, together with a forty page documents request that would require thousands of hours of search, review, and evaluation of the University's recruitment, hiring, and promotion records—in an effort to find a scintilla of evidence that the University tolerated sexual bias or harassment. Danby's predecessor, after stonewalling on an individual settlement, had allowed the case to mushroom into a class action for all female faculty members and candidates for faculty positions, encouraging plaintiff and her aggressive counsel to go for complete capitulation, including millions in damages, an admission that Carter was institutionally biased, and court monitoring of all faculty hiring and promotions. The cost of the litigation in terms of time and focus, never mind the legal fees, had been and would continue to be enormous; on the other hand, a loss of this high profile case would grievously wound the University's integrity, reputation, and ability to govern its affairs.

Three uncomfortable meetings, three major, different, and continuing worries, in three hours. Must be some kind of record.

I left the office tower and stepped out into Kennedy Plaza, noisy with bleating car horns and saturated by the aroma of diesel fumes from the buses lined up at the depot which ran down the Plaza's center. I turned on to Westminster Street in front of the granite steps and columns of the Arcade, and became part of the financial district's noontime bustle of office workers on lunch break and takeout runs, sidewalk vendors offering hot and sweet Italian sausage rolls, walkers and joggers in exercise clothes, bicycle messengers, and construction workers munching sandwiches and commenting on the "skirts" going by at the Sovereign Bank Plaza. At the College Street Bridge, a gust of brine-filled air caused me to linger at its central parapet over the Providence River. The tide was flowing toward the Bay, carrying debris from upriver on a turgid current. The breeze driven water slapped against the bridge's abutments and the blackened, mushroom-like braziers anchored permanently for WaterFire events, and flicked away in a million small waves toward the riverbanks. Further down the river, sea gulls shrieked and swooped, their cries almost lost in the noise of traffic on I-195 and the whomp, whomp, whomp of a helicopter landing at the South Main Street helipad. Above me, the wind sang in the halyards of the bridge's three empty flagpoles.

My hands left the recesses of my pockets and went to one of the wrought iron chains that served as railings for the parapet; the adhesion of finger flesh to cold metal brought to mind my winter sea duty on a cruiser of the Sixth Fleet before I got tapped to defend court-martials. I was so *aware* of myself at twenty-six, a Marine lieutenant, a lawyer, full of expectation that life was meant to be lived well, with a single-mindedness that reduced the entire world to manageable size. Those were easier days, all action or all monotony, with specific responsibilities and ascertainable risks, and, my God, didn't my future seem exciting! I would be a hand of justice, use my talents and good fortune for noble ends! I'd be focused and passionate about whatever I did!

What happened?

It's not what you are, somebody said, but what you don't become that hurts.

Despite the satisfaction of a legal career and successes that others might envy, I had been wrestling with the realization that I was without that focus. My professional life was a series of reactions to others' demands, needs, causes, or outrages: a legal litter box. My relationship with Nadie was unsettled. How was it that *I* wasn't in control? Where had the passion gone? Would I ever again feel that I would make a difference?

The three-story brownstone which houses the Faculty Club once had all the charm of the Irish funeral parlors on Smith Hill. Its dingy, high ceiling rooms, closed in by maroon and gray drapes, dark wallpaper, brownish rugs, and mahogany trimmed furnishings, its bland "welsh rarebit special" menus, and BYO booze policy, discouraged use, except for the gastronomically challenged and bachelor professors of both sexes. In a peace offering to a complaining faculty, the University renovated and decorated the dining rooms, parlors, and reading rooms, added an atrium off the main dining room and a patio annex for summer dining, subsidized the Club's budget so that dues remained manageable, and hired experienced kitchen staff seduced by regular hours, reasonable compensation, and the freedom to plan menus and interesting food-centered events. Eventually, even Providence politics were satisfied; to obtain a full liquor license from the uncooperative and unsympathetic City Licensing Board, the Club, nominally independent from the University and therefore taxable, was persuaded to offer an *ex officio* membership to the holder of the office of mayor, creating the supreme irony that Sonny Russo could, and did, have lunch here occasionally with Puppy Dog and other cronies. Just to demonstrate his disdain, he paid his bills infrequently, and late, with checks from his "Friends of Russo" political fund.

I declined the hostess's offer of a seat at one of the common tables and she found me a place in an alcove off the main dining room. I glanced at the menu, ordered the quiche of the day, a garden salad, and hot tea, and laid out a pocket notebook to record some thoughts on the class action for a memo to Danby and the Provost. I began my scribbles, slowly becoming aware that at nearby table, two faculty members were commiserating. Their complaints, common faculty grievances about time-consuming research, writing commitments, and classroom overload, reminded me why Presidents rarely lunched here and why members of the College Hall cabinet purposefully did so once or twice a month. Fortunately, lunch arrived quickly—the quiche was hot, eggy, and filled with broccoli, onions, and pepper-jack cheese—and I dug in, trying to concentrate on my food and my notes.

The complainants eventually left but other, more rancorous voices were raised from a nearby common table. Two of the louder voices belonged to Ambrose Kyle, a professor of political science and rather famous campus blowhard, and Merton Aggassey, a chemistry professor; they had to know I was within earshot and they were trashing Danby.

"Overblown, if you ask me," Kyle whined between noisy chomps. "An excuse for all the bleeding hearts around here to beat together. I tell you..."—he stopped to swallow—"...they take advantage and the administration lays down and plays dead...."

Aggassey, whose squeaky voice and narrow views were offered freely on most campus topics, agreed. "Just listen to the names of these groups in this Coalition for Justice..., GUTS...Gays United To Survive, Black Nation, FEM...Feminist Equality Movement...."

"Where do they come from?" a table companion grumpily interrupted. Others made almost inaudible comments which probably were assents.

Out of the corner of my eye, I could see Kyle's balding scalp, with its prominent liver spot, above the *Crier*. "Listen to this," he snorted, and read off a list of demands: that classes be suspended, an ethnically *balanced* Security Office force be recruited, a quota system for minority faculty in each University department, the rooting out of any anti-feminist or homophobic faculty speech, and support for Jesse Kingdom's causes. "How 'bout dem apples," Kyle said triggering a general clacking by his tablemates about free speech, political correctness, and the expected wimpy College Hall reaction. "Maybe they could give The Stalker some sensitivity training while they're at it!" Kyle said, and they all laughed.

"Danby's playing into their hands if he gives them any credence at all," Aggassey said plaintively, all the while chewing. "I know that it's a serious matter," he responded to a comment. "I understand the concern, believe me. It's just that we can't let the place go to hell..., again. The cops should do their job, find this guy, and Danby shouldn't let the loonies set his agenda."

Why did I listen? Why did I let them get under my skin? They were just background noise, hollow, insecure men who relished having another victim in the President's office. I closed my note book and left the table; as I passed by them, I directed appropriate recognitions to their raised eyes. I had almost escaped when Aggassey grabbed my jacket sleeve. His oddly prunish face made motions toward a smirk. "Algy, did you see these demands?" He took the *Crier* from Kyle and turned to his tablemates for support. "These people are trying to take advantage of the situation, to put the University on the defensive, and...," he continued, without the guts to say it to my face, "... what is the administration doing about it?"

I could have reminded the self-righteous boob that student

demands popped up every year on a host of social issues—war, poverty, ROTC recruitment, needs-blind admissions, or the cause of the semester—even though I knew I was whistling in the dark about this year's problem. I gently pulled my sleeve away from his fingers. "It's hard to make too much fuss about rape and murder."

Aggassey wouldn't give it up. "This murder victim, I mean, she wasn't even a student here, not anymore. Reading the *Crier*, you'd think it was the President's wife, for God's sake!"

I didn't respond and his companions were silent. Holly Danby, the President's wife, had been buried little more than three months ago. Aggassey's face slowly registered his faux pas. "Well, you know what I mean," he said into his napkin.

No rejoinder was necessary.

I threaded my way out of the dining room. Fifteen minutes of pool on the Club's new Olhausen table upstairs might help my equilibrium but a glance at my watch nixed the idea and, instead, I entered the library, a room that whispered "hush" in its subdued décor of landscape paintings, grouped tables and Parsons chairs, and thick carpet. A copy of the *Crier* lay open on a tufted leather sofa where I sat and read the headline story on student demands. The President hadn't bothered to mention it this morning; that's how pressing he thought it was. I was about to put the tabloid down when I noticed Joe Bucas standing at the newspaper rack near the doorway, picking through various national and international dailies. I raised the *Crier* higher seeking to avoid a conversation not welcomed at any time and, at the moment, potentially compromising since Bucas was a party to speech code complaints due for a hearing within the month.

The incident was high profile and unusual since it arose in the context of the Permanent Curriculum Committee—the PCC—a cockpit of campus ideological wrangling. A majority of the PCC's faculty component are liberal to radical activists who usually portray Carter's undergraduate curriculum as a biased reflection of male-dominated Western cultural aggression; the rest are a few wobbly middle-of-the-roaders from the arts and science faculty who nominally favor a relevant curriculum, with Joe Bucas as the sole representative of the anti-correctness conservatives to whom "Third World" and "multi-cultural" mean "third class". No, that's not quite right because Joe Bucas, a gadfly reactionary nuisance, gives conservatives a bad name. Along with two administrators and three seniors, this ill-matched group had been for years an ineffective debating club but hadn't caused too much harm until Danby's predecessor saw its rancorous debates and procrastination as a way to avoid policy decisions: if it had to do with the curriculum, she decreed, it had to go through the PCC.

Like most speech code appeals, Bucas's case began with an exchange that reeked of insensitivity and bad manners. At a PCC meeting a few weeks earlier, his views had been savaged by a Marcus somebody-or-other, described to me as an obnoxious, opinionated senior. Marcus characterized Bucas's opposition to a new, non-Western culture element in the basic studies program as "fascist" and Bucas, who is Jewish, exploded, as Marcus probably intended. No admonishment to Marcus from the Dean of the College could calm Bucas; his fists pounded the table while he decried the student's insensitivity to the Holocaust and railed at remedial courses for minorities, inflated grades, no grades, and ethnicity majors, much to the snorts and amusement of Marcus. Bucas brought up, for no apparent reason, the tumultuous faculty vote that had led to adoption of curriculum change years ago—and the rhetoric of a young assistant professor of history, Carl Reinman, which carried the faculty resolution and put Carter in the vanguard of curriculum change. "Reinman and his clique almost brought the University down," Bucas thundered, according to the taped minutes, "and we've been wallowing in the muck ever since!" That broke up the party, with the students narrowly beating Bucas in the filing of harassment and hate speech charges.

Unfortunately, Bucas spotted me and plopped his large rump on the arm of the sofa. As usual, his brow was wet and his pudgy face had an unpleasant jaundiced tone. He wore a shapeless brown suit, grayish shirt under a tan V-neck sweater, and a mustard yellow tie. "So, Reinman didn't make it," he said without the pretense of concern.

"No, he didn't," I said, folding the newspaper and putting it on the seat, and started to get up. But Bucas wouldn't let it go. He touched my arm and put his face close to mine, close enough for me to see the hairs that sprouted from his ears and red-veined nose and to get a whiff of cheap cigar smoke.

"You know, Reinman and I almost came to blows once. On The Green, after one of the sit-ins..., CIA recruitment or something. It was late in the day, almost dark, and he was walking across, coming towards me, with a couple of young girls hanging all over him like he was some sort of idol. For some reason, that moony adulation got me steamed. As they passed by me, he said something to the kids that made them laugh. I was sure it was directed at me. I lost it and grabbed him by the shoulder, ready to take a swing. Took him completely by surprise for a second, before he pulled loose. Laughed at me. The girls, they laughed at me, too." Bucas shrugged and said, with a touch of genuineness, "I don't know why I did it. He could have murdered me."

"Forget it, Joe."

"Always had the girls...," Bucas said, obviously exasperated.

I should have left well enough alone but Bucas nettled me — can't help it since he is so unlikable, and besides, I had some vague notion I should defend Reinman since I was to be his executor. "Joe," I said, "lots of people were involved then. Principled people. He wasn't much different, maybe more persuasive and aggressive, but not basically different. And he changed...."

"Yeah, sounds silly now, doesn't it? But," he said, edging closer to me, "for me, he symbolized a lot of what was happening, all the sit-ins and disruption, turning the curriculum upside down, the pass-fail thing, every fad that dropped academic standards. I realized that the night of the faculty vote when Reinman and his hippies won." He paused, then said, "I thought he was a phony even then. And that was before he turns into Reagan's pet."

I stood to leave, realizing that Bucas would relish the opportunity for piling on more scorn, but he was hard to escape. He grasped my forearm. "A few years ago, I had this kid for... second semester creative writing. A cute little redhead, from some farm town in the Midwest." His face hardened. "I think she slept with him. She wrote a short story about a professor and a sophomore and how the sophomore got picked up, seduced—and never told a soul. The professor she described, physically, and in attitude, was a dead ringer for Reinman. I asked her about the story and she said to me: 'write from life,' one of those aphorisms we tend to use. 'Write from life,' she repeated and then she spelled it out. 'R-I-G-H-T from life.' Had to be Reinman!"

It took a second for the spelling of the word to have significance. "You mean, he was dating students? Why didn't this ever come up in some formal way, some student complaint or—"

"For what? To whom?" Bucas' face displayed the meanness which often lurked in his voice. "College Hall put out any regulations yet on faculty-student romance, Algy? Not that you should have to, for God's sakes. Or," he added snidely, "is that sexual harassment? I get confused." I let that pass: I wasn't about to get into a discussion on student vulnerabilities or plain old, unacceptable behavior. "He would have been very discreet, with just the right kind of kid. I would have leaned on him if I had the proof. I think he thought he was just accepting their favors. I don't even say he exploited them, but it's so *lousy* to do it!" He took a deep breath. "So there it is. I don't apologize for it."

"I guess we ought to leave it at that."

"You're right," he replied, his eyes holding mine for a second. "It's all over with now. Maybe there is some justice after all."

CHAPTER FOURTEEN

"Whatever happened to the ivory tower?" Marcie's scribbled note was on a Post-It attached to the cover sheet of a quarter inch thick document on my desk. It was her draft of our annual, federally-mandated, Campus Crime Report.

I put down the Diet Sprite I'd brought up from the canteen, picked up the document, cleared a place on the sofa, and sat.

The Crime Awareness and Campus Security Act, now called the *Jeanne Clery Act* after a murdered freshman at Lehigh University, requires all colleges and universities to tabulate, summarize, and report all crimes occurring on or near their campuses. When it was first proposed, the academic community was split as to its need, with some schools asking why higher education had been singled out for intrusive self-reporting while others, with varied motives, sought to have the campus crime issue publicized. The legislation passed Congress in the aftermath of a couple of street murders of students in Boston which provoked predictable reactions from Massachusetts's powerful delegation. While Carter University had been ambivalent about enactment, its passage required Providence cops to provide the University with reliable data on what the feds refer to as off-campus "incidents," something that the cops had long refused to share with the Security Office. Even with the federal mandate, it took years and Justice Department threats to begin the process and to this day, the cops had sand in their shorts about the extra work.

Marcie, diligent and persistent as always, with a personality that bridges a lot of institutional truculence, had collected data from the police and the Security Office, organized it into the prescribed format, and compared the results with those of each of the prior two years. Her suggested introduction tried to make sense of the pages of graphs, tables, and maps, especially in pointing out that not all the incidents were related to Carter University or its student population.

I kicked off my loafers and began to read her draft critically. It was not exactly heartening. The number of alcohol-related crimes, everything from binge drinking to mayhem, stayed about the same despite an increased University focus on the problem and more counselors, education, and stronger disciplinary actions. Both hard drugs and the recreational variety were still prevalent; the number of drug-related arrests and the mix of drugs confiscated hadn't changed much from past years. Petty crimes, like audio equipment and cash purloined from dorm rooms and student apartments, however, were up by ten percent, and worse, serious crimes, including aggravated assault not involving sex, had bumped up by twelve percent, likely due to a rash of armed robberies around Thayer Street last April and May. Sex-related incidents were up, maybe due to Fingers, and either more complaints or better reporting, or both. There was a zero after "Homicides."

I pinched the bridge of my nose when I considered how the report, due to be filed in less than ten days and made available to students in hard copy and online, would be played up by the media. The *Globe* always compares results for Boston area schools with Providence institutions, the *Times*, now into the Stalker crisis, would compare Carter to other Ivy League schools and their academic competitors, and neither the newspapers nor *SecurityOnCampus.com* would likely make the point that Carter students weren't involved in most of the incidents or that an increase of only one or two could be misleading on a percentage basis. With The Stalker out there, the media would have a field day, despite the spin the Information Office's press release might put on it, sort of like a tutu on a dancing male dog.

Marcie had left the concluding paragraphs for me to handle. What to say? Pat ourselves on the back or wring our hands over the numbers? Defend our programs or deplore the nation's descent into crime? What was the right slant, since Carter does a decent job when it comes to campus security? Our Security Office has over eighty people, including forty campus police officers and twenty-five security guards. We've got over a hundred outside emergency phones, operate shuttle buses and escort services for both the on-campus and off-campus student populations, and all freshmen get lectures in personal safety and property security. Student Life runs a mandatory orientation about booze, drugs, and, of course, sex: safe sex, sexual effrontery, and sexual harassment. However, with all the other things happening in young lives, it has been an unachievable goal to get kids to focus on safety and security in a setting as comfortable, as seemingly secure, as Carter's upper middle-class neighborhood.

I filled the rest of the afternoon with routine work, packed the draft report and my notes in my bag, and left around five o'clock, walking home under leaden clouds that reminded me of a thick, rumpled blanket. During the walk, I called McAllister. One effect of the murder, he said tersely, was a jump in the number of kids signing up for Jesse Kingdom's demonstration at the federal courthouse and Public Safety Building tomorrow. Worse, dorm occupancy among women was down twenty-five to thirty percent.

"Any other good news?" There wasn't and I called Tuttle who reported that his contacts within the Detective Division had largely discounted The Stalker as the murderer of Anne Sullivan, despite the machinations of Chief McCarthy, and the focus was now on Lavelle Williams, who—surprise, surprise—seemed to have disappeared. Tuttle reiterated that he'd get a lot more cops on patrol on Saturday night near the campus but, so far, *nada* for the Kingdom rally.

At a few minutes after five, I unlocked the front door to my house. I picked up the hall phone for messages—there were none—and left Nadie a voice mail invitation for dinner before I went upstairs. I left my briefcase on my work table and recognizing I was out of sorts, and had been all day, changed clothes for a workout.

Despite real effort, I couldn't get into a rhythm on the Nordic Track. I stopped, stretched for a few minutes, picked a *Monty Python* episode from a stack of DVDs, and started again. Somewhere between the "Cheese Shop" and the "Ministry of Silly Walks" sketches, I had a good, sweaty, thirty-minute workout. After a shower, I changed into jeans and a heavy Pendleton shirt and poked around in the Sub-Zero for the makings of dinner. I was in the mood to cook and the latest issue of *Gourmet* gave me a menu that would soak up time and energy and be worth it: garlic soup, broiled chicken breasts with sun-dried tomatoes and onions, and a shredded radish, orange, and onion salad. With an apron decorated by a large Tabasco bottle covering my front, I flattened garlic cloves under a cleaver's wide blade and kept on chopping, slicing, peeling, and pureeing until there was enough for two of everything. A bottle of Marchese Antinori Chianti Classico was withdrawn from the mini-wine cabinet in the basement; the chef enjoyed a large glass of the ruby colored wine after Nadie telephoned to accept my invitation. As the kitchen filled with the aroma of simmering soup and sautéing onions, I prepared the salad, had a second glass of wine, and set the table for two, positive that the dinner and company would be enjoyable.

Nadie arrived around six-thirty and stayed with me as I broiled the chicken. She was not conversational. Even my summary of the draft Campus Crime Report got little reaction which surprised me since Nadie has lots of opinions, often strongly expressed, about campus life and security. But not tonight. The glass of Chianti I poured for her was barely tasted, and despite the lush food smells and a Putumayo CD of French Caribbean music, she picked at her meal and my culinary efforts merited little acclaim. When we finished, she made espresso while I put away leftovers and cleaned up the kitchen. She didn't wait for the coffee to brew and went upstairs to the loft. When I joined her, she had on her reading glasses and was sitting in an overstuffed chair under a lamp which cast a pool of light on a folder holding a number of handwritten pages that she seemed to scan with impatience. The shades on the loft's oversized, cantilevered windows were up; in the blackness of the night, their panes captured the room's walls of books, eclectic furniture and artwork, even the geometric designs and stylized foliage of a red, gold, and olive Anatolian rug. A brushed nickel ceiling fan rotated slowly keeping the room's air moving. I put her espresso on the table next to her and took mine to my work table where the draft report awaited me. I pressed the CD player remote and a Muir Quartet recording of something by Schumann began with a cello's sharp arpeggio; barely a minute into it, Nadie got up, turned down the music so low that it was barely audible, and flopped back into her chair. Okay, I thought, how long would it be before she got it out.

Ten minutes later, after not a word of conversation, as I was finally making progress with the conclusion to the report, she said, too matter-of-factly, "I was at the Center this afternoon and I checked to see if we had a file on Anne Sullivan. We did."

I was stunned. Nadie is not one to bend privacy rules. I turned to her; her glasses rested at her hairline above a face that was troubled. I touched the power button on the remote and the room became still. "And...?"

Her head went back to the chair's headrest and her eyes closed. "I know I'm going to regret this," she sighed. "Late May, just before commencement, she had a consult, said she was pregnant and was thinking of leaving school. She was already looking for an apartment. Maryann Gounoud was her counselor and Maryann, I'm sure, would go over her options. Her notes are really difficult to read, never got into the computer because she left in July for a job in California, but Maryann seemed to think Anne was emotionally stable. Even exceptionally so, under the circumstances. The words underlined are 'cool' and 'determined.'" Nadie's head snapped to attention and she looked at me sharply. "If you ever tell anyone that I took that file, I'll...."

"You know that I won't...."

"Just don't. I still don't know why I did it. I guess I wanted to know if she had been a client before she dropped out and what we did, if anything..." and her voice drifted off.

That ended my thought that she had broken the rules for me!

"There's something else," she said reluctantly. "Apparently, she saw Maryann back in February, beginning of the semester. Depression, sleeping problems, fitful appetite, emotional involvement with someone unnamed that was difficult, serious enough to recommend psychological consultation. No indication if she followed up."

"Complicated kid. Anything else?"

She frowned and slipped her reading glasses down from her forehead. "End of report. End of comment."

She knew I would press her. "How about the referral? If she was going to get an abortion, where would she have gone?"

She turned over a page. "The file doesn't indicate but I imagine it would've been the Planned Parenthood clinic downtown. Student health insurance would cover it, or most of it, but not any extras." Her eyes sharpened. "And don't get any ideas about checking it out because, mister lawyer, the privacy laws don't give you standing to even ask the question."

I knew that! Hadn't even crossed my mind! "If someone was willing to pay her for an abortion and keeping quiet about it, maybe Franks is right."

"Maybe Franks is wrong," she said dismissively. "Or his client was lying. Or, it simply makes no difference."

I remembered Tuttle's lack of empathy for the young woman. "I wonder if her parents knew about the abortion. Tuttle gave me the impression that they are religious Catholics. Her uncle is a priest."

She flipped through the pages before she answered. "She lists her sister Patricia as the person to be notified in case of emergency, not her parents. Same address as her parents. Anyway, it's just speculation but if she was 'cool' and 'determined,' she must have had the abortion...."

I turned back to the work table and locked my hands behind my neck. Knowing Nadie, there might be more to it, maybe some additional insight by the counselor, but she had decided what she would tell me. Okay, it was a good bet that Anne Sullivan's sister would at least know about the abortion. The money? Maybe. My eyes fell to the shelves full of mysteries and thrillers across the room, from Block, Burke, and Cornwell to Sayers, Simeon, and Tey. A Morse or Spencer or Dalgleish or Maigret would have the truth out in a single interview of Patricia Sullivan. Ah, well, so be it. Franks would have to get his information to prosecutors quickly if Lavelle Williams was picked up. Assuming that Franks had loyalty to his nominal clients. What if he didn't? Would Senor Flores be unhappy if Williams disappeared, or if arrested, was permanently silenced by some rogue cops?

I took a sip of espresso that was now lukewarm. Last night, Nadie had berated me when I had been wondering out loud about Ms. Sullivan's character. "Yes," I said, smart-alecky. "You're right. We shouldn't speculate. Not at all professional. Shows a *morbid curiosity....*"

I heard a dismissive breath as her reading light went out. "Yeah. Right. Uh-huh." She got up from her chair. "Listen to the voyeur who rummages around in a dead woman's apartment, the bleeding heart who spends his time with the prime suspect's lawyer and anguishes over his role in delivering him up. Listen to the patrician who spent Monday night in the police station like a knight-errant and worries about being perceived as Don Quixote." She picked up the remote to the forty inch screen Sony Vega. "I hope you don't mind, but I'm in the mood for something not too serious," and she channel surfed until she found a "Mary Tyler Moore" rerun on TV Land and flopped down on the sofa. "You can speculate if *you* want to. I'm all done." A bellow from Lou Grant interrupted her.

I gave up on the draft report, turned off the desk lamp, and joined her on the sofa. She had the right idea; it's a lot easier to laugh at Ted Baxter and Rhoda Morgenstern than it is to ruminate about Ms. Sullivan's personal crisis of months ago. Much easier.

Thursday

CHAPTER FIFTEEN

I woke—alone, since Nadie had gone home last night—with my mind on Carl Reinman's estate. Tomorrow, I'd be appointed his executor. I imagined Eustace Pine in the dusty precincts of the Providence Probate Court, his trademark bow tie bobbing beneath a prominent Adam's apple as he requested a bench conference with Judge Cremascoli, the huddle at the bench, the presentation of affidavits from the witnesses to the will, some side bars about other cases, the clerk stamping the petition, and Reinman's will admitted to probate. When did Pine say Reinman's will was executed? Two years ago? May? Was that around the one time he came to my house?

○ ○ ○

I was slouched on a bench on The Green, delighting in the pleasure of the sun warming my face. With the temperature well into the eighties, kids were in tee shirts, halter tops, shorts, and cut-offs, some noisily tossing frisbees and softballs, others sprawled on the grass, reading, in conversation, many with cell phones at their ears, with one oblivious couple smooching passionately at the base of an elm. Excited talk and music came through open windows in the surrounding buildings as fresh, youthful voices passed by me on the cobblestone walk. The pungent sweetness of newly mowed grass enriched my sense of spring and growth. I was very content.

Abruptly, I was in shadow. Reinman was standing over me, a corona of sunlight streaming over his head and wide shoulders.

"You look so damned comfortable!" he said and deposited a battered briefcase next to me as he sat down. "The last exam books for a whole year!" he said, indicating the bulging briefcase, and stretched his arms along the back of the bench, turned his face to the sun, and closed his eyes.

He seemed put together for a Ralph Lauren advertisement: blue blazer, pink button-down shirt with open collar, khakis, Docksiders, square but narrow chin etched with a trace of a dimple, high cheekbones, well-formed nose, dark eyebrows, and a complexion that was unseasonably tan. His wavy black hair, attractively gray above the ears, was long and combed straight back until it fell into a spray of curls over his collar, giving him an annoyingly handsome, Pierce Brosnan-like, appeal. It struck me that his angular good looks gave him a formidable edge in any argument, especially on television, where his telegenic features radiated charm and his resonant voice conveyed intellect as he jabbed at his liberal opponents.

The Chapel Bell struck three o'clock and I couldn't think of one pressing reason to go back to the office. "Got an idea," I said, startling Reinman, and a few minutes later, jackets over our shoulders, we were cutting between Channing Hall and College Hall to the brick walk which crossed the University's well-groomed front yard, and out through Billings Gate to Prospect Street. Reinman kept up a constant chatter, bubbling with enthusiasm for his upcoming sabbatical year which included September in Tuscany and two months in Brazil for a PBS "American Experience" project on Teddy Roosevelt's post-presidential Amazon adventures. His monologue continued virtually uninterrupted as we entered my house. Reinman used the hall lavette while I mixed a pitcher of kir in the kitchen; he hadn't returned when I finished so I went into the hall and found him at the entrance to the commodious living room, taking in its twelve foot high ceiling, eggplant walls, Persian carpets, groupings of furniture, artwork, family photographs, and tabletop objects and baubles. With a smile, and without comment, he followed me through the kitchen and french doors to the patio where I placed a tray holding the pitcher and glasses on a glass-topped table between two chaises.

We leaned back into the flowered cushions of the chaises facing the lush greens and bright yellows of the patio's flowerbeds and a profusion of irises, geraniums, and daffodils in oversized terra cotta pots. Puffs of wind wove through a pair of early-flowering dogwoods and blossoms swirled down to the sun-burnished bricks. Reinman, after a few moments of silence, raised his glass of pinkish liquor toward the sun, letting its rays diffuse into copper colors on his face, and began to gushily praise my house and its incredible views of the city, which became a segue to the cost of renovations to *his* 1790's house on Benefit Street and to *his* farmhouse, recently purchased, near the wineries in Little Compton.

I realized, as he went on, that most everything in *his* conversation was, sooner or later, about *him*.

He drew a cigarette from a pack of Marlboros in his shirt pocket and lit it with a disposable lighter that he had fished awkwardly from his pants. He didn't ask me if I minded nor ask for an ashtray. He inhaled deeply and blew out a cloud of acrid blue smoke which drifted my way without apology. He was now into *his* over-scheduled life of speaking engagements, opinion pieces for the country's major dailies, on call availability for cable news hot topics—besides those on which he was a regular—a bimonthly column in the *Weekly Standard*, and seemingly most irksome and tiresome, his two lecture courses at Carter. He became more and more puffed up about *his* role as an intellectual touchstone for modern American conservatives, as though his participation and views were vital to contemporary political dialogue.

I made appropriate noises of attention—I've always been good at that—but eventually stopped listening. Had he always been this self-centered? What had triggered his metamorphosis from campus radical to stalwart of the right?

"...And the country still misses Reagan," he was saying, as he ground out the cigarette on the bricks. I winced but covered up by using his reference as an excuse to ask him about Reagan's endorsement of *T.R.*

Reinman apprised me carefully, perhaps considering my motivation for the question, then smiled broadly and poured another kir from the pitcher. Ironically, he said, it was a Carter story, his tone suggesting intimacy. "It was the time of Iran-Contra, with all those rumors about him nodding off at Cabinet meetings, and this White House intern, a student of mine from here, gave the President a copy of *T.R.* It happened to be on the President's desk in the Oval Office and a reporter noticed it during an interview. Then, later, Reagan was asked about the book at a press conference and said it was a *wonderful* book about Theodore Roosevelt, his favorite president. Since nobody had ever seen Reagan with any book, not even a paperback whodunit, it was news! And, zoom!" Reinman's glass became a rocket; when he put it down sharply, the glass tabletop rang. "If you were inside the Beltway, you *had* to read *T.R.* Everybody assumed it gave off all kinds of signals as to where the man was coming from. The flacks at the White House flogged it and the media swallowed it whole. People wanted to buy, sell, digest, record..., you name it..., *T.R.* A best seller for forty-six weeks! A six hundred and sixty-four page, serious, bestseller!" He took a swallow of kir. "When sales went into overdrive, I got on the book and lecture circuits, invited to White House functions, and Teddy-mania is all over the place. Ken Burns does a PBS series on Roosevelt, and I'm the narrator! The President loves it!"

He paused. "Great days."

I waited for him to get to the manifesto of his political sea change, an Op-Ed piece in the *Times* in which he excoriated the cherished liberalism of his colleagues, but he swallowed the rest of his drink, refilled his glass, and said, "Of course, it was a damn good book, too!"

We lapsed into silence. I waited for more but he seemed finished. A purplish cloud covered the sun and it immediately turned cooler. No longer in the sun's glare, I discerned that Reinman's face was flushed and that a smirk was firmly gripping his lips. Unexpectedly, he turned to me.

"I'm glad you invited me, Al-gy." He slurred my name. "It's mostly stubbornness that keeps me at Carter. Let me tell you, they may listen to NPR all day and eat only tofu and vegetables, have a "Hey Jude" self image, and wear those clunky shoes, but they play dirty and for keeps. Political correctness is the enemy of clearheaded observation and I remind them of it all the time so they snub me and criticize my stands on the issues. Not just because it's ingratiating and popular here to do so, but because it makes them feel like they're so much smarter than all the poor schmucks out there. Makes me ill!" He hacked a smoker's cough. "Of course, it's jealousy. In academia, the purist poison. They cling to this 'he sold-out' thing. Can't imagine that I could have principles. Or that my ideas could evolve. They don't get it." His voice took on a tone of earnestness. "You have to take advantage of opportunities, especially if they fit your principles. Reagan preached that. Opportunities! That's what this country is all about. Opportunities! Sometimes..., well, to be absolutely honest..., you *can* be born to it...."

I felt a dart directed at me and he knew it.

He shook his head and waved his hand at me as though to fend off my reaction. "Don't get me wrong. Please. I mean you have your family's heritage. And that is your opportunity. Your family reminds me of Roosevelt's. Tradition, wealth, work, service. Your family's achievements...,"—he moved his head to take in the view of the house—"...all of this. Really, I admire you. But for me..."—

he leaned forward, put out his hand, and quickly closed a tight fist—"...I saw the brass ring. And I *grabbed* it!" He stared at me meaningfully, as though satisfied we shared a common ground, then turned back toward a downtown increasingly streaked with shadows. His smirk became a knowing smile.

In the silence that followed, I fought off my annoyance. He was my guest. I reminded myself that *T.R.* had been published a long time ago, that Reinman's recent work hadn't included much history or biography but were tomes blaming the decline of America's values on an amoral, liberal elite. His television appearances as the conservative talking head, not his scholarship, kept him in beer and skittles and in the public eye. So, why this maladroit attempt at intimacy? Had it just occurred to him on the spot?

Reinman slipped his legs off the chaise and faced me. "And the compensation isn't just emotional. My agent called me yesterday about..."—he mentioned a well-known character actor who'd played Roosevelt in a movie a few years back—"...who's thinking of doing a one-man show on Teddy. Has an HBO contract in hand. And he wants me to collaborate on the script!" He stood up, hands on his slim hips, looking more like a graduate student than a tenured professor of American History. "Good old Teddy! Just keeps rollin' on!" He shrugged his shoulders as though he just couldn't comprehend his good fortune.

I led him back through the french doors; he retrieved his jacket and briefcase from the hall table, and as I opened the front door, I had no doubt he was tipsy. Good thing Benefit Street was a short walk, I thought, as he disappeared around the corner of the yard at East Street and headed down The Hill. I considered that Reinman had most everything going his way. He had grabbed the brass ring and was holding it tightly.

○ ◯ ○

After a morning of routine work, including an hour or so on the procedural issues for the tenure appeal facing the Provost, I drove through downtown, across the gorge of I-95 to Providence's Italian enclave: restaurant-choked Federal Hill and the adjoining mansion lined Broadway. Every two weeks, Fausto Tramonti, the middle Tramonti brother, held Thursday lunch meetings at his law offices in a meticulously renovated Victorian on Broadway to plot his younger brother's mayoral prospects. Early on, the group consisted of Fausto, Tony, Tramonti family friends, some money people, a couple of reform types, and a handful of seasoned politicians who, for one reason or the other, detested Sonny. In the aftermath of the August riot, and the dissipation of our early confidence, the group had dwindled to a core of Tramonti loyalists like myself.

Fausto's office is across the street from Tramonti Corporation's block-filling headquarters. As I parked among the expensive cars, including Fausto's elegant, black Maserati Quattroporte with its coveted, single-digit license plate, I remembered that the patriarch, Angelo Tramonti, had started the business in a garage only a block away with a "pick and a wheelbarrow," as the family often boasted. When Tony and I were teenagers employed for the summer as laborers, the company was run out of a collection of ramshackle corrugated buildings at the edge of the landfill in Johnston, a place of storage sheds, *T* logoed road machines, hoists, derricks and tractors, and noisy with diesel engines, whistles, the bee-beeps of vehicles in reverse, and the profanity of beefy workers in safety hats and overalls. By then, under the leadership of hard charging, ambitious "Aldo the Dynamo," the eldest brother, the company was expanding rapidly, garnering contracts as a construction manager for airports, university dormitories, classroom buildings, stadiums, research facilities and hospitals, initially in New England and then countrywide.

Meanwhile, Fausto, the middle brother, who most resembles his father in looks and mental toughness and is the most tradition-al Italo-American of the three brothers, stayed local in his college education at Providence College, law school at Boston College, and choice of the Broadway neighborhood for his home and office, and developed a law practice which combines his consider-able abilities with that inevitable element of a successful Rhode Island legal practice: influence. Tony, the youngest brother, the one with the robust handsomeness and the natural gifts of a politi-cian, the Harvard footballer and company lawyer who married the prettiest girl at The Dunes Club, seems always to have been desig-nated for elected office.

Today, in a conference room that would make a Roman *avvo-cato* jealous, there were only six of us: Fausto, myself, a dissident city councilman, a young Latino lawyer with ambitions for Congress, a Tramonti cousin who owned the largest jewelry man-ufacturing company in Rhode Island, and state Senator Frank Rotundo, a construction supervisor at Tramonti Corporation who was as a thirty year veteran of political wars and intrigues. Tony was absent; he had to contend with Jesse Kingdom's courthouse rally and march to the Public Safety Building. Since Fausto believed in *la cucina buona*, today's lunch from the Italo-American Club was a spread of veal pizziola, choice of pasta, salad, and *dolce*. Bottles of San Pellegrino and the absence of wine indicated seriousness.

Fausto's secretary operated an elaborate espresso machine to fill tiny cups as we began the political talk. Since for a mayoralty cam-paign, Tramonti wouldn't have to worry about finances, the ques-tions were always the same. Was Tony's candidacy premature? Who out there was unhappy with Sonny? Were there enough votes? The politicos dominated today's discussion with anecdotes about Sonny and McCarthy who, they said, had galvanized the city's public safety and teacher unions as bases of support. This was confirmed by a recent poll conducted by a Providence College think tank which indicated that Sonny was riding high. Not even his latest tax increase seemed to make a difference! Rotundo groused that Sonny had the unions, he had a good part of the ethnic neighborhoods, and he didn't need to worry about the rest of the citizenry. The only good news was that former State Senator Lucca, known to some at the table as *Il Mazziere*, the "card dealer," and his son, the councilman from Federal Hill, were likely to stay neutral in a primary, not out of friendship but because *politica tradizione* has it that the enemy of my enemy is my friend.

When they finished, we argued about what all of that meant. I said that we had in Tony an honest candidate running in a troubled city, that there were enough people who despised Sonny or who wanted a better future to put together a coalition that could win. Tramonti's cousin's face told me I had no clue of political realities, that Tony should pack it in for now; Rotundo squinted and grimaced as though he was thinking *basta* at any point I made. Fausto, however, agreed with me. There was plenty of time, he insisted, for Sonny to screw up. Fausto, in his feisty, take no prisoners mode, seemed to be an Italo-American Bobby Kennedy in his determination that his brother should run in, and would win, the next election. By the time the meeting broke up, he had most of us thinking his way.

Clouds with dark edges had formed and the sun had become a yellowish smudge in an unpleasant, unsettled sky as I got in my car. I started the engine and let it idle while I considered the advice from the politicos at the table. They were up to their keisters in Providence's sometimes odious, often suspicious, and rarely principled politics. They understood better than I the fickleness of Providence voters who are notorious for their tolerance of roguish, rapacious politicians so long as "tings are goin' good." Wheeling-dealing, after all, is our basic form of city government, how we deal with civic issues during infrequent truces in ethnic turf battles and political vendettas. So, why did I think Tramonti could shake things up? Make a difference?

Damn, if I know.... But, I know!

I drove back into downtown with the back-from-lunch traffic. At the Providence River Bridge at Market Square, waiting for a light change, a steady stream of somber-faced Carter students, many toting placards and banners denouncing Sonny Russo and Chief McCarthy or supporting Jesse Kingdom, held up traffic and joined others massed on the RiverWalk in front of the RISD Auditorium. There, under a multicolored, tile-faced gazebo, an impassioned young black woman, her hair in a seventies-ish Afro and wearing a faded Army field jacket, directed maybe a hundred or so into groups with vigorous arm waves and her bull horn. With a chant of "Jess-ee, Jess-ee," they lined up five abreast and started off toward the courthouse. Others, at least another fifty, not as regimented, maybe more sullen and purposeful, followed in groups of three and four.

In College Hall, noisy radiators greeted my return; the building's steam heating system had cranked to life, which meant my office door had to stay ajar and a window had to be kept open to limit the effect of erratic blasts of heat given off by the old cast-iron piping. Accompanied by clanking and an occasional whistle from a radiator valve, I finished the conclusion of the Crime Report and the memo to Danby and the Provost on *Zerma v. Carter University*, and otherwise plodded through telephone calls, e-mails, letters, and reports. Once or twice, my mind went to the demonstration at the courthouse but since neither McAllister nor Tuttle had called, I continued my work. Maybe today, with Ms. Sullivan not on my mind, I could earn my salary.

○ ◯ ○

McAllister didn't knock, he burst in. "It's bad. Some demonstrators got busted charging police lines in front of the Public Safety Building. Likely some of our kids. Don't know much about it yet. Seems like a break-away group from Kingdom's rally at the courthouse. At least a half-dozen arrested, maybe more. I've got to go down there."

For a second, I hesitated. If it was "bad," the kids could be brought up on charges for violations of Carter's Student Code. I wasn't supposed to get involved or intervene since, as University Counsel, the administration of the student justice system was under my purview. On the other hand, goddammit, I wanted to!

"Provost know?"

He nodded affirmatively.

"Tuttle?"

Again the nod.

"I'll go with you. My car is parked on Waterman. I'll call Steve Winter and get some help."

Fortunately, Winter was in his office at Champlin & Burrill and I authorized him to implement the "get'em out of the tank" procedure we had worked out long ago. A justice of the peace and a bail bondsman would arrive for arraignments in less than an hour if McAllister couldn't work out releases. Before dinner, if the plan worked, the kids would be celebrities at the Refectory.

McAllister barely squeezed into the Mini. We drove through Capital Center to avoid the courthouse and downtown traffic lights; other than wondering aloud what had triggered the fight, he didn't say a word until we were in the parking lot behind Trinity Square Theater, a block from the Public Safety Building. I sensed he thought he had misjudged the situation, hadn't expected violence; I said that our kids do a lot of crazy things and are not going to give the Dean or his minions prior notice. As I locked the car, McAllister pulled out a cell phone and punched in numbers. "My only good contact in the department," he said and we waited in the lot until he made the connection and got us a promised entry.

We heard the clamor before we saw the crowd. A black man in a clerical collar—not Jesse Kingdom—stood on the flatbed of a pickup truck with a bullhorn, haranguing a crowd that maybe numbered fifty to seventy-five. Couldn't make out his words except "racist" and "cops" in close proximity. Around the front and sides of the Public Safety Building, cops in robotic-looking riot gear stood side-by-side, shields up, batons in hand, like a phalanx of Spartan warriors. Taunts were still flying at them although nothing physical was going on, probably due to a handful of young, mostly black and Latino, women with white arm bands who patrolled between the police and the demonstrators. All three local television stations were there, their mobile unit antennas sprouting high above the crowd, their video people thrusting cameras at demonstrators and cops in attempts to capture vituperation and reaction. As we approached from Empire Street, the reverend jumped into the crowd and pushed forward to the police line where he began a "Jess-ee, Jess-ee" chant that others quickly joined. Where was Kingdom? Arrested? Despite the noise and angry voices, I got the impression that some of the demonstrators, except those facing the cops, were listless and dispirited; many did not join the chant, their banners furled and their placards leaning against the pickup, or at least no longer bouncing up and down.

McAllister's pal, a uniformed sergeant who addressed McAllister as "Shaz", let us in through a side door off the police hierarchy's parking lot and we walked down a dimly lit corridor and into an empty holding room. I saw Steve Winter pass by and I called to him and went out to the corridor. Winter finished speaking to a red-faced, paunchy, unhappy police captain with gold leaves on his cap brim and introduced me. The cop gave me a once over, sneered, and left. Winter said, "Six of yours arrested out of a dozen or so, and they're looking for the one who threw the Coke can and bonked the cop and set the whole thing off." He paused. "Are you supposed to be here...?"

"Never mind."

We had been partners and friends far too long for debate. He shrugged.

"They'll be kept in the tank for about another hour before we can get arraignments. One or two cops got banged up, one of the kids claims they twisted him to the ground and bruised his arm, another says she got pushed by a cop and whacked with a baton, and another says he was attacked by a police dog. Don't know yet how that's going to play out. At least, we'll get them out of here. If we don't, a few heads are going to get knocked. I've heard Sonny has gone ballistic. McCarthy's holed up upstairs with his commanders and you can imagine what's going on there. Kingdom got the crowd under control once he arrived and somebody on his side had enough sense to use his people from the courthouse protest, the ones with the arm bands, as security. Otherwise...!"

"What happened?"

"Best as I can find out, before Kingdom finished up at the courthouse, a few troublemakers, including some Carter kids, went face-to-face with a police line setting up here in front of the building. Maybe thirty or forty. Somebody threw a soda can, hit one of the cops on the head, the shields went up, batons came out, some idiot got the dogs out of the back of a van, and the next thing you know.... Nobody decided to be peaceful or go limp this time and a dozen got arrested before Kingdom and his people marched here. They had no clue what had happened and got only one side of the story. Began demanding the release of the *hostages*, if you can believe it. Anyway, Tramonti got Kingdom on a cell phone—"

"What...?"

He shrugged. "I don't know. Anyway, Tramonti got Kingdom to agree to get his people out of here if we move quickly on the arrangements. Kingdom did his teevee thing and he's gone. I don't get it. Seemed like a perfect set up for more confrontation. What's out there now are the remnants."

McAllister joined us. "I'll need names and addresses of everyone arrested."

I said, "You can work it out with Steve. Call in a list of charges so we can figure out how to handle parents and the media, and whatever else might happen on campus. I'm going back."

McAllister's broad face was unhappy and strained. "Tell them," he said, "we've got to think twice about Kingdom on campus tomorrow."

I knew that idea would go nowhere. "You can take that up with the President, if you want to. But from what I've heard, Kingdom wasn't the problem here. What we've got to concentrate on is getting the right message out to our kids."

Winter nodded.

I left them and had reached the rear door when I heard Puppy Dog's voice croak from behind me. "Whoa. Not so fast," he said as he caught up to me, with jacket off, tie down two buttons, face beet red, and a loose strand of hair behind an ear; the yellowish glints in his eyes were particularly malevolent. "I warned you about Kingdom. See?"

He took a step closer. His breath needed a wash.

"Now look what we've got. Don't you guys get it? He's poison. Sonny's gonna have the whole council, the whole city this time, when he puts it to you, and believe me he will. I warned you...!"

"So you did."

"You want extra help for Kingdom tomorrow? Fuhgeddaboutit. And if any of your kids come marching down here afterward, we'll be prepared."

"What's that supposed to mean?"

"If they pick their noses or spit on the sidewalk, they're gonna be in the tank. That's what McCarthy's told everybody and I'm telling you right now so there won't be any surprises." He was barely controlling himself. "And don't go complaining to your buddy on the third floor. He's out of this!"

This is what passes for the chief legal advisor in City Hall. I shook my head, opened the door, and was out on the street.

CHAPTER SIXTEEN

Steve Winter was on speakerphone with the Provost and McAllister when I entered the Provost's office.

Our arrests turned out to be seven, and one by one, the kids were being arraigned and released on minimal bail by Winter's on call justice of the peace. The cops, Winter said, had filed multiple misdemeanor charges—disturbance of the peace, illegal parading, refusal to obey a lawful police order, and the like—as well as a felony assault charge for the John Doe who threw the Coke can. In turn, a fistful of complaints would be lodged by Kingdom and the demonstrators with the Attorney General, the Human Rights Commission, and the Justice Department that would take time to sort out. Supposedly—and this was interesting—somebody had captured the confrontation with a video camera on the roof of the Public Safety Building; Winter's comment was that if the cops had been assaulted, we'd see the tape; if the cops had been vicious, the tape would likely be lost in the property room. From what he heard, however, the cops had not been the Neanderthals they can be when surprised and think no one is looking.

No doubt, some of our kids had acted stupidly, crudely, and recklessly for which there was no excuse, and for which—*in loco parentis*, again—comment would be expected from the University. The Information Office had quickly drafted a statement for Danby, which McAllister handed to me, expressing the University's opposition to violence and its commitment to the demonstrators' civil rights, etc., etc., etc. It read like something off the shelf and the Provost asked me to try to make it more specific and relevant. While I scribbled in a few thoughts, the Provost said Danby would be at the Refectory tonight to calm the expected reaction and had tried, in vain, to get through to Sonny to urge a cooling off. Danby also told him that Kingdom's rally would definitely proceed—McAllister looked none to happy—and that Tuttle had carte blanche in terms of getting his people ready. Poor Tuttle, I thought, if Kingdom lets the rally get out of hand, no Event Plan will make a difference.

The ruckus at the Public Safety Building seemed to be of little concern on the third floor of College Hall. Maria, in a heavy, dark red coat, her head covered by a pinkish woolen hat, greeted me by announcing that she was "leavin' early because of the storm."

"What storm?"

Marcie popped her head out of her office to confirm that the weather report had changed from rain to two or three inches of snow and that she would also depart early unless there was some good reason not too. I knew better than to suggest any such thing and nodded okay; in a moment, she was gone. The legend of *the Blizzard of '78* had struck again!

Every Rhode Islander over thirty has a story about the unexpected storm that deposited four feet of drifting snow beginning early on a Friday afternoon, stranded thousands at work or on snow-clogged highways, and shut down the entire state for more than a week in its white flood. While the storm crippled the state's economy, the days that followed were an unexpected respite from work and school and had become, in Rhode Island's collective memory, a time of goodwill, neighborliness, sledding, cross-country skiing on city streets, and lots of parties as the state dug out. To this day, any forecast of snow on a workday means Rhode Islanders prepare for both the possibility of being snowbound and the prospect of a day off. Offices, factories, and government close early, schools are dismissed, and convenience stores' shelves are emptied of milk and bread. "But it's only a couple of inches!" I exclaimed to the empty office.

I thumbed through the message slips on my desk and saw one was from Tramonti with his cell phone number. He answered with a gruff "Yeah." I identified myself. "It played right into Sonny's hands. Just finished his news conference. Said he's 'not gonna knuckle under to anyone', including, ... get this, 'Jesse Kingdom's campus crazies'. That's an open invitation for some of his morons to get nasty. McCarthy, after he calmed down and only after a direct order, will still cooperate this weekend with Tuttle but there will be no extra cops to protect Kingdom tomorrow. If you guys have any influence, either turn that rally off or at least keep your kids from marching downtown."

I said I would speak to McAllister and Tuttle but what could we do; we can't control what Kingdom says and does.

Tramonti was silent for a moment and then switched gears. "Your protégé, Mr. Williams, is going to be coming in for another visit. Got a clerk who identified him as picking up a pizza around seven-thirty Friday night and his fingerprints are on the box found in her apartment, and all around the apartment, with a bunch of others we can't identify, yet. And we got hair matches. You can guess from where. DNA matches come next. We'll get some microscopy fiber matches on him eventually, so it comes down to time of death and his alibi. Because of the sex, McCarthy wants him vetted for The Stalker attacks too. Can you imagine?" He paused, as though waiting for my response. "Unless he's got a couple of nuns saying he was praying the rosary with them late Friday night, he's toast. I'm tellin' you in case he calls. This time, no heroics!" I heard someone call to him and he said, "Got to go," and hung up.

I put down the telephone, thinking that Lavelle Williams has an expensive lawyer and I've got enough on my plate. Lavelle Williams was now on his own.

○ ○ ○

The air was heavy as I drove home; a sliver of a moon was bathed in mist and there were no stars. As I left my garage—it's around the corner from the house, halfway down The Hill on East Street—the first flakes were floating down, large and widely spaced. After checking the mail and putting my coat in the hall closet, I opened a Bass Ale, poured it into a mug, and took it to the loft where I changed into jeans and a chamois shirt. I sat in front of the television, used the remote, and breaking with Channel 11, turned to Channel 7's "News at Six."

Kingdom, W.A.R., and a boisterous crowd—impossible to tell how many were our kids—were brandishing placards and banners and hassling the police cordons spread in front of the Public Safety Building. The cameras had gotten there before McAllister and I arrived because there was Kingdom in the face of a police captain—the same one who had been with Steve Winter—demanding freedom for those detained. Kingdom appeared to be angry but in control.

Not so those who crowded around Kingdom; their soundbite quotes were pure toxin, with one white kid managing to grab the reporter's mike to scream his insults at Sonny and the cops. Others gave purported eyewitness accounts of the melee, arrests, snarling dogs, and police brutality, peppered with profanity that hadn't been edited out. Watching it, I could imagine the reactions of Kevin, Vinnie, and Tony in Elmwood, on Federal Hill, and

Mount Pleasant, yelling into the kitchen to Mary, Rose, and Maria that the college punks were at it again!

This segment was followed by a live report, with the Public Safety Building in the background, from a reporter who read a police statement on the arrests, highlighting the names of six Carter students and one from RISD. The vacuous anchorman who tsk, tsked at the cut-away, made it clear that Mayor Russo had responded to events with bravado, and there was Sonny, at his news conference, his pudgy face twisted in anger, his rotund figure wrestling with emotion for the cameras, denouncing Jesse Kingdom, the "campus crazies", and the "spoiled brats" from the tax-exempt university who were disrupting *his* city. Sonny was at his "stick it to ya" best; with Chief McCarthy, resplendent in white starched shirt with collar emblems, shiny badge, and black tie, standing at his side, he came across as a man in control.

I didn't think it possible, but it got worse. Against a backdrop of College Hall, the co-anchor, a living, breathing, wide-eyed Barbie doll, described "... the death threat that both police and University are taking seriously" as the flyer with Kingdom's photograph and the circle and slashes flashed on the screen. *How did they get hold of that?* She went on to describe the crumbling relationship between City Hall and the "elite" University.

"Give – me – a – break!" I said aloud, and exercised the viewer's veto by pressing the power button on the remote. The riot, or whatever the media decides to call it, and its coverage would feed Sonny's ego and play into his schemes against the University as well as fill his campaign coffers. What would Fausto be thinking? What was his brother going to do?

I was exasperated and needed company. I called Nadie and gave her a quick recap of the day.

"Haven't you looked outside?" she exclaimed when I suggested she come over for dinner. She said she wasn't hungry and then,

"It's really coming down. Up to five or six inches."

"That's what SUVs are for. Snow."

"I just washed my hair."

"So?"

"I wasn't planning on going out, Algy...."

"Bundle up. I'll be over and have you back in minutes."

"No, I think...."

"Please?"

"Algy, I'm really tired." Then, she gave in. "You can come over for a few minutes if you want to but you can't stay and I'm not going back with you."

"Fine," I said, figuring my chances of staying there were close to fifty-fifty, and hung up.

I finished the rest of the Bass and went downstairs. Two or three inches would cover the city's grime for a day or two; five or six inches would paralyze the unprepared city and maybe be enough to cancel classes and Kingdom's rally. As I rinsed out the mug, I pulled aside the curtains over the sink and watched snowflakes silently zigzag their way down onto the floodlit patio. Rummaging around in the hall closet, I found a pair of Totes boots, slipped on a leather jacket, fit the fedora firmly on my head, and locked the front door behind me.

The cold air was motionless. On the sidewalk, I stuck out my finger to catch one of the potato chip sized flakes and saw my breath evaporate in the streetlight. As I turned the corner at East Street and took mincing steps down to the garage, my footfalls making the familiar squishy sounds that go with soft snow, I felt better. Winter had arrived. The world was crisp and clean. I heaved up the garage door, intent on the challenge of seducing Nadie.

The attack came without warning.

As I put out my hand to open the Range Rover's door, I was vaguely conscious of a swishing in the air, ending in a sharp, glancing blow at the back of my head that landed full force on my shoulder. I heeled backward, stunned, as the fedora flew off; both hands went to my scalp, my knees buckled, and I crumpled against the car. I couldn't stop my fall; my head grazed the fender and my forehead struck the tire's nubby tread full on before I slid to the concrete. I was splayed out on the floor, dazed, when I took the brunt of somebody landing on my back; grasping fingers dug into my neck, closing my trachea, and my face was ground into the floor's oily grit. What flashed into my mind? The Stalker.

What happened next was all reflex, part of a repertoire of moves learned as far back as high school wrestling and one-on-one training at Camp Lejeune. Mr. Winslow, the patient wrestling coach at Moses Brown, and D.I. Jones, a despised drill instructor, had hard wired a set of reactions in my physical memory. Without plan or thought, my body arched up, rocked forward, and his head crunched into the wheel hub with its jutting lugs. My knees got under my body and that gave me the leverage to buck upwards, grab his knee, and crack it into the edge of the wheel well. Another wrench yielded a muffled cry and a smash of bone against metal, and I felt him slipping off me. I jabbed back with an elbow that thudded into cartilage, produced a gasp of sucked-in air, and he was off me.

That was all I had. My breath was gone, blood pounded in my head like a steam engine, pain sprinted up my spine. My right shoulder seemed paralyzed. It took a teeth-clamping effort to turn toward the open garage door as he lurched on to East Street.

He should have gotten away; I had no thought of pursuit until he slipped in the snow and went sprawling into the curb. I saw his struggle to his knees and unsteady attempts to stand in slow motion. In those few seconds, something happened—second wind, an adrenaline surge, who knows—but I went from prone to crouch to standing, charged out of the garage, and tackled him below his waist, hurtling him facedown into the snow. I clung to him as he thrashed beneath me and boosted myself on to his back; he tried to bronco me off and I smashed the back of his neck with my hands clenched together in a single fist. Even with the snow cushion, his head hit the pavement hard.

He didn't move.

My lungs were now completely blown, my heart pounded against my ribs, the back of my head throbbed in time with my heightened heartbeat. My face stung as the falling snow wet the cuts on my forehead, cheeks, and chin. Pain helped to cut through my mental miasma, to realize that in a few seconds, whatever strength I could marshal would be sapped and he could break away. My voice would have to enforce my control.

It came out unrecognizable. "Get up!" boomed in the quiet as my right hand went under the hood of the parka and grabbed his neck while forcing an arm behind his back with my left. He yelped and I leaned in close to his head. "On your knees. Real slow, or I'll break your arm!" He squirmed and I remembered that if I could get to his trapezius muscle, I could paralyze his arm and shoulder; instead, I chose the easier option of pushing his wrist up a notch, which brought shaky compliance.

As he struggled to stand under my restraint, my brain caught up with reality: he might have a weapon! My hand shook as I released his neck and reached into a parka pocket; my scraped fingers touched something hard and I withdrew a screwdriver, sharp and heavy-duty, ideal for breaking and entering... and maiming. A snippet from an old gangster movie registered and the point of the screwdriver went, not gently, into his ear. He tried to duck away from the pressure. I muttered, "It's the screwdriver. You're going to stand. Slowly. We are going to walk up the hill. Slowly. If you make any move I don't like, I'm going to push it right into your brain."

His breathing was tortured as I shoved him forward. Lights were on in the houses facing us on Congdon Street but would shouts penetrate any of those buttoned-up dwellings? Would a cry for help reveal my weakness? I didn't want him to think; I wanted him to be terrified that I'd push in the screwdriver. The light was on at my front door and I muscled him up the walk. Through clenched teeth, I croaked, "I'm going to release your arm. You move an inch and the screwdriver goes in," and let go of his wrist. His arm fell limply while I fished for my keys in my jeans' pockets, opened the storm door, and fed the key into the lock. When we got inside, I bullied him down the hall and through the swinging door to the kitchen where the ceiling lights were on. Pressure from the screwdriver forced him into one of the spindle-back chairs at the counter. "Man, you're hurtin' me!" he whimpered. "Watch out with dat tool!"

The voice was young and frightened.

I wiped sweat from my eyes and my fingers tingled in pain. "Drop your pants!"

"Wha'...?" earned him a stab of coercion in his ear. "Stop it, man. Please don't, don't, don't...," he pleaded and unfastened the belt around his floppy pants and pulled them over his buttocks and down his legs to a pair of wet, unlaced Nikes.

"...And your shorts. Down to your knees. Move!" Clumsily, he did as ordered. "Put your hands behind you. Through the chair back, through the spindles." He struggled to get his hands through the narrowly spaced spindles while I pocketed the screwdriver, removed the belt from his pants, looped the belt around his wrists, wove it through the spindles, and tied a good Navy knot. For good measure, I wrenched his parka over and around the back of the chair. It was all makeshift, but it would hold.

My own jacket, scuffed-up and oil-stained, was dumped on the counter as I went around to face him. He looked maybe nineteen, not past twenty. His head was cocked to one side; an open wound above an eyebrow—maybe where his face met a lug nut—leaked blood. His open mouth displayed irregular teeth; a growth of skimpy whiskers covered his chin. At his hairline, where the first follicles sprouted like surgical stitches, his almost-shaved head had two razor cuts on either side, an inch or so over tiny ears with silver rings in the lobes. A tattoo, maybe the tip of a wing, went halfway up his neck from inside a zippered hooded sweatshirt that howled "Lakers." What I had thought was a parka turned out to be an oversized, padded, red, white, and blue Patriots jacket that gave him false heft. He was, in fact, slim, although broad-shouldered.

My inspection produced the beginning of a smirk at the corners of his mouth, and ignited a pent up, raw anger in me. My left hand fingers curled; I took a deep breath, and forced my hand to relax, but when his smirk broke into an insolent sneer, I lost it. I grabbed the front of his sweatshirt, pulled him toward me, and hit him squarely on the jaw with a roundhouse left. His head snapped back and he and the chair toppled to the floor.

The shock of pain that streaked through my hand brought back some control. What was I doing? I shook the pain away, and climbed over his coiling body, went to the sink, catching in the window above it, the reflection of someone I hardly recognized, someone wild-haired, dirty, bloody, and furious, with lips swollen and encrusted with blood. I splashed cold water on my face, and from beneath the dirt and oil smears, felt the sharp bite of scrapes and cuts on my forehead, chin, and jaw. My bruised fingers went to the throbbing at the back of my head and came back streaked with red.

"You gone crazy, man? Are you fuckin' nuts?" came a cry from the floor as he struggled against his restraints, angling the chair away from the counter with his feet.

I was ashamed. My gorge of rage had been spent; I didn't know that something so terribly elemental existed within me.

CHAPTER SEVENTEEN

I grabbed him under the arms and pulled his body with attached chair upright. Sweat trickled from his forehead to his scratched cheeks; his eyes were huge as a purposefully rough search of his jacket's pockets produced a woolen watch cap, a pager, and a crumpled cigarette pack. His eyes followed the pack as I threw it on to the counter; I squeezed it open, inserted a finger, and out popped four lumpy joints. A slit in his jacket's lining produced two plastic bags of yellowish granules and a roll of twenties and fifties, maybe six or seven hundred dollars; he didn't flinch when I flashed the stash in his face and tossed it on the counter. In his jeans was a cheap wallet containing a hundred dollar bill and a New York driver's license. I removed the license and raised it to the light.

Lavelle Williams wore his hair in cornrows a year earlier when the Polaroid ID photo was snapped at the registry.

Somehow, I knew it was him, as far back as forcing him up East Street. If the kitchen telephone hadn't rung, stopping a rush of anger, and jolting him as though a firecracker had exploded in his backside, I could have whacked him again. I ignored the rings and threw the wallet and license on the counter. My hands remained balled into fists. "Why?" I asked.

His chin squeezed his chest, making his voice small and tinny. "I didn't start out comin' here. Da cops got my car, my place staked out. Hadda get out of da hood, started walkin' over to Fox Point when it starts ta snow. My friends...." His voice trailed off, maybe to a different story. "Saw your house. Nobody'd be lookin' for me 'round your house. The Reverend said *you* da big man, told me where ya lived, when we were.... I was gonna stay outta da snow, and den get out." He raised his head and maybe there was a glimmer of remorse in his voice when he continued, "When ya come in..., I... panicked."

Through the fog of my anger, I could imagine him in the darkness of the garage: he hears footsteps, the garage door rolls up, and somebody walks in. Who's that? A cop? Somebody who saw him break in? I caught myself, despite a fleeting recollection of *Native Son*; what difference did his panic make? He had come purposefully to my garage, I had surprised him, and he had attacked me!

"Bullshit!"

He jerked his head away from an expected blow but I was back in control. What I wanted more than anything was to scare the living shit out of him, to make him cower, and I wasn't sure why.

"You sure screwed up. You picked absolutely the wrong guy to mess with. Let's see..."—I picked up the screwdriver from the counter, then dropped it for noisy emphasis—"... breaking and entering, assault, assault with a deadly weapon..."—repeating my performance with the plastic bags and the cigarette pack—"... possession of marijuana and... crack? While out on bail for possession and sale? You've five to ten coming at the ACI. The judge will love how you assaulted someone who tried to help you."

My threat got no reaction, leading me to stoop to his level—in more ways than one—when I put my face within inches of his. "The cops want your ass for Anne Sullivan's murder. Nobody's going to help you now. Not Reverend Thomas, not Franks, certainly not... *Senor* Flores. You're too far off the reservation. You're all alone now."

He had taken it all in with a punk's stolidity until I said "Flores." At that name, his face twitched. I had breached his defenses, but since he had too little emotional range, he reverted to type. His tongue brushed his swollen lips and he muttered, "Go fuck yourself."

My hand went back as if to slap the look off his face but instead I stepped away and grabbed the kitchen phone. I began to punch in 911 when, without warning, Lavelle Williams's street-born insolence evaporated: tears filled his eyes and he broke into sobs. Real honest-to-goodness sobs! "I just can't fuckin' stand it! Every fuckin' thin' is goin' bad. Da cops, da fuckin' spics, dey all want to.... I didn't kill Annie! I didn't rape nobody! But who da fuck believes me? Who gives a flyin' fuck for me?" His body shook maniacally, rocking the chair back and forth in a struggle against his restraints, mucus mixed with sweat and blood erupting from his swollen nose.

I hesitated, then touched the "off" button. I searched his face for a hint of a reversion to smartassness. But there wasn't. It was all self pity.

"I didn't kill Annie. It coulda' been fuckin' anybody, ya know." His head pivoted from side to side like a bobblehead doll. "Anybody dat knew her mighta done it. Annie could piss anybody off. She'd say shit to hurt ya, be in ya face, until ya just can't stand it." He tried to wipe his mouth by brushing it against a raised shoulder but it barely grazed his chin. "She didn't care. She liked ta do it. She was always screwin' around, showin' off how much smarter she was. She didn't care at all if she fucked ya over. She liked ta do it...."

Almost before I realized it, I said "Your lawyer says that somebody gave her money. A lot of money...."

His mouth opened, displaying a row of teeth with spaces. "Ya talked to Franks...?" His bewilderment immediately gave way to an expression of fear and I knew he was through talking. That merited a twist of sweatshirt under his Adam's apple. "One more chance," I grunted. "Who gave it to her?"

He locked his eyes in mine. Little flecks of orange appeared as they widened. "Fuckin' cash cow!"

"'Cash cow'?"

I tightened the twist, shaking his head with force. What was he talking about? "What cash cow?"

"Dat's who sent da money, man! Dis cash cow! Da cash cow! Dat's all she said."

I released him and his head bounced backward.

"Some kinda joke. Always said it widda smile. Wouldn't say no more. Not Annie. Too fuckin' smart for dat. Took da bucks, had da 'operation,' she said. Zip, and it was *gone*, but money just kept comin' in. Lived huge—bought all da shit she wanted, DVD's and computer shit, took off to New York all da time—and the rest went to da bank." His voice slowed and he spoke as though mystified. "Saw da bankbook once. Told dat to Franks. Ten grand at first and she was still packin' it away. Even after buyin' all da shit. Money came in 'round da first of da month. Went down to the post office and picked it up. Just like welfare, I says to her, and she laughs but says she 'earned' it. But she never had to do nottin', no work, nottin'! Sleep all day, da lazy ho'. Never go out except at night, like she was hidin' from somebody. Den, dis month, the cash didn't come in!" His lips smacked together as he started a gaspy laugh. "I told her da cash cow musta run outta milk. She got pissed at dat. Too fuckin' bad!"

He took a long look at the crumpled cigarette pack on the counter. I pulled out a joint and rolled it between my fingers, and considered if a toke would loosen him up. The cabinet drawer next to the counter had matches; I stuck the joint between Williams's lips, lit it, and he inhaled deeply. His eyes closed, and as he exhaled, his shoulders slumped perceptibly. I snapped the joint from his lips. "Da bitch was messin' wid me, ya know. Couldn't let dat happen again...." He nodded towards the joint; I raised it to his lips and watched him inhale and the smoke leave his puffed-up nose. I took the joint and ran water over it in the sink, and stuffed it into the garbage disposal. He didn't seem to care. "If I'd offed her, I'd have gotten my ass outta here."

I gave him that. "Why was she on your case?"

"Who knows? I seen her down at da CVS. 'Bout six. Ain't seen her for awhile but she wanted some stuff so we went back to her place, had a couple joints, and I fucked da ho'. Den, she gotta use my cell, 'cause hers ran outta juice, while I went and got a pizza. When I got back, she had a joint in her face, baked out. Told me dat da cash cow was gettin' milked again. She was goin' to get her 'milk' again, startin' right away. She had some pizza and started dissin' me and talkin' trash. Mean shit. So dis time I gave da ho' a few whacks to remember me by, and I left." His voice sought justification for the "whacks". "It was still early, only 'bout nine or so, and I was pissed so I wanted ta party, got my car and hit a party out in Olneyville, took care of some…business, and went back to my crib and smoked some ganja." He looked up at me. "Not dis shit. Da bomb!"

"That's your alibi? A party in Olneyville? Drug sales? Going home and getting stoned?"

"Man, I *was* stoned," he said, focusing his reddened eyes on me through the lingering smoke, then arching his head way back. "Shouldn'ta been so stoned! Saturday night is a business night. But she got me so fuckin' mad…!" His head looped in a slow circle. "She caused me all dis trouble. Damn me for foolin' around wid a white ho'!"

"When did you start going together?"

The smirk almost reappeared. "We didn't *go together*. It's not like fuckin' 'dates', ya know?"

"Dope?"

"Not junk. After da 'operation', she'd smoke. Smoked alot. Always had some stuff around. It was always the same. She'd smoke and she'd get mean, real mean. I could tell when it was comin' on like Friday, when she'd got jammed. Shoulda left her alone... her old man, da cop, had sent da word on me and dat ain't good for business so I ain't seen her for a couple weeks. Just couldn't take all her shit anyhow." A grin started at his face. "Hey, man, I *supply*! I got da stuff. I got whatever you want. Da good stuff, straight from Colombia. I'm like da pizza man. Page me and I deliver."

"Where's the bankbook?"

The brightness left him. "Man, ya just don't get it! Annie didn't tell me shit." He thought for a moment. "Maybe her sister. She was da only one Annie would trust." He shook his head. "And dat bitch really hated me." He slumped back. "I don't know what happened to Annie. It could've been some junkie, or dis dude dey looking for... dis Stalker. Wouldn't even have to break in. Da crazy ho' was always leavin' da door unlocked."

I pushed myself away from the counter, not sure what to do next. More questions? Why?

He started squirming within his restraints which brought me back to practicality. "Look, ya gotta let me go. I can't get picked up by dem cops. Ya know what dey do...."

I didn't respond.

"...Or call Franks. If I go down dere wid him, dey gotta be careful. He knows everybody. Dat's why dey got him for me."

"Who did?"

He was silent.

"Who did?"

"My friends," he said sourly. "Dey take care of deir people."

"Wise up! They're not going help you if you're going to be charged with murder! Nothing to do with them."

This time, he actually laughed. "Franks ain't goin' to let 'em pin dis on me. No way! Dey is only interested in money, and dey don't get money when dey have to lay low 'cause someone's goin' to da joint. Anyway, I ain't a snitch, 'cause if ya snitch, ya die!

Sometimes," he continued in a low, almost instructional tone, "when somebody has to do time, he might give up someone for a little better deal…and stuff. So, to make sure dat don't happen, we get Franks. Ya get out on bail and…, who knows? 'Course, if ya *do* snitch, it don't make no difference where ya is; dey gets ya in da joint, or outta da joint."

I shook my head, realizing I was out of my league in trying to deal with Lavelle Williams. He was no different from the grim-faced punks I'd prosecuted years ago, people you can't reason with or cajole because they didn't care about what you care about.

"How come you went to your mother's when you knew the cops were looking for you?"

"Couldn't go to my place, had to stay away from…, and… Mistake. Don't know why I told her…."

I went over to the sink and threw water on my face. There had to be more to it. Was there a cache of money or drugs hidden at his mother's apartment? Was he smart enough to figure on Reverend Thomas being his good will ambassador to the Providence cops? Or just scared?

"Call Franks. Gimme a break. I didn't mean ta hurt ya. Ya know what could happen if ya call da cops and dey get a mind to hurt me. C'mon, man, I need Franks." He didn't know it but he had things going his way until my silence let him relapse into his street personality. "What's dis? Some fuckin' game? A story to tell ya snotty friends about? What da fuck does it mean to ya if I get lynched? Just a dead nigger? I ain't *you.* Dey ain't gonna treat me like *you.*" Then, the scorn left his voice. "I ain't like *you.*"

Jerome Franks was not a happy camper. When I called his home on Blackstone Boulevard, only a mile or so away, I hadn't mentioned Williams but assured Franks that it was a matter of utmost urgency. He had been reluctant, complaining about the snow but I was insistent and he finally agreed; possibly, he felt something akin to the curiosity which brought me to his office only two days earlier.

The front door lights revealed a dusting of snow on the tweed cap that crowned his large head, a blue scarf overflowed from inside a camelhair overcoat, and he entered with a flourish of self-importance. With the hall light off, my face, which even after a wash was very much damaged goods, was barely visible. "This had better be worth it," he said impatiently, taking off his gloves to unbutton his overcoat and inspect an oversized gold wristwatch. "Ten-thirty," he intoned.

I snapped on the hall light. His florid face, stubbled by a day's whiskers, lost its pompous expression when he saw mine. "Well, you can decide. The police, as you are well aware, are searching for Lavelle Williams. Since he is sitting rather uncomfortably in my kitchen, I—"

Franks's mouth gaped open, then closed, and opened again. "What the hell is he doing here?" he sputtered.

"I *thought* you might wish to inquire, counselor. Right this way," and pushed open the kitchen door. Williams, with his pants around his sneakers, his undershorts barely covering his knees, and his arms lost behind him in the restraining jacket, looked ridiculous. Before Franks arrived, the cash, pager, and wallet had been wiped clean and returned to his jacket's pocket and the pot and plastic bags, wiped *very* clean, had been tucked back into its lining. The screwdriver, woolen cap, and driver's license remained on the counter.

As nonchalantly as I could fake, I leaned against the doorway with my arms folded and found the insouciance that I knew irritated Franks. "Of course, you understand this is really a courtesy to you as well as a convenience to me, that is, having you take him in, rather than my calling the police and charging him. As you said yourself, the situation remains 'venomous'."

"What...?" said Franks, still staring at Williams who exhibited a mixture of sullenness and downright fear.

"'Venomous'. Your word to describe the atmosphere at the department." A little rub of salt in the wound as I crossed to stand behind Williams and face Franks. "He assaulted me. He—"

"He's nuts," Williams blurted. "He...."

I jammed his wrists upward, garnering a groan, as I untied the knot in the belt. "But we've had such a nice chat! How he lives, how he survives. Shocking! As you said, one of our wasted youth...."

Williams's head snapped straight up. "I didn't say nuttin'—"

"Reverend Thomas was on a fool's errand," I said, and with the final loop of the belt unwound, Williams pulled his arms forward and attempted to right himself. His hands were too numb to brace against the counter and he slumped awkwardly back on to the chair. I remained behind him, ready to make a grab in case he thought of escape.

Franks' lips slid back and forth, his expression not bothering to hide the depth of his anger. "*You* expect *me* to take Williams to the police, for *you?*"

My voice struck the right annoying pitch. "I understand they have more questions for him about the Sullivan murder. And you might want to use the time to discuss other matters, like her bankbook and her abortion. If I were to simply hand him over to the police, well, as you say, no telling what might happen. It is still 'venomous', isn't it? Probably more so after today's events." I smiled, even though it hurt.

Franks' eyes sparked with hostility as he divined my motives: he was being forced to be *my* messenger boy, instead of the other way around.

I yanked Williams up by his sweatshirt and pushed him toward his lawyer. He almost fell into Franks.

"Pick up your pants," Franks snarled and Williams struggled to obey. Over the back of his client, Franks struggled to keep his voice under control. "You're trying to play me for a fool. Nobody does that to me."

"I'll keep his cap and license, together with his...weapon, enough I dare say to give whatever I say some credibility. And surely there are sufficient fingerprints all over my cars...."

Franks' jowls seemed to multiply as he puffed up like an iguana for his rejoinder, and decided against it. He forced Williams through the kitchen door, down the hall, and out of the front door. I watched from behind the storm door as Franks propelled his charge towards a white Lincoln Town Car parked at the curb. It was still snowing heavily; Williams' rubbery legs kept buckling all the way to the car. Franks held the passenger door open to make sure Williams entered and slammed it shut. He glowered in my direction as he high-stepped through the snow to the driver side door and got inside. The engine roared, the wipers cleared snow from the windshield, and the car lumbered forward.

In my smugness, I actually waved, satisfied in my payback to Franks, and remembering that the garage door remained open, I retrieved my jacket from the kitchen and went outside. An overhead light in the garage revealed a broken pane of glass in the rear door window and my fedora, dirty and crushed, on the floor between the Mini and the Range Rover. I scooped up my hat and earned a stab of pain in my lower back. I walked around the SUV to search for whatever Williams had used to deliver the blow to my head and shoulder and spotted a two-by-three sticking oddly out of a box full of old climbing gear. Must have been that, I concluded, and then remembered the tools—like ice axes—that nestled within that box!

I snapped off the light and was closing the garage door when I kicked a small and metallic object and sent it spinning into the snow. I might not have found it except it landed in a footprint where it caught the glint of a distant streetlight. A cell phone, a flip model. I opened it up, touched the power icon, and it flashed on. Had to be the business phone of Lavelle Williams, lost in the scuffle. A souvenir to add to his cap, license, and screwdriver.

I pocketed it and with hurt in every stride, made my way back to Congdon Street. Second guessing had commenced. Maybe it had been a mistake not to have called the police: I had been assaulted and he was wanted by the cops for questioning. Would Franks break his code and reveal the bankbook? Or the abortion? He'd have to, now, wouldn't he, to get Williams out of there? But suppose he didn't? Was the risk to Williams worth the pleasure of putting down the preening Jerome Franks? What kind of payback could Franks deliver? Had I been uneasy about Reverend Thomas's and Sylvia's reactions to my bringing charges against Williams—even justifiably?

As I entered the house, I remembered the joints and bags of junk inside Williams's jacket lining. Suppose, in haste or confusion, they forgot to remove them before Williams was brought in?

What a satisfying thought!

Friday

CHAPTER EIGHTEEN

A hot shower identified and magnified the hurt of every scrape and bruise. I swallowed six hundred milligrams of Advil, swabbed the cuts and abrasions I could reach with Neosporin, then inched my way under the covers. It was beyond my capacity to remember where the heating pad might be or where I could comfortably plug it in. Eventually I slept only to be roused to semi-consciousness several times by twisted images of the attack or by a stitch from a shift of my scalp or torso. About six, a roll to my right side triggered a shock of pain from screamingly-tight lower back muscles that was more effective than any alarm. I crawled out of bed and took baby steps to the bathroom where I stretched what I could and braved another teeth-clenching hot shower.

It took twice as long as usual to towel off and when I wiped away the condensation from the bathroom's pivot mirror, the damage was all too visible: my forehead, chin, and right cheek resembled pieces of basketball cover, my puffy lips would have made a Hollywood ingénue giddy with jealousy, my right shoulder was a blight of purplish-red, and the skin over my right ribs was a mixture of mauve and yellow. Shaving proved to be an adventure as I attempted to avoid the grit marks on my cheeks and chin. I applied Neosporin again, took more Advil, rubbed BenGay on all the tender spots, and struggled into underwear after wrapping my lower back in a surgical corset. In the triple mirror in the loft, I looked like one of my jarhead, Section 8 bound, clients after one helluva shore leave.

But, I had fought, prevailed, and was proud of myself!

The kitchen was flooded by brilliant sunlight. Through the french doors, the patio and garden were a dazzling white; the top of the brick boundary walls measured the inches of fallen snow. I brewed some espresso and tuned the radio to a local AM station which reported "...five inches in Providence..." and "...a record snowfall for this time of year..." every two minutes, along with no school and no work announcements, and a lot about a low pressure system that had sucked in a layer of cold off the Atlantic and turned flurries into winter's first snowstorm. From Foster-Glocester to Newport, the State of Rhode Island and Providence Plantations was closed. I switched the radio's band to FM and tuned to WCAR, our campus station, which confirmed that the University had suspended all classes and activities, including, *mirable dictu*, Jesse Kingdom's rally!

Gr-e-a-t!

With this welcomed news, I was one with the ranks of happy Rhode Islanders. A snow day Friday! It's like recess or a pardon or winning $100 on a scratch card! I suddenly had an appetite and the kitchen soon smelled of coffee, scrambled eggs, sizzling Canadian bacon, and thick toast from Mrs. Pina's homemade bread which I devoured while working the crossword in yesterday's *Journal*. Pumped up by a second espresso, I went upstairs and only then noticed the blinking red message light on the telephone console. I punched in the required code.

"Are you coming over or not? At least call one way or the other!"

Ugh! I had completely forgotten about Nadie! It must have been her call when I was interrogating Williams. I picked up the telephone, ready to apologize, and then imagined her concern when she saw my face. I decided my apology had to be in person.

I dressed slowly and carefully; sore fingers took time to get my jeans over the corset, negotiate the restraints of a red and black checked wool shirt, and tug my Totes over slip-on loafers. A ski parka from the basement closet, gloves, a buffed up fedora, and Ray Bans completed my outfit and I left the house with all the physical mobility of a tiny tot dressed up for play in the snow by an overanxious mother.

Congdon Street hadn't been plowed and it took painful, giant steps to get me through the snow on the front walk to the few car tracks on the street. High silky clouds barely covered a bright sun and I became aware of the quiet, rare and welcomed in the city; only the clucking of squirrels hopping through the snow and starlings rustling about in the hedges broke the stillness. I passed trees wonderfully feathered and plumed by snow and, near Angell Street was hailed by a neighbor, snow shovel in his hands, who shouted something to me about snowplows or lack thereof. His brick house, set behind a white picket fence, could have been taken from a Christmas card; all it needed was a holly wreath on its front door. I waved, keeping my face hidden, embarrassed by how I would have looked upon close inspection.

After slow progress up and over The Hill, I realized that not taking the Range Rover had been a really bad idea; I hurt and with the temperature rising quickly, I was overdressed, and perspiring. Within the shadows of College Arch, a University maintenance crew dressed sensibly in sweatshirts and jeans made loud company as they drank coffee from paper cups and leaned against idle snowblowers and shovels. I stopped to adjust the very uncomfortable corset and faced glass panels behind which "Campus Security Briefs" were posted weekly by the Security Office. Each incident of stolen property or other reported crimes including The Stalker's assaults and rapes merited three or four lines. Next Friday, the murder of Anne Sullivan would be listed with similar terseness.

"Ugh!" I said, and my voice echoed through the Arch loudly enough to deserve a glance from several of the snow removal crew.

I left the Arch under the faded "Stop The Stalker" banner and entered The Green, not surprised that its walkways had been cleared and were already getting student traffic. On the steps of Dustin Hall, a dozen or so kids in ski sweaters, down vests, and turtleneck shirts were engaged in a wild snowball fight that didn't get a truce when I crossed the line of fire; further on, another gang, no doubt its members thinking themselves to be particularly brazen, was finishing off two huge, anatomically correct "snowpersons." Somehow, the antics of the kids, the stark outline of the surrounding buildings against the blue vault of the sky, and the snow-cleaned air seemed to have lifted, momentarily, the smog of foreboding that had enveloped the campus for weeks and added buoyancy to my spirits. In the few minutes it took to reach Nadie's apartment building, the outlandish, impractical plan that had been gelling since last evening now seemed inevitable.

I pressed the call button at the entrance to announce my arrival. "Yes?"

"Algy." There was no response. "It's freezing out here," I said, lying, since I was hot and sweaty.

A raucous buzz offered entry. I stomped the snow off my boots onto the entryway mat, climbed the stairs to the second floor, knocked on her door, and, finding that she had unlocked her two safety locks, walked into her apartment.

The impression I always get, and maybe this is a good sign, is of a transient situation. You walk into a sparsely furnished living area—its only wall decoration a framed poster of a baleful Albert Einstein with the legend: "It is impossible to prepare for war and make peace"—and practically stand in its miniscule kitchen. Nadie, in a faded blue terrycloth robe, was sitting on a stool at a counter which separated the kitchen from the living area. A towel was wrapped, turban style, around her head, suggesting a recent shower. Without make-up, her skin was pale, highlighting the natural pink of her pursed lips. Her legs were crossed; a bedroom slip-per with a fluffy blue pom-pom on the toe and without a heel, dan-gled from her foot. She had a *New Yorker* propped up in front of her and the radio was tuned to a soft-rock station.

"Thanks for the call last night." She turned a page and didn't look up.

I closed the door behind me, took off my hat and sunglasses, waiting for her to lift her eyes to my bruises. When she didn't, I said, "Sorry" and remained silent until she glanced up at me.

"What happened?"

"I had an unexpected visitor last night," I responded, and with grimaces to reflect my real or imagined pain, pulled off my gloves and parka. "Lavelle Williams..., Reverend Thomas's kid..., assault-ed me in my garage as I was coming over here." I grasped the counter, a bit dramatically, to lower myself on to the stool opposite her and proceeded to tell her the whole story, not scrimping on the graphic details of the fight but omitting my moment of shameful rage. Along the way, my narrative got disjointed and when I ram-bled on how unlikely it was that Williams could be Anne Sullivan's murderer, that he was a punk who would never hang around to be arrested and that he had confirmed both the abortion and bank account, Nadie's face displayed complex emotions. My big finish—the scene of an angry Jerry Franks leaving with Williams—brought expressions of dismay and disapproval.

"What has gotten into you? It's one thing for you to perform some misguided act of noblesse oblige, or whatever it is, and another to be assaulted and get into a street fight! As for Franks, you *should* have called the police!"

Her reaction deflated me. Why had I bothered to slog over here!

"Latoya Chapin," she began, "came to the Center yesterday. Wanted to talk to us—Charlene Harris and me—before she gave an interview to the *Journal*." Charlene is a black colleague of

Nadie's. "Scheduled for today's Lifetime section. It might be in the paper but it's not online. She was depressed, scared, humiliated, and yet she wanted to go through with it. The assault was more vicious and racist than you could imagine. We let her talk it through before she left for the interview. She wasn't doing it because of pressure…, although there is some of that. She's convinced that black women are always going to be subject to rape, that it's all driven by racism. She's saying publicly what a lot of the black women are saying among themselves. She made me feel so…sad! That's why I didn't want company last night."

Nadie searched my face for a reaction. I was too dim at that moment to deliver the required empathy so she abruptly loosened the turbaned towel, shook her hair, and began to rub it purposefully. Belatedly, I slid off the stool and stood behind her, my hands on her shoulders to gently knead her muscles. She shrugged me away but my hands remained lightly on her shoulders.

"I need you to help me," I said softly.

Nadie stopped towelling; she must have thought that I needed a sympathetic ear because I felt her body relax.

"Look, I know it sounds absurd," I continued, "maybe even obscene, but I want to speak to Anne Sullivan's sister."

Her back stiffened under my fingers.

"If anyone holds the key to this, it's her. She was her confidante. Remember, it was her name in the Center's file. She knows about the money, if there is money. She may have the bankbook. She might even know who was supporting her sister." My face was at her right ear as I poured it on. "Williams didn't do it. Williams may be a punk, but not a murderer, not the kid that went to his mother when he thought he'd be arrested. He could be convicted only because he was with her that night…"—and I knew this would get through to her—"…and because he's black. Unless we do something!"

She spun around, her green eyes sparkling like polished emeralds and she had difficulty controlling her voice. "Just how do you think you can invite yourself—the University's lawyer—to have a nice little chat with her about her 'moidered sista'?"

A heavy Brooklyn accent is a verbal weapon used when she wants to show me up. She was right; however, she failed to get the drift. "No," I said. "I'd like you to make the call."

Her mouth opened and her eyes became the color of martini olives. She started to say something, thought better of it, and after a disgusted shrug, walked into the bedroom. "You had better go," she said tightly over her shoulder, "... now. Go home, fix your face, read a book, maybe Trollope, something to slow down your imagination!" The bedroom door closed behind her.

Well, I wasn't going to give up!

"Think about it. Nobody has mentioned her money! Why would Franks have gone to the trouble to involve me? Something's not right. Maybe the sister is withholding it. If I call her, you're right, she's not going to speak to me. But if someone from the Women's Center calls, trying to get a handle on what the University might have done to help her sister when she was pregnant, when she didn't register...?" I walked halfway to the bedroom. "Besides, you're a woman. *You* could convince her."

The bedroom door flung open and a pom-pommed slipper went whizzing past my left ear. "Dumb! Dumb! Dumb!" She stood in the doorway in black pantyhose and bra, pointing toward the door.

I made my last plea. "Okay, I am a case study. Write me up later if you want to. There's a black kid—not a nice black kid, I know—who's being falsely accused of murder! The cops can say they got their *perp!* His lawyer doesn't care what happens so long as the kid doesn't rat on his slimeball clients." Then, more plaintively, deserving of a dramatic award, "Doesn't anybody but his mother and me care what happens to this kid?"

I took a step toward her, my hands raised hip high, before she moved away to sit in front of a dressing table. She brushed her hair in long, even strokes, sweeping on the right and then on the left, her face set in a scowling stare as reflected in the mirror. I sat on a large, painted trunk at the foot of her unmade bed, and waited.

Maybe a full two minutes later, she pointed the hair brush at my image in the mirror. "This doesn't have much to do with..., what's his name..., Williams. It's about you, all this family obligation stuff, guilt that goes back to the days of rum, slaves, and molasses. Anyway, it's misplaced. This is a murder, and you're not a prosecutor anymore, or the kid's lawyer." Then, I saw her anger dissolve into something more thoughtful and after several long brushes, she said, hesitantly, "I'll do it."

Huh?

"... I'll do it because it can end this whole fiasco right now. But," she said, waving the brush at my reflection, "the deal is, if I can't reach her on the first try or if she says no, that's it! That's the deal. One telephone call, and if I'm not successful...."

"Agreed," I said, not really meaning it, and stood up to kiss her hair. She ducked away and dressed quickly in stonewashed jeans and a white turtleneck sweater. With her thumbs jammed into rear pockets and fingers spread around the curves of her fanny, she stood over me, repeating that she was not going to cajole the sister; a simple "no" or any sign of reluctance on the sister's part would end their conversation. I nodded, and she sat on the bed and used her cell phone to call the Women's Center; I moved up on the bed next to her as she waited for someone to get the sister's full name and telephone number from the Center's computer. A few seconds later, Nadie was actually speaking to Patricia Sullivan, home today like all good Rhode Islanders.

Nadie was the consummate professional, making the point that while she didn't want to intrude, she was a volunteer at the Women's Center where her sister had been counseled, and that she wanted to speak to Patricia as her sister's referenced confidante, ambiguous enough for anyone to surmise that Nadie needed some follow-up information for her file. As she went on, I remembered that yesterday was her sister's funeral. Damn awkward but couldn't be helped. She agreed to meet Nadie at two o'clock this afternoon and Nadie scribbled an address on a paper bookmark taken from her night table.

When she finished the call, Nadie said, "Obviously, I didn't mention you. I don't know if she will even let you into the family's house..."—she referred to the note—"...Stanhope Avenue in Elmwood, wherever that is. The parents won't be there, she says. Here's the address." She smiled, a little priggishly. "You wouldn't mind waiting in the car, would you?"

"That's ridiculous!" I protested, but I took the bookmark.

"Assuming you do get inside, I get to ask all the questions. You're not going to interrupt, lead, or suggest anything. Absolutely and unequivocally, nothing! Clear? You are there as a witness to protect me. Then," she said somewhat resignedly, "if there are any repercussions from all of this, at least I'll be able to have the University Counsel as a witness that the discussions were proper. It's my show, Algy. Understood?"

Okay; if this was going to come off at all, it had to be on Nadie's terms. Of course, I was intrigued by her motivation. To end my farrago or to satisfy her own needs. "I agree, but at least let me tell you what I'm interested in. She...."

Her hands went to her ears. "No! No! No! Let *me* decide what is legitimate inquiry. You'll have to live with that or I call her right now and cancel." She moved off the bed and led me out of the room. "Now, go home, fix your face, and pick me up around one-thirty; that will give us plenty of time to get there."

I raised my hands in surrender. "I'm going," I replied meekly. "I love you," I said.

She didn't look up.

CHAPTER NINETEEN

As I began the trek home through the streets east of the campus, I was joined by parents with toddlers on sleds, older couples with shopping bags, and troops of students heading towards the Refectory and the day-off delights of Thayer Street. With most sidewalks unshoveled, slush filling the barely plowed streets, and clogged catchbasins overflowing with snow melt, we were forced to compete with trucks armed with front-end plows and splashing cars for the limited street space. Most of the kids favored bright jackets, fleece vests, layered shirts, and sweaters over jeans; many had their heads uncovered showing iPods or Walkmans, and most wore sunglasses. The racket of snowblowers' two-cycle engines from driveways and parking lots increased as we neared Thayer Street where impatient customers, cell phones to their ears, were lined up outside of eateries like Paragon, Johnny Rockets, and Spike's, the sidewalks were crowded with students from the University and the East Side's private schools, and starlings and sparrows, twittering above us on utility wires, waited to swoop down to any morsel, however soggy or nasty, uncovered below. Surprising to me, ten or a dozen motorcycles were lined up in a cleared spot by the CVS, their leather clad riders aboard deep-throated Harley's and higher pitched Yamahas and Kawasakis seemingly unfazed by snow conditions and obviously planning an expedition to some unlucky destination.

At my house, somebody in Mrs. Pina's extended family had come and gone; the front walk and sidewalks were clear and practically dry and a trench had been cut through the mound of snow left at the curb by the belated plows. I picked up the *Journal* which had been placed neatly on the front step, entered, and went immediately upstairs to check my messages. The first call was from Tuttle, asking me to call back. The second was from Tramonti; he said that Franks had brought in Williams, that Williams had been released, "What's going on?" and "Don't you listen to *anyone?*", and nothing about a bankbook or an abortion, until his time ran out. So, Franks *had* managed to involve me. The bastard! No doubt, he had thought of a quick payback of some sort. I should have known. And the dope in Williams's jacket had either been ditched or he never got searched!

I made a BLT on rye and finished it with a Sam Adams while reading the *Journal*. The snowstorm shared the front page with a three column photo of a demonstrator on the ground facing a snarling police dog—a photo sure to be published nationally—and a line of cops with raised shields. According to the story, Kingdom wasn't present when the police lines were threatened, the cops hadn't used their batons but had pushed back with shields when orders to disperse were ignored, and nobody had owned up to calling in the K-9s. Carter students were prominent in inside photos, including one of the black female student in fatigues angrily yelling at the police from behind a row of sawhorses at the courthouse. A sidebar listed those arrested and while not identifying any as ours, I could tell from the ages and addresses that the *Journal* had it right.

All of the principals to the event, including Kingdom, got quotes: "It was provocation by the police. Howsoever it happened, it shouldn't have. People are justifiably angry, and bringing out the dogs reminds me of Selma." McCarthy blamed the "rioters" while Sonny's "Carter crazies" quotes were straight from yesterday's press conference. His challenge to Danby was "keep your spoiled brats out of our downtown!" Tramonti's role as peacemaker-mediator merited no mention; he had refused comment, probably having figured there was nothing he could say that would be helpful one way or the other.

The *Journal's* Lifetime section is a tabloid pullout; its interview with Latoya Chapin was the cover story. It started off like a feminist tract: her rape, she said, was part of a backlash against black assertiveness and the Carter Stalker was a white male instrument of repression. But when she got into the simple narrative of her rape, it was so vivid that I, like Nadie, boiled with anger and frustration.

Around one-fifteen, I was in the Range Rover. The huge SUV, powerful and bulky with an attitude, made me feel more in control. At a traffic light, I slid *Linda Ronstadt's Greatest Hits* into the CD player. The first track, "You're No Good," was playing as I pulled up in front of Nadie's apartment. She was standing on the sidewalk, in a tannish duffel coat, high black boots, and large-lensed sunglasses, holding the straps of a roomy canvas bag. Her hair was gathered at the nape of her neck by a black ribbon. I reached over to open the passenger door when she appeared at the driver side window. I heard her say, "I decided I should drive. Puts things in their proper perspective."

Uh-oh. Her last car, which she gave up when its engine succumbed to a hundred thousand miles of zero maintenance, was an ancient and tiny Toyota Tercel, and she wanted the keys to a Range Rover! In snow conditions! I almost resisted, but my shake-of-the-head hesitation as her hand clasped the door handle wasn't appreciated. Reluctantly, to save the interview, I got out. She brushed by me to step up and get in behind the wheel; I climbed in on the other side, adjusted the leather bucket seat for some leg room, and hadn't yet snapped in the crossover belt when she had us bouncing forward.

Nadie drove hunched over the wheel, with her elbows akimbo and her hands precisely across its diameter, like a kid on a tricycle. I managed to keep my mouth shut and my eyes straight ahead, only once or twice sucking in breath or wincing as she maneuvered down ill-plowed, puddled, and car-clogged side streets to Wickenden Street and up the ramp to I-195. There, we barreled, without reference to any of the car's three mirrors and to a cacophony of horns, right to left across four lanes of highway at the junction with I-95. 'Geezus!' I said to myself as we turned south and she slowed the SUV to a crawl; she was hapless as a driver and was gripping the wheel like she was throttling a snake! The CD began the track for "That'll Be the Day When I Die"!

There was more traffic than I would have thought, even a mini-jam as we passed a pest control company's rooftop giant termite—known to all Rhode Islanders as the Big Blue Bug—and made the long curve at the gas tank farm. We left the highway at the Elmwood Avenue exit just before the Cranston line and made a right turn at the bottom of the ramp into Roger Williams Park. The idea was to cut through the Park, cross Broad Street, and find our way through the maze of streets that constitute the Elmwood neighborhood. It was slow going; with school out and workplaces closed, the Park's narrow, slushy serpentine roads were congested by throngs of kids dragging sleds to favorite slopes and walkers enjoying the sunshine and dazzling snow, particularly around the ponds and up past the Zoo and the Planetarium. Nadie drove even more cautiously—if that was possible—within the Park, which suited me because of the pedestrians, until she got us behind a sander truck. I urged her to keep her distance from the cascading dirt and earned an evil mutter.

Our conversation, despite my attempts, had been nil. She was mute on purpose; her expression was one of peevishness and that annoyed me. The map I was using contained profiles of the city's neighborhoods and, more to irritate her than anything, I read aloud from its scraps of local history. Elmwood, I began, had once been all woods, orchards, and rolling farmland, supplying the rapidly growing mercantile and manufacturing city with produce, hay, and other staples..., not unlike Brooklyn had been for Manhattan Island, I added for her reference. She studiously ignored me and I repaid her with a three minute recitation on the advent of horsecars and trolleys in the area, the division, subdivision, and sub-subdivision of land into smaller and smaller house lots for the families of silversmiths at Gorham, machinists of Brown & Sharpe, and boilermakers at the Corliss Works, and how the neighborhood now belonged to the middle class families of utility workers, hubmakers and moldmakers from jewelry manufacturers, and city employees like teachers, police, and firemen. Her pique became evident by loud breathing as I blithely went on, editorializing, that Elmwood had survived as a stable urban enclave in sharp contrast to the crumbling neighborhoods of South Providence to the north and west. It was a place, I said, offhandedly, "of promise."

At that speculation, Nadie lowered her sunglasses, looked at me, and remarked, "How would *you* know?"

I had no reply which would have kept the truce.

We exited the Park through its open, spear-topped gates on to Broad Street. We crossed and I gave directions from the map—"next right, that's Bacon Street, first left"—until we were on Stanhope Avenue. The plows had been here—after all, this was where city workers lived—and mounds of snow paralleled both sides of the streets in front of neat, vinyl-clad capes and bungalows protected by enough chain-link fence to surround Guantanamo. Each house had a small front yard with a maple or an ash drooping with snow, a garage at the side or rear, and a driveway filled with combinations of cars, pickups, vans, and RVs. Kids played in the snow-banks along the curbs and snowmen were fully dressed in some yards. It wasn't exactly a Christmas card scene but it was kept up, and it *did* have promise.

We arrived ten minutes early in front of a fenced-in white bungalow with blue shutters and a jalousied screen porch between the house and garage. "Heat Wave" began and Nadie huffed and turned off the CD player. A minute of silence went by.

"Anne must have grown up here," I finally offered.

Nadie's response, after tapping the wheel impatiently for a few moments, was, "I just can't sit here!" She grabbed her bag and was quickly on the shoveled sidewalk; despite the pain of rolling myself out of the car, I was right behind her as she slipped the latch on the gate in the fence, marched up a snow cleared walk, and climbed a single step to push the doorbell. Almost simultaneously, the inner door opened and a heavyset young woman in a red ski hat, red scarf, and heavy blue-green sweater and obviously startled to see us, appeared behind an aluminum storm door.

"Ms. Sullivan?" Nadie asked loudly, taking off her sunglasses. "I'm Nadie Winokur."

The young woman used a hand to shade her eyes from the snow's brilliance. "Sorry. Can't talk to you now. Sorry," she repeated and started to close the inner door.

"But we had an appointment...," said Nadie plaintively. "I know that I'm early...."

It must have been Nadie's evident surprise and disappointment—the moral equivalent of the foot in the doorway—that caused Ms. Sullivan's hesitation because the door opened fully. She was short, five-two or five-three, and maybe twenty-five. Her headgear did nothing for her round, plain face with its widely spaced, brownish eyes, pug nose, large lips, and wide mouth. If there was even the slightest resemblance to her sister in the ID photograph—except, maybe at the mouth—I didn't see it. "I called the Women's Center to cancel. Nobody answered. I'm sorry." She started to turn away.

Nadie grabbed the storm door's handle. "Please, Ms. Sullivan, if you could just spare a few minutes...."

She stared at Nadie, then at me. I gave her what I was sure was a winning smile, forgetting that my bruised face was barely concealed by sunglasses.

"Who's he?" she said suspiciously.

"My friend Alger Temple. I had to borrow his car and he came in case I got stuck." Nadie followed her stare to my face and added, "He had a tumble in the snow last night." I continued to smile. Nadie said, "He could wait in the car."

The smile evaporated.

A mittened hand went to Ms. Sullivan's partly open mouth and her expression changed from wariness to resignation. "Look, it will have to be short. My folks are out with my uncle getting the headstone and I don't want them bothered," she said, pushing open the storm door. She glanced at me. "He might as well come in, too."

We wiped our feet on a green plastic mat adorned with a white daisy. Cardboard cartons and stacking bins of various colors and sizes, stuffed with books, shoes, DVDs, CDs, and clothing lined the hallway floor into the kitchen where a Panasonic television and an expensive looking multi-piece audio system shared a table with a computer; more clothes were draped over chairs and hung on a portable rack. Patricia Sullivan steadied herself against a wall, pulled off her boots, put them next to two blue stacking bins packed with books, and shrugged toward the kitchen. "The place is kind of a mess since we got Annie's things out of her apartment," she said evenly. "Haven't had time to deal with it but we couldn't just leave her things there," she said as she passed by me and led Nadie into a parlor. "They'd just disappear."

I followed them and in the process, my eye caught a book on the top of one bin: a copy of Carl Reinman's *T.R.*, with its dust jacket looking printer fresh. I took off my sunglasses and couldn't help but pick it up, and when I did, the book fell open to an auto-graphed flyleaf. "To Annie" was clear, and then "Carl," followed by a squiggle that could have been "Reinman"...or just a squiggle. I returned the book to the bin, felt the prickle of an idea being formed, and promptly banged the wound on my scalp into the rounded archway to the parlor.

"Oh-h-h," I complained and rubbing my hurts, entered the par-lor where Nadie, appearing chagrined at my clumsiness, asked without any real concern if I was all right. I nodded.

The parlor, small and immaculate, lacked touches of welcom-ing domesticity: no plants, books, knickknacks, or pictures on the walls. Sunlight streamed in through an open venetian blind; the lacy, white curtains framed a large bow window facing the street. The furniture consisted of a recliner and soft chair, both slipcov-ered in reddish plum, a console television in the far corner, a low mahogany coffee table with an ashtray in front of a beige sofa, and end tables holding lamps with plain white shades. A reproduction of a Virgin by Raphael and an antiqued frame mirror were on the walls. The two sepia-toned photographs on top of the television seemed out of place.

Patricia Sullivan had removed her ski hat, revealing mousy-brown hair, cut short; her tight jeans didn't flatter her heaviness. She took Nadie's coat—my jacket apparently didn't rate—and laid it on one of the chairs, then motioned us to the sofa behind the coffee table as she slumped in the chair opposite. We almost sank out of sight in the sofa's too-soft cushions; my corset hitched up and stabbed my back. Nadie started right in, explaining her work as a volunteer at the Women's Center as she removed a spiral steno pad from her bag and rummaged inside its vastness until she came up with a ballpoint pen.

"I still don't get it why you people are still interested in my sis-ter. She wasn't a student anymore...."

As her eyes strayed to me, I gave her a concerned, trustworthy look and was about to respond when Nadie, with the coffee table giving her visual cover, dug a boot heel into my ankle. Not missing a beat, she said: "Ms. Sullivan—"

"Patricia."

"...Patricia. When your sister became a client of the Women's Center last February, she listed you as the person to call in the event of any issues that might require family information or counsel. She specifically did not want your parents to be called. She apparently was under a lot of stress and apparently had some problems because...."

"That's when she *thought* she was pregnant," Patricia sniffed. "The *first* time is what you mean. I don't think so!"

Nadie's face didn't give away surprise and her silence invited further comment.

Patricia cleared her throat and raised her voice half a tone. "She...we both have had menstrual problems, irregularity, and I think she was taking Cartocean, a hormone, and it kind of screws up that time of the month. At least, it did for me. And she wasn't on the pill, or she wasn't supposed to be on it, because of the hormones. But, maybe she was. With Annie, who knows?" She glanced at me with lowered eyes, maybe a little embarrassed at the abrupt intimacy, and covered by fumbling in her jeans for a handkerchief.

Nadie sensed her hesitation. "If Mr. Temple's presence makes you uncomfortable...?"

It was my turn to find an ankle under the table.

Patricia wiped at her nose, tucked the handkerchief into her sleeve, and exhaled. "No, it's okay. I don't mind talking about Annie, not to someone like you, someone not in the family or neighborhood. Who knows, it might do me some good. Anyway," she continued, ignoring me, "if she wasn't pregnant in February, it didn't take her much time afterward."

"Is that why she didn't register this fall?"

"You care if I smoke?"

"It won't bother me," said Nadie, and I shook my head "no" even though her question hadn't been directed at me. Patricia left the room briefly and returned clutching a pack of Marlboro Lights, with a lit cigarette between her lips.

"So-o-o-o...," she said as she lowered herself into the recliner before she took a deep drag, exhaled, and waved away the smoke in front of her face. Her eyes had hardened and settled into a stare. Nadie; her face told me not to expect a peachy-sweet remembrance. "My little sister Annie. What can I say?" she began with calm emphasis, a hand cupped around the elbow of the arm which held the cigarette near her mouth. "My only sister. I had an older brother... Steve... but he died in a car crash a few years ago. She is... was... five years younger than me and I was five years younger than my brother." Her moon-face tightened. "Annie was always the darlin' one.... Could charm a nun out of her habit, and got all the good looks in the family. My folks doted on her, at least until...." She shook her head as though trying to get the story straight in her mind, to start in the right time frame, as though the memory, or how she would reflect it to us, was uncertain. "Annie was always difficult to handle, worse after Stevie was buried. As far back as junior high at St. Catherine's, then at St. X's. She got so difficult even the nuns complained, and yet my parents would do anything for her, 'cause she was so pretty and smart and that was enough. Sometime, they'd act like they would crack down but they never did. Annie always got her way. She'd turn the charm on and off..." —she snapped her fingers— "... quicker than that. She'd give them crumbs of attention...." She stopped to pull on the cigarette and appraised Nadie's reaction to her description as the smoke left her mouth. "So, what else?"

Nadie's pen, I noticed, hadn't touched her notebook. She said,

"The pregnancy. What happened?"

Patricia put her cigarette in the ashtray; when she spoke again, she was choosing her words more carefully. "All I know, she was in City Hospital for a couple of days back in early July. Told me it was an 'operation'. Wasn't that just too cute? An 'operation'. Always played with words..., almost told the truth, just to show how smart she was, just to show off. Even when she told the truth, it could be just to mislead you. Always playin' around. Didn't tell me until it was over. She never told the folks and I didn't either." At that, her face registered her exasperation. "With what she had put them through, it would have been too much."

Nadie shifted in the soft cushions of the couch, made some notes and said, with consummate gentleness, "Her counselor saw her last in early June, and the file isn't particularly clear but could she have been thinking about keeping the baby? It seems she thought she had enough money to—"

Her hands slapped her knees as though she was about ready to get up. "What's money got to do with anything?"

Oops, I thought, a sensitive topic, and there *was* something else in Anne Sullivan's file!

"Well," Nadie's voice oozed concern, "most of the Center's clients are understandably concerned about the cost of a pregnancy, especially if they are going to full term, and availability of funds. Anne was on scholarships and loans...?"

As her question hung in the air, I thought "Nadie, you are into this now!"

Patricia Sullivan reached for the cigarette and held it, watching the smoke curl upward. Slowly, an unpleasant smile framed her mouth. "I don't know about that. Sounds like Annie was puttin' her on. She'd do that kinda thing for no good reason but show. Anyway, she wasn't pregnant long." After another drag on the cigarette, she put it in the ashtray. "Okay," she said, "this will relieve you of any guilt. When spring semester was almost over, she phoned Dad that she wasn't going back to school. Didn't say she was pregnant, of course. I got two years at Community College and she's in the Ivy League...and leaving for no reason, just leaving. There was nothing for my folks to do. When Annie made up her mind, that was *it*. Dad went nuts, threw things around, cursing, knocking things over, scared my mom half to death. That's about when I decided to get out of here, 'cause I knew it was goin' to be bad, and I got an apartment over in Cranston." She leaned forward to run her fingers back and forth around the little carved spirals on the edge of the coffee table. "He couldn't believe it," she remembered, irony dripping from her voice, "...his favorite! The one we all sacrificed for, and she was shitting in our bed! Dad wouldn't let her come home, or even talk about her. She'd call Mom, and she'd call me, but I didn't see her over the summer, not until September. She lived in a dump near Carter but she had money, more than enough, some kind of job on the internet, she said. I didn't understand it, but she was making a ton of dough, saving up for a move to New York. Bought piles of clothes at the best stores in Garden City and the Mall, even went up to Boston and Chestnut Hill, sometimes New York. And stuff like her computer and the plasma television and the CD player, for when she made the move, she said...." She coughed and didn't bother to cover her mouth. "Of course, there were always guys, and by then, she was hanging around with this nigg...." She looked up quickly. "This black guy."

The "N" word was narrowly avoided and we all knew it.

"When I found out, I had to tell Dad. Despite everything, she's my sister and this guy was dangerous for Annie, the drugs and stuff like that. I thought maybe Dad could get to him. Dad went nuts... again...but before he could really do anythin', Annie told me that she had kicked him out." The eyes trained on us were now full of resentment. At whom? "You can see how she was all screwed up, leaving school, gettin' knocked up, and then she musta let this guy come back! But she was *always* doin' stuff like that! She wouldn't listen to me or anybody!"

Patricia stubbed out her cigarette in the ashtray, making that squeaky sound that to me is as annoying as chalk on a blackboard. "About three weeks ago, something was bothering her. I thought maybe it was break-ins around where she was living. Gave me her bankbook for safekeeping. Don't think she was scared, though, just not so cocky. Not like she had been." She turned her glare toward the ceiling. "Anyway, the money will help my parents cover her funeral costs."

Nadie said, "I wonder if more counseling might have helped in her situation, or caught her emotional issues earlier. She dropped out, not many do when they're on scholarships, even if they're having problems like a pregnancy, and she did call—"

Patricia interrupted by raising one hand, palm side toward Nadie. "Like I said, don't feel that you coulda done anything. Annie knew what she was doin'. She always had an angle, a fall-back. She was always calculating. Always! She...." Suddenly, as though she felt she had gone too far, she folded her fleshy arms under her breasts and motioned toward the console television. "Don't get me wrong. She's my sister. We got along. She had brains and she was pretty. You can even see it in that First Communion photo on the teevee." She gestured with an elbow. "She's on the left. Mom put it up there so my Dad could remember her like that. When she was a little girl."

Nadie and I turned to the photographs, and they must have reminded Patricia of the time because she stood up. "Look, my folks are going to be back in a few minutes and this would really upset them. Particularly Dad. I really don't want to go on, anyway. It makes me feel like I'm a whiner. We're all in this. People have been two-faced. To my parents, they'd say it was the black guy, or this Stalker, but I heard them, the old biddies and people who know better, gossiping at the wake, blamin' *her*, blamin' the victim. Yesterday was the funeral, then the FOP hall where it was more of the same, only now with a lot of loud mouth, half-in-the-bag, cops. I don't know how we got through it." Bitterness welled up in her voice and tears filled her eyes. "You just don't know what it's like. You don't know what she put us through...."

Nadie stood, grim-faced. "If you'd like to talk to me again sometime, I hope that you'll...."

Without a response, Patricia Sullivan got up, wiped at her eyes with her fingers, and handed Nadie her coat on her way to the hall. As I helped Nadie into her coat, my eyes strayed to the photographs on top of the television. Nadie followed Patricia to the hall; I walked to the television and inspected Anne's photograph. A blonde little bride for Jesus, with eyes uplifted to heaven and white rosary beads in her fingers, a prankish smile at her lips. It probably pleased the parents when taken but it seemed patently artificial to me, especially with its sepia tones and backdrop of imitation clouds looking a lot like mashed potatoes. Anne Sullivan of her sister's tale, as a little girl in a white dress, striking a pose, pretending even then.

CHAPTER TWENTY

A black Chevrolet station wagon pulled in behind as Nadie drove off. In the side mirror, I watched the car nose up to the driveway's gate and a stocky man in a baseball cap and dark windbreaker jacket got out, put his hands on his hips, and faced us. No doubt, Mr. Sullivan.

We headed back toward Broad Street. I ignored Nadie's agitated, one hand in my face, remonstrations for getting her involved with Ms. Sullivan until she made a wide turn on to a nearly empty Broad Street, completely oblivious to the huge snowplow rumbling toward us on her left. I made a grab for the steering wheel which provoked her into a brake slam that sent us into a skid and out of harm's way as the monster swung behind us on to Stanhope Street.

"What are you doing!" she screamed and whacked my forearm before regaining control.

"That plow was going to cream us!"

There was a split second of hesitation before an angry exclamation. "I saw the plow! I *saw* the plow!"

We lurched forward, heading toward the city instead of retracing our trip. Nadie was on the attack, contrasting her careful driving to my carelessness, which expanded into an analysis as to why am I such a control freak and other character flaws. I endured the verbal barrage by shrinking away and staring out of my window.

We entered *Nuevo Providence*, the Latino commercial section, jammed with tiny, brightly painted, heavily signed bodegas, hair stylists, laundromats, restaurants, bars, money-wiring offices, thrift and video stores, and liquor stores with neon "cerveza" signs and ads for Bud Lite specials in Spanish. Sidewalks were bustling and business seemed brisk; apparently, Providence's most recent wave of immigrants had easily adapted to the Rhode Island ethic of snowday. It would have been no different years earlier when the markets, variety stores, and drugstores were owned, operated, and named for Dave or Ginny or Patty, when the barber shops were operated by Joe or Louie, and the local taverns and hangouts had neon shamrocks in their windows.

Nadie braked for a traffic light, pounding the pedal at least six times, probably scaring the daylights out of the driver of the Camry behind us. Her focus had shifted from me as I caught her saying, "... the father must be an abusive lout. Her family has been put through hell. You could see that Patricia had no one to talk to through her ordeal. You could just *feel* her anguish...."

Anguish? Is that what it was? Seemed more like anger, jealousy, and sibling rivalry, but *I'm* not the psychologist.

Her analysis of the dysfunctions of the Sullivan family continued as we drove into the graffittied plywood alley that is upper Broad Street. My mind was tight as a jalopy's engine cranking over as I tried to budge some rusty deductive skills, taking in the street scenes which included one heavily bundled citizen swigging out of a paper bag as he lurched through the snow. "Ugh," I muttered, reminded that this neighborhood, prosperous within my own memory, a place of stately Victorian houses, majestic oak trees, and thriving retail activity, had fallen into dilapidation and become infamous for its curbside businesses of drugs, prostitution, and stolen goods. At least today, the snow hid the broken glass, dog turds, cigarette butts, and fast-food containers which cluttered its gutters. A few kids, a sign of life and hope, were playing, unsupervised, in a vacant lot which also held snowed-in or abandoned cars. Outside seedy bars, stragglers congregated, blowing on glove-less fingers or sucking on cigarettes: business would soon be back to normal.

I made occasional noises to indicate interest in Nadie's mono-logue as the coincidences finally ripened: *Annie*—not *Anne*—on the flyleaf! Williams had called her "Annie," as did her sister. Why would Carl Reinman? And more interestingly, why was the auto-graph from *Carl*? Or was there more? My mind buzzed with Nadie's description of Reinman as a womanizer, Joe Bucas's out-burst about Reinman's dalliance with the red-haired sophomore, and the *Carl* autograph.

We drove past the darkened Central High-Classical High com-plex, through the newly chic Weybosset Hill where art galleries and coffee shops were open and apparently busy, and two traffic lights later, the old chic DownCity arts district where a revival of *Jesus Christ Superstar* was playing at the Performing Arts Center according to its message-popping marquee. Nadie, ignoring my silence as we weaved through the downtown streets, continued her analysis of the effects of the murder on the Sullivan family, refer-ring more than once to a psychological study on police families that I bet she had dug up on her computer since this morning. I was so stuck on connecting the dots between Carl Reinman and Anne Sullivan that I was startled when Nadie parked in front of her apartment building. She unbuckled her seat belt and turned to me with eyes softer than I would have expected. Had I missed something? I fumbled with my seat belt release and she leaned over and pushed the red button on the lock which allowed the belt to retract smoothly across my body.

"Damn things," I said under my breath and reached over to pull the car keys from the ignition.

Nadie grasped my hand. "I didn't mean to sound so shrewish. Really."

I wasn't sure what she was talking about—what had I missed in her stream of consciousness—but I know an out when I hear one. "I'm sorry, too," I said.

"As far as the money is concerned, there *was* a bankbook, whatever that means..., and in case Franks *didn't* tell the police about it, you should call Tony. You did what you had to do; let someone else interpret the facts."

I nodded. It was not exactly an affirmative nod, more like an *I understand you* nod. She patted my hand as though I was being a good boy.

The slamming of the car's doors was like two rapid rifle shots, helping me to regain my bearings. She dropped the car keys in my open palm and we went upstairs. She suggested cocoa and moved a kettle to a two-unit electric range, while I went into the bathroom, uncinched the corset, and stretched, hoping to relieve the strain that had been aggravated by the sofa and the car seat. I realized that she was on the phone to the Women's Center when she called out to me that she'd have to be available for counseling on Saturday night: the volunteer staff was needed before and after Kingdom's rally.

"You've got to be kidding!" I struggled into my pants and waddled into the kitchen. "Saturday night? With The Stalker out there? Can't be!" She had already disconnected and blithely confirmed that Kingdom's rally had been rescheduled for Saturday night! But not on The Green. Inside the Sports Complex!

Tuttle was in his office when I called. "It's a goddamn media circus. All three local stations, plus Boston stations, and reporters from all over the place. We've had inquiries from the *Times*, the *Globe*, *Newsweek*, *U.S. News*..., you name it. Came down from College Hall this morning. Nobody asked me! When they're through, they're all going to march over to The Green. It's going to be a security nightmare! After what happened yesterday? Are they kidding? The deal is that he comes without his..., his...," he struggled for a word that was more neutral than troublemakers, "...people. *Sure*, he will. And they won't be outside, waiting for him? Then, after The Green, maybe more marches! And the organizers won't tell us where! And they want security—?"

"Whoa," I interjected, trying not to reveal my own chagrin about not being in the loop for this important and totally bizarre decision.

Tuttle continued. "Too many variables. Especially if Kingdom gets the kids riled up. And that march will be a perfect setup for The Stalker. Perfect! What an opportunity! I told Gregson and the Provost...."

Nadie deposited a mug of steaming cocoa on the counter and I let it cool. Tuttle was right. It was a crazy idea. *What* was Danby doing? Tuttle went on as to how he was trying to work his way through the security mess, how he had managed to cash in some chits with the Traffic Division and the Patrol Division for help. We also had a deal for off-duty security cops from RISD, Providence College, and Johnson & Wales to work the streets between the Sports Complex and The Green. Actually, he admitted, with the rally *inside* the Sports Complex, they could probably control admissions if Kingdom cooperated. But once outside, fired up by Jesse Kingdom, the opportunities for mischief and for The Stalker picking somebody off were off the chart.

I tried to encourage him before I hung up. I drank the cocoa and became even more annoyed that I hadn't been consulted. Maybe I was wrong about Danby's growing confidence in me.

The rush of shower water from the bathroom finally got through to me. Nadie takes a lot of showers, as though she can clean away whatever troubles her at the moment. The bathroom door opened a crack and Nadie's eyes held an invitation.

I was in such dudgeon that I almost passed. Almost.

My bruises got her appropriate attention while the needles of hot water on my skin and scalp did little to distract me from her body. We started fooling around, barely dried off, and made love. Our lovemaking played out in silence, and was an opiate for my aches and pains. It came on so quickly that for once, the shade in the bedroom's single window wasn't lowered before we clung to one another; the late afternoon light made her skin luminescent and smooth like an abalone shell. Afterward, I slept. It must have been more than a catnap because when I awoke, the light passing through the window had become faint. Nadie, wearing a green silk kimono I had given her last Christmas, was sitting in the room's only chair, under a lamp, reading a novel by Anita Shreve.

"How is it?" I said, startling her.

"It's murky, different than her others," she replied, and went back to the book. I slowly became conscious of the aroma of nail polish, an odor I really dislike, and saw that her toenails were now a bright plum-purple color. I made sniffy noises of displeasure and she put the book down and came over to me, smiling, exuding a fragrance that covered the lingering trace of acetone. She leaned forward and kissed me on the ear, and I reached within the kimono to caress a breast. Her skin was warm and her fathomless eyes reminded me of those of the Afghan girl on the famous *National Geographic* cover. She responded by lying down next to me. I put an arm around her and she snuggled close. Then, Reinman and *Annie* Sullivan managed to crowd my composure. Could the randy Reinman and Annie have been lovers?

"This is going to sound ridiculous, but I want you to hear me out." I hesitated a moment. "Joe Bucas..."—Nadie sat up—"...I ran into him at the Faculty Club yesterday. Detested Carl Reinman. Said that he suspected Reinman of having affairs with students. Then, there's what you said the other night about Reinman, how he seemed to be on the prowl all the time. And

Anne Sullivan, her personality, how she lived, the money, her pregnancy…, or pregnancies….” Nadie moved to the edge of the bed; her fingers played with her purple-tipped toes. “In the hallway at the Sullivan house today. Remember the bins full of books that Patricia Sullivan said she took from her sister’s apartment? On top of one was a copy of Reinman’s biography of Teddy Roosevelt. He autographed it to *Annie* Sullivan. Not *Anne* Sullivan, but *Annie* Sullivan. That’s what both Williams and Patricia called her. From *Carl*—not *Carl Reinman*, at least I think so. It seems so damn personal! Now this may sound nuts, but suppose Anne Sullivan got involved with Reinman, she gets pregnant, and she blackmails him. He would have been vulnerable. He was Mister Morals. And he certainly had enough money to pay her—”

Nadie slapped the covers of the bed, stood up and wrapped the kimono around her as though suddenly chilled. “I can’t believe it,” she said with real amazement in her voice.

“Look,” I said defensively, “consider the possibility. If Reinman was being blackmailed, it doesn’t mean he killed her. I’m not saying that. But it would explain the money….”

“Wait a second! Just wait a second! I thought this was all about justice. So that Williams doesn’t get railroaded or lynched because he’s black! That’s why you didn’t have him arrested for assault! Remember? That’s why I agreed to see her sister. So you could confirm the money angle, to cast doubt, so the police would investigate. You’re not trying to solve a murder!”

I didn’t have a response. She had me. Somewhere, somehow, I had crossed over a threshold without realizing it. Did I really care about Williams’s rights? I had been concocting a blackmail scheme from innuendo and gossip. Dross! Worse, I was targeting someone whose reputation and property I had a legal duty to protect! Well, maybe not quite yet, since the probate court had certainly closed today along with the rest of municipal government.

Nadie got off the bed and took a small wooden box from the middle drawer of her bureau, opened it up, and took out a joint. I sat up at the sound of the match. "I thought you were through with that."

"I am. But I just *feel* like one right now," she said fiercely. She inhaled deeply, then let the smoke slowly leave her nose. There had been a silent truce on the pot issue for months: Nadie was for its legalization and I wasn't. She came back to the bed, bringing the box with her, and lay down after plumping the pillows. "Now, where were we?" she said calmly, her eyes scrunched almost closed. "Forget the moralizing. Let's be very honest here. You have somehow convinced yourself that a drug dealing punk that you were inveigled into protecting, who later *attacks* you, is not a murderer. Why? Because he said so. You find out from his lawyer, now verified by Williams himself and by the victim's sister, that she had some money, actually alot of money, some in a bank account. The victim had also been pregnant but had an abortion. Preliminary conclusion, blackmail. Maybe if the cops follow the money, they have to lay off Williams. Okay so far?"

Acrid smoke curled towards the ceiling. I didn't reply.

"Then, a busybody like Bucas tells you that he thought Carl Reinman was fooling around with young women years ago." She stopped for a drag and again exhaled slowly. "And, from me, you heard that he made a pass at me, also years ago. Well, Dick Tracy, what then? It so happens the victim owned an autographed copy of a bestseller by Reinman who taught at the university she attended. He didn't write out his entire name! Gol-ly! He used her nickname! The same name everyone else used! Can you believe it?" she said in mock amazement.

I didn't like where this was heading.

"Now, *if* Reinman had impregnated her and was unwilling to keep paying blackmail, he'd have a classic motive for murder." She paused for another drag and I remembered something from a

Dorothy L. Sayers mystery, Lord Peter Wimsey and Harriet Vane airily discussing the universal motives for murder: passion, revenge, money, and blackmail. One or two out of four, I thought. "One tiny problem," Nadie continued. "Even if... through some unbelievable mischance... you are right about the blackmail and money, Reinman was at death's door! Barely able to get out of bed, by all accounts. Needed a heart transplant. And, he died the same night she was killed! He had the perfect alibi. *He was dying..., or dead!*"

I opened my mouth and she warned, "Don't you dare say 'Ugh!'"

Ugh! She was right. Getting high, but still right! When I didn't respond, she knew she had me. "This isn't one of your crime thrillers and you're no Spenser! You aren't even Miss Marple! You've got to stop interfering. Does anyone want Alger Temple investigating their lives? I don't *think* so! You have no God-given right to do it... and no obligation, either. You've interfered with the Sullivan family already—now you want a go at the Reinman family, too?" She glared at me. "Aren't you his executor?"

Turn the thumb screw tighter, Nadie, so when it's released, I'll feel better.

The pot smoke hung over the bed like a canopy and that didn't help my growing crankiness. It galled me how she had quickly and thoroughly destroyed my crime scenario. I knew Reinman was a walking skeleton. How could he have taken on Annie Sullivan? Anyway, as Nadie reminded me, he was probably dead when she was murdered. What the hell was I thinking? I turned over, lay on the opposite side of the bed, and brooded.

She didn't let up. "Now, what about me? What am I supposed to do? I took Civics, didn't you? Maybe they didn't teach that at Moses Brown Academy but at Benjamin Cardozo Junior High, they did. *I know* you're supposed to give any evidence you have in a criminal investigation to the police, and not wait for somebody else to trip over it or volunteer it. Maybe Franks spilled the beans but maybe not. You've got to talk to Tony about the money and abortion and be done with it!"

I remained silent and, eventually, she went into the bathroom and I heard the toilet flush. End of the pot. She came back into the bedroom and announced, "I'm due at the Center at six o'clock. I'll be there for at least a couple of hours."

I dressed; she sat on the bed and watched me. "I'll call you in the morning," I said as I left the bedroom. She didn't reply.

I didn't drive directly home; instead, I parked across from the tenement on Veasey Street. The plowed portion of the pavement glistened like oil in the streetlight. Without meaning to, I visualized Reinman's shuffling approach to the apartment last Friday night, his slow ascent up the stairs, the moment of conflict... and then, nothing! Something in that part of my brain that doesn't necessarily respond to direct logical inquiry begged for recognition. Something I could not shake off.

CHAPTER TWENTY-ONE

T he key.

It lay in a pile of pocket debris on my work table. I picked up the string that ran through the ringhole; the shiny brass threw reflections on the walls as it slowly revolved. I didn't immediately recollect what the key locked, and then it clicked: Eustace Pine, the key to Reinman's office. It took a few more seconds to realize what I had twirling before me. Want to know what someone with a private office has been up to? What the family needn't know? Safe and far away from prying eyes? Search the office!

The key dropped into my fist. "Great," I said half-aloud, how the hell was I going to get into Ramsden Hall on a Friday night?

I used my worktable phone. Tuttle, fortunately, was still at the Security Office. Before I could request his assistance, he was into a litany of complaints about Kingdom's rally. The Black Student Caucus, the dorm administration people, even the fraternities claimed that they'll be watching out for black women on Saturday night. "S-u-re" was his reaction. "Off-campus people, a couple of thousand if you count the grad students, half of them women and lots of them minorities, what about them? The Stalker has broken in at least twice!" My lack of response eventually registered. "So?"

"I have to get into Ramsden tonight. I'm the executor of Professor Reinman's estate and I need to...."

"Tonight?" His tone implied *'What's this got to do with the rally? With The Stalker?'*

I lied. "It's a probate matter. An inventory has to get done by Monday. I'm free tonight, and who knows what will happen tomorrow."

That seemed to satisfy him. "Yeah, everything's in flux. I suppose you'll want to be there..., at the rally, I mean." I almost responded that it wasn't *my* problem when he added, "If you want to, you could watch it here on the campus interconnect. I gotta be at the Complex. This is still our center for response and you could get over to the Complex or The Green fast enough."

"Thanks." Did my assent betray my impatience? "How about Ramsden tonight?"

"Oh, sure. Sorry. What time? I'll have somebody meet you there."

I checked my watch. "What about seven? Can I let myself out?"

"You'll need the security code, and there's a deadbolt lock, so you'll need a key when you leave. You'll have to drop the key back here."

"This will save me a lot of time."

"No problem."

○ ○ ○

Ramsden Hall is on the easterly side of the main campus, close to the Wheeler School, near the corner of Angell and Hope, and it took only a few minutes to navigate the Range Rover through the slick streets and enter a well-plowed and empty parking lot. The night was moonless, with a low cloud cover, and the drop in temperature penetrated my leather jacket. A damp wind, heavy and ominous, blew off hardpacked snow mounds and whipped around me as I approached the two-story, granite-faced building with Gothic embellishments, narrow windows of intricately leaded glass, and cathedral-like arches. The snow had been cleared from the four stone steps that led to its vaulted doorway. The promised security officer had not yet arrived.

The few minutes of waiting in the cold gave me ample time to examine my motives and feel the guilt of being downright sneaky. I was there because my ego had been bruised by Nadie and what I sought, a further thread of contact between Carl Reinman and Annie Sullivan, was to prove to Nadie, if to no one else, that Carl Reinman had been Annie Sullivan's lover. Ignobly, I was using my executorship as my excuse to search his office. Suppose it had been me who had popped off? How would *I* like strangers rummaging through my office desk and twenty years of odds and ends that had accumulated there?

Out of the gloom, a uniformed security officer approached me. As he climbed the steps, I recognized him as one of Tuttle's senior people, a sergeant by the name of Ewell. He scrutinized me, took a step closer to check my face shadowed by the brim of the fedora, said "Evenin', Mr. Temple," and used a key from a jingling ring on his belt. He pulled open the heavy door, entered, and punched in numbers on the alarm box located on an inside wall. I followed him inside as lights went on in the reception area and hallway.

"Now, when you leave," he said, pointing at the alarm box, "hit eight, eight, one, zero. Then," he added as he unhooked a clasp on the ring, picked off a key, and handed it to me, "use the key." His tone indicated that this numerical sequence and mechanical action might be beyond my ken.

"Eight, eight, one, zero," I repeated. "Got it," and took the key without showing any smugness.

"We'll check the building again around nine-thirty. If you're still here, the guard will wonder what's up, so you probably should call in to Security just to let them know it's you."

"Thanks," I said, and he left without another word.

An office directory, on the wall above the mail cubbies near the reception desk listed Reinman's office as Room 113. It was at the rear of the building, down the hallway and in an ell off to the right. Unlike the doors I had passed, Reinman's was not covered by clippings from the comic pages, editorial cartoons, tacked-up bumper stickers or other political and social commentary. The key turned easily in the lock and the office door swung open silently. I groped inside for a switch and, when it was found, I was impressed.

The office had to be twice as large as my own, furnished with comfortable looking chairs, a glass table with an arrangement of silk flowers, a handsome light wood desk and credenza, and a sleek Herman Miller Aeron chair. The carpet was grayish-green, with a dense cut pile that didn't shout "office". On a worktable by a window overlooking the parking lot sat a powerful-looking Hewlett-Packard computer and a fax machine and printer, with a shredder on the floor nearby. The wall by the door was lined with bookshelves; the far wall was filled by a glossy entertainment center holding a television monitor that reflected slices of light within the room and an audio system and DVD player. A flashy circle of awards and diplomas covered the wall behind the desk; by the door, Theodore Roosevelt grinned down from a vintage campaign poster, his pince-nez on his nose, his hand raised in challenge, his teeth bared, exuding vigor and drive. "The strenuous life," I remembered. The overall neatness of the office was marred by a jumble of cardboard boxes of various sizes near the desk.

I sat in Reinman's ergonomic chair. Damn comfortable! I recently had bought one at the Design Within Reach store in DownCity for my worktable at home. I unzipped my jacket; the fedora was pushed back with my index finger, a gesture straight out of a B movie. Okay, shamus, where to begin?

The desktop was bare except for a halogen lamp, which I snapped on, and a black blotter. I swung around to the credenza which held a multi-buttoned telephone console and a cluster of framed photographs. Reinman with President Reagan, maybe in the Oval Office, took pride of place, while others showed Reinman in black tie, one with the first President Bush, another with Henry Kissinger, and still another with Larry King. In the middle of the pack was a slightly faded studio photograph of a young Carl Reinman and a fresh-faced woman of twenty-five or so. I picked it up—it took me a moment to recognize Deborah Reinman—and was struck by the incongruity of their pairing, the pretty, but not overly so, girl with her handsome husband. What had brought them together? Reinman, I had learned, wasn't the type to cherish a woman for her personality.

I replaced the photograph and attacked the desk drawers. The top one was empty, as was the deep drawer on the desk's left pedestal. The drawer on the right side, however, was crammed with Merrill Lynch account statements addressed to the office, each wad a year's worth, held together by a thick rubber band. For this year, the statement for January was on top of the wad; the slimmest of all, for May and dated June 15, was at the bottom. Where was June? That had to be when Deborah Reinman took over the family's financial affairs.

For reference, I started with the January statement. It was comprised of eight or nine computer-printed pages. The first few listing stocks, bonds, and other investments totaling well over a million, investment transactions during the month, and a flow of deposits close to twenty thousand in total from the University, a variety of publishers, Fox News, and what could have been the producers of television news shows; the last page covering debits to the account, including a transfer to Deborah Reinman for six thousand and other payments that appeared to be routine. I put January aside and checked the subsequent months for consistency; except for federal and state tax payments in April, each statement showed virtually the same credits to the account and similar payees. Nothing was out of place until the next to last transaction in May. On May twenty-seven, a ten thousand dollar debit to cash!

My breath caught. I thumbed through the statements for prior months and exhaled loudly. A single cash entry in all that time! And not for chump change! Franks said the first deposit entry in Annie's bankbook was early June. Ten grand! Slow down, boy. Reinman could have used the cash for something normal and everyday; it didn't necessarily have anything to do with the money that ended up with Annie Sullivan. You need a lot more to make a case. I reassembled the statements, snapped the rubber band around them, and put them back in the drawer, except for the one for May. That went into my jacket pocket.

The carton nearest the desk caught my eye. Ah, that's why the desktop was clear and the drawers empty: their contents had been dumped into the cartons. Maybe Pine's paralegal had gotten here after all. I pulled the closest one toward me and found it contained memo pads, a pen set, pencil holder, letter openers, an address book, glass paperweights, and a stamp box resting on a bed of rubber bands, paper clips, business cards, caps from discarded ball-point pens, and similar desk drawer cheese. The address book was a thin, expensive-looking one, with the gold initials *CRR* embossed on its worn black leather cover. Definitely, Reinman was pre-Palm Pilot and it led my now overheated imagination to its identification as a proverbial "little black book." I ran a finger down its alphabetical, cut away pages, to "S."

There were three pages of names, some scribbled while others were printed neatly, with telephone numbers, some crossed out and restated. No Sullivan. Ugh! Disappointed, I was about to toss it back when my eyes focused on the name "Samantha." A first name! I went to "A." Again, lots of names on the pages, mostly scribbled, and bingo! "Annie," and two local telephone numbers! I stared at the printed name for a few seconds.

Annie!

I turned to the credenza, reached for the telephone, punched in the second listed number, and waited, thinking that if an Annie answered, I was dead wrong. A recorded message told me the number was no longer in service. Ugh! I tried the first number, and after four rings, a young woman's voice said, "Hi, Jason, Joanne's waiting downstairs." She was chewing something, and music throbbed in the background.

I paused. In which dorm did Tuttle say she lived last year? "Is this Johnson Hall?" I said uncertainly.

"Yeah, who do you want?" The voice had cooled.

"Well, I'm trying to find someone who lived there last year and...."

"Last year? Who's that?" Now, she was suspicious.

"Someone who lived on the floor last year," I repeated numbly.

"Look, I wasn't here then. You'll have to call back," she said and hung up.

I put the receiver back on the console, turned away from the desk, and raised my arms in a *hoo-rah!* Vindicated! I wondered about the first number I tried but who needed that? Johnson Hall in Reinman's address book under *Annie* was enough for me. As the precious little book joined the Merrill Lynch statement in my jacket pocket, my gaze fell on the lineup of photographs on the credenza. Reinman, the defender of America's public virtue and family values, the relentless critic of the permissive liberals, had been rutting with undergraduates, getting one pregnant and then paying for her abortion and silence!

I returned to my task. Okay, I had enough to give me credence with Nadie. What else? Forget the computer since without his password, it was a dead end and there was neither a personal journal nor a pocket calendar among his effects. Realizing I didn't have the time to check everywhere, I decided to concentrate on the remaining cartons and I moved to squat next to one which was filled with thick manila folders of resumés, book offerings, departmental meeting notices, and schedules. Nothing there. The next carton contained two extra-large ring binders, one, with its cover emblazoned with the name of T.R.'s publisher, held plastic protected reviews of T.R. from *Time, Newsweek*, the *Sunday Times*, bestseller lists, and so on, and related news clippings recounting President Reagan's interest. The other, more randomly put together, held reviews of T.R. from *Modern History, Journal of American History, American Historical Review*, and other academic journals. A pattern emerged as I flipped through the second binder and sampled the reviews. Upon publication, T.R. merited favorable scholastic reviews, praise from colleagues that ran along the line of "an important biography", "rich with insights", and "a witty, accessible account of a complex man." After the presidential endorsement and the notoriety of Reinman's political conversion, an academic reaction clearly set in, with letters and notes in the same journals reflecting anger and skepticism as to Reinman's sharp turn to the right. Why did Reinman keep this stuff? To remind him why he had such contempt for his peers?

The largest carton was packed with dated folders from a news clipping service, mostly xerox copies of magazine articles and newspaper op-ed pieces written by Reinman, some fairly recently. Hard to believe that he wrote so much for the popular media, and..., then, I remembered the magazines in Annie Sullivan's apartment. Could they have contained some of these articles? Is that why they were so varied? What a damn shame I had let them be carted away to the Central Landfill!

"Ugh!"

I shuffled folders to put them back into the carton and something made out of thick paper stock to fall on to my lap. A greeting card. On its front was a squiggly cartoon of a little girl, with a pug nose, long Mary Jane curls, doleful eyes, and downturned mouth, sitting on the floor with a banana peel behind her. I opened the card. The tag line was, "I slipped up. Sorry!" There was a caret after the *I* and the hand-printed words "might have" inserted. Below that, also hand-printed, was "Need to see you" and under that, an "A" in cursive. I fingered the card for a moment, trying to put its message into context and searched the carton for its envelope without success. My mind raced with the prospect that Annie was "A." How had she "slipped up"?

The greeting card went with the rest of my cache and I tackled the last carton. Unlike the others, which were standard packing cartons, this one had once held Sterling Vineyard Merlot and was empty except for a single manila folder. Inside was a pamphlet with a smudged yellow-gold cover. It read: "Information for Patients: Your Vasectomy." The name of a well-known East Side urologist was printed below the title. Tucked into the middle of the pamphlet were two folded pink receipts from the doctor's office. The first one I opened was for a sperm test in May of this year. The other receipt was worn and faded, made out to Carl Reinman for the surgery, and dated almost twenty years ago!

CHAPTER TWENTY-TWO

he voice mail had two impatient demands from Tramonti for return calls and a curt message from Nadie saying she'd call tomorrow.

I stripped, filled the tub, and eased myself into hot sudsy water scented with a capful of sandalwood bath oil that Nadie keeps in a basket hanging between the hot and cold faucets. I let the heat penetrate and closed my eyes. After a few quiet minutes, I didn't feel quite as foolish as I had on the drive back through a daunting rain from Ramsden Hall. Reinman's inability to father a child demolished my theory of the abortion hush money. He couldn't have impregnated her. Probably was retested to make sure. So how could Annie hold something else over him? Was he, vasectomy or not, the cash cow? Who knows. Hey, at least with the address book, I could show Nadie that he was more than a book autograph to Annie.

That last thought salvaged my ego. But how to tell Nadie without being accused of being a voyeur—which I was.

"Ugh," I said aloud. One thing for sure was that Williams was on his own. It was beyond me. A sleuth needs ingenuity, patience, an investigative routine, and time. All I had was serendipity. Williams had Franks to out-maneuver and overpower the prosecution. I would make sure Tramonti knew about the bankbook and the abortion tomorrow morning and that would be that. My tilting at windmills would stop. Anyway, who was I to complain about the lack of justice in this world?

Having made the decision, I soaked up heat and felt better than

I had at any time since Monday's meeting with Reverend Thomas. After another shot of hot water and a few more minutes of soaking, I climbed out of the tub, toweled off, rubbed in more BenGay, dressed the cuts and scrapes again with Neosporin, donned pajamas and a red silk robe, and got comfortable for an hour or so of television before bed, only to be interrupted by the ring of the front doorbell. Must be Tramonti, I thought; he'd be bound and determined to get to me. I started to think of excuses for not returning his calls as I walked downstairs and snapped on the hall and outside lights.

Bill Tuttle stood on the other side of the storm door next to another man, shorter and wider than Tuttle, with sparse ginger hair and hands in the pockets of a dark blue windbreaker with a faded yellow logo that I couldn't quite make out. Tuttle, in a dress shirt and tie under a dark brown raincoat and holding a furled umbrella, barely greeted me as he entered; his burly companion, wet shoulders hunched forward and eyes searching his shoes, silently followed.

One look at Tuttle's face and I knew he was on a mission. "This here is Terrence Sullivan. He'd like a word with you. Asked me along." The other man's beefy, glistening face angled up at me, his eyes startling me with their anger. I extended my hand but his didn't move from the windbreaker.

I ignored the obvious insult, took the umbrella and placed it in the hall stand, and led them into the living room where, as I put on table lights, they took in the room's formality and the generous space that permitted it. In the awkward silence, I gestured to a seating arrangement of a roll arm sofa, chairs, and table, and they chose opposite ends of the sofa as I took one of the wing chairs across from them. I thought about igniting the gas fire but decided that coziness wasn't likely at the top of their agenda. Tuttle removed his raincoat and placed it in his lap; Sullivan, who kept his windbreaker zipped up tight—the yellow blob turned out to be a faded Fraternal Order of Police logo—sniffed at the room, radiating resentment. By now, I was acutely conscious of my foppish attire, my facial bruises, and the clashing scents of BenGay and sandalwood. Fortunately, neither of my guests seemed interested.

"Terry would—" began Tuttle.

"I can speak my own piece." His voice was strained; his eyes stared at me above half-moons of purple. "You came to my home today." He hunched forward, waiting for me to respond, and the smells of whiskey and damp clothing reached me. "You came with some cock-'n'-bull story and scared my daughter half to death. I'm tellin' you to your face," he said, with his chin jutting out and his hands leaving his pockets to become fists on his unpressed khaki trousers. "You got no call to butt in, to bother my family. Especially now." His eyes darted around the room. "Who d'you think you are? What gives you the right to—"

Tuttle quickly placed a hand across Sullivan's fists. "Hold on, Terry. You're bein' insulting. You don't give a man a chance to explain." He gave me a pained look.

"Alright, explain," Sullivan said snidely and sat back, folding his arms across his paunch.

I remained silent as I looked him over. Maybe fifty-five, pugnacious, rude, in need of a shave, double chinned, with the skin of a boozer with high blood pressure. Purplish swiggles webbed a reddish nose. Then, I remembered that yesterday, he had buried his daughter.

"First, my condolences to you and your family. I want to assure you there was nothing sinister or inappropriate about my colleague's interview, Mr. Sullivan." His face told me I was a liar; that unsettled me and involuntarily my voice slipped into that dry preciseness that would play to Sullivan's expectations. "I simply provided transportation, an... accommodation to Ms. Winokur from the Women's Center because of the snow. I was invited inside by your daughter. I didn't say more than a word or two. My understanding is that Ms. Winokur was inquiring as to whether the University or the Women's Center might have helped your daughter when she didn't return for this semester—"

Sullivan shook off Tuttle's restraint and threw up his hands in dramatic disbelief. "Will ya' listen to this guy! He's been mucking around in this since it began—even arranged for Williams to get a meet with the Commissioner—and now he wants me to believe he's only *helping* out somebody who's on some sort of stupid project. An *ac-com-mo-dation*...," he drew out the word, "*ac-com-mo-dation*, mind ya. What a bunch of bullshit!" He glared at me. "What is it with you? What kind of game are you playing?"

"No game."

"Well, I'm having none of it." Sullivan stood up. "Let's go. I said my piece. And he's got no answer."

Tuttle remained seated. His face had the unsettled look of someone disappointed in himself or maybe his colleague. "Bill," I said in a level tone, "if Mr. Sullivan is prepared to listen, I'll be glad to talk. But if he intends to be offensive, then—"

Sullivan made an awkward grab for my robe. Missing by six inches, he went crashing forward, clearing the table of its family photographs, to lay across it floundering like a beached seal. Tuttle bolted up, seized Sullivan at the waist, heaved him back on to the sofa, and roughly braced his shoulders against its cushions. The lout's fall seemed to knock both the breath and the fight out of him; sweat broke out on his forehead. As I picked up the photographs and put them on the seat of the other chair, Tuttle's face flooded with embarrassment. He needed support so I said, "Maybe a drink might do us some good."

"I won't say no," said Tuttle quickly. Sullivan looked up, his face sullen and pale, and nodded. Tuttle looked murderously at his charge and muttered, "Hair of the dog."

I left them and went to the drinks cabinet in the dining room, returned with a bottle of Macallan and three glasses, and poured a good measure in each. I hoped the ritual of alcohol would get us settled. Tuttle took a glass and handed it to Sullivan who, slumping further into the sofa, his stringy hair falling into his face, swallowed greedily and wiped his mouth with the back of his hand like he had downed a beer instead of some of my best Scotch. Tuttle, obviously pained, glared. "I've known Terry for twenty years. There's blather but no harm in him. Been a tough day. This sort of thing can affect even a good man."

Sullivan raised his hand dismissively, eyed me with a sidelong glance, and unzipped his jacket, revealing a red plaid shirt. Sweat now beaded his face.

"Did ya' know my Annie?" His voice had lost none of its surliness.

"No, I didn't know her."

"Why get into this, then?"

I took a deep breath. By now, I could summarize the story in twenty seconds or less. "I was asked by the minister at Lavelle Williams's mother's church to escort him to the station where Williams was to be questioned about his relationship with your daughter. As I'm sure you know, it didn't work out that way. Then, Williams picked my garage to hide during the snowstorm when he found out you..., the police..., were going to bring him in again." There was no need to mention Williams' assault on me. "When I found him, I called his lawyer who brought him in."

"And that's why you go to my house? Ask all those questions?"

"I didn't ask any questions. I told you—"

Tuttle intervened. "You heard the man, Terry. He was with his friend from the Women's Center. Your daughter wasn't forced to say anything. She volunteered. She let them in. You know that."

Sullivan finished the Scotch and played with the empty glass in his hands. His face was now sickly pale; the sweat beads had broken and streaked his face. "Fool of a girl, lettin' perfect strangers in the house," he grumbled.

"So, what was the harm?" Tuttle asked.

Sullivan glared at me and shook his head. "I dunno. Sounds very peculiar to have you doing all this." Then, the meanness on his face slowly formed into a sneer, a look that seemed habitual. "People like you—"

"Terry...." Tuttle's rising voice carried a warning. He took the glass from Sullivan's hand. "We're going."

Sullivan remained defiant. "Well, I know enough to see that all this doesn't wash. He...," he gestured towards me with a shrug of his shoulder, "...his kind never helped our kind. They used us in the shops for generations and then threw us away. There's something in this for him. Something—"

I said evenly, "And what's in it for you?"

"Eh?" Sullivan snapped.

"How much did Annie have in the bank?"

His eyes ballooned. He leaned forward, put both hands flat on the table, and his whiskey breath poured out at me. "What—?"

"Her bank account!"

His eyes became slits. He started to get up but his legs were like rubber and he fell back on to the sofa.

"What bank account?" Tuttle asked both of us.

Sullivan shrugged. "Forget it. Let's go," and he struggled to gain his feet, using the arm of the sofa for leverage.

"What bank account!" Tuttle demanded.

Sullivan's face was suddenly the color of rotten melon; the stubble of his beard glistened in sweat. "Geez," he said, eyes rolling upward, "I think I'm gonna puke."

We got him into the lavette just in time and stood in the hall through an eruption of gagging noises and coughs. Tuttle's face had become hard. I asked him, "You've followed all this. What do the police know about his daughter's bank account? With maybe twenty grand in it? Monthly deposits?"

"I've heard nothing about it."

"Or that she'd had an abortion?"

That stopped him cold. "No, not that. They might have found it in the autopsy..., but I don't know. They'd likely not tell me, with her being Sullivan's kid...." He was thoughtful for a moment, then set his jaw and eyed me suspiciously. "How'd you know about all this?"

My reply was interrupted by the whoosh of a toilet flush, guttural phlegm clearing, and water splashing in the sink. Sullivan appeared, white-faced, hair matted, reeking of vomit, holding the windbreaker, while hanging on to the lavette doorknob for support; his plaid shirt, barely covering his belly, showed his undershirt between lower buttons. "Sorry," he muttered, without meaning it.

Tuttle's eyes drilled him. "The bank account, Terry. C'mon, let's have it!"

"Whaddabout it?" Sullivan responded.

"Which bank?"

"Citizens."

"Where did the money come from?"

He was keeping his head down, hiding his face. "I dunno. Pattie had the book."

"C'mon—"

"I tell ya, I dunno!"

"How much?"

Reluctantly, still hiding his face, he sighed. "Near to twenty thousand...."

"Twenty thousand! Did you tell anybody downtown?"

He pushed his way by us into the living room and turned to

defend himself. The room's eggplant green walls emphasized his face's sallowness. "Christ, don't you understand?" His shoulders sagged. "It's... it's owed to us. It's blood money. Blood money!" His voice pleaded even as his eyes showed cunning. "All we got is the funeral bills. We need it. It's ours." He dropped the windbreaker on the sofa and found a dirty handkerchief in a back pocket which he used to wipe his face. "If the AG got it, we wouldn't have the money for months. It'd get impounded, just when we need it. Do you know what a funeral costs these days? I got a lawyer who prepared some kind of affidavit and Ginnie brought it down to the bank this morning and cashed it in. It's barely enough to pay all the bills."

Tuttle walked past me into the living room, picked up the windbreaker, and thrust it at him. "When did Pattie get the book?" he said sternly. He turned to look at me, embarrassed. "Why?"

Sullivan looked around the room, and when he faced Tuttle, a lie flickered in his face. "A couple of weeks ago. Annie gave it to her for safekeeping. She must have been afraid... of something...," he hesitated but said it anyway, "... like that piece a shit that was botherin' her." He turned to me. "I gotta sit down. My head is killing me," he said and sat on the arm of the sofa. "I was gonna say something to the Chief about it, ya know. But with the wake and funeral and everything happening, I just didn't get the chance."

Tuttle replied icily, "They got to know—"

"I was goin' to give them the canceled book. When I went back on Monday. That's all they need, right? I'll talk to McCarthy first thing. He'll understand."

"You see McCarthy tomorrow with that bankbook and if you know anything about when she got the money, you'd better tell him straight. I'll check myself tomorrow." Tuttle's face betrayed disgust. "And maybe you'd better apologize to Mr. Temple before we go."

Apologize? You gotta be kiddin', his eyes responded, but apparently realizing he didn't need another problem, he murmured, "Sure, it was the drink, Mr. Temple. It's been hard on me and Ginnie, last couple days..., real hard. With me on the force and people asking about it all the time, the autopsy, the wake, then the funeral, and this thing about you comin' to the house, talkin' to Pattie...." He sucked in a heavy breath. "I've been drinkin' too much," he said in a voice that quivered as tears came on cue. "Annie was so smart. Coulda gone to PC, URI, or some other place, but she wanted to go to Carter. We let her. If she hadn't done that, she'd still be with us." He wiped his face with a sleeve. "If she'd only gone someplace else, like we wanted her to—" and he put his face in his hands, his shoulders shaking with sobs.

His audience recognized this was theater. Tuttle shook his head and said in a tired voice, "That's it then, Terry. Let's go." He helped Sullivan get his arms into the windbreaker and pushed him out to the hall. "I'll call if there's a problem," Tuttle said to me, and guided his charge out the front door into the rain.

When I closed the door behind them, I leaned against it. Ironically, Nadie's well described "lout" would tell McCarthy about the bankbook, and Tuttle would check into the abortion. I was off her Benjamin Cardozo Junior High moral hook. I went back into the living room and sat on the sofa to finish my Scotch, wondering if I should tell Nadie that Sullivan had been here to complain about her interview. No, she would react as though it was all my doing. And, my mind started to work again on who killed Annie Sullivan.

Saturday

My eyes darted around in the darkness. I had awakened with a start after a no-REM night of restlessness. Annoying questions crowded my mind, like hooded shadows, fast moving and vague. My cache of evidence was ridiculously trivial. I had been a snoop, a voyeur, trying to show Nadie how smart I was, smarter than her, smarter than the cops. Did I owe Reinman something? His family? His reputation? He had trusted me for some reason. Or had it been the whim of a thoughtless egotist?

I turned on to a side and a stab of pain reminded me of Williams. A drug dealing punk. He assaulted me! Couldn't I remember that? Annie Sullivan. She'd brought a bag of tricks with her to Carter. Her sister and father were a pair, too. So what if Reinman had been her lover; he couldn't impregnate her. And in his condition, he couldn't have killed her. Nadie had nailed that. Or had she?

Another spasm shot up my spine and I grabbed my pillow and bunched it up behind my head. Why am I going on with this? The victim wasn't exactly virtuous and my suspect isn't guilty. But, neither was Williams. Or The Stalker, according to Tuttle. Maybe one of them did it and I'm just flat out, stupidly wrong. Did my agitation boil down to satisfying my vanity, to be the one who put all the pieces together? Or was there an echo of the lawyer I had been years earlier, a need for simple justice, a recognition that murder couldn't be condoned, even if the victim was, by all accounts, a miserable human being.

And it went on and on.

By seven-thirty, I had narrowed my options. One person could put Carl Reinman and Annie Sullivan in context last Friday night. I had to confront her, otherwise, I'd never detach from the tar baby.

○ ○ ○

Mrs. Cabel's voice was wary and cool to my early call. My excuse was that I had some probate papers for her daughter's signature. As I spoke, I fingered the cut-out alphabet of Reinman's address book. How many of Reinman's dalliances were in here? Before she could question me, I said I would be there within the hour, got something of an assent, and said goodbye.

I showered, medicated myself—the bruises were turning a yellowish blue and the abrasions remained raw to the touch— strapped on my corset, and dressed in casual clothes, leather jacket, and the fedora that now seemed to be my talisman, was soon walking through the slush of East Street down The Hill towards Benefit Street. My takings from Reinman's office were in a leather case under my arm. The sky was a dome of cloudless blue, the early sun glowed, there was no wind, and the temperature was moving up rapidly. The snow had been reduced even further by a night of steady rain; lawns were once again visible under a bluish-green glaze; what remained had been protected by shade or overhangs or was piled—darkened by sand, exhaust, and soot, and tunneled by the runoff—at curbside. Predictably, at the bottom of East Street, the storm sewer was inside a snow bank and a puddle rippled from one brick sidewalk to the other, a pond that would take another day or two to drain off.

The northern part of Benefit Street is famous for the nearly identical eighteenth-century clapboard residences built right to its sidewalks. The two and a half story dwellings, painted in preservationally correct shades of dull red, brown, yellow, and blue, have four windows on a floor with another over a decorative entryway. Reinman's home, at the corner of Friends Street, was slightly larger than most, with a full basement, rear entry, and driveway down the slope, and had been recently painted a pale blue with a darker blue front door and had shiny black shutters. A boot scraper was affixed to the single granite front step and a Preservation Society plaque proclaimed that one "Jared Wilson, Cir. 1794" was its first known occupant. One rap with its brass pineapple-shaped door knocker produced movement in the curtains at the window to my right and, a moment later, the door opened.

She plainly expected me to hand her an envelope, give her instructions, and leave, and was surprised when I took off my hat and breezed by her, only to stumble against a large cardboard box filled with clothing. "Carl's clothes. For the Goodwill," she said with some exasperation, realizing that I had come for more than a quick delivery. She gestured to her left and I entered a low ceiling living room, austerely decorated and not particularly welcoming. Its pale red drapes were partly drawn and a blade of morning light sliced into the room, brightening a suite of showroom-new furniture, two walls of filled bookshelves, and a blue carpet. A porcelain banjo clock ticked off the seconds from the mantle over a slate fireplace. She passed by me and snapped on a table light, her expression one of impatience. Dressed in the gray woolen cardigan in which I had first seen her, and a white blouse, she put her hands in the pockets of a pleated gray skirt, holding herself stiffly.

I put the fedora and case on a drum table in front of the greenish sofa and made small talk about the snowstorm. I said that the probate court session of yesterday must have been postponed and lied that I'd taken a tumble on a patch of ice yesterday on my way to Carl's office—"just to get things going." She nodded as she directed me to the sofa. I asked after her daughter and she replied that Deborah remained in Vermont and that the movers were coming on Monday. A brief silence was relieved when she said she had boiled water for tea and asked me to join her. I accepted, and when she left the room, I slipped off my jacket, putting it next to my hat and case. My eyes immediately fixed on the botanical watercolors of orchids behind the sofa; closer inspection confirmed that they were exquisitely drawn and colored, particularly the delicate throats of the blooms. The artist was D. Cabel. That was unexpected.

I heard her say, maybe after a second or two of watching me at the watercolors, "Do you take sugar or lemon, Mr. Temple?"

"Just milk is fine," I replied, and shortly, she returned, setting a tray with cups, milk, tea packets of Twinning's English Breakfast, and a pot of hot water on the table. As she poured water over the tea bags, I continued with prattle about the houses of Benefit Street, that I had rented one when I first came back to Providence, how they had been saved from demolition back in the fifties by earnest preservationists, and what an upscale neighborhood it had become. All the while, I thought: *Why* am I doing this? I felt inane even as the words kept flowing; after all the Simeon's and P. D. James's I had read, why hadn't I picked up Maigret's and Dalgleish's methods of confronting the critical and usually reluctant witness? A copy of *T.R.* was half hidden under magazines on the table. I picked it up and, still into a flow of words, gushily, went on about what an *important* book it was and how *proud* the University had been of Reinman's successes, praising her son-in-law lavishly. I really laid it on and it was all bull! Damn, I couldn't get started!

Her eyes narrowed as I went on about Reinman and her impatience had been replaced by a vague animosity. "You said you wanted me to have some papers?"

This was the moment. I picked up the case, unzipped it, and...

weakened. "The watercolors," I said, "are beautiful. Your daughter's work?"

Her face brightened. "Yes," she gestured toward the botanicals, "from years ago. I don't know where she got the talent. Deborah was always interested in flowers, then, it was botany, and she could always draw beautifully." Her voice faded; it was too obvious that she was speaking in the past tense.

The room was silent again and I knew I had to get on with it. It came out bluntly. "Mrs. Cabel, did Carl ever mention a student by the name of Anne Sullivan?"

The clock ticked off seconds.

"She is…was…a former Carter student who was murdered a few days ago. Lived off Thayer Street. You've read about it…."

I opened the case and laid out the Merrill Lynch statement, address book, and greeting card, one by one, next to *T.R.*, explaining where I had found them, and the disjointed events that led me to uncover a relationship between Anne Sullivan and Carl Reinman. She listened intently even as her face clouded, as though my story was beyond her powers to comprehend. "Anne Sullivan's dormitory telephone number, from last year, is in here," I said, picking up the address book, opening it to "A" and holding it out toward her. She didn't look at it. I put the address book back on the table and picked up the brokerage statement. "I know she received a sizeable amount of cash within days after Carl took the exact amount from his Merrill Lynch account. The only debit to cash in five months." I picked up the greeting card. "I believe she sent him this card." I opened it and showed it to her. "Look at it. She 'slipped up'. What might she have been telling him? I can tell you that in May, she was pregnant, that—"

"What are you getting at?"

"Look," I said, aware that I'd never get anywhere trying to bully or bluster her, "she was murdered last Friday night. I believe your son-in-law had a very recent relationship with her and maybe gave her a lot of money. If I turn over what I have to the police, they would investigate the relationship, even if it's only to exclude a possibility. I'm his executor, or will be, and that makes it very awkward, but I'm not going to hide anything that would be relevant to the investigation of a murder. On the other hand, if Carl has... had... an alibi for last Friday night and early Saturday morning, I see no reason to get the police or the family involved."

Our eyes locked; I half expected an angry order to leave. The mantel clock took this inopportune time to chime. Slowly, the dull quality in her eyes cleared and her face tightened. One hand went to the chair arm for support and she stood.

○ ○ ○

I followed her to the second floor and down a narrow hall to an austerely decorated room—it didn't need a placard to say "guest"—with a bed covered by a tight blue spread, a bureau with an attached mirror, a ladderback chair with a cane seat, and a faded blue and maroon braided rug; a single window with its shade up let in a harsh light which almost erased the color from pinkish walls. The bureau top held multiple plastic bottles for prescription medicines and a single photograph in a silver frame. She picked up the photograph and handed it to me. "My daughters," she said in a threadbare voice.

It was a studio portrait of two girls in white pinafores sitting primly on either side of their mother. Deborah was easily recognizable, and pretty, at about eight, her smiling face had not yet acquired its pinched look; her sister was younger, maybe four or so, with curly dark hair and a natural, unposed smile. Mrs. Cabel, her hair drawn back in a bun, with her arms around the girl's shoulders, beamed with a mother's pride in her daughters. The photograph must have been a memory of better times, precious to her, something brought along on trips. I was reminded of Annie Sullivan's photograph in her First Communion dress as I handed back her keepsake.

Mrs. Cabel sat on the edge of the bed, holding the photograph, and I sat on the chair. She was composed, her eyes calm and trained on me, her hands primly in her lap, when she began. "We're farming people, been so for generations. Hay, vegetables, dairy. Good land right on the Connecticut. Early on we knew the farm wasn't for the girls. Both are smart, always into books, not practical like you have to be to farm. Deborah graduated from UV the year my husband died. She had made up her mind she was going to get a master's in botany and then teach at the college level. She got into Cornell with a scholarship and got a job as a teaching assistant. Her sister had a full scholarship to UV, so with the life insurance money and the farm, we could make ends meet. Deborah was on her way, happy, intelligent... full of life when she met Carl. My daughter became infatuated with him and she got pregnant. For some reason, she waited too long to tell him and when she did, she went back and forth on what to do. Finally, at his urging, she decided to have an abortion."

A drop of perspiration appeared above her lip as she revealed this uncomfortable family story. What did *this* have to do with an alibi for Friday night?

"She was further along than they thought, and the abortion got complicated and she ended up hemorrhaging and in the hospital. Nearly died." She looked down at the photograph and put it aside. "Within a week of leaving the hospital, she was filled with guilt and shame and had a breakdown. Tried to kill herself with sleeping pills. I went out to Ithaca to help out. Carl stood by her..., I can't imagine why..., but he did and they married after she recovered." Her eyes flickered towards me. "I've never understood that; even then, he was so full of himself. Of course, Deborah was obsessive about him. She would do anything for him. Maybe, that was what he needed," she added snidely.

"By the time he got his position here, Deborah was back to normal, got a job teaching elementary classes at a private school and things seemed okay for awhile. She wanted children desperately but I *knew* he didn't; especially after he became a celebrity. Even so, Deborah told me they tried for quite a while, especially since Carl absolutely refused to consider adoption...."

The vasectomy pamphlet remained in my case downstairs; the date on the doctor's receipt told me Carl didn't try for very long.

"At some point, Carl began taking up with other women, or maybe he always had. My daughter Beth teaches at UV, and she heard about it...that's how I found out.... Deborah became depressed again, quit teaching, became reclusive..., I don't know what all. I think she knew about his philandering and that's how she dealt with it. Gave up her few friends, probably because she wouldn't hear anything negative about him. Nothing. She'd say that other women were jealous because Carl was so handsome and a perfect husband. She couldn't..."—she struggled to find a word—"...judge him."

The emotions boiling inside her made her voice strained. "All the publicity for *T.R.* was devastating for Deborah. Before that, she could cope. Now, Carl was traveling all over the country, on television, and at the White House, and never at home for more than a few days before he'd be off to some meeting or conference or party. Her depression got worse, and she got treatment at a psychiatric hospital. Sometimes her medications agitated her, sometimes they sapped her strength. They went on for years like that..., he'd be doing his thing while she became more and more remote..., only occasionally well enough to be in any kind of society. Maybe it worked for Carl. She was an uncomplaining servant, devoted to him, out of the way, never complaining, never interfering with his image, and he could carry on as he pleased."

Her narration abruptly stopped as she looked out of the window and I found myself staring at her pale reflection in the glass. *What was going on?*

"Then, one night in June, there he was on the kitchen floor, desperate for breath, alive only because Deborah gave him CPR until the ambulance arrived."

A dry, out of context laugh seemed to mark a turning point in her story. "Deborah saved his life! Deborah, whom he had neglected and cheated on and prevented from enjoying a real life! But when he left the hospital and came home, totally dependent on her, she changed. She became purposeful as she nursed him, read to him, picked up his books and mail at the office, typed his letters and answered his e-mails, and worked with a young woman the University sent over. Drove him to the doctor and down to that place they have in Little Compton." Her fingers went to her temples, dramatically emphasizing how Deborah's turnaround was perplexing. "I could see that she had regained a sense of identity, even stopped her medications. And, she made plans! She managed their finances, had this house painted, started to redecorate..., things she hadn't cared about in years!"

"As she improved, it was Carl who became depressed, especially in September, after weeks without improvement, the doctors told him that he needed a heart transplant. That was devastating. His speech remained halting. He had lost thirty pounds and he was gaunt. Fatigue made writing difficult, if not impossible. Worse for him, important people no longer called, and his attempts to reach them, now that he was out of the public's eye, were rarely successful or short and barely polite. He couldn't keep up with events. A heart transplant was the only possibility for a better, longer life, but, even if it was successful, he knew his life was changed forever. So, Carl being Carl, he took his frustrations out on her. I came down on some weekends and saw that he'd become coarse and abusive to her. Yet, she had gained the strength to ignore it and to lay down the law to him. She was no longer a servant...and he knew it!"

Mrs. Cabel paused to take a handkerchief from a sweater pocket; she pulled it open but didn't use it for her eyes or nose, instead, she tugged at it. "Then, a few weeks ago, something happened between them. She became at once distant and consumed with anger towards him, barely speaking to him, making him fend for himself, and he reacted by threatening a divorce! Can you imagine it? A divorce? In his condition? He still thought he would punish her! She wouldn't confide in me. I begged her to take her medications, see her doctor, but she refused. I knew she was heading for another setback, maybe worse than before, even when she went back to her medications. Finally, I got her to agree to come home last weekend—her sister would be there—while I came down to handle Carl's needs. But, he made such a fuss when I arrived Friday afternoon that instead, Deborah drove down to their place in Little Compton...."

Finally, we get to last weekend.

She was now pulling the ends of the handkerchief with enough ferocity to split it at the middle and her eyes stared ahead like I wasn't there. "Deborah was long gone when the telephone rang about nine-thirty or so on Friday night. I was getting ready for bed, Carl was upstairs in his room. It was a young woman, asking for Carl. I asked her name, and she giggled when she said 'Anne Elizabeth Sullivan'. Giggled! Then, she said, 'Tell him Annie,' and giggled again. I thought she was drunk and I almost hung up, but she insisted it was important so I put the phone down and went upstairs and told Carl. He recognized her name, seemed confused, then angry, and ordered me out of his bedroom! Ordered me! I hadn't hung up the downstairs phone…, and so I listened." Her face screwed up at what must have seemed to her to be a shameful act. "This Annie told him that she needed money. He said that he had given her all the money she was ever going to get and why was she calling him now? She said that he owed her, that there were plenty of people who would be interested in her story, like some of those scandal sheets…, the kind you see in the supermarket. Then she laughed, and told him to calm down or he'd have another heart attack; maybe all she'd have was a talk with Deborah! It went on like that until Carl agreed to meet her that night and she told him where."

Mrs. Cabel pulled herself up with the aid of a bedpost. "I'd like a drink of water," she said and left the room; seconds later, I heard the sound of a tap running from down the hall. I stood and stretched and sat back down. The coherence of her account baffled me; on a moment's notice, most people can't tell a story with multiple strands without digressions and repetitiveness. Mrs. Cabel's tale had a rehearsed quality and she seemed determined to give me every sordid detail.

Spots of color were high on her cheeks when she returned and sat on the bed; with hands playing over the bedspread, her gaze was directed at the floor. "A few minutes later, Carl came downstairs to the kitchen. He had his overcoat on, looking ashen, sweaty, his eyes huge. He went out through the pantry, down the back stairs, and I heard the door open but when I didn't hear it close, I went to look and found him sprawled on the threshold. I knew he was dead. I just stood there, I don't know how long, staring at him. All I could think of was that he had died *trying to see that girl!* How could I ever explain that to Deborah?"

Her eyes sought a measure of understanding but the disconnect between her anguished voice and the paper thin set of her lips keep me impassive. "God help me, I stayed with him the whole night! Somehow, I managed to get him upstairs, undress him, and left him by the bed. In the morning, I called his doctor. He came right over and I told him that I found Carl just as he was. The doctor had been treating him for months so there were no questions. He helped me with the funeral arrangements, then I drove to Little Compton and told Deborah. She took it very badly, as I knew she would. I had brought her medications and forced her to take sedatives that calmed her enough to get her home. Beth came down and we managed. I never told Deborah about the girl. She was barely fit for the memorial service on Tuesday but we got through it and Beth took her back home..." She looked away toward the window. "What else could I do?"

No answer was required.

"The morning of the service, the murder was in the newspaper. How could I forget her name? Somebody would surely investigate, somebody would call here. But nobody did, not that day, not later, and I realized that, as time went on, it would be less likely that Carl would be linked to her. I searched Carl's bedroom and his study and found nothing to connect him to the girl. I was going to go through the things at his office—"

Our eyes met; her face was an accusation.

We sat in silence. She had to be Yankee tough to stay overnight with the corpse cooling upstairs, call the doctor, and move on. But not tough enough to overcome a need to condemn Reinman, to destroy his stature, even if it put her in a compromised position. Why? Was it because I had praised him so effusively only minutes ago? So that at least *one* of his colleagues had to know the pain he had inflicted on her daughter, that even his death was a catalogue of duplicity and shame?

She rose from the bed and smoothed its cover. Her manner said expiation was over and her voice was icy calm. "You have a telephone number and your suspicions but he didn't murder her. He has an alibi and you have your answer. Whatever happened to that girl Friday night has nothing to do with us."

She stepped into the hall. I followed. At the top of the stairs, we awkwardly paused for the other to proceed. Behind her, the door was ajar to an empty room, newly and brightly painted in yellow, with a stenciled border of balloons and stars in red and white, and a Picasso clown print on the wall. She saw my glance and moved quickly to close the door. Her face came close to mine when she said, "Don't bring more pain to my daughter. Let the police find their murderer and let my daughter have her memories. Surely, she deserves that much out of life."

I couldn't frame an answer so I didn't reply. I passed by her and went down the staircase, retrieved my jacket and fedora from the living room, and tucked my evidence into the case. I saw Reinman's photograph on *T.R.*'s dust jacket with new eyes. The angle of the photographer's light shadowed a part of his face, accentuating his high cheekbones and filling in the cleft in his chin, giving him a too-clever, saturnine expression. I covered the photograph with a magazine.

Mrs. Cabel remained at the top of the stairs when I closed the door behind me. On the sidewalk, I paused, not knowing if I should feel relieved, compromised, or manipulated. There was her Stella Dallas melodrama to it all, the protection of a daughter at all personal costs. I looked up at the dark blue door and its brass knocker. Inside, I had expected surprise, defensiveness, protest, even anger. I hadn't expected her overwhelming need to smash the reputation of Carl Reinman or to expatiate a hatred that had been mute for too long.

CHAPTER TWENTY-FOUR

Whyen I got home, my emotional tank was on empty.

I worked out for an hour, hard, until the sweat poured off me and my muscles felt like liquid, my brain focused only on the next push and pull. Then I shot pool for twenty minutes, beginner exercises because I didn't have any concentration left and I needed to shove Annie Sullivan and Lavelle Williams, Carl Reinman and Ms. Cabel, Tramonti, Sonny and Puppy Dog, Jesse Kingdom and The Stalker, into a separate folder of my mind.

Getting on with a Saturday routine seemed best for my psyche. I got dressed, plunked the fedora on my head, and took the Mini Cooper up to Federal Hill to Gasbarro's for wine and the political wisdom served up by owners Lom and Marco. Plied with a glass of an aged vin santo and a plate of cantucci, I listened to the give and take of the father and son with customers who arrive from all parts of the city and beyond for the best in Italian wines and raucous political conversations. The chatter revealed that Sonny had scored points in his verbal barrage against the demonstrators, the University, and Kingdom, although the sloppy plowing job brought complaints.

I left the wine shop unhappy with the gossip but with a good variety of Chiantis and two Barolos, as well as a Capezzana vin santo, and went on to Whole Foods at University Heights for groceries, sundries, meat, and fish and Wayland Square to pick up dry cleaning. The streets were virtually clear of snow although huge puddles filled intersections; the end of the parking ban brought out cars that angled into the streets, making their side mirrors likely casualties to the growing traffic. It was now past noon, the temperature was in the high fifties, and the sun was playing hide and seek behind rapidly moving, puffy clouds. Instead of heading home, I drove to Jimmy's.

Jimmy's wife, Maria, had the lunch trade and joined me at the counter facing the open kitchen for a few minutes of conversation over a bowl of her renowned Portuguese kale soup with chiarco and red wine, with a basket of hard crusted bread. We chatted about food, politics, the Patriots, and Young Jimmy bringing in more talent for pool exhibitions. I was about to leave, with my check paid and fedora on, when Tramonti's voice came from behind us. Maria looked up, greeted him, and excused herself. His usual driver, a thickly built cop in his thirties with a dark complexion and slicked-back hair, wearing a green, satiny Celtics jacket, stood next to Tramonti and stared down at me with toothy interest.

Tramonti slid into the nearest booth and beckoned me to follow. Reluctantly, I did. Ugh. I don't need this right now.

"Loci, get yourself something to go," he said. "I'll only be a few minutes." Loci reluctantly sauntered to the counter and spun the stool around to face the kitchen.

Tramonti's face was tired, with shadows under his eyes.

"I saw your car in the lot. Tuttle called me last night about the Sullivan girl's bankbook and the abortion, and her old man's stupidity..., and what were you doing Thursday night with that punk Williams! I warned you not to...!" His eyes widened when he turned to my roughed-up face. "What the hell happened to you!"

I knew I couldn't expect much sympathy so he got the condensed version. From his less than pained expression, I realized that not only hadn't Franks mentioned the assault, he had placed Williams with me, maybe as a place of refuge. Did Tramonti think I had intervened again? He didn't ask questions and didn't let me finish.

"Goddamn it, Algy! If you had pressed assault charges, I could have held on to him! Why are you being such a first class pain-in-the-ass about this scumbag?"

That sat me back in the booth. A *first class pain-in-the-ass!* After what I've done! Because of me, her bank account and abortion had surfaced! Annie Sullivan's murder should now get a by-the-book investigation. I had given the police..., Tramonti..., credibility!

"Listen to me," he said through clenched teeth. "Get this in your stubborn head. My bet, and it's a good bet, is Williams snuffed her. His alibi stinks, even if our fainthearted AG says we still don't have enough to arrest him until the DNA test gets back. And Williams has got Franks, so Lavoie won't let us hold him on the drug counts. But if *you'd* pressed charges, I could have held him on an assault charge since he's on bail...."

When my face didn't register wide-eyed shame, he jammed a cigarette into his mouth. I said, a little too snidely, "No smokes, remember."

Those black eyes reacted with anger. He waved the cigarette in my face, then put it on the table. "You have no clue what this is all about. Hector Flores. Remember that name? Williams's boss? He runs the biggest drug operation in Rhode Island, right into New Bedford and Fall River, all out of a bar in Olneyville. As vicious as they come. Part of the Medellin cartel. Direct connections to Colombia and San Juan. The junk is flown in, the mules drive it up here from New York, and he spreads it around."

I didn't react so he used his large hands for emphasis and thrust his face closer to mine.

"Flores is scum, Algy, worse than scum. Murders without a second thought. Uses the street gangs for runners and to get rid of competition. We've been trying to get at him for years. Your boy's got his own string of sellers—gangs don't blend in on the East Side, it's all quick hand-offs on the street—and he sells enough to deal with Flores's second-in-command, an hombre by the name of Manuel Hones. They call him "the Cutter" for reasons we don't have to get into. If we could get to Hones, we might bring Flores down. We got the state police and the DEA all over this!"

He was really working himself up while I was getting pretty damn defensive.

"Flores and Hones gave Williams his alibi, two of Flores's girls, the kind of crud who hear nothing, see nothing, remember nothing most of the time. They'd do anything for a hit of crack, or anything else Flores has got. Now do you get it? With Anne Sullivan, we're looking at murder one as a charge. Even if he didn't do it, we've got leverage with Williams at the very least. We could get the Cutter. We might get Flores!"

His harangue, in a nutshell, was: *Algy, you are a jerk messing up an important investigation.* He wanted to sweat Williams; I could have delivered him up but didn't. It was my fault that Williams wasn't giving up Hones and Flores. It had little or nothing to do with Annie Sullivan.

"None of my business. Your guys screwed up a murder case. They're so convinced it was Williams or The Stalker that they let one of their own conceal evidence. Now *you* tell me that getting Williams isn't about the murder. I thought this had been screwed up because of plain old crassness, bureaucratic bullshit, and incompetence. Maybe I was wrong!"

Tramonti raised his hand to my face with two fingers a few millimeters apart. "I owe you this much. It's remotely possible somebody else had an interest in her. The autopsy is a mess, nothing to indicate an abortion. Maybe it got deleted; maybe somebody was doing somebody a favor. We're checking on it now. She could have been stashing the money for Williams. Maybe he was holding out on Flores which would not be a good idea, by the way—"

"So what happens if you don't make an arrest?"

"What?"

"If you don't get Williams and it's not The Stalker? For the murder, I mean. When does it all go stale?"

Suspicion grew in his eyes. "No statute of limitations on murder, you know that. Cold case after a year. That ain't going to happen. We'll get Williams..., whomever...," and he stopped, as anger splashed across his face. "What aren't you telling me!" and slammed his hand on the table top, loud and hard enough for customers to turn in our direction. Loci got up off his stool but a wave off from his boss sat him down.

Tramonti managed to keep his voice low and in control even as he lapsed into his tough guy cadence and shook his finger at my face. "Just listen to me for one fucking minute! This is a murder investigation. You don't get any special dispensation. You can't withhold information!" My deadpan made him apoplectic. His hands went high over his head. "Christ, why do I bother! You never pay attention to anyone. At least press charges! If we pick up Williams, I can hold him long enough to check on the money. That ought to make you happy!"

If only he hadn't added that parting shot. It triggered hubris and resentment and I lost any thought of coming clean as to Carl Reinman and his connection to Anne Sullivan. *I* had been consistently right and constantly ignored, *I* was the guy who delivered the bankbook evidence, *I* made her abortion an issue, *I* got beat up, *I* had to deal with Jerry Franks, *I* had Nadie on my case, and now had the burden of dealing with a mother's guilty secret, all of this resulting in being chewed out by my best friend!

It took two deeps breaths for me to say quietly, "Let me think on it," and I was out of the booth so fast that Tramonti barely had time to smother his profanity.

○ ◯ ○

I drove home, put my purchases and clothes away, opened a Sam Adams, and settled down in the lounger to watch Carter at Yale on ESPN 2. I caught it before halftime, Carter with a surprising two-touchdown lead, and used the break for another beer and a plate of crackers, Thompson seedless grapes, salami, and jalapeno cheese. Before the second half, I surfed channels with the remote.

"...And in this racist society, the police are the defenders of the power structure which keeps our black brothers and sisters from enjoying their inalienable human rights." It was an intense Reverend Jesse Kingdom, framed by huge blowups of Martin Luther King, Malcolm X, and Nelson Mandela. I checked the channel; it was the cable local access station. The LCD clock in the DVD read two fifty-five; the program was near its end.

The interviewer sat across a low table from Kingdom. "Your methods, which I would call 'confrontationally-aggressive', are not appreciated by a lot of folks in this town. I guess they're not ready for your message."

"They weren't ready for Frederick Douglass. They weren't ready for Martin Luther King. They weren't ready for Malcolm X. They weren't ready for Jesse Jackson. They haven't been ready for anybody until that somebody got in their faces!" I thought, I'm getting a preview of tonight! "What we've got to do is to be in their faces. We've got to let them know that they can't intimidate us, treat us like animals, that the brothers and sisters won't take it anymore in this town. If that requires militancy, so be it. If it requires confrontation, so be it."

The camera moved in for a closeup and Kingdom's scowling face filled the screen.

"What happened Thursday, the arrests of students and other

folks, was reprehensible. Disgraceful! What Providence has to realize is that this police case is only the beginning. We're going after everybody and everything that harms people of color. All poor people." He turned from the interviewer and looked into another camera. "We know that there are people who hate us and we know that there are people who will support us. I'm looking for support. I'm ready for action." The camera faded back so that Kingdom, his large mouth set in a line, was framed in the background picture of Malcolm X.

"Final questions. What happens if there are no convictions? What do you propose to do?"

"Well," Kingdom replied, drawing out the word, "I expect that they will be convicted because I believe they are guilty. But if there is another miscarriage of justice, if the system again doesn't work, then I don't know what's going to happen in the black neighborhoods. I don't know how the people will contain the rage which they will feel. But, I predict the city will never forget it, if it goes down that way."

He said it so calmly that a shiver ran down my spine.

As the credits rolled on the screen, Jesse Kingdom remained stern-faced. *That* Jesse Kingdom … tonight … could bring chaos to our campus. Would Danby's decision unleash a torrent of anger? Would it be his last as President of Carter University?

I touched the power button. My interest in the game had been trumped by Jesse Kingdom's threat. I pulled on a wool sweater and went out through the kitchen to the patio for some needed fresh air. Within the patio's walls, the snow had been reduced to smudges of white under dull ivy leaves and the yellowish stalks of late blooming flowers. Jet vapor trails were drifting high in the pale blue above me, with waves of clouds forming in the southwest. A fresh, cold breeze rose from off the Bay and a flock of juncos landed in the oak next to the garage and began a chorus of twitters. I tucked my hands into the back pockets of my slacks. I knew I was on overload and decided to walk it off.

I got as far as Prospect Park, a block down Congdon Street, which at this time of year is two acres of faded grass, spindly maples, oaks still clutching some dead leaves, and scattered wooden benches in need of repair; patches of snow covered shady spots and a couple of lumps and a raggedy scarf were all that remained of snowpeople. True to its name, it not only has a great "prospect" of the downtown, its views also included the harbor, the City Hospital complex, and the entire south side as well. With the warm temperature, I was surprised that, except for a persistent terrier busy marking every shrub, the park was deserted.

I walked past a granite pergola that covers a twice life-sized marble statue of Roger Williams, his hands blessing the city he founded three and a half centuries ago, to the wrought iron railing that keeps kids and college drunks from a thirty foot tumble down to Pratt Street. The city which stretched out before me looked as though it was primping for a tourism video: shimmering rivers winding through the snow covered parks to the blue-gray Bay, a brace of starkly outlined high-rise buildings in downtown, the bulk of the Mall over the gleaming train tracks and ribbon of river, and the white, seemingly touchable, marble State House. An attractive, buoyant, parochial, and tribal city, I thought, a survivor and full of itself in its self-proclaimed renaissance, with Sonny, Puppy Dog, and McCarthy types in control, and far too few stand-up people like Tramonti with the determination to find solutions for its problems.

The terrier barked at an incautious pigeon, igniting a chain reaction of yips and barks from up and down Congdon Street. I looked up at Roger Williams. Somewhere in the ancestral chain, he was there, with his stubborn single-mindedness that took a swampy, mosquito-ridden salt river and tidal cove and turned it into a settlement of crusty, hardworking, and independent free-thinkers. Was he the source of our family's stewardship *thing* and my urge to finish whatever I began? So boss, what do I do? Choke on my pride and call Tramonti? Or, let it all play out without me?

Then and there, I knew I had to be satisfied with a private sense of accomplishment. I had been right about Anne Sullivan and Reinman. Chalk one up for me! Williams would get a fair shake on the murder charge—even if his drug connections would put him at risk—because the hush money and the abortion would hang out there. Chalk up another one! Pine wouldn't like it but I would resign the executorship. The old lady would wonder if I was going to keep her secret. I would unless Williams was going down and I had to come forward. Okay, not a chalk up, but... something.

Gusts of cold wind pushed at my back all the way to the house. I went downstairs and played eight ball against myself for an hour and then watched a Clint Eastwood spaghetti western on AMC. When the DVD's clock read a minute past six, I switched to the early news.

Against a photo montage of what was obviously Thursday's confrontation, the weekend anchor, his dark blazer with a monogrammed 11 on its vest pocket, intoned "... And now a Channel 11 EyeWitness exclusive. While President Charles Danby of Carter University and the Reverend Jesse Kingdom may appear to live in two different worlds, in fact, they have been friends since their early childhoods in Philadelphia. Channel 11 has learned that Kingdom, the outspoken and controversial leader of W.A.R., We're Against Racism, and Danby have been in close contact since Danby's arrival here in Providence last May. Kingdom's alliance with University student groups has been a matter of growing public concern, according to Providence Mayor Arthur Russo who has denounced Kingdom's college allies as 'campus crazies.' Thursday's riot and arrests involved Carter students. With the University and the City butting heads over a host of issues, sources have told Channel 11 News that Mayor Russo is intending to press his plan to have the University's property tax exemption revoked. Tonight, Reverend Kingdom is scheduled to address a rally of students at Carter despite the delivery of what has been called a 'death' threat against him. All of this comes against the backdrop of the continuing menace of The Carter Stalker who has committed six Saturday night assaults this fall and may be implicated in the murder last weekend of a former student." He blinked and continued, "In other news, ..."

Off it went.

"Ugh!" How the hell did they find out about Kingdom and Danby! Did Kingdom let it slip? Danby? Danby was now inevitably associated with Kingdom. Danby's campus foes would draw their own conclusions. As for Sonny, McCarthy, and their allies, ...!

I tried Nadie's cell phone number without luck. I called the Women's Center, where I was told she was expected. I left her a voice message that I was going to be at the Security Office for the rally and would call her later as to where I would be. I put down the phone and sat back. Danby was back, where he should be, at the top of my list of stewardship issues. He and Carter should have been up there all along.

ndoor tennis, racquetball, or squash? Sure. Quarter-mile track? Absolutely. How about laps in one of two Olympic-sized pools? Climbing wall? Weight room? Of course, and while the same amenities are available at other college sports facilities, add indoor soccer, lacrosse, and intramural basketball courts all under one roof and you have the Smithson Sports Complex. The rally would be in the center concourse of the multi-domed building, an area which could easily hold a thousand standees. The notion of Carter students rocking and rolling with Kingdom's W.A.R.—more accustomed to demonstration than discourse—after the tensions left over from Thursday's confrontation, was chilling. No Event Plan could foresee all the possibilities.

Poor Tuttle!

The night sky was as black as onyx and the air was sharp as I walked to the Security Office with a wool lining zipped into my Burberry, the fedora squared on my head, and Totes for a walk to the Security Office and wherever else I would be this night. I barely noticed the cold because my brain was still trying to parse out the logic of Danby's imprudent, bordering on reckless, decision. Why had he created this tinderbox? Had he decided to be the focal point of the Sunday news stories, now that his relationship with Kingdom was public? Danby was leading with his chin and trying to counterpunch. That didn't work, in the ring or in academia.

But, nobody asked *me*.

At seven forty-five, I was in the waiting area of the Security

Office. Its rows of molded, green plastic chairs were empty; officers flowed in and out and a speaker system caught static and fragments of radio voices. Sergeant Ewell, in starched uniform shirt and black tie, was at the control desk behind Plexiglas; behind him glowed a console of blinking red lights. "The Chief said you might be by," he said soberly by way of greeting. "Nice hat," he added. "And don't you owe me something?" In fact, the key to Ramsden Hall was in my hand and I slid it through an opening in the Plexiglas. Ewell seemed vaguely disappointed that I had remembered; he moved slowly to pick it up, then swiveled in his chair to open a metal cabinet under the console.

"All set for tonight?" I said to his back.

He found the appropriate hook for the key. "The Chief is down there on Thayer Street with about everyone they could get to come in." He turned to look up at me, scratching his balding head. "You know, I don't quite get it. It's goin' to be a circus. 'Specially after that trouble downtown. What are we supposed to do? We can check IDs at the door, but suppose Kingdom's got all his folks there and they want in. Suppose there's a ruckus outside or on their march or at The Green. Maybe The Stalker tries something while they're rallyin' and marchin' and trashin'?" He touched a button on the desk, causing a buzzer to sound and the door at my right to unlock. "No firearms," he continued, as we entered the corridor, "Okay, I understand that, not even nightsticks anymore. Everybody's worried about Jesse Kingdom. They're worried about The Stalker. They want to protect the women. But us—black, white, whatever—what about us? Who do we rely on, the cops? They belittle us!" He touched a peaked cap on a hatrack as we walked by. "Just what are we supposed to do?"

He asked the right questions. Carter's inability to deal with the authority, needs, and morale of the Security Office was a continuing problem. University policy for the security force was: no firearms, no truncheons, travel in pairs, don't use force, call for reinforcements, and, most importantly, *take good notes.* Semi-permanent commissions advise the Security Office on racial profiling, sensitivity training, stereotypes, attitude readjustment, and, believe it or not, note taking. Not too helpful when a mugger brandishes a weapon or is about to wreak havoc on a victim.

Ewell opened the first door on the right into what turned out to be Tuttle's office, a graceless room smelling of secret smokes, with poor lighting, nothing on the wall but a plastic message board with arrows and Magic Marker jibberish. "You know," he continued with increasing frustration, "they want us to respond to every problem in a ten block area, and there ain't enough of us to do the job. Somethin's gonna give!" He shook his head. "Make yourself at home," he said wearily, and left.

I laid my coat on a plastic seated chair in front of Tuttle's cluttered desk. Must be my week for photographs, I thought, as I saw his collection of framed snapshots and studio photographs of a plumpish, attractive wife, two daughters at various ages and locales, a young boy with his father's freckles, and a more recent shot of the family, arms behind one another at a dress-up affair — a happy and glad to be with one another photograph that any parent would cherish.

A television was on top of a bookcase across from the desk; I touched *Power*, 6, and 5. WCAT-Channel 65, our campus interconnect station, is owned by and licensed to the University's Telecommunications Department. Before my time at the University, its program schedule had been turned over to a Program Selection Committee consisting of students from the Department and appointees of the Student Council and advised by a lonely member of the administration, McAllister. Not surprisingly, the Program Selection Committee is comprised of people with tracts in need of pulpits; their meetings and selections are often polemical and controversial with constant First Amendment and media access issues, enough so that I keep a local law firm on retainer to deal with libel and slander and keep the station from losing its license. The committee's constant wrangling and bizarre programming didn't keep Channel 65 from being mostly uninteresting; yet, I had to credit its coverage of campus events like graduation, major guest lectures, and otherwise not televised Ivy League basketball, Eastern League hockey, and other league and intramural sports where it did an adequate job despite wobbly cameras and none-too-lively commentary.

I sat on the edge of Tuttle's desk—after last night's excursion into Reinman's office, I was uncomfortable sitting behind *any-body's* desk—as the screen sharpened to a dozen or so students, male and female, black, white, and Asian—Martine Danby among them—huddled around a podium bristling with microphones over a large brass Carter University seal. What must have been a handheld camera pulled back and slowly panned the crowd which might have numbered two to three hundred kids—predominantly white, with a goodly number of black kids and other minorities. Predictably for a Saturday night, their dress was casual: droopy jackets, sweatshirts and sweaters, baseball caps on frontwards, sideways, and backwards, jeans and baggy trousers. Both sexes had placards and banners which I couldn't make out in the camera's shaky moves. At a media stand near the podium, Channel 11's reporter spoke directly to a camera; behind her, kids stood in the background in a raucous conviviality until they were admonished behind the camera, leaving them to grimace and squint in the harsh lights. And not a security officer's peaked cap in sight!

I found the volume dial under the screen and turned it up. Two student commentators seemed to be losing the audio battle to earpiercing hip-hop, rap, and pop rock from boomboxes, drums, something akin to air horn blasts, and a pep rally chant of "Jess-*ee*, Jess-*ee*, Jess-*ee*!" The camera jerked back toward the crowd for no apparent reason and returned to the podium where a black student in a yellow dashiki and cap, arms outstretched and hands waving, was attempting to gain attention by shouting into the microphones. He was no match for an eruption of clapping, chants, whistles, and drums as the camera searched the crowd and found Jesse Kingdom, somberly dressed in a black suit and clerical collar, parting a sea of outstretched hands. He stepped up to the podium to stand solemnly, even as he took in the crowd's adulation. Eventually, his silent presence stopped the persistent "Jess-*ee*" chant and allowed the kid at the microphone his chance.

The introduction was an excited condemnation of the Providence police, Sonny Russo, and old friends "Whitey" and "Uncle Tom" which produced groans, boos, angry shouts, and whistles at each mention, followed by an introduction of two black women and a Latino male who had been arrested at the Public Safety Building demonstration. Finally, after some impatient applause and whistles, he got to "the man you came here to hear" and the masonry walls of the Complex echoed with cries for "Jess-*ee*, Jess-*ee*, Jess-*ee*!"

Kingdom solemnly shook hands with the three arrested kids, moved to the podium, and stood there, his hands squarely on the lectern, his head lowered as though in meditation, until the crowd was mostly quiet. His magnetism took hold as the camera zoomed to the podium for a closeup and, on cue, he slowly raised his head—a move which gave his body an extra measure of height and stature—and thanked the crowd for its support in a rich voice that quickly found the right pitch and cadence. He brought his palms together, raised them above his head, slowly lowered them down to the lectern and began with a story about growing up in Philadelphia with another boy—whom he did not identify but whom the crowd clearly took to be Danby—and the night his mother's younger brother was rousted at their home. Yes, his uncle had brushes with the law, what child of that ghetto didn't. He didn't resist his arrest, yet he was clubbed in front of his family by a "thug" policeman. Why? Because he was black and the cop thought he could do so. The image of that violent moment had been with him during his adolescence, his college and seminary years, his ministry in Philadelphia, and now, Providence. That man with a nightstick was *the man* who symbolized prejudice and injustice and it was *that man*, he said in a voice rising in fervor and indignation, who must be humbled.

The crowd roared its agreement in a "Jess-*ee*, Jess-*ee*, Jess-*ee!*" chant that echoed and re-echoed so that it seemed it would never stop.

Kingdom stilled the chant by raising his arms—it was amazing how the crowd responded to his rhythms of speech and silence. In a voice subdued and gentle, he got to the heart of his message. People of all colors had to deal with brutality and there were kinds and grades of brutalities. Some, the ones which created hunger, family breakdowns, economic stagnation, and lack of opportunity were the insidious brutalities. They were more universal than the vicious, aggressive brutality of violence like "... the brutality you face here—with The Stalker!"

I braced myself.

In a voice that hushed his audience and chilled me, he said, "The Stalker is the ultimate brutality. One of bestiality." I held my breath. "You," he said, his voice finding new depths of power, a single finger pointed straight into the silent crowd, "... it's going to have to be *you* who will stop him. You *know* you can't depend upon anyone or anything else, including..."—his voice dropped an octave—"... the nightstick. But *you can stop him* by doing what any small child can do: be smart and not alone. *You can stop him!*

Not with weapons, but with the courage to love and protect each other, to do the sensible thing, and not let him rule you. He will be brought to bay... *like... any... other... beast!*"

A single male voice rang out "Jess-*ee!*" and the whole place exploded with yells that went on and on.

I was thrilled. What a great message! Cooperation! Responsibility! Couldn't have been better!

But, when the roar finally died down, Jesse Kingdom threw red meat at the crowd. With his voice resonating, soaring in its power, Thursday's "police riot" became his target. In language that would trigger a rabid response, he challenged the crowd to fill the streets in front of the federal court before and during the upcoming trial, not to protest only the "aimless brutality" represented by the defendants but also the "brutality of a system" that fosters *ex*clusion instead of *in*clusion and imprisons one out of four black youths, finishing with a thundering call to stand with him for justice.

He was answered by screams of allegiance and shouted pledges to join him at the courthouse.

I reminded myself I should be satisfied with his cautionary words on The Stalker and checked my watch. Under ten minutes!

Kingdom stepped back from the podium and the kids swarmed forward; he escaped off to one side and plowed into the crowd followed by the lights from a dozen camcorders. The Channel 65 commentators gushed in admiration as the camera followed Kingdom's slow progress towards the Complex's rear doors. And suddenly, he was gone.

He *had* come alone!

Martine Danby's voice brought the camera back to the podium, even as some of the camera lights were being shut off and a technician removed microphones in front of her. She held an unlit candle in her hand and urged her audience to pick up candles at the exits, light them, and march to The Green to show solidarity with Jesse Kingdom and the victims of The Stalker. She was cheered by those paying any kind of attention as she left the podium.

So far, Danby, I said to myself, had been right, but this might be the easy part. I reached over to turn off the television.

I drew back my hand. The WCAT commentators, now at the podium, were rudely brushed aside by a determined-looking young black male with a do-rag, wrap-around sunglasses, and a padded jacket who shouted into the microphone and blasted the Complex with an unintelligible roar of words. As he struggled to become understandable, the camera pulled back to show a phalanx of young black males standing below him, shoulder to shoulder, arms folded across their chests, dressed in similar bulky, loose-fitting clothes, a few in full "gangsta" mode with pants down by their crotches and black berets over Afros, shiny scalps and do-rags. W.A.R.? Carter students? And I realized with the ID checks at the door, they must be ours. Showing off or serious?

Their leader raised his arms and shouted that they were the *Black Posse*—as twenty or so right arms with black armbands shot skyward and his followers cheered for themselves—and that black sisters would now be protected by their black brothers in the Posse. *We take care of our own from now on* was the clear and menacing message which produced a few yells of support but mostly hung in the air, which led him to raise his fists for more threats—when the microphone went dead.

He didn't realize what had happened at first, then he shook the mike, blew into it, then angrily batted it away; his rant went on, his mouth forming shrill words, maybe more than a few vulgarities, inaudible as the wide-open space of the Complex took his voice away. His fists continued to pump up and down and his face became distorted; on the screen, he looked ridiculous, like Mussolini on a balcony exhortating a crowd in Rome in a thirties newsreel, as pop rock blasted from the Complex's speakers, completely drowning him out. In frustration, he jumped down to his gang. They huddled—and were gone.

Oh, Tuttle, you clever bastard!

CHAPTER TWENTY-SIX

Ewell had watched the rally on a monitor on his desk. Tuttle, he said, had called in to report that Kingdom had arrived alone and had left the area immediately after his speech, the marchers were getting organized, and he was leaving for a Thayer Street command post to coordinate with the Traffic Division cops who would stop anything on wheels approaching the marchers. The Black Posse apparently did not follow the marchers as Tuttle had feared but he had no idea of its destination or purpose. Ewell made it clear what he thought of this new development. "A bunch of kids like that can get carried away, like Guardian Angels," he said with a mixture of dismay and disgust, and I was left in apprehension as to how the tired and demoralized security officers and the Black Posse might interact.

The temperature had dropped a few more degrees, trees shivered in the wind, and the night remained moonless with only a few stars glittering coldly as I left the Security Office, crossed Brook Street, and headed toward The Green's entrance on William Street. In the distance, the beat of a bass drum marked the progress of the marchers. Security Office red and white Fords were parked at most intersections; at Thayer Street, where police cruisers blocked traffic, I better understood Tuttle's security nightmare: while no vehicles were getting through, anybody on the sidewalks could join or follow the marchers, enter the campus with them, or slip between the campus buildings where there was no fencing, and mix right in.

A group of ten or twelve kids preceded me through the South Gate where two security officers requesting IDs, as allowed by the Student Handbook, were being informed by several women with emotion-laden voices that ID checks were harassments. Inside the gate, maybe a hundred or so kids were gathered on the terrace in front of Prince House, with dozens of others standing or sitting on the steps of facing buildings where the snow had been cleared or had melted. Rap vibrated from two huge speakers on the terrace steps; a stand of microphones glinted in the rings of brightness from floodlights located on the building's cornices. Television crews had arrived and were setting up in front of the terrace; one was videoing taping the banners that hung from the windows of Prince House and dangled from tree limbs: "Women United Against the Night," "No More Rape," a two-story "V"—which I didn't need to guess at—"Jesse," "Third World Action," and more of the same.

Artemus Vose, in a quilted parka and his leonine head topped by a Cats baseball cap, was suddenly standing next to me. He had watched the Sports Complex rally on the interconnect but had turned it off before the unexpected appearance of the Black Posse; I told him what I had seen as we walked to the steps of College Hall. I didn't have to see his face to know his expression didn't change. The drumbeat was now louder as we took our position; the marchers had to be turning on to Waterman Street from Thayer, which meant that the vanguard would be through the College Arch in a minute or two to join those on the rapidly filling terrace. "Okay," I asked Vose, "what are we supposed to do?"

"We wait, listen, and follow the crowd to President's House where Danby expects to address them unless something really serious happens here, in which case, I make the call." He pulled out a cell phone and then put it back in his coat pocket. "That's his decision," he said with a sigh that was almost drowned out by the pounding drum as marchers, marked by clusters of flickering dots of light, emerged from under the College Arch, followed by the banner and sign carriers, more candleholders in twos and threes, and finally, those who had joined the march empty-handed. Counting the new arrivals, I estimated the total crowd at no more than four or five hundred, many fewer than I had expected. The Black Posse had not put in an appearance.

"Manageable," I remarked to Vose as Martine Danby approached the podium. Had the campus been emptied by the threat of The Stalker? Or was it apathy? Or the other attractions of a Saturday night?

A bearded white student, dressed like someone from the Beat Generation in his black turtleneck shirt, black leather jacket, black beret, and goatee approached the podium. After feedback squeals from the address system, he shouted, "Yesss!" pumped his arms, and rocked back from the mike. Again, "Yesss!" and this time, a few in the crowd responded with shouts of encouragement. When they quieted down, he congratulated all for their show of solidarity with Jesse Kingdom and "the women of Carter," declaring that Jesse Kingdom's battle was a cause for all of "Young America." After a few more yells, whistles, and, belatedly, drumbeats, he introduced the three arrested demonstrators—they were "heroes," "committed to change," "victims," and "examples"—and they took the applause holding each other's hands high over their heads in solidarity. Next, he introduced Latoya Chapin.

I half-expected a repeat of her *Journal* interview. Instead, in a voice that trembled but never broke, she had a simple message. "Don't let it happen to you. Don't be fooled. Don't have a false sense of security. Don't let someone else try to protect you—because only *you* can protect you." Her thin voice cracked as she recounted her feelings of shame, her terror at the forceful invasion of her body, and asked the males present to try to imagine being the victim of an act of rape. When she stepped back from the microphone into the arms of friends, there wasn't a sound and I got a sense that raw emotions were gripping the crowd. Somebody started to applaud, and in seconds, everyone joined in; no whistles or drums, only clapping and yells of support.

The restless crowd was probably at a critical point; it would either slink away sullenly or be led as Martine Danby stepped to the microphone.

"There's one more stop," she began. Her father had asked her to invite the students to President's House, she said, in a voice growing stronger. "He's on the line for me, for you, for all of us. Our committee thought it was right not only to demonstrate that we *care*—not just about Jesse Kingdom's cause but also about our University and what's happening here. My father knows what racism is." She let that sink in. "He needs your support. Not only to make the University better but also to bring an end to The Stalker. He should see that it makes a difference to us, too." The crowd's uncertain response was a low murmur, along with a few isolated shouts of support. "Hear his words! Join us. Join Latoya. Support the black women of Carter. Make up your own minds!" she challenged, left the podium, and walked down the terrace steps followed by Latoya and others. As she reached the first rank of the crowd, the bass drum boomed and hip-hop exploded out of the terrace's speakers.

Vose looked at me with arched eyebrows, nodded as though he had his answer, and we started across The Green as most of the kids—I could see now that it was largely a female crowd—coalesced behind Martine, heading for the South Gate. Then, a campus *thing* happened; a young male took over the microphone and, trying to outshout the music, began a hysterical and maybe drunken, confession about his participation in a date rape. He went on until, mercifully, someone slipped up behind him and turned off the mike. His interruption had not broken Martine's progress nor the enthusiasm of the bass drum nor the clapping of those she passed. I found myself ready to applaud; Vose touched my arm to shush me and we followed the crowd through South Gate.

Dwayne McAllister joined us as the marchers turned onto dormitory-lined Carter Street; he had been at the rally and at the rear of the march. "So far, so good," he said.

From the Quads came noise, music, and laughter through open doors and windows—this was Saturday night after all. Not surprisingly, the parade picked up additional kids. One or two snowballs were tossed at the marchers, maybe as a compelling target, not in rancor. With the drum marking our cadence in a resonance that surely could be heard and felt for blocks, the march had almost attained a festive mood as we neared President's House. When Martine and her group turned on to Gower Street, they visibly hesitated until the crowd's momentum swept them around the corner. The drumbeat abruptly ceased. Puzzled, we looked at one another and pushed our way forward.

The Black Posse, arms raised and hands rolled into fists, filled the sidewalk, front walkway, and the five steps up to the entryway of President's House. Its scowling leader stood under its entry light, a bullhorn close to his mouth; next to him was a not-at-all concerned Charles Danby in a dark sweater under an open Carter warmup jacket, encouraging arriving marchers to approach the steps. McAllister left us to barrel his way forward up to the chain of Black Posse members until he was halted by Danby's upraised hand. Not a security officer nor cop was in sight.

No question, a whiff of confrontation was present. A few in the march left despite Danby's vigorous, arm-waving welcome. Vose took the cell phone from his pocket and was punching numbers, which I presumed were for Tuttle, when I put my hand on his wrist. Maybe I was wrong but the faces of some of the Black Posse members appeared to have relaxed since I saw them on television, maybe because some of the black women in the march called out to them and mixed with the young men. Martine squirmed through their barrier to join her father on the porch, embracing him, producing scattered whoops of approval from the uneasy crowd.

Vose's cell phone was at the ready as we found a place on the lawn of the Episcopal Bishop's gray stucco mansion across the street from President's House where we could see and hear everything and still be out of the way. Danby appeared to be very much in control; he said something which caused his do-ragged guest to reluctantly pass the bullhorn to him. Martine attempted to pull the bullhorn from her father who, playfully tugged it back, then gave in and handed it to her. She raised the bullhorn above her head in triumph, earning the crowd's approval. The girl had *style!* Only the Black Posse on the steps of the house maintained their attitude; those members on the sidewalk were now stamping their feet in the cold, talking to the girls and friends among the marchers, giving every appearance of being ready to join them. McAllister remained close, looming above them.

Martine raised the bullhorn to her mouth, praised the students for coming, smiled, and gave it back to her father. Danby waited for the crowd to settle. His "friends," he said, obviously referring to the Black Posse, had heard his remarks a few minutes earlier so he would spare their ears and they were welcome to wait inside the house. At that, he opened its door, revealing sparkling lights in the crystal chandelier in the front hall. His gesture caught the self-appointed guardians on the steps by surprise; there was uncertainty among them as to how to maintain "presence," although not one accepted his invitation.

Then, Danby took over.

With his arms punctuating every point, he described growing

up in Philadelphia with Jesse Kingdom. He had known mean streets, he had known cold, poverty, and discrimination. He praised them for their solidarity against violence, even complimenting the Black Posse which caused a few high-fives and some head-bopping among its members before he got to the heart of his message: brotherhood against racism and violence, common sense against a common enemy, the real boogiemen being ignorance and despair. He was mesmerizing. He was simply himself, as Kingdom had been, and I wondered how that Philadelphia neighborhood had produced two orators like Danby and Kingdom. If I had any doubt before, it was gone: Carter University had a leader who could break down campus barriers, turn youthful passions into lifetime missions, and provide the sense of community, pride, and leadership it sorely needed.

His message finished in applause, shouts, whistles, and the upbeat tempo of the drum. Even the Black Posse caught the mood as heads and shoulders bobbed and arms pumped; only their leader remained sullen. Martine hugged her father, producing extended *ta booms* from the drum; all were welcome to stay, he said, and "dialogue" but I thought it was clear the kids were through with tonight's commitment to virtue. Martine kissed her father and went down the steps through the Black Posse and into the crowd, which rapidly dispersed toward the campus. The Black Posse's leader started down the steps but Danby took him by the arm and said something that produced a grin, a shake of the head, and a high-five.

"*In loco parentis,*" I said to Vose, who let that go by without rejoinder.

We watched the Black Posse regroup on the sidewalk and noisily shuffle off toward the campus. "Where?" I wondered aloud as Danby motioned to us to come inside. Vose, true to form, held off, saying he was going home; McAllister, clearly relieved and in an upbeat mood, said he was going back to his office, so I was alone when I followed Danby to the family room at the rear of the house. He squinted at my facial bruises and, again, I dissembled. Danby, fortunately, was too pumped up to inquire further; he checked his watch and said, "Can't believe it's only ten-thirty." He opened a cabinet to a shelf of bottles and a tray of glasses. I asked for a Scotch and he poured two Johnny Walker Golds and handed me a glass. I declined ice. Danby looked both fatigued and happy. "I gather Jesse was at his best tonight," and he raised his glass in salute.

"It was as though he had a script from Junior," I replied.

"Well, I can assure you that he didn't, but we did talk a bit today." His eyes narrowed. "You seemed to have made your own impression on him." I was flattered by that and took a seat on the sofa; he slumped in a recliner. The Scotch tasted good and it hit my empty stomach with a smack. "Bringing his people up here," he continued, "right in the middle of The Stalker's mess, would have made it impossible for Security and the police ... and maybe dangerous."

I swirled the Scotch inside the glass. There was no need to comment.

"Well, it'll be interesting to see how this all plays out. Jesse Kingdom on campus, the march, The Stalker still out there, the press.... Sonny Russo called me yesterday morning. You would think he'd have his mind on the snow cleanup but it was on me. Let me know his views on the state of our relationship. 'Shitty,' he called it, so long as Kingdom is welcome on campus. That was when I decided on the rally at the Sports Complex, something I had been thinking about. 'Shitty,' and that was before he knew about my friendship with Jesse. Sonny thinks that I'm personally pissing inside his tent. Threatened the usual—the man knows no bounds."

I sipped my drink and didn't comment. Perhaps my silence signaled my unease about not having participated in his decision on Kingdom's rally because he began to explain it. "I felt it had to happen. You would have wanted checkmarks in all the little boxes in your Event Plan. Jesse made it clear to me that he would come alone, and that he knew what he had to say. Also, I figured Tuttle would be better able to control problems inside a huge, enclosed place like the Sports Complex. And Saturday night? I was trying to raise the kids' consciousness of The Stalker problem. Hard to pick on one when there are three or four hundred in the group." He looked at me over the rim of his drink. "The Black Posse was a surprise. Thank God for the campus interconnect. When they showed up, I was ready and, you might say I disarmed them." He grinned. "I was hoping they'd stay until the marchers arrived, and when they did..., well, it all fell together."

He raised his glass to me. "Whew! But never again without my counsel's advice. I've been wetting my drawers, figuratively speaking, of course!"

I relaxed, and raised my glass to clink his.

"And now, it's up to the kids, Security, and the cops. If The Stalker is out there, there's no better night to nab him."

CHAPTER TWENTY-SEVEN

The late game on ESPN, 76ers at Lakers, was viewed with the Johnny Walker, a water carafe, an ice bucket, and an extra large bag of Annie's Cheddar Cheese Popcorn on the table between us. Near the end of the first quarter, I telephoned Nadie at the Women's Center and she agreed—*consented* would be the right word—to join our vigil. At eleven, Danby surfed the late news on all three local channels, and the coverage wasn't that bad—clips of Kingdom, the candlelight march to The Green, brief glimpses of Martine on Channel 13 and Channel 7, a lot of chatter about the relationship between City Hall and the University—until our channel flipping hit a Channel 11 interview with Latoya Chapin.

It was painful to watch. She barely held back her tears as the reporter snapped a series of loaded questions like "will you ever be the same" and "why doesn't the University support you". At the interview's conclusion, the anchor added that Channel 11 would be on "stakeout" all night at the Carter campus. This produced snorts from both of us since the media was ensconced in the comfortable surroundings of the Information Office, with the delights of hot food, a refrigerator, and a bar to ease discomfort.

Around eleven-thirty, a doorbell rang, and I followed Danby into the back hall off the kitchen to answer it. Nadie, in a black wool walking coat and red tam, was on the tiny back porch in silhouette against the floodlit driveway. She tucked the tam in her coat pocket, handed her coat to Danby, and fluffed her hair; she looked put-together in olive corduroy slacks and a dark green

333

turtleneck, with gold hoop earrings that I hadn't seen before. I made a cautionary remark about her walking the four blocks from the Women's Center alone, which she ignored.

We returned to the family room. Danby asked her if she wanted anything to drink; she asked for a Frangelico on ice and reported that the "word" was that many of Carter's black women were away for the weekend while those remaining on campus were socializing in groups. The campus escort service was busy, she added, the women who had been in the march were likely to hang together, and she had seen a half-dozen Security Office and police cars on her walk over here. The Stalker, she concluded as the buzzer sounded for the second half, was going to have to search for a victim who hadn't been paying attention. What she didn't have to add was that there were plenty of likely candidates.

Danby, I quickly learned, was a rabid Sixers fan and was enjoying the duel between Kobe Bryant and Allen Iverson who were attacking each other as though it was a playoff game instead of the season's first meeting. Nadie had her nose in a magazine. Twice during the third quarter, the telephone rang: Vose checking in and Tuttle reporting that the campus and its environs were well-patrolled and quiet, with a scattering of parties going on at fraternities and around the Quads. The Black Posse, he said, had ended up at a black fraternity house, mostly making noise, but occasionally providing escorts for black women party goers. "Can't hurt," he concluded.

The next call was to Nadie's cell phone. Nadie listened for a few seconds and said resignedly, "Okay, I'll be right over. Thanks." She put the cell phone away and said, "Nothing too important. We've got a case of hysteria at Student Health, and I'm on call."

Danby left us to retrieve her coat. Since I was feeling sheepish about how we had left each other yesterday, I was relieved when she gave my forehead a light kiss, and smiled, straightening up quickly as Danby returned. "It's never as bad as they think. I'll just look in for a few moments before I go home."

I checked my watch. "Let me call Escort, or better yet, I'll walk back with you...."

"Finish the game. Anyway, you're both probably going to be up late. I promise to be a good girl and walk right down the middle of the street the whole way." She slipped on her coat and adjusted the tam to a jaunty angle. With a wan smile at me, she said "Wouldn't it be wonderful if this was the last Saturday night you had to camp out like this?" I followed her into the kitchen and I kissed her—this time the passion was there—and she said, "See you later," as she let herself out into the darkness.

Back in the family room, I found Danby shaking a bag of Cape Cod potato chips into a bowl and saying something about Kobe's last drive to the basket—when the coin dropped: the driveway! Nadie had walked into pitch black; when she arrived, the driveway had been brightly lit by floodlights over the garage doors! No one had been in the kitchen to turn the lights off since she arrived. So how—?

I rushed back to the kitchen, opened the outer door, and careened around the porch into the driveway. I called "Nadie!" but there was no response. Only the meager light from the kitchen gave any visual definition to the house and driveway.

Danby caught up to me. "What's going on?" he said, his voice booming over a wind that had picked up to a howl in the past hour. Feeling a little embarrassed, I explained about the driveway lights as we went back inside and tried the switch next to the door. It was up. I pressed it down. Nothing happened. Up again, and down. The driveway remained dark.

I was perplexed, if no longer as concerned, and went back outside. My eyes had adjusted somewhat to the night and I could distinguish the tall box hedges and hollies which narrowed the width of the driveway as it curved around the corner of the house. I found my way to the sidewalk to where the snow at the curb had been trampled by the crowd. Nadie must be on Carter Street by now, I thought, in the safety of the Quads. The wind whirled fragments of leaves around me like a flock of birds; tree limbs creaked and smacked against each other and leaves swooshed as they collided. Maybe a nor'easter had blown into town.

I had retraced my steps to the turn of the driveway when a scream, higher and more piercing than the wind, came from the direction of the garage. Before I could react, a rush of steps came at me and I never saw the body check that sent me careening into the hedge.

Stabbing stems of hedge dug into my face and shirt as my weight pushed me deeper into its maw. I struggled within the bush for leverage to stand and when I did, I was knocked right back into it by a banshee who threw herself on to a shape slumping to the driveway. As I freed myself from the clutches of the hedge, throaty grunts came from the lumpy shadow. Nadie yelled, "Grab him!"

Grab him? What? I groped forward, saw Nadie roll away, and fell to my knees to lay across his back. He—it was definitely a *he*—shuddered with deep, wheezy breaths under my weight; he was stunned or unconscious.

Someone ran towards me and after the two knocks into the hedge, I braced for a blow. But, it was Danby, waving something long and heavy that might have been a baseball bat. "Call the police!" I shouted over my shoulder and heard him run up the driveway toward the kitchen.

"He...came up from behind me...," Nadie gasped in an almost unrecognizable falsetto, "...got his hand over my mouth...dragged me back toward the garage...had me against the wall...."

A rattling groan interrupted, followed by two heaving breaths. *Was he in shock?*

"You came outside and he saw you, he about smothered me when...I bit him..., his hand slipped, and I got enough leverage to get between his legs.... Threw me down and ran.... You blocked him...."

I blocked him?

I pulled myself up on his torso; inching closer to his face, I barely made out a puffy lid over a closed eye, a large nose, an earlobe the size of a nickel, and brown, stringy hair that stuck out from under something that could have been a hairnet or a rolled-up stocking. He gave off a musky, garbagey odor; his breath was as described by every victim. His jacket creaked with his jerky breathing and I yelled to Nadie to call an ambulance. I heard her inhale sharply, then her rapid footsteps.

No longer concerned he might escape, I got to my knees and straddled his back. The wind rushed around us, picking up a sweetish, strangely familiar odor that emanated from him, one that I couldn't for the moment identify. Nadie and Danby returned as a siren, then another, pierced the night through the blasts of wind. My hands pressed his lower back and I felt breathing that seemed less frequent, maybe funereal.

We kept an impatient silence as sirens came closer; then, tires squealed in the driveway and dazzling blue and white lights barreled toward us, stopping not ten feet from where I sat on my captive. My hands went up to block the blinding lights. Nadie rushed forward, waving her arms and shouting; car doors were thrown open and two cops charged at us, their shouts unintelligible in the wind, sirens, and Nadie's cries. I started to roll off my captive when a steely blue Smith and Wesson was thrust in my face.

"Freeze!" shouted the voice above the gun as an arm went around my neck and yanked me upright. *My spine!* Nadie pounded the shoulder of the cop who was strangling me, screaming that she had been assaulted by the guy on the ground, and it took long, *long* seconds before her words penetrated the cop's intensity. Finally, the gun was lowered, my neck was roughly released, and I fell to my knees, barely missing another crunch on the body below me.

"I think he's in shock," I gulped as my vocal chords relaxed. Meanwhile, more sirens sounded from the street, cruiser doors opened, strobe lights revolved and illuminated the house and hedges, flashlights were turned on, radios crackled, and cops and security officers filled the driveway until there had to be at least a dozen uniforms in a knot around the body, listening to its gasps for breath, nobody touching it and nobody doing anything but gawk.

I jostled my way forward. He remained motionless but the ever-moving flashlights revealed a scarlet stain spreading on the asphalt and I saw my hands, shirt, and trousers smeared with blood. I now recognized the smell and almost manically wiped my hands on my trousers. My stomach rumbled and began a heave; my fists clenched in embarrassment. *Please, God, don't let me make a fool of myself!*

Nadie grasped my arm and demanded loudly, "Do something!" encouraging someone with authority to step into the overlapping circles of light, stoop, and pull back an eyelid for a second only to let it drop. He fished under the torso, shifting it slightly on one side, and blood sprayed from beneath the jacket.

That about finished me! I was so woozy that I was barely aware that EMTs were charging their way through the uniforms with gruff yells of "get the hell out of the way"s.

The cops elbowed one another to make room and a jumpsuited EMT entered their dancing lights as he snapped on latex gloves, and thrust a white bandage inside the bloody jacket; another EMT shouted for a gurney, checked for a neck pulse, and reached into a satchel for a syringe. The EMT working on the wound withdrew his gloved hand and raised a black-handled knife; the flashlights captured drops of shiny blood dripping from

338

its blade on to its handle and his glove.

My stomach churned! I wasn't going to make it.

Another siren wailed in the distance as a gurney clanked up the driveway and the injection was jabbed home. Two EMTs lowered the gurney to knee height, placed a stretcher on the asphalt, then inched the limp figure on to the stretcher, lifted it to the gurney and fastened velcro straps; the gurney, raised with another 'get out of the way," was pushed down the driveway. The cops milled around the bloodstains on the driveway as a blast of horn erupted from the street, signaling that the ambulance was on its way to City Hospital, while yet another cruiser noisily braked to a stop. There had to be six by now!

I was still fighting nausea when Danby appeared at my side. We started back toward the kitchen, with Nadie in tow, only to be confronted by a cop at the door. "Where do ya think yer going?" After some nonsense about being available for questions, he followed us inside. Nadie took off her coat. Her chin was scratched, her cheeks scraped, and her hair fell in her face. One earring was missing. Yet, she seemed to have eyes only for me. Her touch was gentle at my forehead and I saw blood come away on her fingers.

The goddamn hedge! I had been mauled by a goddamn hedge!

Danby left the kitchen as I washed my face at the sink, feeling the stings of old and new cuts, and used a dish towel to wipe away sweat and blood. The cop, who had blond hair, a bushy, blond mustache, a new looking uniform, and the clear eyed gaze of a rookie, slouched by the door. He obviously didn't have a clue what to do; after assurances we would stay where we were, he went back outside for instructions and returned, saying he had orders to search the house. He drew his pistol.

Nadie and I had the same thought. Loudly, we shouted to his back "be careful," that *President* Danby was somewhere in the house, maybe in the study or the family room, because if this kid saw his own shadow, we'd hear a shot!

Two older, rugged-looking, cops in scruffy leather jackets came into the kitchen from the driveway and ignored us as they decided who was going to do what. One, who was a dead ringer for Danny Aiello, took down our names, addresses, and telephone numbers in a worn, black leather notebook and told Nadie she could make her statement downtown or right there, once the detectives arrived. The other, a skinny guy with acne marked cheeks and an overbite showing bad teeth, kept looking Nadie over until Nadie stared him down and said calmly, "Downtown," and added that first, she was going to clean up. She left, to his disappointment, and I gave them a brief rundown of what had happened. Danby—alive—returned with the rookie, confirmed my story, and left us again. The older cops snickered to themselves about what a "wuss" The Stalker had been, put down by a "little girl, fer Christmas sakes", and flicked the light switch to the floodlights a half-dozen times or so for the benefit of the rookie. He was told to escort Nadie.

Nadie looked less disheveled when she entered the kitchen and said to me, "Why here? Why was he *here?*" I had remembered Tuttle's insight that The Stalker was picking his victims, even as I was scissored over The Stalker's back. But, first things first. I didn't want her in the Public Safety Building alone, and said so, under my breath since the rookie remained in the kitchen. "These bozos can wait until tomorrow—"

"I have to do it," she said firmly. "All they need right now is me. If I'm questioned with you and Danby, especially here, there's bound to be a lot more interest. I want to get this over with. Tonight."

She was right, as usual, as expected. And how can you argue with a woman who weighs a hundred pounds, and who had just taken out The Carter Stalker!

She put on her coat—the tam was probably in the garage or on the driveway—and leaned forward to give me a kiss on the cheek.

She left with the rookie, passing in the doorway a squat, bald guy with ball bearing eyes in a floppy raincoat over a too tight green jacket. A shiny ID badge clipped to his lapel identified him as Detective Sergeant Joseph Palumbo; that and his attitude shouted he was *important!*

Danby, looking less anxious than before, and I went through our stories again; Palumbo, hearing Tuttle's name, said that he had worked with Tuttle and his expression didn't hold any affection. Must be one of McCarthy's boys, I thought, as we went over the same stuff in twenty, grunt-filled, minutes. Palumbo, who didn't bother with notes, muttered something to the effect of "too many nut cases these days" and left without more. I glanced at Danby; he just shook his head.

Tuttle arrived and we repeated our stories; did they get better in the telling, I wondered? I left them at the kitchen table and retrieved the Scotch we had been enjoying less than an hour or so earlier. "It was Martine he was after," Danby was saying thoughtfully as I returned. "That's why he was here. Must have loosened the floodlight bulbs. He must have known she usually used the rear door." I found glass tumblers in a cabinet over the sink and poured large drinks for all, neat. "She was the target. Bill, you were right about the direction this was taking—higher up the visibility chain—but I never considered Martine in that context. God, what a chance I took!" He took a hard swallow. "I should have known!"

It made sense. Why else would The Stalker be lurking in the garage of President's House? He was in a darkness of his own making, and there was Nadie, coming out of the rear door, not much different in size from Martine ....

"Curfew is one o'clock. I expect she'll be home as soon as she hears that we got The Stalker!" His face finally showed relief and a smile. "Still can't believe it!"

The Scotch and adrenaline rush I was on must have been taking hold because I asked why the goddamn media wasn't banging
on his front door. Danby replied that he had telephoned Gregson
at the Information Office with instructions as to a media statement
and had decided on a press conference for tomorrow afternoon.
"We'll build some momentum if we keep quiet now and then hold
it right here," he said. "Lots of praise for the police and Security
Office. And Nadie. And you. And for the kids who acted so respon-
sibly tonight." I protested my involvement and he nodded in
understanding. "Maybe, I'll even call Sonny! Let him know that I
plan to get on with business." Tuttle grinned; maybe he was thinking of making a similar call to Chief McCarthy.

○ ◯ ○

A few minutes later, after a vain attempt to blot out the stains
on my shirt and trousers, Danby lent me a shirt in exchange for the
bloodied one; there was nothing to be done with the trousers. As I
left, Danby was pouring on praise for Tuttle's perseverance and his
deft handling of the rally and the march; outside, a genius had gotten the floodlights back on. A solitary cop stood near a chalked circle around a blood stained patch of driveway. I put up my coat collar, tamped down the fedora, and started for Congdon Street.

The wind was blowing hard, kicking up grains of frozen snow
from piles remaining at curbs and spraying it fiercely against me,
as I mulled over The Stalker's last assault. The darkness in the
driveway where the light should have been. If I hadn't noticed, or
if I hadn't made so much noise, what would have happened?
Nadie could have been raped or killed! All *I* had done was be there
for him to crash into, even if Nadie was giving me more credit.
Was that when he got the knife wound? When he fell to the driveway? His wheezing lungs, the dazzling headlights, the blinding,

flashing whites and blues lights, the creaking of his jacket, the knife with its crimson drops, spun through my mind, and I was half way to nausea when I made the conscious effort to think of something else, and, of course, it was Annie Sullivan's murder.

Now, I realized, everyone would know—for sure—that The Stalker had not killed Annie Sullivan.

I went into the dining room, opened the drinks cabinet, removed a decanter of Aux Vieux Calvados and a snifter, and took them downstairs. I snapped on the lights over the pool table and opened the case of my favorite cue, a Schoen, a twenty year friend, and screwed it together. The balls gleamed within the triangle on the felt. I drilled the cue ball, smacking the set up into a wide spread. And that's when it came together. As the balls hit the rails and caromed, with two disappearing into pockets, I *saw* connections! It was no longer a stream of consciousness, it was chronological and logical. The play had been there, I just hadn't worked it out. I straightened up after that shot, took a long snort of Calvados, chalked the cue tip, and smartly cleared the table as the elements of the case became clearer. Annie Sullivan had sent lives caroming in a game she had been playing until she made a fatal error. She had been so sure of herself that she had not prepared for her next shot. A good player always prepares for the next shot. And that mistake had killed her.

I left the cue on the table, turned off the lights, and went up to the loft. I took off my bloodied trousers and sat in the recliner in my skivvies to work it out. To do so, I would pry into the malicious, manipulative mind of Annie Sullivan. I would know her in her mean, twisted essence. Across the room on my worktable, my evidence case lay next to Williams's wool cap, license, screwdriver, and cell phone. I was drawn to get up and touch them. I picked up the cell phone and pressed "on"; its screen brightened, and like metal fragments drawn by a magnet, my insight became a certainty.

I called 411 for Patricia Sullivan's number at her apartment in Cranston and punched it in. Would she be home on a Saturday night? I heard a television in the background when she picked up. I identified myself and she was immediately defensive; no longer the practiced storyteller, she sounded scared. Maybe the "lout" had gotten through to her. I cut her off and asked my questions; slowly, reluctantly, she answered them. One was the bull about her sister's job. No, she wasn't "sure" there was a job but she also didn't know—"...I'm telling the truth..."—or how or where the money arrived—..."I think it was sent to her." Yes, she said, when pressed, her sister once had used the term "cash cow" without explanation. I asked one final question, and after a long pause, she answered, "No."

I told her that The Stalker had been caught and described Nadie's part in his capture. She didn't seem all that interested. I thanked her, said goodnight, and hung up the phone.

Next came Tariq Faud. When we got through his fussing about the late hour, he listened with impatience and growing interest as I gave him the background that hooked him before I asked for the favor. He objected and complained about the privacy of records in the Pathology Department and hospital rules and that there could be "trouble" and finally promised to call me back if he could get the information, which he said might be in a few minutes or tomorrow morning. I said I needed it tonight, if possible, and he said he'd try, although I shouldn't plan on it.

An hour later, Faud called and his information, a little too

344

graphic, fit once I had the essence of Annie Sullivan's mind. Now, I had facts; I was no longer pressing to jam pieces of the puzzle together so they fit. They slid in easily.

I finished the Calvados and went to bed.

Sunday

CHAPTER TWENTY-EIGHT

Annie Sullivan's eyes are open and gaze at me reproachfully, asking why I'm there and why am I not doing something to save her life. Her blonde hair is lank, her complexion wan, her eyebrows raised; in her stillness, she is a mannequin. A pillow floats above her head before her face vanishes beneath it. I can taste the pillow and experience flashes of color that dance behind her eyes.

"You—?"

But who does she say it to?

A human shape appears hovering over her. Hands press resolutely on the pillow. Blood from her bitten tongue fills her mouth. Her eyes redden with ruptures of tiny blood vessels. She struggles, then accepts. The pillow drops by the bed and her murderer turns to me. A doorknob squeaks, the apartment door opens and scrapes against the uneven floor, and I wait to see who has joined us. I hear a moan....

Mrs. Cabel didn't have the opportunity to protest as I marched into the hall, around two suitcases, and into the living room. It was barely eight o'clock; the room was saturated with morning sunlight. She followed me, her mouth agape in surprise; neither the hollows in her sagging cheeks nor her tired eyes gave me pause.

"Just what do you think you're doing?"

I felt profound anger; any pity or empathy had evaporated. My mouth was surely drawn in disgust. She had composed a minuet of deception and almost pulled it off. The fedora remained on when I sat on the sofa, my right arm draped along its back affecting an air of confidence.

"I went for it hook, line, and sinker." I picked up *T.R.*, which remained on the top of the drum table, and thrust it at her. Holding that book gave me moral authority. "The most believable lie is always clothed with truth. That was the whole idea." I replaced *T.R.* on the table, pointedly turning Reinman's face toward her. Her eyes strayed momentarily to his photograph before returning to me.

"Last night, the police arrested The Stalker. In no time, they'll know he had nothing to do with Annie Sullivan's death. That means they'll start from scratch, examine everything again, including her past associations, and this time, they'll pay attention to the money they now know she was receiving—"

"Carl didn't do it!" she shrieked. "Can't you get that through your head?"

It was time. Like a jury summation, after the confusion of confrontational and contradictory witnesses at a trial, I had to lay out my case and I was only going to get one chance.

"Annie Sullivan," I began evenly, "was as intelligent as she was perverse. She lied for the pleasure of it, because she could get away with it. She had the confidence required of a good liar and believed in her ability to manipulate almost anyone. She played with her victims, teased them, ridiculed them, and was capable of deceit as your son-in-law." From my inside jacket pocket, I pulled out the vasectomy pamphlet and flattened it on the coffee table next to *T.R.* "From Carl's office."

She stooped to pick it up, read its cover more than once, and didn't comprehend its significance until she flipped through the pages and unfolded the invoices. Then, as though some life force had evaporated, she sank into the chair opposite me, tightly grasping the pamphlet and receipt, staring past me across the room.

"Carl and Annie Sullivan had an affair. It must have been discreet. That would have fit their personalities—for her to have an affair with the University's most well-known faculty member while other students had their schoolgirl crushes, and he was as randy as ever with his secret escapades showing his disdain for campus convention. Maybe he told her not to worry about the sex because of the vasectomy, maybe he didn't. She wasn't, or shouldn't have been, on the pill because she had hormonal problems and the pill would have had side effects."

At that, Mrs. Cabel's brow furled with a question which I ignored.

"Toward the end of the school year, Annie knew she was pregnant. Carl must have vigorously denied his paternity, and if he hadn't before, he made it..."—I pointed to the pamphlet—"...known to her. That's why the pamphlet was in his office. And to make sure, there was a second visit to the urologist in May. He probably thought Annie had been sleeping around if she was pregnant and would go away; Annie may have thought the vasectomy was a ruse because she hadn't been and knew she was pregnant. Seems likely she also discovered his vulnerability. A paternity suit would have destroyed his morality guru image, ended his public career. When Carl paid her for the abortion and silence to get her out of his life, she knew he would pay more if there was a child." I shook my head, disparagingly. "Smart as he was, he underestimated Annie."

As I continued, the old woman's face showed that her mind was working feverishly on where I was heading.

"His heart attack spoiled everything. If Carl died, or if he was too sick to care, her doublecross—to keep the baby, insist it was his, and blackmail him—was blown."

Mrs. Cabel's mouth opened and she put up a hand to stop me which I ignored.

"So, she took a chance with another ploy. She told your daughter that she was carrying her husband's baby and proposed an arrangement. Annie would deliver the baby to your daughter, a surrogate of sorts, and was to be paid each month until the baby was born, and probably more when the baby was turned over to Deborah. How did she know that Deborah wanted a child so badly? Something that Carl said? Had he abused Deborah's confidence? Since Deborah controlled the family's cash, the payments would be no problem. It was for her a bargain with the devil and one she accepted for a baby. Carl's baby! Even if Carl died, she would have the baby, and alive, Carl would be in no position to deny her the child, even as an adopted child, not now, not after all these years, not in his condition...."

"Conjecture," she croaked back at me, "... complete, absolute conjecture. This is so absurd...."

"The scheme broke down when Annie found out she wasn't pregnant! Everyone thought her hospital stay meant a problem in the abortion or a miscarriage, some sort of euphemism when she said it was an 'operation'. They forgot she always liked to play with words in her manipulations. It *was* an operation, an operation for an ovarian cyst. It had stopped her menstruation, made her puff up, fooled her body into false pregnancy symptoms, and she was still on student health insurance when she had her operation. Just an irregularity, an abnormality, and the operation took care of it. A few days in City Hospital and she was out."

She was staring at me, her face a mask of varied emotions; I continued with growing certainty in my voice.

"The threat to her meal ticket was real so she dug deeper into her repertoire of deceit. She probably told Deborah that there were complications in her pregnancy, that she needed rest and expensive care, and Deborah could send money to a postoffice box while Annie was being cared for. Annie stayed out of sight during

the day so no one would be the wiser. Your daughter, unsophisti-
cated and wanting the baby so badly, went along. She even started
planning for its arrival." I pointed toward the hall. "That room
upstairs, the one with the yellow walls, with the painted balloons,
the Picasso print. At her age...? You *must* have wondered...."

Still no outburst of indignation, of defense from her. So, I wanted the next part to sting.

"While the money came in, Annie enjoyed herself, bought
things, took trips, just had a blast—at your daughter's expense—all
the while mocking her gullibility and her weakness. Yes, mocking
her. She boasted to her boyfriend and her sister that the money
came from the 'cash cow'. *Cash cow!* The Vermont farmer's
daughter was the *cash cow*. Annie demeaned your daughter, where
she came from, her size, her vulnerability. It was all part of a great
scam! When the jig would finally be up, when there was no baby,
what could Deborah do about it? Complain to the police? Or to
Carl? Admit how badly she had been duped?" I shook my head. "A
perfect scheme—"

Mrs. Cabel threw the pamphlet on the table, nearly hitting
Reinman's photograph. Her eyes sparked with malice; when she
spoke, her voice was steely. "You've read too many Agatha
Christies, Mr. Temple!"

She had no idea that was a good hit on me. And, it angered me.
Here's what Hercule Poirot would do, Ms. Cabel.

"Annie's plans went awry, maybe because Carl discovered the
payments Deborah made to Annie and confronted your daughter
or Deborah found the vasectomy pamphlet in Carl's office—it was
as though he'd kept it handy as proof of his inability to father a
child, evidence which might be useful someday. I think the latter,
on one of her many trips to his office. Either way, after a lifetime
of guilt over the abortion, with barrenness and an unfaithful husband as punishment, Deborah discovers her husband deliberately

frustrated her attempts to get pregnant. And, since Annie couldn't be pregnant by Carl, Annie was a fraud, too!"

The hate Mrs. Cabel's face registered helped me to go on.

"When November's money didn't arrive, Annie guessed something had gone wrong. She decided not to push her luck by pressing for payment. She had enough cash to get out of town in style. Then last Friday night, when she was high, and her boyfriend taunted her, she couldn't resist one last gambit for more money and another malicious twist. She used the boyfriend's cell phone..."—I took it out of my shirt pocket and held it to her face— "...this phone. Later, she told the boyfriend that she was again milking the *cash cow.*" I pressed the phone's memory button, scrolled back, and read aloud the Reinman's listed phone number and the time, "Seven forty-eight. Not nine thirty, Mrs. Cabel, seven forty-eight. It retains the last twenty numbers and the time of calls. *That* was the nineteenth. For thirteen minutes."

The cell phone was placed on top of the pamphlet, next to *T.R.* She remained silent. I had failed to goad her into the expected denial. Yet, I knew it would come as I drilled deeper.

"You told me that you were Carl's alibi. I forgot that you were Deborah's alibi, too. And that Deborah is your alibi. Never occurred to me to ask about it. Annie's phone call had to have been the detonator. So who killed her? Carl was too frail, no match for Annie. You? Physically, you'd be no match for Annie. That leaves only Deborah, with the motive and the physical strength. She had been robbed of her baby, abused by her husband, violated by everyone, and she went over the edge. Was it before or after Carl's death when she went to Annie's apartment, found her tormenter zonked out on drugs, and used a pillow to smother her."

My voice almost cracked as I accused her daughter of murder and I braced myself for her reaction. "That's what bothered me.

The pillow. From the beginning. Although I didn't focus on it. The cops didn't tumble to it because of their mindset. A rapist doesn't use a pillow. A drug dealing punk doesn't use a pillow. But a crazed, humiliated, jealous woman...?"

Her breath caught for the first time, confirming that I was close to the truth. "Why was Annie's room ransacked? Why were her panties removed, her slip lifted over her face? It had to be someone's idea to phony up an assault, probably with The Stalker in mind. I can't see Deborah, in her confused mental state, having the clarity of mind to fake a crime scene." I paused for effect. "Someone else was there."

I stood, feeling extraordinarily tired and angry at the woman whose eyes latched on to mine, the accomplice, the liar. Would she admit her duplicity, her complicity? "Carl, if he wasn't already dead, couldn't have made it over to Veasey Street by himself, or stagger up two flights of stairs to get control of Deborah. No, there had to be someone who could manage her, someone who'd take her or follow her, who maybe got into the apartment too late. Someone who could think rapidly enough to cobble together a scene the cops might buy...."

Her knuckles whitened as she grasped both arms of the chair and slowly hunched forward. "What is it that makes you do this?" she hissed. "Why do you persecute us? You can't prove any of this. Deborah was never in that apartment, and that cell phone doesn't prove anything! It was like I said. I was just wrong on the time!"

"They'll be no alibi for Deborah since you told me and Pine, and no doubt others, that Deborah was in Little Compton when Reinman died. That was when Annie was killed. You hid Deborah from Carl's doctor or maybe even whisked her away that night or early on Saturday, dosed with her own medications? Don't know how you did it, don't care. The money will lead the police here and the records will document the source. And as for Deborah, or someone else, being at Annie Sullivan's apartment...." I reached over, picked up *T.R.*, placed the palm of my hand directly over Reinman's photograph, and pressed down. I took away my hand and a palm print and five fingerprints blotted the shiny paper. "There were unidentified fingerprints all over the apartment. Despite your efforts, some will match Deborah's and...whomever else was there. You'll never explain that."

Her right hand rose as if to strike me. She held it aloft, unable to bring it forward. Her face admitted everything.

The summing up was over. I thought it would bring me relief but instead I felt drained. The pamphlet, receipts, and the cell phone went into my jacket. I left for the hall; she grabbed my arm with a force that practically spun me around. "If you could have seen her before she met Carl, her sweetness, her talent, her confidence—"

I shook off her grasp. "Sorry, but nobody else should be punished for a murder that belongs here."

"You're *sorry!*" she said in a voice so hoarse that I scarcely recognized it. All pretense was gone. "You're *sorry!* You've been wondering about Deborah. Where she's been...?"

Maybe I should have wondered but I hadn't thought about it....

"On the afternoon of the memorial service, we found her in bed, staring at the wall. She couldn't hear me. Catatonic. I thought it was an overdose of her medications but it wasn't. We managed to get her into her sister's car, and drove her back to Vermont. She was admitted to a psychiatric hospital that afternoon." She pointed to the two suitcases on the hall floor. "Hers. I'm taking them to the hospital." She shuddered, and forced out her words. "She hasn't recovered. It could be days or weeks, or even longer, because something terrible happened, something so terrible that it took her mind away. If..., when..., she recovers, *if* she remembers, and *if* she can live with it, that's the time to be dealing with your sense of *justice.*"

That was as near to an admission against interest as I was going to get. She'd never come close again.

I swallowed a retort and got to the hall with Mrs. Cabel following me. "She's the real victim." As I opened the front door, her voice dripped with scorn. "But you'll do what you want, Mr. Temple, won't you? You don't care about *real* justice, about how the scales should even out. Your life will just go on...."

CHAPTER TWENTY-NINE

I wasn't surprised that Nadie, in black slacks and a red shirt, with her hair held back by a red barrette, was at the kitchen counter behind the *Sunday Journal* with a celebratory box of Krispy Kremes. Except for the scrapes that cosmetics couldn't quite hide and wisps of strain showing at the corners of her eyes, she appeared none the worse for wear from last night's adventure. She responded to my bleak stare. "Where have you been?" When I didn't answer immediately, she took a second look. "Are you alright?"

I lied and told her I couldn't sleep—well, that partly was true—and had gotten up for a much-needed walk. I asked how she felt and she said, "Fine" as she slit the tape on the donut box with a fingernail; there was enough sugar in those things to rot teeth and I said so. She ignored me, devouring a jelly-filled donut as she recounted her interview at the Public Safety Building "...what a dump!" and appraised her interrogation "...weak!" and added flatly that she'd been told that The Stalker was in intensive care at City Hospital. When she finished a second caloric monster, she licked her fingers, got up, and made espresso for two while jibber-jabbering about the moronic cops and what the capture of The Stalker would mean to the women at Carter. It was evidence of my funk that I found her good spirits maddening; in the last nine hours, she had been attacked by The Stalker, questioned in the friendly confines of the Public Safety Building until one or two a.m., and here she was, green eyes sparkling and acting like nothing much had happened!

I unfolded the *Metro News* section as Nadie delivered my espresso to the counter. "You should read that," she said, pointing to a column by one of the *Journal's* feature writers, Mark McCormick. I was immediately on guard. Nadie has been known to refer to him as "a wise-ass, macho conservative" and thus beneath contempt; either she was taunting me or it was actually interesting. It took me only a paragraph to understand: his subject was Annie Sullivan's funeral Mass.

It hadn't been much like the dry-eyed memorial service of Carl Reinman. In cavernous St. Michael's, there would have been *Dies Ires*, incense, flowing vestments, and High Mass candles. According to McCormick, the priest's homily was emotional, the faces of the congregation were pained and intense, and the anger of those on the church steps ill-concealed. Most assumed she had been killed by The Stalker, or another of the depraved, ignorant, and destructive people in our midst, the marginalized people who just don't understand the rules or who don't think any rules apply to them. Police families, he wrote, have learned to accept that a cop could go to work any morning and end up being laid out at Skeffington's Funeral Home that night. That's the risk. When the victim is the son or daughter or wife of a cop, the family's grief is infused with bitterness that goes beyond the ordinary, with their reactions revealing an innate sense of futility at the seemingly endless, and losing, battle against lawlessness and evil. McCormick's last paragraph concluded, "One of their own is gone, a victim of urban, undirected violence that swirls around us all. These cops will go to work tomorrow, a little more jaded, hardened, beleaguered, and belligerent. How will they do their jobs?"

I put the newspaper on the counter, numbed by the irony it was Annie Sullivan's funeral—the funeral of a blackmailer—that produced this paean of praise and sympathy for the cops and their families. I would have told Nadie everything if she hadn't said, with unexpected solemnity, "There's something else. Page six in the *Local* section."

It took me a few moments to find the right headline and a second longer to stop breathing. "Providence Man Found Murdered in New York." I flattened the newspaper page on the counter. Lavelle Williams, 20, of Providence, had been found, with .22-caliber slugs in the back of his head, in the trunk of a stolen car in a parking lot at Kennedy International. Crack cocaine and other drugs were found on the body and in the glove compartment. A New York homicide detective said that leaving a corpse at the terminal had become the favored modus operandi of Colombian hit men who murdered and then boarded planes for Bogota, Medellin, or Cali. The last paragraph noted that Providence police wanted Williams for questioning in the Sullivan murder investigation.

I felt my body sag. Ugh! Nadie, who could not have seen my face blanch, came around and began to massage the back of my neck and shoulders. Lavelle Williams might have been in custody—instead of dead—if I had only delivered him up to Tramonti after the assault! My hubris had gotten in the way! For a few minutes, I had unknowingly held his life in my hands and I had let it slip away. My little escapade in detection, my diversion—for that was what it was—had condemned Lavelle Williams!

She continued to knead my shoulders. "I read it, hon," she said, very sympathetically. "I'm sorry about the kid. But it must happen all the time. They get into this drug system and he probably was dangerous to somebody, and...."

I wanted to respond, to seek her consolation and understanding, when Annie Sullivan intervened. Her perversity was the root of all that had transpired. As I considered it that way, my guilt began to ebb. Annie Sullivan, victim and victimizer. Annie in the First Communion photograph. Annie, as described by Franks, by

Williams, by her sister, by the old lady. Annie, the daughter of a lout who must have shaped her environment no differently than what wind does to desert sand.

A few hours later, we were upstairs watching the Patriots-Jets game when Tramonti and Oboe arrived. Tramonti wore a crimson Harvard sweatshirt over a white shirt unbuttoned at the collar and khaki slacks; he looked tired, rumpled, and pleased. I got him a Sam Adams from the fridge; Oboe, after his ritual sniffs of the room, flopped down at Tramonti's feet.

"His name is Naylor. He lost a lot of blood but he'll make it. Been employed at the Refectory for about five years, a third cook, cleanup guy..., the guy who empties the Fry-o-later, takes out the garbage, that kind of stuff. Good employee. Quiet, kept to himself, like they always say. No rap sheet, nothing at all. Into weights and body-building stuff. Right under our noses all this time and no one ever suspected he had a problem. The goddamn knife came right out of the Refectory kitchen!" He took a swig of the Sammy and continued. "Box full of Stalker clippings and videotapes of the news broadcasts in his apartment, lots of pictures of Kingdom and Danby, and even one of Martine out of the *Crier*. And a lot of copies of that flyer, you know, with the cross hairs. Must've hated those black college girls he was serving every night or is just a pervert. We're trying to find out if he's involved with any of the skinheads or other crazies. I doubt it."

He took a long pull on his beer. "Oh, and we also got a positive ID on him as Fingers, too. Anyway, the way we figure it, after Latoya, there was only one black female student with greater campus visibility—Martine—and he was going to get her." He shook his head. "You look at him and he's a nothing. You'd never notice him in a crowd of two. Everyone figured him for a wimp. Fat, not

too smart, and burning inside. Must have repressed something."
He glanced at Nadie and grinned. "Sorry."

"Not another one," she said resignedly, and curled up in her chair.

"Why the pattern, nothing last summer, the missing weekends…?"

"That's something you'd never guess," he responded. "He's a mess corporal in the Army Reserve! Spent all summer at Camp Drum, and he was on duty at the Armory down in Bristol the last two weekends when The Stalker didn't strike. He was there Friday night to Sunday afternoon, the whole weekend—cooking! There's no way he could have left the facility without signing out, and he didn't." Tramonti's face then got a touch more serious. "That means we're back to square one with Ms. Sullivan," and his eyes shifted from his beer toward me.

I shuddered, remembering his lecture at Jimmy's.

"Did you see the newspaper?" Tramonti asked.

I nodded.

"Sorry about that," he said, not quite evenly. "No, that sounds crass. I know you tried your best for the kid." He took another swig. "Don't waste your pity. He didn't come from nothing. He could have done something with his life. He chose not to. His mother will grieve for him. Nobody else will much care. No angels singing in heaven. He knew what he was doing when he hooked up with the worst, was headed for prison or an early death…." My unspoken protest must have been plain on my face but Tramonti didn't flinch. "That's the truth. You don't want to see it that way, but sit where I sit and it's true."

"It's over," I replied glumly. "It was something I had to do. Too bad it turned out piss-poor."

"Even if you *had* pressed charges, Franks probably would have gotten Lavoie to let him out."

That sounded as though he was trying to be sympathetic. I looked at him squarely and his eyes avoided mine.

"Well, maybe. Who knows? Anyway, now, I'm not sure he did kill her or that we could prove it. Time of death is still a problem. Can't pin it down better than a span of four to five hours. The DNA would only prove that he slept with her, not that he killed her. And the room was full of unidentified prints. Everything is circumstantial, not even *good* circumstantial. So Franks would have ripped us up with Williams's so-called alibi, no eyewitnesses, the other prints, and the uncertainty as to the time of death. With Williams either out on the street because of Franks or on bail, Flores and Hones would have gotten to him eventually. He was just too hot and too close."

"Who?" Nadie asked.

"Two of his bosses," he answered, fingering the bottle. "As for the savings account, how are we going to find out where she got the money if she didn't tell anybody? The sister swears she doesn't know, now that this baloney about an internet job has been shelved. It could have been Williams's dough but I doubt it. He wouldn't have trusted her. Punks like him can't trust anybody."

Nadie looked quizzical and then frowned. Tramonti had slipped into a cop's straight from the shoulder attitude which Nadie would not like. "So, what happens now?" she asked.

"Hey..."—he turned to me—"... didn't I have this conversation with you yesterday?" Then, he repeated to Nadie the mechanics of a cold case and how the file never officially closes. "As for Naylor," he said to Nadie, "I don't think you'll be bothered. He's charged with attempted assault on you but my guess is we'll get a confession on the other assaults. Then it's only a matter of how many of the rapes and assaults the AG goes with. You'll almost certainly be out of it. We have him, and that's enough."

"The press...?" she said uncertainly, and I realized that she came here so early to avoid reporters who must be hanging around her apartment.

"They'll be all over you. You'll be Superwoman for a day," he chuckled and glanced at me, "despite your..., what should I call it..., *statement?*"

Nadie's face crinkled into a smile. "Our guys don't think too highly of *you* either, Ms. Monosyllable." He checked his watch. "Danby should be having his press conference just about now." He put down his beer and Oboe, sensing his master was about to go, got up, stretched, and put his head in Tramonti's lap. "Well, one less problem. I've still got McCarthy, the brutality trial, and the Reverend on my case. Not to mention my next to zero rating in the polls." I must have winced because he continued "Should be some lessons in all this but I'll be damned if I know what they are."

I knew one big one! Despite Tramonti's easy excuses, Williams might be alive if I hadn't acted out of arrogance or some misplaced loyalty. I owed somebody, something.

A few minutes later, Tramonti left.

"You never did tell him about Reinman, did you?"

"It was just so remote. So what if he knew her. Or paid her off. In his condition...."

She nodded. "I'm glad. Why do it now? It would only make things more difficult for the family," she said and used the remote to raise the volume on the television.

Some part of me wanted to tell Nadie that I would not let a victim be forgotten even if the police were stymied and prepared to leave her murder unsolved. While Nadie had prepared lunch, I made phone calls from the loft: Deborah Reinman had been admitted as a patient at the Vermont Psychiatric Center in

Middlebury on Tuesday; no visitors allowed except for immediate family. That verification of Mrs. Cabel's story had resolved my compulsion to protest the taking of a life. It would have to wait. What use is justice for the dead, anyway? To satisfy the living?

Annie Sullivan's perversity had infected Reinman, destroyed Reinman's wife, and killed Lavelle Williams. Looking at the shelves of thrillers, I remembered the bleak comment of a detective that every victim carries the happenstance of the person he or she has become and becomes a victim because of where he or she is at a single moment in time. Know the victim, and you are close to the murderer. It could be reversed, too; this murderer was a victim—another victim of Annie Sullivan—and she deserved to tell her own story, in her own way, if her mind ever let her remember. The great detectives of fiction—Maigret, Morse, Dalgleish, even Sherlock Holmes—had cases when fate prevented the killer from being convicted for the ultimate crime. Which one had remarked that murder is often the logical end of an accurate mind overstretched? And that sometimes a detective's only satisfaction is to know that there is nothing more that can be done?

I had to take solace that the accomplice would be living with demons as she awaited the moment when her daughter awakes. "Thou shalt fear day and night, and shall have no assurance in this life," says the Old Testament. Mrs. Cabel had nothing to hope for in this world and little, except God's mercy, in the next.

I got up and bent over to kiss Nadie's forehead. "It's over, sweet thing. Time to concentrate on real life. It's all been a movie and the credits are on the screen."

"What...?"

"Never mind. Remember that weekend in New York...?"

She looked up and caught my arm, her green eyes intent, her lips in a slight smile. "I hate to admit it but when you focus on something, you are not a really bad detective. Good instincts, and...."

Focus. Somehow she knew!

"Can I be a 'not a really bad detective' and still woo you?"

She smiled again, and that was all the encouragement I got. It was enough.

ACKNOWLEDGEMENTS

No work of fiction ever gets to print without a band of hardy colleagues who suffer the author's whims, foibles, and peccadilloes. To all who gave me succor along the way, many thanks.

Particularly, Donna Beals, Brenda Almeida, Zelia Taveres, Sue McCarthy, Judi Adams, Linda Delgardo, and the late Sue Anderson, among others, deserve my thanks for patiently putting up with my handwriting and too many changes in text.

Special thanks to David J.W. Partridge for his patient editorship; he made it come together

Thanks also to Regina, Greg, and Sarah for their support, edits, artwork, and comments.

Finally, Providence truly is in a renaissance but maintains the murky charms of the old world captured by Don Henley years ago.... How did he know? It has been fun to create characters, institutions, and myths for literary purposes and at the same time reflect that the city has been shaped by its unique history as a place of first impression for immigrants, going back to the very first who embraced it with the passion of new beginnings.